MW01042667

THE HAND OF ATUA

CHARITY BRADFORD

Fidem Press

The Hand of Atua

Copyright © 2019 by Charity Bradford

All rights reserved. No part of this book may be reproduced in any form or by any electronic or mechanical means, including information storage and retrieval systems, without permission in writing from the publisher, except by a reviewer, who may quote brief passages in a book review. Electronic distribution of this book or the facilitation of such without the permission of the publisher is prohibited.

This is a work of fiction. Any similarity between the characters and situations within its pages and places or persons, living or dead, is unintentional and co-incidental.

Cover design: SelfPubBookCovers.com/RLSather

ISBN: 9781730972645

For Katie. Thanks for asking me to finish this story every time you saw me for months on end. It helped. Sorry it took so long. :)

PART I

1

AMIRAN

Everything I loved about Manawa could disappear in a week. This planet felt more like home than the palace on Rawiri. I escaped my duties as son to the ruler of the galactic empire by hiding on this scholarly planet.

The blue-green grasses outside the window rippled in the breeze, the shades of color changing with the light of the sun. There were several moons in the sky. Some glittered like distant gems, others loomed like bloated orbs waiting to fall and crush the planet. The contrast had always bothered me, but now that the heavy hand of the Hatana's fleet approached, it seemed prophetic.

I never should have stayed on Manawa so long. My continued presence brought it to my father, the Hatana's attention.

Turning from the window, I faced my only childhood friend. His shuttle had landed half an hour earlier. "Are you sure, Ev?"

Evander nodded. His blond hair flopped across his forehead. "We've been monitoring the fleet's communications, but one of our inside sources confirmed it this morning. They'll be here in eight days or less."

A vice cinched around my chest. There wasn't enough time to evacuate the entire planet, but we had to do what we could. "We need to get Ephor Adoser to sound the alarms."

"You do that while I get your glorywinger ready."

"Can I fill your ship with refugees? We need to save as many as possible." I knew Evander would do everything he could.

"We can fill the cargo holds with several hundred people. Where should I take them?" he asked.

I stepped to my desk and retrieved a datacom. After flicking through several screens, I turned back to Ev. "I've sent you contacts on several different planets. One of them will be willing to take the refugees in."

Ev nodded. "Amiran, the Hatana would have come here eventually. This isn't your fault."

"Maybe, but if I hadn't questioned his right to enslave Attalea and Cassia, he might have spared Manawa a bit longer." The acidic taste in my mouth turned my stomach. I should have known better, but I had been stupid enough to think I could reason with my own father. Now Manawa would pay. "Get your ship ready. We have to get the leaders off planet today."

"Yes, Your Highness." Evander clicked his heels and saluted. Ev was a couple years older than me, but he'd always been there for me during the lonely palace days. Until the Hatana sent him into the fleet at age sixteen. I was fourteen and felt his loss as strongly as when my father, Hatana of the Allegiant empire, sent my mother away.

"Stop. Not here, not ever." The sight of him behaving like a fleet soldier turned my blood cold. We'd worked too hard to free him from the military's grasp by faking his death two years earlier. Now at age twenty, he should have been here with me, studying, living the life of a student. Not the life of a ghost, striving to earn the respect of a crew years older than him.

"I might call you Am, but that doesn't change who you are. You are Amiran, the Hatana Tama, heir to the throne that currently rules the known galaxy. Neither of us can forget that." He grabbed the duffel he'd dropped inside the door. His steady voice reminding me of his quiet strength and maturity beyond his years. Evander already had the respect of his crew. That's the only way he could do what he did every day.

Ev pointed at me. "You're the only hope the Coalition has against your father. I'll use the shuttle to ferry people up to the *Krahvuus*. You talk to the Ephor and then get to your ship. These people may have welcomed you as one of them but how long will that last once they know the fleet is on its way?"

A heaviness settled in my chest. "I don't know."

"I'd better see you in," Ev glanced at his COM, "two hours. If you're not there, I'm sending men to collect you."

4

I waved him toward the door. "Go."

As soon as he left, I called Imon Adoser, the Ephor, or elected leader, of Manawa. "The fleet is a week out. You need to sound the planet-wide evacuation."

"Atua in heaven, save us all." He hung up without another word, and I was grateful he trusted me that much.

When sources said the Hatana had turned his sights on Manawa, Adoser invited me to sit through hours of meetings with the council discussing plans. A lot of good it did us.

I punched the wall. Pain radiated up my arm, but the wall remained unchanged.

There was nothing on Manawa the Hatana wanted. No rare minerals he couldn't get elsewhere, no special technology. Just people he could enslave, and he already had two planets of slave workers. My sources thought he'd raze this planet, leaving it uninhabitable for centuries, just to punish me for running away. Manawa's military would be no match for the Hatana's war machine.

If only we had more time!

Struggling to breathe, I fled the apartment in search of Professor Canto Talrano. He'd been the opposite of my father, teaching me about things that had never been a part of the Hatana's tyranny. When Talrano spoke, it was to encourage free thought and debate. When my father spoke it was to drill home some military strategy for bringing the weak under control. One man believed there was strength in the diversity of thought, while the other strove to destroy any and all opposition.

Talrano was the main reason I'd remained on Manawa. He and his family filled the void created when my mother left the palace and my father turned cold and mean like his general.

I found Talrano in his office. "Professor?"

"Am, come in. They've activated the sirens again. Do you think it's necessary?" He sounded calm, a testament to how quickly things had escalated.

We'd only learned about a possible attack two months ago and sent the first load of children and women away a month later. Everyone thought we had of time to prepare. We'd been wrong.

Talrano continued speaking before I answered. "If it gets worse, I'll send Sora and Eleena away. Atua willing, that day won't be soon."

"It's here. My father sees Manawa as a threat because I've questioned his methods."

The color drained from his face, and the book slipped from his hands. It landed on the floor with a thunk.

"How long do we have?"

"The fleet will arrive in a week. I'm sorry I didn't know sooner." Shame burned up my neck. "There won't be time to get more ships to help with the evacuation. It's now or never. Evander can get you and your family away today."

Talrano sank into a chair and buried his face in his hands. "I can't leave."

"You have to."

"No. Sora's on the other side of the planet. She left yesterday for a symposium." His transparent anguish weighed me down further.

Sora, Talrano's wife, always welcomed me into her home with a smile. She spoke with a soft voice and cooked better than the palace chefs. Many nights I'd sat with the two of them and their daughter enjoying discussions on literature over dinner. Eleena was twelve, but her parents included her in the conversation as if she were one of the university students. They'd become my family. I couldn't leave any of them behind.

"There has to be a way. We can send for Sora, or Evander can take you to her." I swallowed my desperation.

Talrano looked into my eyes. "It'll take too long. Get Eleena to safety. I'll get Sora. We'll rendezvous with Evander as soon as we can."

I could tell he didn't believe the words even as he said them. By the afternoon, every available ship would be filled and fleeing the planet in an effort to put as much distance between them and the coming fleet.

Ephor Adoser had a plan, and it couldn't wait for one man and his wife.

Every private space vessel had assignments to take government officials, scientists, artists, anyone that could help preserve the Manawan culture. In addition, every freighter on the planet was currently offloading cargo to make room for people and food. They would scatter around the globe and take as many as they could hold to safety. Even so, only a fraction of the planet's population would escape before the fleet arrived.

"Professor," my voice faltered. I had failed him. I had failed all of Manawa.

Talrano walked around his desk. He rested his hand on my shoulder. "In the coming years, you must remember this wasn't your

6

fault. Don't forget the pain, but don't accept the guilt either. Because of you, many of our people will be saved."

Despite his words, my guilt remained. "It's not enough."

"Then do more. Stop your father." He grabbed a satchel. "I'll send Eleena to the spaceport."

He hurried through the door, and I followed him down the hallway. "Professor, Evander will get her off Manawa. Come with her. You can continue your work."

Talrano paused. "I won't leave without my wife."

My stomach churned. "We need you to teach others, help them see there are ways to fight the Hatana."

"My son, there are many who can do that. You can do it." He shook his head then pivoted to resume his journey. "I only have one wife. We made a promise to each other."

My feet were rooted to the floor. I couldn't let him stay. We'd lose one of the greatest teachers I'd ever known. And he just called me son. My own father hadn't used such a term of endearment since I was five and my mother still lived in the palace.

Talrano spoke over his shoulder before entering the lift. "Save Eleena for me."

"You'll make your daughter an orphan. Let me come with you." I ran to catch up.

"No." Talrano stood with his hand against the lift door. "Where's Evander's shuttle?"

"East side, near the tree line."

"Sora's brother, Beck, lives close by. Eleena won't be alone."

"I'll watch for them, but after I get her on the shuttle, I'm coming for you. We can use my ship to get Sora and meet up with Evander."

"Fine, but make sure Eleena leaves first. I'll wait for you at my home."

2

ELEENA

"Mima, can you see the ocean from your room?" I asked my mother. She called first thing in the morning, just like she promised.

"Do you want to see?" she asked.

I nodded and she took the datacom to the large window of the apartment she was staying in. The wide blue sky glowed with shades of pink and orange next to the sea.

"I forgot how beautiful it is!"

"Next time I'll bring you with me." She smiled and returned to her desk. "Make sure you finish your school work before you run out to the park."

"Yes, Mima." I knew better than to roll my eyes, but she must have heard it in my voice.

"Eleena." Ug, she used my full name instead of the shorter version. "Your education is important."

"But it's so boring doing it by myself." Most of my friends had left with the first evacuation a month ago, including my best friend Corvey. So many kids from our city left that we no longer had group classes, but that didn't mean I got to quit school. "What if I did a teleclass with Corvey?"

Mima frowned. "I wish you could, but she's in hiding with her mother. There's no way to—"

The sirens outside wailed. I clapped my hands over my ears. Sirens echoed over the datacom as my mom glanced at another screen beside her. All the color drained from her face.

"Mima, what's wrong?" I yelled over the noise.

"I need to call your father. Stay in the house, Leena. I love you, talk to you soon." The screen went dark.

My mother wasn't usually so abrupt with her goodbyes. I stared at the datacom, the desire to call her back coursing through me. Loud shouts wove through the sound of the sirens, sending a shiver down my spine. The noise sounded different than the last time. More fearful. I glanced out the window. People ran from their houses, filling the streets quickly.

I entered the code to call her but got the busy signal. She must have called Popi as she said. The noise grew louder. There was no way I could concentrate on my school work. Instead, I left a note for Popi on my datacom telling him I was in the park and slipped out the back door.

The REC area sat behind our home. The blue-green meadow of tall grass had become my special place. Nothing was fun anymore, but at least I could hide from the noise. All I had to do was run across my yard and access the field.

A large energy shield surrounded the park like a bubble. You didn't need a gate to enter; you simply stepped through. That shield blocked out the sounds of the city, and more importantly, the chaos from the evacuation horns.

I ran to the middle of the park, slipped off my shoes and lay down in the swaying grass. The tall stalks completely surrounded me, cutting off the rest of the world. I tried to forget Mima's fear by counting the clouds above me. The bubble warped them into melty blobs. It helped a little. Breathing in the smell of fresh grass and dirt, I closed my eyes and prayed.

Don't let the Hatana come here. And please keep Mima and Corvey safe.

I don't know how long I lay there. My thoughts bounced between Mima and Corvey. Both too far away to comfort me.

"Eleena, come to the house now!" My father's voice shattered the peace, sending a flock of birds squawking up from the grass. "Hurry!"

I jumped up. He stood inside the bubble waving me toward him. My heart pounded too hard in my chest. He rarely came home from the University before dark. First Mima, now Popi.

"Yes, sir!" I grabbed my shoes and ran. He didn't wait for me. As I stepped out of the bubble, the stampede of feet and people yelling filled the air. At least the sirens had stopped screaming. I caught up to Popi and grabbed his hand. "Did you talk to Mima?"

"Come inside quickly and put on your shoes." He squeezed my fingers, then jogged toward the back of our house.

I slipped on the shoes and followed. Mima's brother, my uncle Beck, stood in the kitchen. The tall red-headed man threw food into a bag. Popi put my datacom inside my backpack and handed it to me.

"You have to go with Beck. He'll explain everything on the way." He spoke over the rattling of dishes as one of the evacuation transports flew overhead.

I glanced from him to Uncle. They stared at the ceiling until the shaking stopped. Popi looked pale, and Uncle's smile didn't reach his eyes.

"Are you sending me away like Corvey?" I asked.

Popi pulled me into his arms. "I'm sorry we can't go with you. Promise you'll always look forward with hope, not fear."

Fear was the only thing in my heart at the moment. However, I nodded my head, even though the words wouldn't, couldn't, pass my lips.

"Why are you sending me away?" My voice cracked.

"There's no time to explain. Listen to your Uncle and you'll be fine." Popi swiped at his eyes before returning his attention to Uncle. "Am will meet you at the spaceport. You can trust him. Take the ship he tells you to."

"What about Mima?" I asked.

"I'm going to get her, but I want to know you're safe first. We'll catch up when we can."

"I don't understand. Where are we going?" I clung to him.

"I don't know," he whispered.

"Then how can you find me?" The fear twisted in my stomach. "Popi?"

"Eleena, no matter what happens, no matter what you see, stay close to Atua. That's what your mother would tell you right now." Popi squeezed one more time, then stood straight and tall, his dark hair sprinkled with silver. His eyes no longer watery. "Beck, go around the back way to the spaceport, try to avoid the largest crowds."

Uncle Beck nodded his head and reached for the bag on the table.

Popi gave me the other one. "Keep her safe. Peace on your path, brother."

I waited for the standard reply, but Uncle didn't give it. He caught me staring and jerked as if I had surprised him.

"Burn a light to guide me home, Canto." It sounded like Uncle had swallowed his gum berries without chewing them.

Tears pricked my eyes. Why didn't his answer make me feel better? The saying had always sounded nice before today.

"When will I come home?" I asked.

"Go quickly." Popi moved to the door as Uncle Beck walked through it. "Be a good girl, and remember we love you. See you soon."

Uncle grabbed my hand and pulled me into the crowded street. It looked like the whole world ran toward the spaceport. The other evacuation days hadn't been this frenzied. Something made this one different. Was it because I had joined them?

My feet beat a rhythm that matched time with my heart as we ran. The pack slapped up and down on my back.

Good-bye. Good-bye. Good-bye.

UNCLE'S HAND was sweaty against mine. He pushed his way between people as he dragged me toward the escape shuttles.

"Eleena, hold tight!" Beck readjusted his grip.

I nodded, but the noisy crowd made his words sound like static. How long until the screaming and crying all around made me deaf?

Thoughts scattered when someone stepped on my foot. My yelp fizzled into the already overburdened air. I jerked my hand from Uncle's grasp. The crowd carried me with it, preventing me from checking my throbbing toes. People pressed closer and I lost sight of Uncle.

"Uncle!" I tried to wiggle my way past the person in front of me. "Uncle Beck!"

My heart now beat as fiercely as the crowd pushing forward. I struggled to get my bearings. Above the head of the woman in front of me, I saw one of the security lights that lined the fencing surrounding the spaceport. I ducked under a man's arm and veered toward the pole.

People shoved me forward on the way toward the gates. I missed the first security light and the second, but I grabbed hold of the third one, climbing up the base and wrapping my arms and legs around it. Bodies brushed past me. I closed my eyes, but the fear didn't go away.

An elbow jabbed my side, knocking the breath out of me. I tumbled to the ground. Another foot landed on one of my hands. Gasping for air, I scrambled to my feet and climbed back up. This time I kept my eyes open while sucking on my crushed fingers.

Strangers stared at me as they pushed by. My throat hurt from trying not to cry.

Popi had sent me away.

I didn't get to say goodbye to Mima.

Silent tears gave a little relief, but a pressure built in my head. There was too much noise, and crying didn't help me feel better.

A man and woman pressed close. The woman held her arms out to me. "Come with us little girl. We'll get you to a shuttle."

"No!" I gripped the light pole tighter. Mima had warned me about people who stole children to sell on other planets. Did they want to sell me?

The man tried to pry my hands from the pole.

"Stop, please!" I yelled and kicked at them while trying to hold on.

"Eleena!" Am pushed his way through the crowd until he reached us. He shoved the man, knocking him into the crowd where he was carried away.

Am was my favorite out of all of Popi's students. He talked to me like a person and not a child. Corvey and I had spent several nights giggling over how cute he was with his intense gray-blue eyes. I'd always been happy when he came to visit, but I'd never been so glad to see him as I was at that moment.

"Am!" I screamed and reached for him.

The woman flailed her arms, hitting Am as she ran at him. She screamed over and over. "Help, someone, help me!"

A small crowd gathered. Am grabbed the woman, twisting her around until he held her arms to her side so she couldn't punch him anymore. Then he yelled to the people over her cries. "Wait, she's trying to take Canto Talrano's daughter. Ask Eleena."

Everyone knew my father because he'd been interviewed for the nets the week before.

The woman stopped fighting. "I only wanted her so I could get on a ship."

12

Am relaxed his grip. The woman elbowed him hard in the stomach and wiggled her way past the others.

"Should we stop her?" someone asked.

"No, let her go." Am waved them away, rubbing his side. "I'll make sure Talrano's daughter is taken care of. Hurry to the spaceport."

Half the group had already moved on, but one or two nodded at Am before leaving. Then he turned back to me. "Eleena, are you okay? Where's your uncle? Your father said he'd be with you."

"We got separated." I blurted, "Am, Popi wouldn't come."

"I know, but don't worry. After I get you on a ship I'll go back for him." He stepped closer so he wouldn't have to yell. The flow of the crowd almost tugged him away, but he gripped the pole to stay in place.

"What about Mima?" I asked.

"I'll take your father to get her. They'll both be with you before you know it." Am looked around. "What does your uncle look like?"

"Tall, red hair like Mima's."

"Climb on my back, and hold tight." He wasn't as big as Popi, but he'd been strong enough to save me from those people. I moved from the pole to him, wrapping my arms around his shoulders.

"Help me look for him." Am's voice was harder to hear from behind.

"Okay." My hands grew numb from holding on so fiercely. I wiggled my fingers to relax them.

"It'll be okay, we'll find him." Am shifted this way and that, weaving his way through the crowd.

The sea of people pressed against me. I was pushed and shoved. Arms, shoulders, back. Someone was always touching me. Am clutched my legs tighter. I tried to keep my body close to his so I wouldn't get knocked off, but it made it hard to look for Uncle. My fingers were locked in a death grip around his neck.

"Eleena, not so tight." Am twisted to try and see me. "It's hard to breathe."

"Sorry." I loosened my hold a little.

Am turned again and movement drew my attention to a tree across the street. Uncle Beck sat on a low limb waving his arms at us.

"I see him! He's over there." I waved to let uncle know I'd seen him. "Uncle Beck! We're coming!"

Am waded closer until Uncle dropped to the ground in front of us. Before I knew it, he had me in his arms.

"Eleena." He hugged me so hard I couldn't breathe. Then he spoke next to my ear, "what would your mother have done if I lost you?"

My feelings got tangled. I was glad to find Uncle, but now that I was safe, I wanted my parents. Am talked with Uncle Beck, but I didn't pay attention to what they said. I clung to Uncle wishing for those easy nights sitting at home listening to Popi teach Am and the other students. Then Uncle Beck knelt in front of me.

"Hop on," he said. "I'm not losing you again."

I climbed on his back and we followed Am into the throng of people. Am pushed and shoved, fighting his way to a side gate with us close behind. Soldiers guarded it.

Am pulled a paper out of his pocket and handed it to the men. "This is from Ephor Adoser. Let us pass."

One of the men looked over the paper then nodded to the others. They opened the gate to let us in but kept the others out.

"Why do they get to pass?" someone yelled.

Another voice hollered, "It's because of who he is. Seems like that would be a good reason to make him stay!"

We hurried away and those voices blended in with the others around us. The crowd grew thicker inside the fence. I only saw a few ships left on the ground. Uncle could barely move forward anymore. We passed one of the shuttles as it closed its doors. Most people ran to the next spacepad, but some fell against the metal, crying and screaming. My heart thumped hard in my chest each time a fist beat the side begging for entry.

"There's Evander's ship." Am pointed to something in front of us. "Hurry!"

Another young man stood on the gangway of a small shuttle. He had light hair and more soldiers stood around him. They used their weapons to keep people away from his ship. That man flicked his hand forward and the soldiers cleared a path for us.

Uncle Beck set me down inside the protective circle of men. He turned to Am. "Thanks for your help."

"No problem. Be safe." Am shrugged and turned to me. "Eleena, don't worry about anything. Evander will let me know where to bring your parents so you can be together."

The other man, Evander, stepped forward. "Am, we've intercepted communications from Rawiri. Your father sent an envoy ahead to collect you before the fleet arrives. It could be here any moment. You need to leave now."

"I'm not leaving Talrano." Am shook his head. "We'll take my ship to get his wife. We can do it by the end of the day, tomorrow at the latest."

"Am, don't be stupid. Your father wants you back. If you don't leave he'll get what he wants. Send someone else for Talrano." Evander stood his ground.

Uncle pointed at the people surrounding us. "They know who your father is, and it won't take long for them to turn on you. If you go back, you won't make it off the planet. "

Am turned away. I waited and silently prayed he wouldn't break his word. He said he'd get my parents.

"What about Eleena? I promised her." Am's voice cracked. He coughed and stepped farther away from us.

"Eleena," Beck knelt and looked me in the eye. "One day this man will save planets from Hatana Anaru's wrath, but if he tries to get your parents he will die here. Who will save those other people if that happens?"

A tear slid down Uncle's cheek. He knew Mima and Popi would be left behind. I looked at Am. Who was he that he could do this? I'd always looked at him as just another one of Popi's students, but the others acted like he was something more.

Now, his eyes pleaded with me as if everything were up to me. My parents or so many others? Who were they and how would he save them? I didn't know. I only cared about my family.

Atua, what do I do? I want him to get my parents, not save strangers. My eyes scanned the crowds of people. They were scared but grew angrier with each moment. They pushed closer and the soldiers now fought back. I didn't like them, not any of them.

A voice, softer than a whisper, touched my heart. *But I love them. Let me save as many as I can. I will need him to do that.*

The voice filled my entire body with warmth. With Atua's love for me. For my parents. For Am and everyone on Manawa. It was so full, I thought it might be for everyone in the universe.

Tears flowed down my cheeks, an extension of what filled me so completely. I wanted my parents, but I didn't want Am to die.

Atua, keep my parents safe. I silently pled.

The reply was immediate. *They are in my hands.*

"It's okay." I launched myself at Am, hugging him tightly. "Peace on your path, Am, and may Atua be with you."

"Eleena?" He squeezed back, and when he spoke his voice sounded rough, like it struggled to pass his lips. "Atua willing, one day we'll find the light leading all of us home."

The sadness didn't go away, and the voice didn't speak again, but I felt peace. Mima would be proud of me for listening to Atua.

I let Am go. His eyes looked sad, and I wanted to tell him Atua would protect my parents, but my voice had frozen in my chest. Instead, I waved as Uncle Beck led me up the ramp into the ship.

3

ESCAPE FROM MANAWA: AMIRAN

E leena disappeared into the shuttle with her uncle. She looked so much like her father with the brown hair and eyes, but her heart and faith was all her mother's. I'd never forget the look on her face as she forgave me for not going for her parents.

"That's one strong girl," Evander whispered. "I'll watch out for them."

"Thanks." I squeezed his shoulder. "Eleena is Talrano's world."

"Don't do anything stupid. Think of what she gave up so you can stop your father. Get off the planet." He waved over two of his men. "They'll escort you to your shuttle."

What if I let her down? What if I couldn't do anything to stop the Hatana and General Schirra? I swallowed hard, knowing that wasn't an option.

"Atua be with you, Ev." I followed his men around the back of the ship and into the forest away from the crowds. A new determination filled my veins. With Ev's help, we'd build our own fleet. Then I'd be ready to take on my father and his Allegiant planets.

Ev's soldiers cut a path through the trees to another spaceport where the *Fortissimus*, my glorywinger, waited. I couldn't stop thinking about Eleena. She could lose both parents because I was running away.

"I won't do it," I mumbled.

"Won't do what?" one of Ev's men asked.

"Run away before I save Eleena's parents." I turned around.

"Your Highness?" The soldiers stayed close.

"It won't take long." I jogged the way we'd come.

"Don't be stupid." The voice was right behind me.

"Help me or go back to Ev."

He tackled me, throwing me to the ground. "You're going to the *Fortissimus*."

"How dare you!" No one manhandled the Hatana Tama.

"Sir, you're getting on that ship. Captain's orders." He glared and pulled me to standing.

"Not without Talrano. Let me go or I'll have you sent to the mines." I shoved his hands away and straightened my clothes.

"No offense, but I don't take orders from you." He had the audacity to smile.

"Evander takes orders from me, so you do too." I sputtered. He was wasting time. "I order you to help me now."

The second soldier raised his blaster. "We've got trouble."

A couple of civilians walked toward us. I ignored their glares, confident I'd get my way with Ev's men. "We pick up Talrano, then we get his wife before I leave."

Both soldiers shook their head, but the first one answered. "Evander said to leave now. If needed, I'll knock you out and carry you to your ship."

"You wouldn't." No one had ever disobeyed me before.

More people found the path connecting the spaceports. Perhaps they wanted to see if there were ships on the other side, maybe they heard our raised voices. Whatever the reason, there were now at least ten men and a couple of women surrounding us.

"Mynor?" The second soldier grunted.

Mynor nodded but didn't shift his attention from me. "Sir, your energy would be better served focused on the greater threat." He moved his hands to indicate the growing crowd.

The people held desperation in their eyes.

One of them pointed at me. "The Hatana's son will have a ship."

His statement was followed by other expressions of surprise, anger, eagerness. None of them bode well for me. I stepped in line with Evander's men, taking up a fighting stance. The soldiers' rifles were enough to keep the mob at a distance for the moment.

"Thoughts?" I asked.

Mynor grunted, "Too late for the best course of action."

Yeah, get on the ship like I'd promised Ev. Even with a small crowd after me, I didn't want to leave Talrano behind. I wouldn't let Eleena down.

"I vote fight forward," I said.

"Of course you do." Mynor studied the situation. As we spoke, more people entered the woods from both directions. "Still not going to happen. Riggs, call for backup."

"Already did, sir." Riggs kept an eye on the group behind.

"Amiran," Mynor only nodded his approval to Riggs while keeping his eyes on the men closest to us, "when the others arrive, cut to the left and backtrack to the *Fortissimus*."

The group of men surged forward before I could argue further. Mynor stunned several before they reached us. The first man caught me with an uppercut that made my teeth rattle. Mynor pulled him off before I could mount my own counterstrike, but there were more of them than us. Someone punched me in the side while another man grabbed me from behind.

Instinctively, I dropped my center of gravity and twisted to break his hold, sending my elbow into his stomach. The man grunted but didn't let go. His companion stomped my foot, then jabbed at my head.

I barely dodged in time.

"Come on!" I growled in frustration.

This wasn't like my years of defense training at the palace. People didn't wait their turn. They pressed close, bumping me, grabbing me, then falling away as Mynor or Riggs dispatched them. They took care of one of my attackers, leaving me to deal with the other one.

I swung my arm, elbow connecting with his face. He let go and I spun to see him clutch his nose. I seized his head and slammed it into my knee. He stumbled and fell to the ground.

Mynor and Riggs continued to stun people when they could. I engaged two more men. The years of training took over but exhaustion set in quickly. There were just too many of them.

Several hits to the ribs and head had my body screaming. I wanted to shut down and curl into a ball.

"Amiran?" Evander's voice bellowed over the sounds of fighting.

"Looks like the calvary's here." I dodged another strike aimed at my face. My arms felt like lead weights. I gave in to the fact I was about done for. "Here!"

More shots rang out. The woods grew blessedly quiet as the last man went down.

"What the *reinga* are you doing?" Evander swore at me then turned to Mynor. "Get him to his ship!"

"Ev, I've got time to—" A motion to the side distracted me.

Mynor flicked his hand forward so fast I couldn't stop it. I felt the bite near my ear. The stinging sensation started there and spread. By the time it made it to my shoulder, sunbursts sparkled in my peripheral vision. I felt lightheaded and the forest tilted.

"What did you do?" Even my mouth moved strangely.

"Captain's orders." He hefted me off the ground, slinging me across his shoulder like some animal.

I tried to twist around to see Ev, but my body wouldn't obey.

"It's for your own good." Evander's voice floated somewhere above me. "I'm not taking the shuttle up until you're off the planet. When I've filled the *Krahvuus* with refugees, I'll send you rendezvous coordinates."

My mouth dried out and my limbs hung like dead weight. "Did he—"

"Go on, the drugs are making him loopy. Drop him at the *Fortissimus* and return to the shuttle. I'll wait for you." Ev stomped his way down the path.

I slumped over, exhausted and disoriented. I tried to swallow. The ground moved below making me nauseous. I squeezed my eyes shut, concentrating on not throwing up.

Mynor's steps jarred my insides. This guy was strong. I was easily four inches taller. What was Evander having them do for training?

He had me drugged. Ev had gone too far. Hadn't he?

The leaves crunched under Mynor's boots. A blaster fired. Was that Riggs or another of Ev's men? People yelled but I couldn't make out the words. My ears didn't even work. Everything sounded muffled and warbled.

Ev didn't leave because he had to rescue me. That meant Eleena was still on the planet. If only Mynor had cooperated.

"I'll have you court-martialed for drugging me." My words came out slurred.

Mynor chuckled, "Only if we return to Rawiri, and I don't plan on going there until the Hatana is dead."

Sunlight highlighted random leaves as we left the tree cover. Bright green bounced around, then boots clanked on metal before everything went black.

4

SHUTTLE TO SHIP: ELEENA

The shuttle was dark but just as loud as outside. The engines rumbled as they cycled up and down. Air burst from pipes and vents. The hiss momentarily drowned out the murmur of voices. The passenger area was about the size of our gathering room at home. All the seats were full, most had two people in them. More men and women stood between the aisle and filled the other empty spaces.

"Hold on best you can for takeoff." The soldier waved us in before addressing the crowd. "Liftoff in five minutes."

We squeezed in with everyone else. It was hot and smelly. Uncle pulled me forward until I was crushed between him and another man. I tried not to breathe. The air tasted sweaty. I tucked my nose under the collar of my tunic.

The ventilation kicked up, pouring from the ceiling. Everyone fell silent. The engines revved then stopped.

"Please be patient." A voice spoke over a speaker. "There will be a slight delay, but we should lift off shortly."

"Atua help us!" a woman cried.

Another one wrapped an arm around her. "We'll be fine. It's a delay. He didn't tell us to get off. Have faith."

Uncle Beck squeezed my shoulder. "It'll be okay, Eleena."

I nodded. The warm feeling I'd felt outside when Atua spoke to me was fading, but there were many things to look at. Maybe this could be an adventure. It would be better if Mima and Popi were here, but there'd be lots of stories to tell them when I came home.

"What do you think happened?" I asked Uncle.

"I don't know, but your father said we could trust Am and the ship he put us on."

"Am comes over a lot." I shrugged. He used to come over, but he'd been busy the last couple of months. I never thought of him as anything other than one of Popi's students, but the captain had treated him like he was important.

The speaker derailed my thoughts. "We are ready and clear for liftoff in three minutes."

"Here we go Eleena." Uncle seemed to talk just to talk.

The minutes passed quickly. The engines cycled up again right before a lifting sensation. I grabbed uncle's hand. Everyone swayed and jerked with the ship's movement. Then a great pressure pushed me down from my head all the way to the floor. I wouldn't have stayed on my feet if not for Uncle Beck holding me tight. Eventually, gravity let up and I no longer felt like someone was trying to smash me flat.

In fact, I felt a little floaty. I looked down, relieved to see my feet still on the floor. "Uncle Beck?"

"We've reached orbit. We'll dock with a larger ship soon." He squeezed my shoulder again.

We stood a long time. The thrill of being in space evaporated. There wasn't even windows to see Manawa. I sagged against Uncle, too tired to hold myself up anymore. The shuttle was strangely quiet, with only a few whispers and an occasional soft crying.

The stillness of it all echoed a numb emptiness that had taken root in my chest. All I could think of was Mima with the ocean sunset behind her and the feel of Popi's last hug. Maybe Am would send someone else to get my parents since the others said he shouldn't?

And if he didn't, what would it be like when the fleet arrived? How long until I could go home to be with them again?

Atua said they were in his hands. I'd have to have faith in that, like the woman who had been scared with the liftoff delay.

"Uncle, how much longer?" My entire body hurt.

"Won't be long now, Eleena," Beck whispered. Shortly after, the shuttle thudded down on something solid. "See, we've reached the ship in orbit."

We waited for the door to open. Since we were at the back, we got out quickly. A soldier led us into a loading dock. I stopped, mesmerized by the huge square of stars behind the shuttle. Manawa peeked from the top corner.

That was my world. A place I'd thought so big that I'd never get to see all of it. Floating in a sea of billions of stars. My mind couldn't grasp how small we were in the scheme of things.

I know your name, Eleena. And every other name spread across this galaxy. Atua's words took my breath away.

"What do you think?" Uncle asked.

I pulled my gaze from the glowing orb to look at him. "It's like…"

There were no words to describe how I felt. So small and yet big and important because Atua knew my name.

Uncle smiled. "Yeah."

"This way, the shuttle needs to return for more refugees." A different man waved us toward another set of huge doors. "We've converted the cargo bays into living quarters. I'm afraid it will be crowded, but Jakaru is only a month away."

An entire month without my parents.

"Jakaru?" Uncle asked him.

"They've agreed to take you in." The man smiled but kept waving us down the hallway. "Follow Riggs."

"I wish I had a picture of Mima and Popi." I didn't speak loudly, but Uncle heard me all the same.

"Maybe you can connect to the nets and save a photo to your datapad while we're in orbit." He put his arm around my shoulder. "Observe everything and record your thoughts for them. Hopefully, you'll be able to send the messages to them when we get to Jakaru."

It would be better to have them with me.

Instead of dwelling on that, I walked, taking in everything I could. These corridors were larger and better lit than the shuttle. They were filled with compartments, doors, computer terminals, blinking lights, and fewer hissing pipes. People in uniform slid past us, looking hurried and frazzled.

We turned several corners then down a level to another wide open space. There were lots of people already in the room. Groups huddled together in the middle and a line had formed on one side. A huge bin of blankets sat inside the double cargo bay doors.

I wondered what Mima would think of it all. She'd probably start organizing people first thing.

"One blanket per person. Grab it and claim a spot of floor." The man who'd led us pointed to the bin, then to the line of people.

"We've built temporary latrines and showers to the right. Meals will be brought down since the mess hall isn't big enough for everyone."

I noticed his clothes were dusty and he had a fresh cut over one eye.

Uncle pointed at the thin trickle of blood running down the man's face. "You should get that taken care of."

"On my way to medical after this." The guy smiled like it was no big deal.

Uncle Beck nodded, handed me a thick blanket, grabbed one for himself, and set off across the room away from the bathrooms. "Let's try to find some space along the far wall."

"Are we waiting for a room?" I asked.

Uncle didn't answer until he'd set his blanket next to the far bulkhead. "No, Eleena. This ship, large as it may seem, isn't outfitted for travelers. They probably have three cargo holds this size, one on each level. We'll have to do the best we can until we reach Jakaru."

"You mean I have to sleep in here for a month?" The noise level increased as the rest of the people from our shuttle found places to rest.

"You'll get used to it." Uncle patted my head like I was a baby.

I jutted my chin out and sat down. "Do you think there's a chance Popi and Mima will get on another shuttle?"

Uncle Beck choked. When he stopped coughing, he stared at the people surrounding us. I decided he wasn't going to answer, then he focused on me.

"No. We have to pray for them. Hopefully, they'll be safe until we can go home."

"I can do that." It would be easy to pray because Atua had already promised he'd take care of them for me.

5

WAKING TO DEFEAT: AMIRAN

I woke in my quarters on the *Fortissimus*. My body ached from the
pummeling I'd taken, but my mind was clear of the drugs.
Reaching to the side, I turned up the lights and grabbed a datacom. I
stared at the timestamp, the hum of the ship's engines thrumming
through my body.

"It can't be." I swung my legs to the side and rested my head in
my hands. It had been a full day since I passed out. We had traveled
far from Manawa by now, making it impossible to return for the
professor and his wife.

I rushed to the desk and pulled up the COM to call Ephor
Adoser.

He looked tired and haggard when he answered. "Amiran?"

"What's happening? How did the evacuation go?"

"It went well. The police were able to handle the expected riots.
The last freighter left orbit this morning."

"Do you know if Professor Talrano made it off?"

Adoser shook his head. "I've tried to contact him, but he disappeared yesterday."

"He needed to reach his wife."

"There are a few private ships left. We've encouraged them to
take at least one other family with them. I expect they'll all be gone
by today. No one wants to be close when the fleet arrives."

"Will you leave?" I asked.

"No. My place is here to clean up and rebuild after the fleet."

"From your mouth to Atua's ears." I murmured but had little hope.

Adoser logged off. Next up, I called Evander.

"Finally awake?" Evander scowled at me on the screen. "Why did you risk it?"

"I had to try for Eleena's sake."

"No, it was for your own stubborn pride. She had accepted it and you almost made her choice worthless by getting yourself lynched."

I sank into my chair. That's not what I did. An unbearable weight settled on me. I didn't want to let her down, that's all.

"You know I'm right." Ev drove his point home. "You have to stop reacting, and think before running into things."

"Don't treat me like a child. I've already got one unbearable father."

"Isn't that the problem?" he paused, giving me time to accept the truth. "We're heading to Jakaru. After I unload I'll meet you at Olea. Be careful. Last we heard, your father was still after for you."

"I've stayed one step ahead for the last two years. He's not going to get me back on Rawiri any time soon."

"I hope not." Ev ran his hand through his hair. "I'll contact you after we arrive. Transporting several hundred people is a lot more work than I thought."

"It's only been a day." I pushed away my irritation at being lectured by a friend. He was right anyway.

"The scrubbers weren't made to handle this many people. My crew is working overtime removing, cleaning, and replacing them. I won't even get started on the kitchen staff. We'll deplete our food stores by the time we arrive on Jakaru. So far the people have remained calm, but it's only a matter of time before they get restless."

"Do you have a plan to keep them happy?"

"Working on it, but being packed in a tin can like dinges will get old fast. None of us were prepared for this." He looked tired. For the last year, he'd used a different skill set building a secret base and training our soldiers. Taking care of hundreds of displaced citizens would stretch him.

"Thanks for stepping up."

He grunted, "Get your head together. I'll talk to you later."

After the conversation with Ev, I tried to come up with a reason for my father to leave Manawa untouched. I feared he would unleash his full fury on them, but I couldn't think of anything that would sway him. I sent a message anyway.

"Hatana, I ask you to reconsider your position with Manawa. I've left the planet. They pose no threat to you. Their military is weak, and I've not heard any plans to challenge you." I paused, realizing there was one thing my father wanted. Could I do it? Swallowing my revulsion, I continued. "Father, if you'll spare Manawa, I'll return home. I'll serve my time in the fleet as you've asked. No complaints. Just say the word."

I hit send. My hands shook and my stomach twisted. There was a reason we faked Evander's death in order to get him out of the fleet. I didn't want to be under Schirra's thumb any more than Ev had. Fleet soldiers were one of two types. Those conscripted against their will and those who loved the power to hurt others with no consequences. The second kind of man flocked to Schirra's fleet, outnumbering the others five to one.

Remembering some of Ev's stories made me shiver.

I can do it for Manawa.

My father didn't respond. However, I received a message from Talrano three days after I left Manawa. He stood on a beach with his wife.

"Amiran, thank you for getting Eleena to safety. We need you to tell her how much we love her." Talrano hugged Sora as she silently cried beside him. He shifted the datacom and Sora's arm came up to help support her husband's outstretched arm. "There are no more ships. No way for us to join her until this is over." He choked on the last word.

Sora took over. "We know our chances aren't good." She wiped at the tears rolling down her cheek. "No matter what happens, tell Leena…tell her we've found peace knowing she is safe."

Talrano relaxed his arm, bringing his face closer to the screen. "May Atua be with you, protecting and guiding you. Keep asking questions, Am. It's the only way to find your answers. And if possible, take care of Leena for us."

The screen went dark. I never put much faith in Atua, but I hoped for their sake there was a being out there that could protect them.

Eight days after leaving Manawa, I received the Hatana's reply to my plea for leniency, a vid packet of the two-day siege.

The images were gruesome—a testament to cruelty. Not even a

promise of giving him what he wanted had made a difference. I watched in a state of numbness.

Atua, don't let it be real. I sank to the floor and watched again, thinking of Talrano and Sora. Remembering Eleena as she cried for them. *How will I ever tell her they're gone?*

Schirra's fleet attacked with twice the number of ships normally sent to subjugate a rebel planet. It was clear from the moment they made orbit they didn't intend to take prisoners. Squadron after squadron bombarded the planet and her meager defenses with laser and ballistics fire, only returning to the carriers to recharge and reload.

Manawa's military didn't last the first day, but Schirra continued to raze the globe. In the end, he sent down the eradicators ensuring nothing was left alive on that world. Schirra sent the vid packet of the attack to all the Allegiant and Coalition planets.

The message was clear. Speak against the Hatana and reap the fire of the damned. And on a personal note, my wishes didn't matter.

Thanks to Schirra and the nuclear fallout, I'd never walk on Manawa again. Never feel the sun or breeze. Never laugh with my friends at the local hangouts. I didn't know if any of them made it to a ship. As I took the time to remember every face, every name, the sadness turned to anger. Not only had the fleet wiped out a civilization, it had done it in the most cold-blooded way possible.

Why had Schirra saved the eradicators for the last? He could have sent them in first and ended the siege in minutes instead of days. The planet would be just as dead, but the people would not have suffered.

6

IRI AND HARPER: ELEENA

It had only been two days, but it was long enough to decide living on a ship was the worst thing I'd ever done. There was nothing to do. The grownups nagged at us kids to sit still or be quiet. We weren't allowed to leave the cargo hold either.

There was no way to tell if it was day or night other than the ship's lighting cycle. We slept when they dimmed. I couldn't even look at the stars because there were no viewports.

Each day was the same. Crew members brought in carts of food twice a day from the kitchens. It wasn't much—sandwiches, soup, or a meal bar. The rest of the time we sat, listening to the low hum of conversations. There was always a line for the toilets.

By day three I'd gotten used to the smell of antiseptic from the latrines mixed with the stale recycled air. Uncle stayed with me about half of every day. Then he'd disappear for a couple of hours to help Captain Evander with stuff. My job was to protect our spot while he was gone.

"That's my blanket." An older boy glared at me. His hair was too long. He was taller than me and a little on the chubby side.

"Where?" I asked.

"You're sitting on it. Get up." He folded his arms.

"No, it's not." I looked around the room hoping Uncle was somewhere in sight, but he hadn't been gone long enough to be headed back yet.

"I say it is, and you'd better move or I'll make you."

"No. This is my spot, and Uncle told me not to leave it."

"Liar. Last chance." He leaned forward. "One, two,"

"I'm not giving you my spot." I tried to glare back. My heart beat in my throat.

"Three." He swooped down and grabbed me by the arm, dragging me off the blanket.

Stumbling in the effort to get my feet under me, I tried to hit him with my free hand. He blocked it easily. Next, I tried to kick him. That only made him laugh.

"You kids, keep it down." A lady yelled at us, then lay back down on her blanket covering her head with her arms.

"But he's trying to take my spot." I pled with her hoping she'd help.

"One spot is just like another." She turned her back on us.

The boy squeezed my arm but spoke quieter. "No one cares."

"You can't take my place." Hot, angry tears burned down my face.

"You can't take my place." He mimicked in a high fake voice.

"Why are you being so mean?"

"You've got a better spot than me, and I want it."

"See, you just said it's mine."

The boy growled and pulled me away from the wall. Even though I tried to stand still, he was stronger. Finally, I bent down and bit him as hard as I could. He shoved me to the floor.

"You'll pay for that." He rubbed his arm but jerked around when someone laughed.

Another girl, close to his age, stood behind him. She had blonde hair streaked with brown.

"Looks like you finally met your match. You'd better run back to your mommy before she gets your other arm." The girl put her hands on her hips and cocked her head to the side. "Oh, wait, I forgot. You don't have a mother."

"Neither do you, Harpy." The boy fisted his hands as his face turned red. He stepped forward ready to hit her.

My heart pounded and my head buzzed. Then I heard the voice of Atua. It was just as startling as the first time I'd heard it.

Help them.

I jumped at the command, grabbing the boy by the arm. "We don't have to fight. I don't have a mom anymore either."

"Yeah, but you have a dad." The girl waved her hand in the air.

"He's my uncle." I slowly let the boy go, hoping he wouldn't attack again. These were the only kids I'd seen close to my age. I was

30

sick of being alone. Is that why Atua asked me to help them? "Do you have anybody with you?"

"No." He growled, and the girl shook her head.

"You can stick with us. I don't think Uncle Beck would mind."

The girl squinted at me. "I don't think it works that way."

"Maybe." I shrugged.

The boy grunted. "I don't need your help."

"I know." I sat on the blanket.

"I don't need help either, but I like you for biting him." She pointed to the boy and sat beside me.

"That's all this ship needs. A harpy and harpy wannabe." The boy stormed away.

"Why does he keep calling you a harpy?"

"My name's Harper. That's Iri. We were in the same class before school disbanded. He didn't use to be like that." She picked at a string from Uncle's blanket. Harper kept glancing across the room. I knew she was watching Iri stomp around. "He used to be nice."

"Oh." I didn't know what to say. Uncle Beck had explained that some people would act mean because they didn't want others to know they were scared.

"So, what's your name?" she asked.

"Eleena. Did your parents stay behind too?"

"Iri and I don't have any parents. We were both in the *pohehe* children's home."

"Where's *Pohehe*? I've never heard of that city."

Harper fell backward with laughter. She hugged her stomach and rolled to her side, still laughing. "*Pohehe* isn't a place. It's another word for crappy."

"Oh." My face warmed. I stared at the floor. She must think I'm stupid.

"It's okay. I can teach you lots of good foreign words. There was a girl at the home that spoke E'tchlic. She taught me lots of stuff. For instance, when you're really mad, you can shout or say *reinga*." She spit the words out.

"What's that mean?"

She whispered, "hell."

"I'm not allowed to swear."

"That's why you use E'tchlic. Plus, as you said, you don't have a mom anymore."

It hadn't hurt when I'd said those words, but somehow it felt like a punch in the stomach when Harper repeated them. I'd tried not to think of my parents the last few days. Now I couldn't stop. Were they okay? The tears surfaced, and I turned away from her.

She touched my elbow. "I'm sorry. I forget it's different for kids that knew their parents. When you've always been on your own, this doesn't seem like such a big deal."

I nodded but didn't look at her. *Atua?*

The peace I sought came gently. It was a soft, barely there kind of thing, only dulling the bite of my heartache. The tears didn't stop right away.

"How old are you anyway? I'll be fifteen in four cycles like Iri. Wonder if that will change because we're going to another planet?" Harper continued to chatter, distracting me further from missing my parents. She didn't stop until I turned and faced her again. Then she paused and stared at me.

"I'm twelve and four cycles," I told her my age, a little afraid she'd stop talking to me.

"Huh. I'm impressed with how you stood up to Iri like that." She looked me over a little closer.

"What?" I asked.

"Nothing. Just, most kids would have given him the spot."

"But it was mine."

Harper smiled. It made her pretty. "Yeah, it sure is. Don't worry about him. I bet he'll go back to being the old Iri I used to know before long. Maybe then he'll take you up on the offer to share an uncle."

7

RETURN TO RAWIRI: AMIRAN

A member of the crew rushed into the galley. "Your Highness, another ship has appeared below the port bow."

"Identification signature?" I asked.

"Fleet registry out of Rawiri."

"*Aukati*." I shoved my breakfast away. How did they find us? "Any chance of outrunning them?"

"No, sir. We're at full engines and they're almost in firing range."

That meant stabilizing range as well. "How did they sneak up on us?"

"They must have stayed out of range until ready to attack." The man stared at the ground. "What do you want us to do?"

"Wipe all data files, including personal ones, and prepare to be boarded." I waved him away and hurried to my own quarters to do the same. Before wiping my computer, I sent Talrano's last message to an encrypted server on Olea, vowing I'd show it to Eleena one day. Finally, I sent a message to Evander.

SCOUTS BOARDING. RETURNING TO RAWIRI.

At least he'd know not to contact me until I reached out to him.

It had been two years since I'd last seen my father. Two years of avoiding my homeworld and the mind-numbing palace politics despite the Hatana's demands to return home. I wasn't sure what I would return to, but knowing my father it wouldn't be a happy reunion.

The wipe was almost finished when the *Fortissimus* shuttered from the stabilizing beam.

"Computer, broadcast." I waited for the ping before continuing. "All hands prepare for boarding. Do not antagonize the fleet soldiers and you should be fine. Out."

When my computer finished rebooting, I left my room and headed for the docking airlock, uneasy that the other ship had not yet tried to contact us.

"Sir, they've engaged magnetic locks." The same man that informed me of the approaching vessel joined me. "The others stayed in their quarters."

I nodded. It was probably for the best. General Schirra wasn't known for negotiating and neither were his handpicked mercenaries. A dull thud echoed in the corridor as the last lock clicked into place signifying the two ships were coupled.

"Here we go," I murmured. "Let me do the talking. As soon as I'm gone, head to Olea but make at least three other stops before."

"Yes, sir."

Seconds turned to a minute. Two. Three. My stomach clenched in anticipation. Finally, the red light flipped to green and the airlock door slid up to reveal six fleet soldiers.

"Take the Hatana Tama," one ordered. Then he flicked his wrist to the hallway. "Dispose of the others."

"No!" The word was barely out before the man beside me crumbled beneath blaster fire.

I lunged, catching hold of the extended blaster and shoving it upward into the soldier's face. He stumbled back, blood oozing from his lip. Before I could shift my focus, I was slammed to the ground. It felt like half the fleet sat on top of me.

"Prince Amiran, we are authorized to subdue you any way we see fit."

I twisted to glare at him. "There's no reason to kill my crew."

"Maybe, maybe not, but I follow the orders given to me by the Hatana. Perhaps you should have as well."

"The *reinga* with you." I spit out.

He rolled his eyes, flicked his wrist again, and everything went dark.

I came to as they dragged me through the airlock into their ship. The back of my head pounded. Before the hatch closed I heard screaming and the distinctive whine of blaster fire. What little fight I had left drained out of me.

We stopped in front of a door. It slid open to reveal the standard fleet officer's room. Bed, storage, desk, and sanitation cubicle. This one even had a viewport.

"Meals will be brought to you. The captain wanted to make sure you could watch your ship as we left." One of the men laughed as he shoved me into the room. His next words were heavy with derision. "Welcome back, Hatana Tama."

The men departed and I didn't bother to try the door. Even if it opened, I wouldn't join the others on this ship. Moving to the window, I caught my reflection in the glass. A trickle of blood ran past my ear. Tenderly, I touched the area and found the source of my headache. The lump seemed to grow as I probed it. I cleaned up at the sink before returning to the viewport.

The stars shifted and the *Fortissimus* came into view, drifting slightly askew. She didn't look any different on the outside, but I knew the inside had forever been tainted by the Hatana and Schirra's men. Were they going to let her drift?

When the *Fortissimus* was the size of my fist, a momentary flare ignited. It was nothing more than a spark quickly snuffed out in the coldness of space, followed by three more down her length. My ship shivered, sinking inward as if pulling in a breath, then it shattered outward. Debris flew in every direction, spinning off to every corner of space.

THE LAST TWO days of the trip were torture. I stopped mourning because it hurt too much. Instead, I focused on the anger and desire to stop the Hatana. Hours of pacing didn't help me relax. By the time we landed on Rawiri and the soldiers escorted me to the palace, I was coiled so tight I stomped through the halls to the council room.

The guards opened the doors and I jerked free of their grasp to stalk forward. My father sat on the dais. General Schirra to his side. The room was full of the military and civil staff that kept the war machine running smoothly.

"What gives you the right to slaughter billions of innocent people? Women, children? Only a handful spoke against you, but you wiped out their entire civilization." My fists clenched. It took all I had to stand still.

"The prodigal returns." Hatana Anaru glared at me from his higher ground. His shoulders stiff, but the rest of him appeared relaxed. "Pity Schirra's men didn't teach you respect before your arrival."

The venom in his voice pushed the air from my lungs. I hadn't felt loved by the man who contributed to my existence since the day my mother left, but I'd never felt threatened before now.

Schirra stood. "Hatana, the prince's loyalties have been contaminated more than you thought. It would be wise to discard him and try for a new heir."

My father's eyes narrowed. He studied Schirra's placid face. I don't know if he found what he searched for, but he waved a hand in the air dismissively.

"The boy is young. There's time to train him properly. Perhaps a year in the mines on Cassia will bring him around." The Hatana motioned to the side of the room.

The soldiers I'd left behind stepped out of the shadows and flanked me. The entire room held its breath. My mind and body froze. Surely, he wouldn't? The mines were a death sentence.

Schirra bent to whisper something. Hatana Anaru's face contorted before he hid all emotions once more. He simply nodded.

Schirra stepped forward. "Prince Amiran, you have been sentenced to one year in the mines of Cassia for treason against the Hatana. A light sentence and we all know it." He sneered at me before continuing. "After which you will serve the required five years in the fleet to better prepare yourself as the Hatana's heir."

The anger and guilt I felt changed to terror. If I survived the mines, I'd become Schirra's slave. There would be no preferential treatment in either place. It was one thing to sacrifice myself to save Manawa, but that world was gone.

"Hatana, Father. I only wished to discuss alternative ways of ruling. Ways that don't necessitate so many mindless deaths. I'd never act against you."

"Speaking out is an attack in and of itself. If you were not my only heir, you'd be lying in a pool of your own blood. Speak again, and it will be done." The Hatana stood, the epitome of the warrior. Tall, broad-shouldered, and built like a mining frigate—all muscle and brute strength. His eyes glittered like steel, and I didn't doubt his words.

The Hatana jerked his head and the men grabbed me. How could I have been so stupid? I'd only been on Rawiri half an hour and I was being reminded of how things worked. I strained against their hold.

A kick to a soldier's instep freed one arm. Grabbing the second guard, I shifted my weight, dropped low and sent him flipping to the ground. Four more guards rushed me, pinning me down.

In the struggle I thought I caught a glimpse of a smile from my father, but when I focused my gaze he looked as angry as Schirra.

"Get him out of here," the Hatana bellowed.

I suppressed the instinct to continue fighting, knowing Schirra would need very little encouragement to carry out my father's threat of death. The men dragged me to my feet and led me out the door. We passed Timoti, Evander's father. He nodded and hurried the other way. I stood straighter. From now on, it was just me. I couldn't count on anyone else.

We left the palace, entered a transport, and drove to the cell block. Schirra hadn't wasted any credits on building the detention cells. No one stayed long. They were executed or put on one of the daily shuttles bound for Cassia. The mines drained the rest of their life.

"You'll stay here tonight." A new soldier opened a door. He was young and let me walk in under my own power. "Your Highness," he checked to see if the hall was clear, "be careful on Cassia. Keep your head down and you might make it out alive."

He nodded once before locking me in. I glanced around the steel room and considered his remark. Did he want me to make it? Perhaps I wasn't alone. With a sigh, I sank onto the thin mat. There were no windows, but there was a latrine in the corner.

Hatana Anaru had taken away everyone and everything I'd ever cared about. Mother, Evander, my crew, and Manawa.

I kicked the wall until my toes hurt. Not many people survived the mines. I didn't expect to fare any better. Ev wouldn't know what happened to me, and Eleena gave up her parents for nothing. I'd die before ever getting the chance to stop my father and Schirra.

8

CAPTAIN EVANDER: ELEENA

Iri hovered near our spot for another day. Maybe he wanted to see how Uncle Beck took to Harper before throwing his lot in with ours. Maybe he was still mad about me biting him. I never asked. Eventually, he let Beck draw him into a conversation. Then he followed my uncle around everywhere, helping him do whatever it was he did every day.

Harper just smiled behind Iri's back. She loved being right and was kind of bossy, but I loved her like a sister after that first day. She made everything more interesting. We made up stories about the other people in the cargo hold. Mostly about what they had been or done before leaving Manawa.

When we grew tired of that, I pulled out the datacom Popi put in my pack. I felt a little guilty I hadn't recorded any messages for my parents. Harper and I made one together.

"Mima, Popi, this is my new friend Harper." I started and Harper waved at the camera. "There isn't much to do on the ship. We just kind of sit here, but having a friend makes it okay."

I paused, not sure what to really tell them.

Harper nudged me and whispered, "show them what everything looks like."

"Good idea." I flipped the camera and panned around the room pointing out the groups of people, hygiene facilities, and massive doors. "I think Uncle Beck is helping Captain Evander with some-thing, but I don't know what."

I turned the camera back toward Harper and me. "Hopefully, I'll be able to send this to you when we get to Jakaru. That's where we're going. Uncle said you wouldn't be coming."

Harper wrapped an arm around my shoulders, giving me the strength to continue.

"That's okay. I'll record it so you can see it when we get there." I tried to hold onto the excitement of seeing a new world but it was hard. "Well, I love you both. Talk to you soon."

After that, we were so bored even school work sounded good. Harper was the same grade as me, even though she was older. We decided to learn about Jakaru.

Iri didn't join us. He rarely talked to me, but I figured that's because he didn't like me much. Most of the time he only grunted at Harper. Sometimes though he'd say just enough that she knew what was going on. It was like they had their own code. The most words he ever spoke were to Uncle Beck. I think Uncle was more comfortable with Iri than me and Harper. It didn't bother me, they were both boys anyway.

When we'd been on the ship a little more than a week, Uncle came through the cargo hold with Captain Evander. Iri trailed behind them. They stopped and talked to different groups of people. Harper and I watched them work their way around the room until we lost interest and turned our attention back to the datacom.

"What have you got there?"

I looked up, surprised to see the captain and Uncle standing in front of us.

"They do school work," Uncle answered for me.

"Really?" Evander knelt down to our level. "What are you studying?"

"We're reading about the ecology on Jakaru." I flipped the datacom around so he could see.

"Why did you pick that?" he asked in that tone adults used when speaking to a child.

I tried not to roll my eyes. "That's where we're going, right? Popi says you should always be prepared for new things. We didn't know anything about Jakaru." I elbowed Harper, hoping she would speak up, show the captain we weren't silly kids, but her eyes were big and round. Was she scared of him?

"Your father was a wise man." Evander glanced at Uncle when he stood. When he refocused on me, his voice sounded more normal. "Eleena, do you think it's better for people to know the truth, even if it hurts them?"

39

"Popi says if you don't know the truth, you can't make the right decisions, but Mima says Atua can guide you no matter what. Do you think that's true? Do you think Atua can talk to us?" I'd thought about this a lot, wondering why no one ever talked about hearing him, and what it meant that I had twice.

"Some people claim to hear his voice. However, most of us have to live with the hope he's there. Do you think he cares what happens to you?" The captain's gaze pierced me.

Not sure of what his stare meant, I answered, "I know he does. I think he cries a lot though."

"Why's that?" Uncle Beck asked.

"Because people make bad choices and hurt others." I couldn't stop the shiver that ran through me. Where were my parents right now? Had they made it off the planet or was Uncle right? Were they trapped and waiting for the fleet?

Captain Evander rubbed his forehead, his smile long gone. He looked tired and older than when he'd stood with Am all those days ago. "I hate how soon you'll understand the truth of those words."

I tried not to squirm since the captain kept watching me. Then he nodded and turned to leave.

Uncle patted my head. The lines around his eyes had grown deeper. Or maybe it was just the shadows that pooled there. Iri glared at us before they followed the captain out of the cargo hold.

"That was weird." I shook my head.

"Leena, you were awesome! I couldn't say anything with the captain staring at us like that." Harper clasped my arm.

"He's just a guy like Uncle and Popi."

"Yeah, but he's the captain. Even your Uncle listens to him. He's important."

"Oh. I never thought of that. He's not much older than Popi's students, like his friend Am. Am and some other students came to our house lots of times." My stomach growled. I wondered how long until our second meal would be delivered.

"He listened to you. Adults don't listen to kids like us." Harper stared at me the same way the captain had. "But then again, I guess you're not like me."

"Of course I am." The way Harper looked at me made me feel weird. I picked up the datacom and flicked the screen. "Look at these birds!"

9

VIBRO-SICKNESS: AMIRAN

M y body ached from lying on the ground. The same soldier who'd given me advice the night before handed me some hard bread and fruit.

"They wouldn't allow anything else." He ducked his head as if embarrassed.

"Thanks." I tasted the bland roll and wondered why he bothered. Wasn't he as scared of my father and Schirra as the rest of us? I studied him as he pulled gray pants and a shirt from a bag, along with a pair of work boots. "Are those for me?"

"Yes, your Highness." He set them on the mat. "When you've changed, knock on the door."

He turned and left me alone. Setting the bread and fruit down, I picked up the shirt. As it unfolded, a piece of paper fell to the floor. I scooped it up and glanced toward the door.

Timoti's clear writing greeted me.

"Be smart. Will get help to you."

It was short and vague, but the weight on my shoulders lifted a bit. If he could, Timoti would find a way to get me out. I quickly removed the attire worthy of a prince and pulled on the coarser work fabric. It was appropriate. I'd failed as a royal. If I couldn't make a difference for the people I cared about on Manawa, the mines were a just punishment.

I wadded up the note and flushed it down the toilet. Then I knocked on the door to let the guard know I was dressed.

He pointed to the food still on the mat. "You should finish that."

"I'm not hungry." I picked up the half of bread and the slightly bruised fruit.

"You will be." He glanced down the corridor and back at me. "They're going to make an example of you. Eat. It may be a while before you get anything as good."

The knot in my stomach churned again. How could food get worse? This was as basic as it got. I forced down another bite of bread, followed by the bittersweet fruit. All it did was feed the acid in my stomach, threatening to send it all back to the surface.

"Why are you helping me?"

"Not all of us are here by choice." He scanned the hallway again. "We respect that you tried. If you live, you might make a difference someday."

"Or I'll get another planet laid to waste." I ground my teeth.

"At least you said something."

"It didn't help."

"There are many waiting for someone better to follow." The sound of doors opening brought us back to reality. Other soldiers marched past, releasing prisoners and leading them away. "I'm sorry, but I have to shackle you."

I nodded and held out my hands. He placed vibrocuffs around my wrists. The hum of low voltage electricity zipped through my body. It was a barely there kind of thing, but it was enough to make me feel off-kilter. My body knew something wasn't right, and I stumbled as the guard led me out the door.

"Try not to think about it. The cuffs make your brain work over-time to regulate your biorhythm, but the oscillating current makes that impossible. The energy output is only point zero one greater than normal, so you'll barely feel it." He kept his voice low.

"It isn't unpleasant." I managed to say before stepping outside. In fact, I felt hyper-buzzed—like the time Ev and I snuck into the kitchens and drank an entire bottle of Waina.

"Give it time." He nodded toward a transport waiting to take me to the spaceport. "Good luck."

I climbed in and joined the truckload of prisoners. The other men's eyes widened, then shifted away. They clearly recognized me. I didn't know any of them, but they appeared to be civilians.

My calm dissipated over the short trip to the spaceport. Twenty minutes in vibrocuffs was enough for my arms to start tingling as if waking from sleep, and even though I felt physically energized, the mental exhaustion set in.

The others exhibited similar internal battles. One sat ramrod straight, his knee jerked up and down, but his eyes remained shut. Others wiggled and squirmed as if they couldn't stay still if their life depended on it. No one made eye contact with anyone else.

What had these men done? Were they innocent like me? But I wasn't really faultless. I'd been foolish enough to open my mouth and others paid for it.

The transport bounced to a stop, sending us swaying. One by one we climbed out of the truck. I shuffled to the ship slowly, trying to take in as much of my homeworld as I could. It wasn't that different from Manawa. However, the fear on Rawiri hid behind a tranquil facade.

Soldiers directed us up the ramp and into one of the newer hybrid ships. I couldn't recall its designation, but it was larger than a firebarge while smaller than a full-blown mining frigate. It was a good size. I bet Evander would like a few of them.

My thoughts were cut off by another shove from behind. "To the left."

I turned and a door opened. The room didn't look much different from the cell, only smaller. One bunk and a toilet, with maybe three extra square feet of floor space.

"Fit for a prince, no?" The soldier laughed and closed the door. The magnetic locks clicked into place.

He hadn't remove the vibrocuffs. The magnets in the door sent new twinges through my arms when I got too close. I backed up and sat on the bed. How long could my body function with the current running through it?

THE VIBROSICKNESS STARTED with a headache and nausea, followed by the inability to sleep. At first, I walked the three steps back and forth across my room. It didn't bring relief. Eventually, my muscles gave out. I lay shaking on the floor in a puddle of sweat and urine until a guard came in with food. He helped me onto the bed and force-fed me some soup.

It didn't take long for me to throw it up. That's when the ship's medic visited. He had me cleaned and administered meds for the fever and nausea. However, it did no good since the vibrocuffs remained on my wrists.

After two days, I tried to gnaw my hands off. I'd barely broken the skin when the medic returned. He cleaned and bandaged me up before calling the guards in.

By the end of day three, I begged to die. My body had grown so weak I couldn't lift my head. I lay curled up, eyes shut, praying for release.

"You have to remove the restraints," the ship's medic told the soldier yet again.

"Schirra's orders are to leave him shackled." The soldier's voice didn't sound confident.

"He's the Hatana Tama, do you want to be responsible for his death?" the medic argued. "Take the blasted things off. The other prisoners don't have to wear them. What are you afraid of?"

"General Schirra," he stuttered.

"I'll do it then."

Cool hands wrapped around my wrist. The vibrocuffs fell away, along with the electrical current that had been my constant companion. The sudden stillness shocked the tears from me. Sobs of relief followed.

"Not much of a prince is he?" The soldier sounded surprised.

"He's just a kid. I'd like to see you last three days with these contraptions on." The medic pressed a hypospray into my arm. Cooling waves flowed through my body. "Amiran, by the time you wake, you should be able to eat."

They left, and I lay there like a dead dinge. I didn't have enough strength to climb under the thin sheet when the shivering started.

Time drifted by, interspersed with dreams and bouts of awareness.

Evander walked the corridors of a ship with Eleena's uncle. The medic came and went, hooking me up to some contraption to feed me. Eleena sat huddled with a blonde girl while a boy glared at them. Ev sat alone in his quarters watching the feed of Manawa's siege. Men came and went from my room. Eleena cried while her uncle held her.

Did she know about her parents?

It became hard to differentiate between reality and dreams. The medic gave me several shots, and eventually, the headache subsided. My body returned to its normal biorhythm.

I lay in bed, eyes closed, pretending to sleep.

"He won't be strong enough for the mines. Not without another day or two for recovery." The medic talked to someone in the room.

I opened my eyes just enough to get a glimpse of the newcomer. It was hard to focus on his face, but I recognized the deep red rank epaulets. The captain looked every bit the military man as the Hatana and the General. He stood taller than the doctor, his arms crossed over his chest, and his brow furrowed in thought.

"We can't do anything about it. We arrive tomorrow and it's out of our hands."

"What if we," the medic stopped mid-thought and shook his head. "Never mind."

"Help him the best you can with supplements, but we can't disobey orders." The captain's next words were scarcely more than a whisper. "Not yet."

I coughed to hide the gasp that slipped out before I could stop it, turning toward the wall in an effort to hide.

The medic touched my arm. "You might as well open your eyes."

Slowly, I faced the men and struggled to sit up. "I don't understand."

The medic helped me lean against the wall. My muscles were still weak, refusing to work properly.

The captain nodded. His eyes weren't as cold as my father's or Schirra's. "If you survive the mines and Schirra's fleet you might one day. We can't take a chance on you until then."

My thoughts moved sluggishly. Possibilities slipping through before I could grasp and make sense of them. I shook my head and cringed as the dull ache returned.

"It'll come to you." The captain moved toward the exit. He held up a disk and the door slid open. "Listen for the voice of Atua and you might save us all."

The medic followed, the door closing and locking behind them.

Listen for the voice of Atua? Even though I'd spoken his name in the trite phrases of my people, I'd never really put stock in a supreme being. My father thought being Hatana made him a god. That was enough to turn me off all the other gods in the universe.

If there really were a god in heaven, why would he let men destroy so many things of beauty?

I sunk back to the pillow, enjoying the coolness against my cheek. It would take more than the captain's words to turn me toward an imaginary being.

10

MANAWAN NIGHTMARE: ELEENA

The overhead lights dimmed then brightened followed by a shrill whistle of three short bursts then one long siren. Harper wiggled closer.

"What's going on?" she yelled.

"I don't know!" I'd covered my ears with my hands until the noise stopped.

Uncle Beck and Iri hurried across the room to our corner. Uncle practically fell to the floor and grabbed one of my hands. Iri sat on the other side of Harper.

"I'm sorry for this. Truly I am," he whispered. The lights went off and stayed off as the room fell silent.

"Uncle?" I scooted closer, feeling Harper come too.

Projectors from the corners of the room lit up. A 3D image of Manawa appeared in the middle of the room. It was as beautiful as when I'd seen it after getting off the shuttle. It hung there, frozen in place inside the cargo hold.

Captain Evander's voice drifted from the amplifier. "The senior officers are not in agreement. However, a wise little girl told me that if you don't know the truth you can't make the right decisions. I hope she will forgive me for what I am about to do. You deserve to know what has happened to your world. The good, and the bad."

There was a pause, but the holovid didn't start. Uncle wrapped his arm around me tighter. His body shook, sending a chill of fear straight through me.

"What..." I started to ask.

46

"Shh, give him a minute. It's not easy for him." Uncle squeezed my shoulders. "It's won't be easy for any of us."

The captain continued. "We've picked up an Allegiant transmission from the Hatana's fleet. Time-stamped four standard days ago. Watch and know that even in the face of this evil, Atua's hand has saved your lives and twenty-thousand others. We only mourn that he did not save all."

The vid started with the breathtaking image of Manawa, then everything changed. Silence permeated the room as the horror played out in front of us. Twenty or so fleet spacecraft surrounded our world. I recognized war cruisers and eradicators from my school studies.

We watched as the Manawan defenders rose from the planet to fight the fleet. They didn't last long against the hundreds of saber-bolts flowing from the larger ships.

There was no sound with the vid. There didn't need to be. Our hearts and minds filled in the sound of crunching metal and explosions.

The battle didn't look like I thought it should. Each time another Manawan ship was destroyed, it didn't go out in a blaze of flame. Instead, there was a brief fizzle, then darkness as the debris simply drifted into space.

When all our fighters had been destroyed, the fleet directed its lasers at the surface. Those images held more meaning for me. Made more sense to my mind. Towers of black smoke gobbled up the white clouds, obscuring even the smallest glimpse of land or sea. I didn't know if the lights from the cities were obliterated or simply hidden by the encroaching darkness.

Ships shifted in orbit, more smoke rose to be trapped in the atmosphere. It was as if Manawa had developed its own bubble. It kept all the smoke and sound inside.

One of the largest ships moved into the upper troposphere and released a huge fireball. Uncle's grip tightened around my waist. My attention followed that flame as it flickered through the black clouds. The explosion blasted away the smoke, once more revealing land masses. The wave of fire expanded outward, devouring everything for hundreds of miles.

Other ships sent down their own fireballs.

Although the explosions were silent, the room around me filled with wailing and sobbing. The vid ended and the lights came up half way.

47

Captain Evander's voice sounded rough even though he talked softly. "When we reach Jakaru, you may stay with us, or you can book passage to any planet in the system. The Coalition is gathering forces to fight the Hatana. The thousands that escaped Manawa are scattering throughout the galaxy to ensure the survival of your culture and race. I'm sorry for your loss."

I couldn't feel Uncle's arms around me anymore. The sounds in the room came from far away. My head felt tight, strange, and the same clouds that covered my world, my parents, surrounded my vision.

"Eleena, breathe." Uncle turned me to face him.

I could see the individual streaks the tears had left on his face, but everything else was blurry. Blinking didn't help. I was vaguely aware of Harper and Iri crying behind me.

"Breathe." He didn't promise it would be okay.

I gasped for air. My voice squeaked out the only thing that mattered. "Mima, Popi?"

Uncle Beck shook his head. It was so slow he barely moved. My heart shattered into a million pieces.

"Atua promised." There were no tears for me. Only a great emptiness.

"Eleena?" Beck hugged me closer. "I'm so sorry. I should have made Canto come."

I didn't understand. Maybe I hadn't heard the voice of Atua. It must have been wishful thinking that my parents would be safe if I left. I thought of the boy from school who always told me I was a stupid girl. He'd been right after all.

They are in my hands.

The voice sounded as gentle as the first time I'd heard it, but this time it lanced through my heart, releasing the pain. It hit me in waves. Shivering and sobbing, I collapsed into Uncle. He cried with me, whispering little things he'd miss about my parents and what he'd loved most about Manawa. I ran out of tears long before he ran out of memories.

THAT NIGHT I dreamed I lay in the REC bubble behind my house. The same blobby clouds moved overhead, and the air buzzed with the sound of insects. The wind blew the grass around me. It was like the perfect days from my memory.

As I lay there, the blue sky was eaten up by orange and red. The air heated. Everything around the edge of the barrier took on a strange glow. I ran to the boundary behind my house, but I couldn't step through no matter how hard I pushed. The bubble shifted and warped under my hands, but it kept me trapped inside.

My house, the grass, trees, everything outside the sphere burned. I didn't see any people. Were my parents in the house?

"Mima!" I screamed and pounded on the bubble wall. It reverberated but didn't release me.

Sweat poured down my back and pooled behind my knees. It dripped from my forehead, mingling with my tears. My skin burned, my lungs stung, and the heat increased.

"Popi, I'm here." I kept beating at the clear surface until my hands bled. The house crumbled. All I could see was blackened lumps. And yet it grew hotter.

My skin dried and blistered. I sunk to my knees, struggling to breathe. There was no air. Only heat waiting to spark into flames.

"Eleena, wake up." Someone shook me. "You're dreaming."

It was hot, but only because someone held me tight. The air didn't smell of smoke. Instead, it smelled like sweat and cleaning solutions.

"Eleena?" Uncle Beck rubbed my back. "Breathe. Please, you have to breathe."

Not Mima, or Popi.

I sucked in great lungfuls of air and sobbed. I couldn't help it. They were gone forever and nothing I did would bring them back.

"It's okay. Cry it out." Uncle rocked me in his arms. "It's going to take time, but Atua can heal your heart."

I cried harder. Atua hadn't saved them. Why, why, why?

Their work was done, but yours is just beginning.

I startled at the voice in my head, too hurt to be comforted completely. However, my crying changed from sobs to silent tears streaming into Uncle's shirt. Even though Atua's words didn't bring peace, his presence did.

Atua, why?

His love enveloped me, covering me like a warm bath. *They are with me, watching over you.*

Uncle Beck's words from the first day on the ship came back to me. He'd told me to talk to my parents as if they were there. Now I knew they were. Even if I couldn't see them. Like Atua, they would stay with me.

I gave Uncle another squeeze. "I'll be okay now."

He looked down at me. "You sure?"

"Yes." I nodded. "Atua says my parents are with him."

"Atua?"

"I was mad because he told me they were in his hands before we left home. But he didn't save them."

"You've heard the voice of Atua?" Uncle's brow dipped as he looked at me with an intensity I'd never seen before. It was as if he tried to see inside my head.

Harper and Iri stared at me as well.

"Are you okay?" I asked Harper.

"Eleena," Uncle placed his hands on my face and turned me toward him again, "have you heard the voice of Atua?"

"Yes," I whispered.

Uncle Beck's eyes got watery like he was going to cry but didn't. Instead, he hugged me tightly.

"This is wonderful and sacred. Don't tell everyone, but listen to Atua. He'll let you know who you can tell. Who can know how special you are."

I squirmed, the heat rising up my cheeks. I didn't want to be special. I wanted my parents and my old life back.

The next night I had the same nightmare, but this time I saw my parents trapped in our house. Harper woke me and she too had to remind me to breathe. Uncle called it anxiety. I hated the way it made me feel. Helpless, scared.

Atua, I don't want to dream of them. It hurt too much and made it hard to remember the good times we'd shared together.

I'll send a different vision.

I didn't know what kind of dreams Atua would send, but I wanted to trust him. They had to be better than the burning ones.

Harper and I lay back down. Her breathing smoothed out quickly. Fear kept me awake longer, but eventually, I closed my eyes too.

Am lay on a bed in a tiny room. Without his smile, he looked very different from the boy that used to visit. His face was covered with a splotchy beard that hadn't filled in yet. Another man wiped his forehead with a cloth. Am's body shook. His face twisted with pain. My mother would know how to help him. She always knew how to make me feel better. Her loss hit me anew. I tried to push away the pain by concentrating on Am.

What's wrong with him? I asked Atua.

Vibrosickness.

I didn't know what that was, but it didn't look good. A new fear took root, threatening another anxiety attack. What if Am died? Who would stop the Hatana then? *Will he get better?*

Yes, the doctor will heal him.

"Eleena?" Am whispered and stretched out his hand. "I'm sorry."

Can he see me? I looked around the room, but I couldn't see me, so how could he?

No, he dreams.

"Evander?" he asked again and tried to push himself off the bed. The doctor pressed a hypospray to Am's arm and he calmed. The scene faded away.

Atua? Was the dream real? I stood by the side of the ocean. My parents had taken me for my last birthday. It looked a lot like the view from Mima's window. Atua didn't answer, but the sound of the waves soothed me until I fell into a deeper, dreamless sleep.

THE CARGO HOLD was a strange place the day after we learned what happened to Manawa. People sat and stared at nothing. Children cried, not understanding why their parents ignored them. Others whispered and moaned, rocking back and forth.

Even though I'd slept, my body felt wrung out. I couldn't concentrate on the datacom.

"Eleena, we could make up stories about the others. We haven't done that in a few days." Harper wrapped her arms around me.

I shook my head. "I don't think I can. Not yet."

"Okay." She rested her head on my shoulder and we sat quietly.

I must have drifted to sleep because I woke snuggled up with Harper and Iri. Uncle Beck was still gone. Panic set in before I remembered there was nowhere he could go.

"Leena?" Harper sat up. "You okay?"

I nodded, but the lump had returned to my throat. I didn't want to accept everything I'd ever known was gone.

We sat with our backs to the wall. Iri stayed with us, but he still didn't talk. I wondered if they were as sad as I was. They didn't lose parents. Just Manawa. When I glanced at Harper, her eyes were red.

Uncle Beck joined us for the mid-day ration. There was some kind of baked bread with meat and gravy in it. We still had to fill our water bottles up at the sink in the washroom, but it was one of the best meals we'd had so far.

"Evander thought it would be worth using the food replicators today. It's depleted our stores, but this kind of meal is more comforting than protein bars." Uncle had taken to rambling to fill the silence. I don't know if it made him feel better, but it helped me.

"Will Captain E do rounds today?" Iri rarely said so much in front of me. I noted he didn't use the captain's full name. Probably his way of cutting down on words.

"No." Uncle wiped the crumbs from his scraggly beard. "The destruction of Manawa wasn't the only bad news he got yesterday."

"What could be worse?" Anger tainted Harpers' voice.

Uncle looked at her until she lowered her gaze to the floor. He took another bite of food, chewed, and swallowed before speaking again. "The death of our world is truly horrible. The only thing that could be worse is for it to happen again. Who is to stop the Hatana?"

All three of us stared at him, food forgotten.

"Am will stop them. That's what you told me, Uncle." I watched him frown and recalled the dream I'd had. Did the captain find out Am was sick?

"We all hoped so, but he was captured by the Hatana. He's been sentenced to the mines on Cassia."

"But he's alive." Harper kept her voice neutral this time.

I grabbed her arm. He was alive, but really sick if what I'd seen was true.

"It's a death sentence." Uncle shook his head. "No one else could have gotten close enough to the Hatana to put an end to this madness. We will need our own army to stop him now."

"I'll fight." Iri sat up taller.

"Me too," Harper and I said it at the same time.

Uncle smiled, but it looked sad. "I'm afraid we all will."

11

THE COALITION: AMIRAN

T he medic returned with a real meal and a concoction of hyposprays that gave me enough strength to stand on my own. It took effort to move, but at least it was possible. Instead of the vibrocuffs, the soldier escorting me off the ship placed a zip-tie style restraint on my wrists. It chafed more than the wider band of cuffs, but the absence of current was worth it.

I joined the other prisoners outside. There were about ten of us. We all sported scraggly beards and bloodshot eyes. They kept their gazes to the ground, but I needed to see everything.

We'd landed at a spaceport in a mountain range on Cassia. The lavender colored sky reflected off the cliff looming above the airstrip. The copper rocks were interspersed with mirrored sheets of metal. A triple star system beat down with merciless heat. Mountains dominated one side of the landing area, a vast desert the other. Sweat dripped down my back after only a moment under the suns' assault.

Our guards led us toward the cliff face and a set of large hanger bay doors. The area was busy, but I only saw fleet soldiers. No civilians and no other prisoners.

A group of men marched our way. I could tell by the stripes on their sleeves they were higher ranking officers.

"We're short-handed in sector five." The CO thumbed to the left and a primitive looking cart system on rails. "Load them up."

The cars stood waist high, less than two meters wide, and maybe three to four meters long.

"Get in." A soldier motioned with his gun.

I fell in.

Another prisoner helped me sit up so I could lean against the side. A trickle of blood dripped from the side of my face. I swiped it away.

The inside of the cart was covered in the black and silver dust of celestium. Clumps of it lined the corners and pressed into my back. The soldiers waited until all of us were crammed into one cart, shoulder to shoulder, even though there were four more connected to the line.

"You'll be unguarded, but don't think this is the time to escape. There's nowhere to go. It'll simply be a quicker death." The soldier slapped the side of the cart, then signaled someone we couldn't see.

The air screeched as the dusty wheels pushed against the rails. The sound dissolved as we picked up speed leaving the base and all the soldiers behind. I was too weak to consider climbing out of the cart.

We rode in silence. I'd lost everything, but Ev and Eleena were safe. Or was that a hopeless dream? I couldn't be sure, but I hoped it was true.

After the cliffs fell away, there was nothing to mark the passage of our journey. Even the sky was bereft of clouds. The void of anything meaningful laced my mind with despair.

"You're the Hatana Tama," the man in front of me stated, pulling my attention back to the cart.

I sensed other gazes directed my way. What to say? The truth could be as deadly as lying, and I had no idea what would be the best or the worst thing. I finally nodded, too tired to think of a lie.

"I can't believe the Hatana sent you here." The man continued to stare. "What did you do?"

Images of Manawa's destruction and a tear-streaked face with large brown eyes filtered through my mind. I swallowed the lump in my throat.

"Not enough." I shook my head. "Others paid for my mistake."

"The Hatana's men paid?"

"No." I turned my face back to the sky, struggling to push away the pain.

"Ah. You speak of Manawa?" I heard him shifting around. "That was my home. You helped get many off-planet before the attack."

"It wasn't enough. How do you know what I did?" I took a closer look. He was in his forties, maybe fifties, but he still had thick hair only slightly gray on the edges. He didn't look like a soldier, more like the soft politicians I'd seen wandering the gardens on campus.

"Imon Adoser was my brother. My name is Na'mune. Schirra's spies found me before I could escape from Rawiri."

"They arrested you because you were from Manawa?" I tried to stretch my legs, which had fallen asleep.

"The Hatana needed no other reason." Na'mune nodded. "I'm just glad they didn't execute me."

The next few minutes passed with the rhythmic clacking of the cart. We swayed and bounced around a curve and the sides of high mountains rose up on both sides of the track. It brought shade and a brief respite from the ruthless beating of the suns. My heart kept time with the wheels, each beat more painful than the last until I had to speak.

"I'm sorry for your loss." It felt like empty words even though I meant every one.

"Imon chose his path. He told me how many were saved."

The ache in my chest turned to a stabbing sensation. I rubbed at it and concentrated on breathing. Not Talrano. Not his wife. Only Eleena.

"Without your help none of those would be alive now. Instead, twenty-thousand people lived and our culture will be preserved." Na'mune nodded as if it were enough.

The sharpness in my heart turned to anger. "Saved for what? To be arrested and sent to the mines? I failed them and they will continue to suffer at my father's hands. What was the point?"

The other men turned away. They'd listened silently, and I accepted their condemnation. Na'mune shook his head, but there was a hint of a smile on his face.

"Amiran, the point is you tried. You defied your father the only way you knew how."

"A lot of good it did." Why did everyone keep saying that? Trying and failing was worthless. It didn't change anything.

"You have no idea." His gaze darted around the cart at the other men. "We should tell him."

Gazes turned my direction once more. They studied me with respect instead of the hatred I thought I'd see. Several of them shared that same half smile that was starting to irk me.

"Tell me what?" I searched every face, waiting for the answer. "Are you all from Manawa? Is that why you've been sentenced to the mines?"

"No, but we are council members from Coalition worlds. The Hatana condemns any man who dares challenge his methods." The man next to me spoke. "The Coalition has watched you for years. We feared you would follow in your father's footsteps, become even more brutal with his and Schirra's guidance. We were prepared to make sure you never took the throne."

"Did you arrange to be here the same time as me?" I gasped. People were prepared to assassinate me?

"No, dumb luck on our part. We didn't leave Rawiri soon enough and your father's soldiers rounded us up." Another man laughed bitterly. "We'll never see our families again."

"So, you're not here to kill me?" I couldn't let that thought go.

"Relax. When you ran from Rawiri and went to Manawa, we knew there was a chance to show you the other side of the coin so to speak." Na'mune soothed. "Canto did a wonderful job of it too."

"Talrano was part of a plan?" My heart sunk. Had his friendship been a lie?

Another man across and several feet down spoke. "No. He didn't know anything about our years of watchfulness, but we couldn't have chosen a better teacher for you if we'd tried. Canto Talrano's passion for the truth couldn't be faked."

The weight fell from my shoulders for half a moment before his loss hit me once more. "I couldn't save him."

Heads nodded and we abandoned conversation. The only sound was the steady rhythm of the wheels spinning along the rails. My thoughts churned just as quickly with the new information. The Coalition would have killed me. Why me? I was only eighteen and had no control over any aspect of the government or military. It didn't make sense.

"Why me?" I asked.

"What do you mean?" Na'mune was the clear leader.

"Why not take out the Hatana or Schirra instead of me?"

"You were easier to get to, and we hoped with you out of the picture, Rawiri's rule would end with your father. Eventually."

It made sense. Sort of. But my father was healthy and could live for decades. He could always produce another heir as Schirra suggested.

"My choices still don't change anything." I surveyed the motley group.

"It changes everything." The man beside me spoke again. "You've given the Coalition planets hope."

I laughed at the irony. "Hope. What good is that?"

"One day you will put an end to the empire." Na'mune spoke with conviction.

"And if I can't?"

"Atua will not leave us desolate forever. You need only follow his guidance."

Atua? Why did it always come back to him? First the captain, now Na'mune. The others nodded in agreement.

I shook my head. "It'll take more than an imaginary god to put an end to my father's cruelty."

Na'mune chuckled. "You're right. It will take faith in a god as real as you and me. He's waiting for you. Don't let us down, Amiran."

DEHYDRATION HAD BEEN my friend for days thanks to the vibrosickness, but Cassia's suns took it to a new level of discomfort. By the time the car jerked to a stop, I'd ceased to sweat. My throat and skin were both dry and gritty.

Soldiers with vibrosticks waited at our destination. They ordered us up and out. If it hadn't been so painful, I might have laughed at the way we all stumbled and fell like drunkards. A sharp volt of electricity quickly wiped the image from my mind. Miles of nothing surrounded us. All I could see were pillars of rock, tables of rock, cliffs of rock, rock, rock, rock, and the bright lavender sky.

"Rules for the mines," a man with captain's stripes on his sleeve addressed us. "Make your quota and you'll avoid a beating. Stay in the well-lit areas and the *Itzalak*, or shadow men, will leave you alone. There's nowhere to run, no way to escape. Welcome to *reinga*."

He waved his hand and the soldiers divided us into smaller groups. A door slid open in the tower of rock behind the captain. Four prisoners and two soldiers entered and disappeared behind the closing door. The rest of us stood in the heat.

I'd never been to Cassia. The strange sky clashed with the red rock and I wondered if there were places that looked nicer. Pretty even? I couldn't imagine it. What I wouldn't give to see blue sky dotted with clouds pushed by a light breeze.

The doors opened and closed while groups of prisoners went down. Each second passed slowly. I found myself willing the lift to hurry back so I could escape the heat. When my turn came, I stepped inside willingly, welcoming the respite.

The scent of sweat and dust filled the air. No one spoke. We simply stared at the walls. The doors opened onto a large cavern. A new smell assaulted me. Mud, mold, and something that hinted of mineral or chemical. Probably celestium.

Low hanging fluorescents hung from the cave ceiling, giving decent light to see several rows of cots. The chill pricked at my skin. It had to be forty or fifty degrees cooler than topside. A large heating system wheezed and belched out warmth near some tables serving as a mess area.

This won't be that bad.

The elevator doors opened again and the captain stepped out with the last group. "Keep moving."

We followed the soldiers away from camp. The corridors blasted into the rock were dimmer than the large cavern. The longer lights were gone, replaced by smaller yellow bulbs. They were scattered around, casting shadows as much as light. Two lines of glow tape marked the edges of the narrow pathway, and the damp air grew colder without the heaters.

"Stay between the lights or you'll find yourself at the bottom of a pit. Only the *Itzalak* will look for you." Our guard prodded us farther down a series of turns and tunnels.

I didn't think I could find my way back to camp if I tried. My eyes grew accustomed to the darker world. I could have sworn I saw one of the shadows move.

"What are the Itzalak?" I asked.

"Venture into the shadows alone and you'll find out." The soldier's voice didn't sound as confident as before.

The clatter of tools striking rock reverberated throughout the tunnel long before we reached a brighter area of the cave system. Spotlights had been set up on stands directed at the walls instead of the open spaces. Men moved from light to shadow as they worked. None of them spoke, but they grunted with the effort of swinging axes and hauling away the stone they dumped into wheeled carts.

"You'll find tools in the crate over there." One of the soldiers pointed. "This is a new tunnel and you'll need to clear the surface to find the ore. Use the larger picks to start. Once you find a celestium vein, switch to the smaller tools. Remove it carefully, with as little of the surrounding slag as possible."

Another soldier chuckled. "Be careful you don't strike the vein and blow your hands off." He headed down the tunnel, his fellow soldiers joining him.

As soon as the sound of their movement and laughter dissipated, the other prisoners dropped their tools and surrounded us. They were a dirty lot—tattered clothes, boots split at the soles, long facial hair hiding their expressions. It was hard to differentiate one from the other, but a tall man stood front and center, the rest flanking him a step or two behind.

"I'm De'truto. I'm in charge. Disobey or cause trouble and I will personally deliver you to the shadows." The man squinted at me and his eyes grew round. He recognized me, and by the scowl that followed, I doubted that would play in my favor.

Na'mune stepped to the front. "De'truto. It's good to see you alive."

"Na'mune?" De'truto moved away to grasp the older man by the shoulders, clapping him on the back and smiling. De'truto's teeth almost glowed in contrast to the caked on dirt that covered his face. "Tell me news of home. Have we convinced more planets to side with the Coalition?"

"No." Na'mune grunted in despair. "The Hatana has made an example of Manawa."

De'truto's shoulders tensed. "What do you mean?"

"None of us will ever return home."

De'truto jerked around to me. "You."

He lunged, his fist connecting with my chin. I stumbled back, then his large dirt-encrusted hands wrapped around my neck. My back slammed against the cave wall. I clawed at his hands, but his grip was like a vice. I pounded at his side, his back, his face, but he only squeezed tighter as he growled in anger.

No matter which way I twisted, he stayed with me. There was shouting, but the sound was muffled. I held onto his arms and wrapped my legs around his body, hoping I could shift our weight and take him down. The man had an iron grip and was as strong as a frigate. I dropped back to the ground and swiped at his feet while he searched for a new balance. We went down, but he didn't release me.

De'truto rolled, landing another blow, and locked me in a death grip. I was aware of only two things. The sound of each breath I struggled to gain and the intense desire to live.

Amiran, it's not your time to die. The voice pierced my heart and mind. The shock of it stilled my hands.

"Truto, stop." Na'mune and two others from our shuttle pulled the man off. I remained on the ground. "When I said none would return home, that included Amiran."

Men surrounded us. Everyone tensed to fight, several holding others back.

De'truto's eyes cut through the shadows like blades of fire. His chest heaved with the effort to breathe, and his hands continued to reach for me. He spit out his next words. "He is the Hatana Tama. We will make an example of him."

The men flinched ready for action.

"Stop!" Na'mune yelled before the fighting spread and slapped the back of De'truto's head like a father reprimanding a child. The others paused, clearly shocked at the motion. "Look at the boy. His own father sent him here for helping Manawa. Calm down and let us talk."

De'truto strained against the men holding him. His eyes glazed over, but he stopped fighting. "There's no way to stop him. No weakness to exploit."

"Perhaps not, but Atua has breathed hope into my heart because the boy is not like his father."

De'truto's face reflected my own disbelief. *Atua?*

"Ask. His voice will pierce you, teach you." Na'mune stared at me as he said the words.

Is it possible the voice I heard belonged to Atua? Would he offer me comfort after my failure?

De'truto sat with eyes closed for several minutes. The quietness of the cave was unnerving. As I looked around, I saw other men standing with eyes closed, faces raised to the darkness above. They were the very image of despair. Dirty, ripped clothing hanging from their thin bodies. Their faces covered in the black streaks of celestium powder, proof that their insides were slowly being eaten away by the very substance that powered our spaceships.

And yet, their countenances exuded peace.

De'truto nodded. When he opened his eyes, they were directed at me. His voice, though steady and firm, no longer held anger. "How did he help Manawa?"

"He helped organize the evacuation that saved many of our leaders and artists. Without him, there would be no survival of our culture. Amiran fought for Manawa."

A murmur moved through the crowd. One of the miners reached down, offering a hand up. The man pulled me to my feet, held my hand a moment longer than necessary then moved on. Another man stood in his place. He too clasped my arms and looked me straight in the eye before moving away. This process continued until only Na'mune and De'truto stood before me.

My heart was full of many things I couldn't name. "Na'mune?"

"Patience, Amiran. The mines will teach you all you need to know." De'truto spoke as he too gripped my hand in his. "For you, the shadows will not hold danger, but the wisdom you seek. In the meantime, we dig for celestium."

Na'mune took De'truto's place in front of me. "Listen for the voice of Atua. Only he can bring you out of the mines prepared for the next step in your journey."

That was the second time in twenty-four hours someone had told me to listen. Having heard my name whispered in my mind, I didn't scoff this time.

12

SHIP'S LESSONS: ELEENA

Even though I knew my parents were with Atua, the nightmares continued. Uncle said it was because I had a strong imagination and the vid of Manawa's destruction gave me too much material to work with. Every time I had one, I asked Atua to send me a different dream. They were always of Am. He looked better, but he was surrounded by shadows and dirty men. Sometimes I felt his sadness.

After the second dream about Am, I told Uncle what I'd seen. The captain came to visit that day. He and Uncle pulled me into the corridor to talk.

Evander stood, his brow furrowed. "Beck says you've dreamed about Am. That he's alive and well."

I glanced at Uncle and he nodded. "Yes, sir."

The captain didn't say anything, just stared at me. Finally, he took a deep breath. "I don't know what to think."

"He was sick on the ship, but he's better now." I tried to remember what I'd seen. "I don't know where he is though."

"I know where he is, but I can't get to him. Not yet." He turned to Uncle. "Thank you for telling me. I believe and that will have to be enough for now."

Uncle patted the captain on the shoulder before turning to me. "Return to Harper and send Iri out."

"Yes, sir." I slipped through the doors and picked my way through the crowded cargo bay. The noise level had increased since the vid. I wondered if other people dreamt about home. Maybe that's why they grew restless. Those previously content to wait until we reached Jakaru now caused trouble. Some argued in the food lines. Others tried to expand their living area, pushing people closer together.

Evander's men had to stop fights all the time now. Those who caused trouble didn't get rations for the day. Uncle didn't like that. He disappeared for a long time after Captain Evander announced that rule.

Iri couldn't always go with Uncle. The three of us studied star charts and other lessons on my datacom on those days. I don't think Iri enjoyed it much. He looked up when I got close to our spot.

"So?" he grunted.

"Uncle said to send you out," I answered.

Iri jumped up and was gone before I could say anything else.

"I don't get it." I pointed after him. "Why doesn't Iri talk more?"

"He does when it's important." Harper shrugged.

"I guess." I didn't really want to talk about Iri even though he was a puzzle. "How much longer do you think we'll be stuck on the ship?"

"I don't know, but I've never missed the sky so much in my life."

"Me either."

We clicked through random lessons and vids on my datacom, both of us lost in our own thoughts. The hum of the crowd rose and fell, but we had grown used to it. I hardly noticed the noise or the smells anymore. Sometimes I missed being alone. Most of the time I was glad I wasn't though. I was relieved to have Harper and Uncle to talk to. Even reassured to have Iri brooding nearby.

Uncle and Iri brought our dinner rations when they returned. We were back to shapeless lumps that were meant to be meat sandwiches. They settled in and Uncle told us how the other cargo bays were holding up. All of them were pretty much the same, except for the one with lots of children. They had a different set of challenges. I thought it might be fun to move to a room with more kids, but Uncle said they fought more than played.

After we ate, the lights dimmed again. Captain Evander once more spoke to the whole ship and introduced a new routine.

"People of Manawa. We only have a week until we reach Jakaru. Each day we will show vids on the planet and people so you will know what to expect.

"A temporary place has been prepared for you. However, the Jakarun council has invited you to move to any town or city you wish. They will grant you a starter allotment of credits, help you find jobs, and begin a new life. You'll need to decide what's best for you when we arrive. There will also be transports to other Coalition worlds available."

The whispers and conversation swelled. I looked to Uncle, wondering what we would do. He didn't say anything. The vid started. It was one Harper and I had already watched on the various climates of Jakaru. I lay back on my blanket, with my hands behind my head, and concentrated on the sky in the vid. I was glad the Jakarun sky looked like Manawa's.

Later that night, after the lights had dimmed, one of the ship's crew burst into the cargo hold. "Beck, come quick!"

Uncle jumped up. So did Iri.

"Stay here, Iri." Uncle jogged across the room and out the door with the crewman.

Harper sat up and leaned against the bulkhead. "What do you think happened?"

"Fighting," Iri said the one word, laid down, and ignored us.

I sat up too, determined to wait until Uncle returned so we could ask him questions.

"Harper," I whispered, "think that's it?"

"Iri told me that's one of the things Beck won't let him hang around for."

"When?"

She shrugged. "A couple days ago."

When had he done that? I was always with Harper. Well, except for when I went to the toilets. I didn't think there could be secrets on a ship but it seemed there were.

We sat forever. My eyes got dry and heavy. Finally, I gave in and lay down. I drifted to sleep before Uncle returned.

The next morning, Uncle woke me in order to give me my food rations. "You don't want to miss breakfast." His beard had grown in thick over the weeks. There were shadows under his eyes, and the whites were full of tiny red veins.

"You're tired." I took the protein bar and put it in my pack. It took a while for me to feel hungry in the morning.

Uncle nodded. "It was a long night. We've decided to let the vids run all day."

"Why?" I glanced around, noticing Harper and Iri were both absent.

"It'll keep people occupied thinking about something other than Manawa and this ship."

It made sense, but I'd already watched most of them. I would get bored.

13

DEEP IN THE EARTH: AMIRAN

The mines were worse than I'd imagined. My eyes strained to see into the shadows. De'truto reminded me to stop trying. He trained me how to dig for the precious ore hidden in the mountains of Cassia.

"Celestium has to be dug out by hand due to its delicate nature. We start new branches of the mine with blasting until we find a vein. That's followed by heavy pickaxes to clear the surrounding rock. Once you get within four to five inches," he pointed where the spotlight shone directly on a blood red and black line of minerals cutting through the brown and blonde stone, "you switch to the finer chisel and hammer set."

He handed me a belt with the tools he'd mentioned. "This work is more delicate. Get too close before switching and you could lose a hand or worse."

"How hard do you have to hit to ignite it?" I asked.

"A little nick with the small chisel is safe enough, but a full body swing with the ax will spark. Don't do that. The explosive wave will travel throughout the vein. So it's not just your life at risk."

I nodded, the sense of dread growing. Even if I was cautious, someone else could kill me.

"We're all very careful." It was as if De'truto could read my mind. "The old-timers keep an eye on the newbies, and everyone reports reckless or erratic behavior."

"What's considered erratic?"

"Good question. You'll learn soon enough. Just be on the lookout for any suicidal tendencies."

"I've got to think that would be fairly prevalent down here."

De'truto laughed. "True enough, but most of us have a mission and something to look forward to. That keeps us alive."

"What's that?"

"See the reign of the Hatana and Schirra come to an end." The laughter was gone from his voice. "Start here. Eventually, you'll have to use the pickaxe, but you look too weak for that now."

Before I could protest, he drifted away, leaving me and my bruised ego to chip away at the vein in front of me. I pulled the small hammer and chisel from the belt.

"He forgot to show you how." A voice startled me. "There is an art to mining."

I looked around but didn't see anyone standing close or looking my way. This voice had not sounded inside my head, or been accompanied by the burning rush of the one that spoke my name earlier. Instead, it was gravelly, as if from non-use. It came from a shadowy place to my left.

"Hello?" I whispered.

"Place the chisel close to the vein, tip pointing away from it. Lightly tap at the detris to free the ore. The bigger pieces are worth more and better for the ship's engines." There was no sign of the speaker.

"Who are you?"

There was no answer. After a moment I shrugged and started the process of freeing the celestium from the wall. I did as the voice had instructed. Tiny bits of rock broke free as I chipped away at the mountain. An hour later, I'd managed to outline a fair chunk of celestium, but it was still embedded in the rock face.

"Good work, Amiran."

I jumped at the voice, dropping the chisel. A throaty gargle indicated the speaker might be laughing at me.

"You will learn to pay closer attention to your surroundings. It's a skill to look absorbed by what's in front of you without being clueless to the rest of the world."

"It would be easier to recognize company if I could see you." I tried to hone in on the direction of the voice.

"Ah, but the things you must worry about are the ones you can't see. We will prepare you. Taking the empire from your father and Schirra will be like mining for celestium. Although there will be a time to swing away with a heavy ax, you must build up your strength first. Most of this process will be tedious, chipping away bit by bit, with the chisel facing away so they don't know you're after them." The voice moved as it spoke, making it even harder to locate where the *Itzalak* stood.

He had to be in the shadows, maybe even behind the wall of rock. If so, how was he projecting his voice through it?

Peace, Amiran. Trust. This voice came from inside my mind. I shook my head. Shadows and disembodied voices were getting to me.

The outside voice continued, "I see you're thinking, asking questions, seeking answers. That is good, but we must teach you to do those things while keeping your expression blank."

"That will help me stop the Hatana?"

"It is only the beginning. Work now." The voice disappeared and a few minutes later other men moved to work closer to me.

I settled into the monotony of movement. The metal hammer pinged against the chisel. I worked for hours, making progress at a glug's pace.

14

LANDING: ELEENA

"Stay close, Eleena." Uncle clipped straps to hooks on the wall behind him. "This is going to be worse than the shuttle."

Harper and I huddled close. Iri wore his usual 'I'm tougher than everyone' scowl, but when Uncle touched his shoulder and pointed to one of the loops, Iri sat and wrapped it around his wrist. Uncle attached two more.

People crowded around us, attaching their own safety devices to the wall. Many of us had bags or packs strapped to our backs or across our bodies. We'd packed everything we could to keep things from flying around during landing.

"Harper, you take that one. Eleena, you're going to hold on to me."

"Okay." I nodded.

His overly serious expression made me nervous.

Captain Evander had decided to land the entire ship on Jakaru instead of shuttling everyone down. Uncle didn't agree with that. He said it was cheaper to keep the big ship in orbit, but Captain E feared what the people would do if they had to wait for the shuttle to unload them little by little. Landing would allow everyone to get off right away.

The ship shuddered as the engines shifted to reverse thrusters. The lights dimmed to power saving mode. Yellow beacons flashed around the room. Everyone stopped talking. They clung to ropes and leather cording that had been strung across the room in a grid pattern for the people without access to straps on the wall.

It wasn't so bad. Each time the thrusters fired, the ship swayed and creaked, but that was it. I tried to wiggle free of Uncle's clasp.

"Eleena, hold still."

"I'm okay. Let me hold the strap there." I pointed to where one of the cords stretched from one wall across the cargo hold to the other side.

Hold onto Beck. The voice startled me. I stopped fighting Uncle and clung to his arm. Had he heard Atua's voice?

The ship tilted. People screamed. Some fell, sliding across the floor into others. If not for Uncle's firm grasp, I would have tumbled away too. I vowed to listen to Atua more closely from then on out.

"Here we go, hold on." Uncle glanced at Harper and Iri. "Don't let go."

I clutched him tight as the ship rattled and shook. Every part of my body vibrated from the ship's effort to re-enter a planet's atmosphere. Then gravity disappeared. It was eerily still as we drifted off the floor. People held on to the ropes. A woman screamed and flailed her arms as she floated higher. She couldn't reach the safety lines or anyone else. I saw others drifting upside down.

"Harper, Iri, hold yourself as close to the floor as possible," Uncle ordered as he hooked a foot around one of the cross straps.

I twisted around to see them mimic Uncle by grabbing another cord with their other hand or looping their leg under it. Then gravity reasserted itself. I slammed into Uncle's chest as he hit the ground.

With the weight of Jakaru pulling on us, everything grew louder. The ship resumed shaking. People screamed.

The clanking soon drowned out all other voices. All that existed was trembling metal and shrieking engines. Finally, there was a thud, accompanied by a bounce of sorts and then stillness. The air grew full of the hissing and popping noises of the ship cooling.

"People of Manawa," the captain came over the intercom, "we'll be able to disembark soon. Please wait patiently."

Uncle checked all three of us until he was satisfied we were unharmed. "Double check our packs, but stay here. I'm going to get medical help for those who need it."

He hurried away, leaving us alone to wait for him.

"That was cool." Iri's face was contorted in a look I'd never seen. A smile.

Harper and I laughed with relief. It was good to see Iri happy, but

I never wanted to do that again. I grabbed my pack. It only contained my blanket and datacom, but when we fell it had been crushed between me and Uncle. I sighed with relief when I checked and the screen wasn't cracked.

"That was scarier than I thought." Harper sat down to wait. "Do you think we'll get beds on Jakaru?"

"I hope so." I'd gotten used to the floor, but a bed sounded wonderful. Whatever this new planet was like, I decided to do what Uncle asked. I'd be kind. I'd find ways to keep learning, and I'd do what my parents would have done if they were here. Whatever it took, I'd help others.

DURING THE MONTH IN SPACE, I'd learned Jakaru was a smaller planet than Manawa. The people were mostly farmers, but there were larger cities too. We didn't land near any of them. Perhaps that's why I loved Jakaru the moment I stepped off the ship. The sky was blue and wide. It stretched forever. Nothing blocked it from view, not buildings, trees, protective bubbles, or anything else. The biggest, fluffiest clouds I'd ever seen scurryied across it.

"We're heading toward the gate over there." Uncle Beck pointed to a large fenced off area containing hundreds of white tents.

"Beck, hold up." Captain Evander jogged down the gangway. "Now the others are unloading, we can find a place for you and Eleena on the ship."

"That's not necessary." Uncle Beck waved him away.

The captain grabbed Uncle's arm. "Look, I promised Am I'd help you as much as I could. So far, you've been more help to me. If you need anything, anything at all, let me know."

"Thanks, I'll keep that in mind. And Captain, the same goes for you. None of us chose this life, but we're here." Uncle clapped a hand on Evander's shoulder. "You're doing something good. I'm more than willing to help wherever you need me."

"How about you keep doing what you've been doing. When you see a need, let me know."

Uncle gave a little salute and ushered us into motion. I was glad to head down a hill to the encampment. The air was comfortably warm with a cool breeze. It felt wonderful to be off that stuffy ship. I'd much rather sleep in one of the tents than stay on board. We followed the others and got in line.

"What are we doing?" I asked.

"The Jakarun's need to know how many of us there are. They'll assign us a tent and food rations. Those who want to move here permanently will be added to the job listings around the globe. Others will be given passage to any planet they wish."

"What about us?" Harper didn't look at Uncle but scanned the camp.

"What do you mean?" Uncle asked.

"Iri and I aren't old enough to live on our own. Will they give us jobs, or will they put us in a home?"

Uncle shook his head. "I thought you'd stay with us. Eleena needs the company, and it's nice having Iri assist me."

"We'd like that." Harper's eyes glittered, but she didn't cry. I'd only seen her cry the one time. The day we watched Manawa die.

I glanced at Iri and caught another of his rare smiles. We reached the gate, and Uncle stepped up to a table. A skinny man sat behind it with a large stack of papers.

"How many?" he asked.

"Four," Uncle replied.

The man wrote something on the top paper, stamped it with a blue circle and handed it to Beck. "You'll be in 42C. Cots will be handed out tomorrow for those who choose to stay. There'll be a meeting in the center of camp tonight at sundown to discuss options other than this place."

"Thank you." Uncle wrote his name on a clipboard.

"Your tent is four rows in. We've placed maps of the camp inside for you." He waved us away, already turning to the woman behind us.

"Come on." Uncle glanced at the paper before folding it and slipping it in his pack. "Let's look at our tent."

All the tents were white with a black square near the zippered flap. The designating number had been stenciled on the square in a bright green paint. We found ours, passing many others that were now home to our shipmates. The only thing inside was a wooden stand with an empty square basin on top for sponge baths. A five-gallon container of water sat on the shelf beneath the bucket.

"Uncle, why aren't the beds here? They knew we were coming." I stared at the basin. Was that the only way to get clean? Even the ship had showers. Iri moved off to the side and my face grew hot. I'd better get used to not being clean.

"The Jakaruns plan on most of us moving into apartments in the city. They'll bring beds for those who choose to stay with Evander instead of resettling." Uncle picked up a paper from the basin. "Here's the map. Looks like there's a REC area, mess, and a medical tent around here. Not much else."

"Why would we stay with the captain? Will we stay?" I shivered thinking about going back to the ship.

"I'm thinking about it, but we don't have to decide today." Uncle patted me on the shoulder. "There are things I'll have to explain to you so we can make the decision together."

"Really?" Harper looked up at him. "Me and Iri too?"

"Yes. I meant what I said to the captain. We're all in this together, but let's enjoy the day before we get too serious."

Harper leaned over for a peek at the map. "Wonder what they have for recreation?"

"Let's go check it out." Instead of dropping his pack, Uncle left it on his back, so we kept ours too.

It took a while to walk around the tents. Few people stayed in the shelters even though they offered the most privacy we'd had in a long time. They took to wandering like us. We passed the central patch of grass that served as the mess area. There wasn't a tent there, but several long tables where they could serve the food. I hoped it wouldn't rain too much. Lots of people congregated there. I watched Uncle as we walked. He didn't smile. His brow wrinkled more as we went.

The REC area was just a big field. Nothing else.

"That's disappointing," Iri grunted.

"It would make a great garden." Uncle rubbed his chin. "Iri, go back to the ship and let Captain Evander know we've found some needs."

Iri nodded and took off.

"What can we do?" I wanted to help like Iri.

"We need to find the bathroom facilities. I didn't see them on the map." Uncle turned in a slow circle.

"I didn't see any as we walked." Harper followed Beck's example and turned to look at everything again.

"That's another thing we need to fix." Uncle strode back toward the front gate. "We'll need tools and supplies."

I glanced at Harper. She shrugged and we ran to catch up. At least Uncle would find stuff for us to do.

15

THE MINES: AMIRAN

"Hungry?" Na'mune startled me.

I'd been concentrating so hard on not blowing myself up, I hadn't noticed him approach or how dry my mouth and throat had become. My nose also burned from the dust I'd inhaled.

"Yeah." It came out a croak. "Any water?"

Na'mune jerked his head to the side. "Follow me."

We walked through several passageways. Men came and went, working, resting, talking.

"This seems relaxed for a prison camp," I mused.

"Yeah. De'truto says the guards leave us to ourselves as long as the required quota of celestium keeps rolling out."

Na'mune stopped and pointed to a barrel. He lifted the lid and I saw the water. "No fancy cups here."

He thrust his hands in and raised the liquid to his mouth. Inwardly, I cringed. However, my parched throat didn't care. I dipped my hand in, drinking in big gulps. The water was cold, with a chalky metallic taste.

"Llandula said you'd need time to recover from the vibrosickness." Na'mune rested against the wall, watching me.

"Who?" I bent for another handful of water.

"The ship's doctor was, is, an old friend of mine. He and the captain visited me before we landed." Na'mune turned me down the tunnel. "This way."

"Couldn't they have helped you disappear instead of coming

here?" They didn't sound like great friends to me, even if the doctor did save my life.

"Probably, but I was needed here."

"There will be plenty sent to the mines. My father is just getting started."

Na'mune laughed and clapped me on the back. "Not once have you assumed anything is about you."

"Huh?"

"Llandula thought it more important I stay with you than escape. Once you've survived your year here, I'll simply disappear into the shadows. I'll become an *Itzalak*, like many before me."

We stopped at a smallish cave that had only one small light. Several threadbare sheets were spread around in clumps. There were no cots, no pillows, no blankets to provide real warmth. From the smell, the latrine was close by as well.

De'truto stepped out of the shadows. "We won't be able to pamper you here."

I shook my head. "I didn't expect it."

Na'mune rested his hand on my shoulder. "This will make you wise. The work will make you strong. And there will be plenty of time for reflection. Time to hear the voice of Atua. He's been waiting for you to listen."

"Maybe." Would he believe me if I told him I'd already heard Atua's voice? Probably, but I wasn't ready to fully embrace the fact I might be talking to a god. It was easier to think I was going mad. Perhaps we were all crazy.

They left me to the quiet darkness, my thoughts tumbling over everything that had happened since I'd left Manawa. The short journey to Cassia was a blur of disjointed images. I had never been so sick. So humiliated. Doctor Llandula saved my life. I only hoped it hadn't been a waste of his time.

I wadded several of the thin sheets under my head. The cold rock pressed cruelly against my hip and shoulder when I turned on my side.

"Atua?" I whispered.

There was no reply. No voice or feeling inside or out. I swallowed my foolishness and tried once more to find a comfortable position.

Sleep eluded me. I didn't worry about myself. My thoughts centered on Ev. Was he safe? Did Eleena know about her parents as the dream suggested?

Eventually, my lids became too heavy to keep open. The darkness slowly brightened, revealing Ev's giant ship resting in a meadow. There were blue skies dotted with clouds as far as I could see, and row upon row of tents. Hundreds of them spread across the green. Ev and several men worked on a wooden structure. Others dug trenches and laid pipes. While they didn't look happy, they appeared satisfied.

The vision flew over the camp to a large open area in the middle of the tents. Children sat in groups or ran in clusters. My gaze scanned them, searching for dark hair with mahogany highlights. Eleena lay beside the blonde girl I remembered from the other dreams, looking up at the sky. She pointed and smiled when the girl said something. A group of boys approached them. One of them also looked familiar. He kicked the blonde girl's foot. Both girls jumped up and chased the boys.

Seeing kids running, playing, and laughing the way they should helped me feel better. Manawa was lost, but part of that world lived on in Eleena and her friends. My father hadn't destroyed everything. Maybe there was a god in the universe that protected the innocent.

TIME BECAME meaningless in the bowels of the mountain. There were no clocks, no rotation of the sun to track the days. I worked until I couldn't, then I'd eat from the food rations the soldiers provided. De'truto divided it out between us, keeping a pile for the *Itzalak*. It wasn't much on flavor, but the Hatana provided plenty. He wanted us strong enough to mine the celestium.

When I was too tired to work, I slept, often dreaming of Ev and Eleena. Seeing them safe gave me strength, especially since I was convinced it was more than wishful thinking. The visions were too detailed. Too specific. And I never would have imagined some of the things I saw. I would have chosen to only see Eleena happy.

Most of the time she was, but there were other times she wasn't. At least she had Harper and Iri to help her. I'd learned their names through bits of conversation I'd overheard in the dreams. Once they carried Eleena to the med tent after she passed out and hit her head. My own fear beat out of control until the nurse brought Eleena around.

She turned away from her friends and cried—her embarrassment coursing through me as if it were my own. She needed her parents.

Amiran. The voice pierced through my guilt. *Eleena is in my hands, as are her parents.*

There was nothing else, but peace calmed my troubled soul. The voice must belong to Atua. I'd heard it a few times, and every time it was accompanied by a burning warmth that radiated through my body. It comforted. If he was real, then I could trust the dreams were true. He must be the one sending them to me.

Days and nights blurred together. My body grew accustomed to the swing of the ax and the cold ground. I took solace from the dreams and found companionship with the men when I worked.

The *Itzalak* visited me daily, teaching me how to school my attention and expressions. Some of them, for there were many different voices that visited, told me things I'd never known about the palace and the hidden politics. One suggested my father was Schirra's puppet. I didn't believe it, but Schirra did control the fleet. What did my father have?

I chose not to dwell on questions I couldn't answer.

It didn't take long to feel as if I'd always been a student in the caves. Memories of sun and sky, tree and life, all faded to memory, living only in the dreams of Ev and Eleena.

"Amiran." A soldier bellowed into an amplifier.

"Over here." I set down the pick.

He jerked his head up the tunnel. "You're a lucky tama. General Schirra ordered you taken topside every three weeks."

"Why?"

"Who knows." He shrugged and marched away.

Had it only been three weeks? I followed the soldier until we reached their camp. The floodlights stung my eyes.

"Wait here." He grunted and moved toward a mess hall of sorts. Tables held real dishes and food that smelled good. These guys didn't have to live on protein bars and scummy water.

Four soldiers stalked over and prodded me toward the lift. No one spoke on the ascent topside. A charged energy filled the confined space. My skin itched with it.

The doors opened. Squinting, I stepped out of the elevator. The light and heat from the suns beat down. Thawing me from the outside in, showing me how cold I'd become. I stood with eyes closed, soaking it up.

"He's smiling. How sweet." The voice came from in front of me. "Open your eyes so you can see."

"See what?" I blinked, but couldn't get my eyes to stay open. Cupping my hands, I made a shade and focused on the man in front of me.

"Schirra's other gift." His fist slammed into my face.

My head snapped back. I stumbled into the guard behind me. He shoved me forward. Another punch connected with my ribs. Someone swiped at my feet and I fell to the ground. I tried to get up, to fight back, but a boot to the groin had me writhing in the dirt. I curled over, wrapping my arms around my head. The kicks came faster. From every direction.

The men didn't yell or berate me. They only grunted with their efforts. My thighs, ribs, back, and arms blended into one massive pain. Eventually, the beating stopped.

I concentrated on breathing.

The three suns now burned instead of warmed, and jagged rocks cut into my flesh.

"His eyes still aren't open." The soldier sounded out of breath.

"He gets an hour. There's time to see the sky."

Someone laughed. "Schirra thinks he can make a man out of the prince."

"I don't think that's possible." The voices trailed away. "Come on, Kolo brought up lunch."

Did my father know Schirra ordered this? I thought of the brief smile I thought I'd seen that last day. It almost looked like he was proud of me in that moment. Doubts churned in my mind. My father hadn't said a kind word to me since I was five. There was no way he felt anything other than disappointment in me.

I curled up, listening to the men laugh. The clink of dishes echoed off the surrounding mountains. When I tried to move, every muscle protested. I rolled to my back. The brightness of the day hurt, even with my eyes closed. Rocks dug into my body, and blood dripped from my lip.

I didn't care.

It will make you strong. The voice whispered.

My eyes flew open, but the overhead sun blinded me. It took every ounce of strength to turn onto my side.

Atua? For the first time, I spoke it without the derision of unbelief.

Grunting and groaning, I crawled to the shade of a nearby boulder. I touched the side of my face—one eye swelling and my lip split open.

The intense heat dulled my aches and pains as long as I didn't move. My eyes adjusted to the daylight, and for the first time in weeks, my sweat didn't make me shiver.

"Get up." The CO towered over me.

I tried to stand, but my body didn't obey.

"I said get up." He bellowed again.

I made it to all fours before another kick knocked me down again.

"I don't have time for this. Get him on his feet."

Two men pulled me up. They half dragged me to the lift when my knees buckled. Once inside, they leaned me in the corner. The support of the walls helped me stand, and the words of Atua kept replaying through my mind. How would this make me stronger?

The jolt of the elevator reaching the bottom almost knocked to the ground again. The doors opened and the maw of darkness waited. The previously bright lights of the soldiers' area were dimmer after the world above.

The CO nodded to the caves. "Take him to the medic for an anti-inflammatory. We need him to keep working."

They dragged me forward. The medic pressed a hypospray to my neck without a word.

One of the men gave me a shove. "Go on. We'll see you in a few weeks."

I shuffled into the tunnel. The cold collected in my sweat soaked clothing, seeping deep into my bones. Each shiver revealed new pain while aggravating the ones I'd already discovered. At that moment, I wanted to die. It would have been easier.

I need you alive. The voice returned.

A brief image of Eleena opened up. I stopped walking to cling to the wall while I watched her kneel on the floor of her tent. I heard her pouring out her heart in prayer to Atua. She prayed for her uncle, Harper, Iri, Evander, all those in camp.

"Atua, be with Am. Don't let him be scared or sad." Her hair lay in braids down her back, her face turned up to the roof of the tent while her eyes scrunched shut. "And, if you can, don't let him die like my parents."

My heart filled with a warmth that slowly spread to the rest of me. I hurt, but it could be worse. Millions had died like Eleena's parents, and yet she prayed for me. The vision faded, but the warmth stayed with me.

Eleena's pleas on my behalf carved a permanent spot for her in my heart. She was family now.

"Atua, watch over her," I whispered.

She is in my hands.

16

DREAMS: ELEENA

"Eleena, wake up. You're dreaming." Harper shook my shoulder. I gasped for air and curled over to hold my stomach. They were beating him again. It felt as if I had been kicked the way he had.

We'd been on Jakaru several months and things were pretty good. The four of us stayed with Evander's camp. Uncle trusted him. He said it would be safer with the captain if we needed to evacuate again.

Although life fell into a routine of school and play, my dreams of Am did not get better. I enjoyed the sunshine and light rains of the planting season. He lived in darkness. On the good days, he worked hard and sometimes laughed. But the soldiers beat him often.

I hated those dreams. My body often ached afterward as if I'd been bruised with him. I cried for him more than I wanted anyone to know. Harper already taunted me about my imaginary boyfriend. I teased her about the way she watched Iri all the time and she shut up.

"Why do they hurt him?" I brushed the hair from my face.

"What are you talking about?" Uncle walked into our tent.

I jumped up from my cot and ran to hug him, needing comfort. "The soldiers keep hurting Am, but he didn't do anything."

"Shhh. Calm down and tell me what you're talking about." Uncle pushed me away but kept hold of my shoulders. "Are you still dreaming about Captain Evander's friend?"

"Yes, Uncle. Why is he being punished?"

CHARITY BRADFORD

"Because he helped us." Uncle's brow creased.

"I know that's why he was sent to the mines, but he's doing what they tell him. Why do they beat him too?" The images of Am curled on the ground, men kicking him until he passed out haunted me.

Uncle took me by the elbow and guided me outside. "Let's talk to the captain. He'll want to know what you've seen. Just yesterday he told me he thinks he can get someone in to help Am. Would that make you feel better?"

"Can they rescue him? Bring him here?" I quickened my pace. Captain Evander would save Am. He wouldn't have to be sad anymore and the soldiers couldn't hurt him.

"No, Eleena. The captain can't bring him here. It would put us and Am in too much danger. Believe it or not, he's probably safer where he is."

"But they kick him. Hit him until he can't breathe or stand up. He can't open his eyes. Then they send him back into the caves to work. Why?"

"Because that is what the Hatana does."

"I hate the Hatana." Usually, Uncle told me it was wrong to hate, this time he didn't say anything after my outburst. "Why doesn't someone stop him?"

Uncle only shook his head. "People are scared he will do to them what he did to Manawa."

The breath caught in my chest. How had I forgotten so quickly? A few months and I'd pushed my parents and home to the back of my mind. It had been easier to forget than continue hurting. Moments like this always brought the pain back with crushing force. If a man could destroy an entire world, he'd think nothing of beating one man.

We found Evander walking the perimeter of the camp. He saw Uncle and changed course to meet up with us. I was struck again how young he was, surely not much older than Am. How had he become captain? He must have been someone important for the older men to follow his orders.

"Beck?" Captain Evander glanced at me, then focused on Uncle.

"Eleena has dreamed about Am. I thought you should be aware of his struggles." Uncle rested his hand on my shoulder.

"Come, let's talk in the ship. I don't want to take any chance of being overheard."

17

CONFIRMATION: AMIRAN

Time passed. Between the beatings I worked hard and learned from the *Itzalak*. They moved on to strategies for negotiating as well as intrigue. I listened. I learned the importance of silence and observation. The shadow men drove home what my father's lectures never could. To win the war, sometimes you had to give away a battle. It went against every instinct I had, but it was sinking in.

They encouraged me to seek the will of Atua. It didn't come easy at first, but when the beatings left me unable to stand, I felt his presence stronger than other times. He continued to comfort me with dreams of my friends. Ev's camp appeared well organized. I watched Talrano's daughter attend school and play with other children in the large field. She was always with Harper. Sometimes Iri hovered about. I couldn't hear them every time, but Atua always allowed me to hear Eleena's prayers for me.

Those were the dreams I requested when the beatings got bad. Because of her faith, I started pleading regularly for her and Ev. The more I did, the more often I felt Atua with me, even when he didn't speak. Little by little I became a believer.

After the sixth trip topside, the CO called in a more experienced doctor to set a broken arm, tape up cracked ribs, and repair some internal bleeding. Through the haze of pain, I recognized Llandula, the ship's doctor from what felt like a different lifetime. He worked on me quickly and quietly as a soldier observed from a few feet away.

Before leaving, he bent close. "There's a letter in the bandages."

I nodded and whispered, "I've heard his voice."

"I bet you have." He smiled sadly and turned to give instructions to the CO. "He needs at least ten minutes before you send him off. His bones should be fine by tomorrow."

The meds kicked in. My body tingled from the nanobots coursing through my body repairing the damage.

A strange sense of peace washed through me. I closed my eyes and tried to put words to the emotion.

Atua, thank you for good men like Llandula. Protect him. Give him peace. Help me become the man he and the others think I can be.

My thoughts turned to Eleena. She was my link to a brighter and happier world. I was thankful she was with Ev, but I knew even their safety was precarious. *Atua?*

My hope failed and I couldn't ask. The anxiety faded as I heard that piercing voice once more.

They are in my hands.

I yearned to have a full conversation with Atua, but he only spoke a phrase at a time. Most often it was that someone or something was in his hands. I had to have faith that was enough. What would I need to do to receive real guidance?

A soldier pulled me to my feet. "Time's up."

I made my way back to the comfort I'd found with the others. They'd be waiting to hear about anything I'd noticed while topside, as well as the state of the guards at the exit. It would be torture to wait for the letter, but I'd only trust Na'mune and De'truto with it.

Sure enough, as soon as I entered our tunnel, men dropped their picks and gathered around. I sat and leaned against the wall.

"Looks bad this week." Na'mune sat next to me. "Broken ribs as well as the arm?"

"Yep." I tested how deep a breath I could take. "The nanobots are working fast though."

"They gave you nanobots?" De'truto's brow shot up.

"No, but the ship's doctor they brought in did."

"Interesting." He nodded. "How many soldiers at the exit. Are they the same, or have they been switched out?"

We talked about the guards for a long time. I was learning how patient De'truto could be. He'd gather intel as long as it took to plan an escape from the mines. Until then he'd pretend to be the perfect slave. They all would, and it worked. The soldiers didn't give us much thought.

Eventually, talk turned to what it felt like to sit in the sun. To feel its warmth sink into my bones. I'd grown quiet poetic over the months, and my audience ate it up.

One of the men slapped my uninjured shoulder before heading back to work. "I'd take the beating to feel the sun's warmth again."

I chuckled. As bad as it got, I felt the same. I looked forward to the heat of daylight all the way up the lift. Twice, the soldiers had been lazy, barely roughing me up. Those times, I sat most of the hour soaking in the bright contrast of the purple sky and red rock. The scene was no longer ugly to me.

"I'll walk you to the mats." Na'mune offered a hand up.

"Thanks." I grabbed it with my good arm and clasped the broken one to my side as he pulled. The old man was strong, but my body protested.

De'truto followed us. "What do you think about when they're pounding on you?"

"Talrano's daughter."

They nodded silently. I'd shared Eleena's story and the way it felt when she gave me permission to leave her parents behind. Would it have been different if we'd both known how things would end on Manawa? De'truto and Na'mune didn't know about the dreams, or the way I thought Eleena was strong in ways I'd never be.

I held out my hand to stop them before we entered the sleeping cave. "We'll need the light."

The shirt I'd been given was worn thin. I struggled to pull it up.

"What are you doing?" Na'mune asked.

"Llandula put a note in the bindings." The exertion made me dizzy and I had to hold onto the cave wall to remain standing. "I guess the nanobots aren't working as fast as I thought."

"Llandula was here?" Na'mune asked again, and I nodded.

De'truto stepped forward. "Be still, we'll find it."

Na'mune ended up supporting my arm as carefully as he could while De'truto unwound the bandages. "You know, you could have waited for the nanobots to finish their job before fishing the paper out."

"I'd go nuts not knowing what was in the note." I groaned as the bindings grew looser. "I hope you can pull those things tight again."

De'truto laughed. "You'll see soon enough. I've got it." He handed me the paper. "Now wait a bit longer and I'll rewrap you."

As soon as he finished, I sank to the ground near one of the lights and unfolded the paper. I recognized Evander's handwriting.

"Found a way in. Can't take you out, but can bring supplies.

We've set up camp. Not sure how long we can stay. The Hatana is on a rampage, but the secret is secure. Artemese is no longer neutral. They've called for the Coalition to gather their own fleet. I'm worried they're moving too slowly. Pray for them. I'm sending a man with the guard change. He'll know the codeword and will give you more intel. I pray for you daily and hope you are surviving. ~E"

The air rushed out of my lungs. Evander had found a way to infiltrate the fleet. It meant part of our plan was possible. The rush of emotion almost undid me. Now if anything happened to me, Ev could still move forward with our efforts to end the suffering my father dished out.

"What's it say?" Na'mune asked.

I passed the paper to him, leaned back and closed my eyes. Evander and Eleena were safe a while longer. I trusted the dreams, but the note confirmed they were true. I hadn't failed Talrano completely.

"Artemese is foolish." De'truto grunted. "Mark my words, they'll go down before they ever get a chance to build a fleet. Learn from their mistake, Amiran."

"De'truto is right, I'm afraid. Schirra will not give them time to prepare a defense, much less a force large enough to go on the offensive."

"Then more will suffer at my father's command." My short-lived peace shattered. "How many will die before we put an end to this?"

"More than your heart can stand. Fortify yourself. Know the blame rests with Hatana Anaru and Schirra, not you." De'truto handed the letter back to me. "Let each death fuel your determination."

Na'mune held onto De'truto's hand, as if to calm him. "Don't lose your goodness. Find a way to walk with Atua. Allow him to lead you through the coming war one battle at a time."

"I'm working on that, but Atua hasn't given any instructions. I don't know where to start, what to do."

"Keep listening. It will come."

I nodded at Na'mune, grateful for his faith in me.

De'truto rubbed his chin. "Can I ask about the secret?"

Atua? I silently asked. A warm feeling of assurance came over me. If nothing else, I'd learned to trust other people based on Atua's whisperings.

"After we faked Ev's death, our first priority was to find a safe place to train men to fight my father and Schirra. At first, Ev trained them on his freighter. Then we found the perfect location a few months before Manawa. Only four people know it's location."

"We'll not mention it again while you're here." De'truto gave me a thumbs up. "Now get in there and rest. We can't cover your entire quota tomorrow."

We all laughed at that, knowing I was still the slowest celestium miner in the caves. I spent far too much time talking with the *Itzalak*.

18

REASURRANCES: ELEENA

Another two months passed with no word on whether Captain Evander had reached Am. I stopped asking for dreams because I didn't want to see him hurting.

Atua sent them anyway.

Most of the time I only saw Am, sometimes sensing his emotions, but once or twice I heard him.

His voice had deepened, and although the dust and beard hid his face, it didn't hide how thin he had grown. Am looked more like a man than the student he had been on Manawa. I preferred those memories of when Am and other students visited our home. Mima cooked for them and Popi discussed books.

"You've got that look again." Harper stepped into our tent. "What are you dreaming about now?"

"Nothing." I bristled at her tone. She was always teasing me about daydreaming. All it did was make me want to keep my thoughts locked away even more.

"Are you thinking about Captain E's friend?"

"You shouldn't call him that." I ignored her question.

"Iri calls him that all the time and Captain E doesn't mind." Harper shrugged.

"Iri barely talks. Captain Evander's probably glad to get anything out of him." I folded my blanket and placed it at the end of my cot.

"What do you have against Iri?"

Uh, oh. I'd stoked her protective side. Harper was a bear when it

88

came to defending those she loved, and I'd been lucky to stay on her good side since meeting her.

"Nothing! I actually like Iri a lot."

Harper's brow creased even more. "You like him, or you *like* him?"

I rolled my eyes. "Don't be silly. Iri's older than me."

"Maybe he's not old enough for you?"

"What are you talking about? Anyway, Iri's like the brother I never had."

"You know what I'm talking about. The only boy you ever talk about is Am, and you ignore the boys who flirt with you in class."

"I'm not ready for all that like you, that's all. Anyway, the boys in the camp could move away at any time." I headed for the tent flap, but Harper stepped in front of me.

"Leena, I've seen your face when you talk about Am. I'm worried you like him because he's your hero. No one else will stack up."

"You sound like an old woman. And he's not my hero. He couldn't save my parents." The words felt like the lie they were the moment they passed my lips. My face heated and I spun back toward my cot to avoid Harper's gaze.

"I don't believe you."

"It doesn't matter. I'm just a kid to him, and he's not here. He's in the mines on Cassia, living in the dark, getting beaten for no reason, and Captain Evander can't save him."

Everything I didn't want to feel rushed through me. Sorrow for my parents, fear for Am, anger at the captain. I stopped short of calling out Atua, but the emotion was there. Why did Atua let so many bad things happen?

So my punishment will be justified.

I gasped at the strength and clarity of the voice in my head. Atua's spirit had always been soft, comforting up to this point, but now I heard and felt the power behind the voice.

"Leena, what is it?" Harper grasped my arm, concern etched into her face.

"Atua." I gulped down the rest of my reply. I didn't know how to explain what I experienced.

Tell her you now know the power of my hands.

I found myself nodding. "Atua spoke, and I could feel his power. I guess I didn't understand before what he meant when he said they are in my hands."

"And now?"

The tears welled up. Atua's spirit filled me, teaching a truth I'd not yet grasped. "It means more than I thought. Not just that my parents are with him now, but their deaths mean something to him, and he will do something about it."

Harper hugged me. "I'm glad, but I hope it doesn't take too long."

Atua?

Peace. There must be time for the Hatana to repent and return to me.

If the Hatana changed, would he be forgiven? I shuddered.

Harper moved away but kept my hand in hers, pulling me to the tent flap. "Let's skip class today and you can tell me all about Am. Did you know him before evacuation day?"

I appreciated her attempt to return things to silly girl stuff. Corvey and I used to talk about boys, but so much had happened since then. We'd lost so much. Harper might sound like an old woman, but I felt like one.

You're still young. Be a girl today. Atua's voice returned to the soft fatherly tone I'd grown to love.

"Okay. I'll tell you about the time Am came to visit when my friend Corvey was over. She was the only one who knew Am was my favorite out of all of Popi's students. She giggled all through dinner. I was terrified she'd tell my secret." We left the tent and headed for the meadow.

"Did she?"

"No. I don't think Am even noticed, but the next time he came, I hid in my room."

Harper asked questions and I talked about Am. I told her about the times I'd seen him on Manawa, then I shared lots of the things I'd seen in dreams. I'd almost worked up the courage to ask her how she felt about Iri when he showed up with Uncle and the captain.

"Girls, you didn't go to class today." Uncle stood with his hands on his hips, but he didn't quite pull off the disappointed look.

"No, sir." I tried to look sorry.

"Leena needed a break. She's been worried about Am." Harper looked expectantly at the captain. Over the months she'd gotten over her fear of him.

Captain Evander smiled. "There's no need. One of my men is now a guard on Cassia. He can help Am. Make sure he's got plenty of food and medicine to help after the beatings."

"Can he stop them?" My heart pounded in my ears, making my head ache.

The smile fell away. "I'm afraid not."

The dam broke with a ragged sob. The tears I thought I'd banished flowed freely. I turned and ran. Am had help, but he wasn't safe. He'd keep hurting. No one could stop it.

Eleena, Am is in my hands. I will comfort and sustain him.

I hid behind the lavatories we'd built and continued to cry. Even knowing Atua was with Am didn't stop my tears. My heart longed for so many things—to return to my home and the arms of my parents, to be ignorant of the pain in the world. But most of all, I wished I wasn't a stupid girl who wanted something she couldn't have.

19

LEAVING THE MINES: AMIRAN

"The guards are changing." A second *Itzalak* interrupted the one who'd been teaching me.

"Am, pick up your ax, we will continue another time." The voice grew softer, then disappeared.

I did as told and worked fast enough to work up a sweat by the time the guards entered our tunnel. One I knew well from my beatings showed several new ones around.

"Line up!" the old guard barked the order.

We turned from the walls to face the soldiers.

"Drop the tools." Another order. One man who stood closest to the soldiers didn't comply fast enough and they struck him with the vibrostick.

I dropped the ax and moved to help him. The guards were never patient and I'd learned the unspoken code between the miners. Help quickly, but quietly. Try not to draw attention and fade into the background like the *Itzalak*.

The new soldiers stared at us while the old guard walked our line. "Where are the rest?"

"The other tunnel." De'truto answered.

"Am step forward." He growled. "You have a message from Schirra."

I took a calming breath and stepped forward. One of the new guards advanced. He looked me up and down, a scowl on his face.

"You're as dirty as the dark side of the moon," he spat.

I barely contained my surprise. A flicker of recognition might have crossed my face before I resumed my mask of indifference. It didn't last long though because the man punched me across the jaw. I staggered but remained standing.

"Schirra sends his greetings." The man's gaze flicked to the ground then back to my face.

I glanced down and noticed a piece of paper sticking out of the hem of his pant leg. When I looked up he winked, then punched me again but in the stomach. This time I went down, landing at his feet. I grasped the paper and slid it under my shirt as I lay curled on the ground.

The soldiers laughed, but it sounded like they were leaving. I stood slowly, keeping my arm pressed to my stomach. When they were out of sight, I slipped the note out. There was a crude drawing of the water barrel and a rock leaning against it.

De'truto drew near. "What was that all about?"

I handed him the note. "Not sure yet."

"Want me to check?"

"No, I'll wait to make sure they're gone, then I'll go." I retrieved my ax from the ground and studied the wall. There was a fat line of celestium ready to be chipped out of the mountain. It only needed a few more swings with the larger tool before switching to the smaller ones.

"Keep me posted." De'truto clapped me on the back and returned to his own work.

Some time later, I walked the tunnels to the water station. After a good drink, I knelt to feel for the stone. Sure enough, a new rock rested against the barrel and wall. It was light when I lifted it. Hollow. Inside I found hyposprays with painkillers and anti-inflammatories. There were also some multivitamins and vaccines.

Life didn't get easier, but I no longer felt disconnected from my old life. Ev didn't send messages but what he did send was a godsend for all of us.

I counted the passage of time by trips to the surface. They'd beat me, then leave me to bake in the sun while they enjoyed their lunch. When we returned to camp, they gave the medical attention I needed to keep digging in the mines. They rarely talked to me. I never spoke to them.

As my body grew stronger, the damage from their punches grew less apparent. They still left their mark, occasionally breaking bones, but I found it easier to recover thanks to the meds Evander snuck in.

We didn't speak after that first day. He avoided me, and I never looked his way. One day the *Itzalak* brought me a message while De'truto and Na'mune worked beside me.

"Your friend found a hiding place above. He's dug a tunnel and wants you to send strong men for the cause." The voice whispered but the words were clear.

De'truto stared at me wide-eyed. "Do we dare?"

Na'mune answered. "If we're careful we could send one or two a month without raising too much suspicion. They might not even notice until the next guard change."

"The rest of us will have to work extra hard to keep the quota going out." De'truto nodded. "Let's do it."

The *Itzalak* spoke next, "Send one now."

My heart pounded, hoping for a brief moment I could be the one to go. I immediately squelched the thought. My absence would be noticed.

"De'truto, you know the men better than anyone. Who do you trust to send?" I swallowed my childish desire to flee and focused on the fact we could save these men and recruit for Ev's army.

"I'll take care of it." He put his tools down and addressed the wall. "Where do I send them?"

"Send them to the sleep cavern and I'll take it from there." The voice faded away.

De'truto left and Na'mune watched me. I tried to continue working as if nothing had happened, but I couldn't shake my own disappointment.

"Amiran, trust in Atua. This won't last forever." Na'mune's words sank in.

"I know. Thank you though." I needed the reminder. The work moved on as I fought my fears and frustration.

Not much longer. Atua comforted. *Patience.*

De'truto and Na'mune stayed with me until the end.

"When I'm gone, you must leave with Evander." I knew my last three weeks were drawing close to an end.

"I've been down here so long, I'd probably be blinded if I left." De'truto showed his reckless smile. "Having said that, I'll be more help to the Coalition down here. Make sure Evander keeps coming to collect men."

Na'mune nodded. "When we can all leave, I'll join you topside."

Atua, is this what you expect of good men? My heart was heavy, but I kept silent out of respect for my two friends.

They will have their reward.

Cassia had seventy-two weeks in its year. My twenty-fourth trip topside came and I said goodbye to them both. I left with a simple 'peace on your path,' one of my favorite expressions from Manawa.

I expected something different from this trip to the surface. Would the attack be more brutal? A punishment for surviving? The lift doors opened and I squinted against the glare of the sun. It always took a while to readjust, and usually the beating started before I'd reached that point.

Not today.

I heard the rustle of clothes as someone approached. The guard beside me knocked me to my knees, but the hits never came.

"Your Highness. General." The captain of the guard spoke. "This is an honor."

"Amiran, stand up." Hatana Anaru ordered.

"Yes, Father." I kept my voice and face neutral even as the men around me gasped.

My guard had changed twice over the year, and I wondered if they missed the memo on my identity. I no longer looked like the boy who entered the mines.

Holding my hand over my eyes, I forced them open, blinking and wiping away the stinging moisture from the spasms brought on by the light.

I focused on my father. General Schirra stood to his left. Both glared at me.

"It appears the mines have made a man out of you." Schirra circled me. "Now I'll make a soldier out of you."

My skin crawled, but I didn't move. The mines had done more than build muscles from hard work. They'd taught me the value of patience. The beatings had taught me how to keep my face free from all emotion. The human predator tired of the game faster without the bonus of watching the prey suffer. Schirra would be no different.

He returned to the Hatana's side. "Amiran should be sent to the fleet immediately."

Hatana Anaru nodded, then waved dismissively with one hand. "Keep me posted on his progress. He never paid much attention to tactics before."

"He'll learn. One way or the other." Schirra smiled. "I promise not to go easy on him."

"Never thought you would." The Hatana turned and walked away.

The guards that came topside hovered near the lift, afraid to leave, but trying desperately to go unnoticed.

Schirra pinned them with his gaze. "Step forward." The men snapped to attention and did as ordered. Schirra paced their ranks. "Captain, these are the men who carried out my orders?"

"Sir, yes, sir."

"Would you say they gave it their best effort?"

"Sir, yes, sir."

"And yet the prince stands before me healthy, strong, and not remotely broken."

The silence stretched. The Hatana entered his shuttle. Only Schirra stood to pass judgment. The men stared straight ahead, but one's eye twitched. It was the only sign of their fear.

"Captain?" Schirra prodded. "Is it possible they slacked off because of his rank?"

"Sir, no, sir. These four did not know this was the Hatana Tama."

"Then I have to ask how he could survive regular beatings by four men."

"They beat him until he couldn't walk. However, a dead man can't mine celestium, sir."

"And who gave you permission to make that decision?" Schirra stood toe to toe with the captain.

I had to give the man credit for not messing his pants. He blinked a second before Schirra's fist connected with his nasal cavity in a brutal upward motion. The captain's head snapped back, then he collapsed in a heap. The other men visibly trembled now.

"Please inform the First Lieutenant he has been promoted." Schirra turned his back on the men. "Come, Amiran. You won't find life in the fleet as soft as the mines."

THE TENSION ROLLING off Schirra was palpable. It was evident in his fisted hands, stiff body language, and piercing gaze. He sat across from me in the cramped shuttle, my father having left in his own luxury Glorywinger.

My skin chaffed from the stiff uniform I'd been given, and my face burned from the first shave in over a year. They cropped my hair in the close cut of the enlisted military. I had many questions, but kept my mouth shut.

We hadn't cleared the atmosphere before Schirra lost it.

"I should have had them all executed." He glared at me. "Obviously, they're too soft on the prisoners. Be assured, I may have missed my chance to kill you outright, but there are other ways."

I didn't doubt he'd do all in his power to be rid of me. However, it was a relief to hear he wouldn't personally stab me in the back or pull a blaster on me.

"Do you have nothing to say?" He growled.

"Sir, no, sir." I mimicked the soldier's words from earlier.

Schirra grunted. "You'll learn sir, yes, sir, but don't think I'll believe it."

I didn't comment, keeping my expression calm, neutral. The inner peace I'd achieved during my days listening for Atua helped.

We sat in silence for the next ten minutes. After docking with his fleet cruiser, Schirra left me with two low ranking officers. The men led me to a room and gave me a general rundown of my work schedule.

"You've been assigned two shifts on, one off for the next three months. During this time you'll train in ballistics, hand to hand combat, tactics, and strategies, as well as serve your time on KP and the other work crews." He handed me a datacom. "You have five minutes to report to deck four, cargo bay ten for your first shift."

"Is there a ship's schematic?" I asked.

"Yes. Your access code is 081696420. This room is on deck twelve, room forty-two."

"Thank you."

"Don't thank me yet. Welcome to the next five years in *reinga*."

20

MIRIMBIA: ELEENA

2.8 Years after Manawa—Mirimbia

"LAST CALL FOR EVAC. Lift off in twenty." The voice echoed across the spacepad from the amplifier.

It would repeat instructions in another five minutes, counting down until time ran out. Everyone had already loaded onto one of Evander's two ships. However I waited on the ramp of the *Vapaus* for Uncle and Iri while Harper saved our spot in the cargo hold.

The Jakaruns sold the *Vapaus* to Captain E's cheap when we left them after eight months. We'd been on Mirimbia two years. Long enough to have my fifteenth birthday.

Mirimbia was high tech, one giant city. The complete opposite of Jakaru. We had access to the nets again, improving the quality of education. I found studyied everything I could in an effort to make my parents proud.

A lot of refugees found jobs and moved away. Even Uncle considered settling here. Then Captain E got word the Hatana had set his sights on Mirimbia and their tech facilities.

Uncle Beck decided we'd stick with the captain. I felt good about that until a few minutes ago. Uncle and Iri hadn't returned to the ship, and it was time to go.

"Eleena, come inside." Captain Evander stood at the top of the ramp.

"We can't leave." I wouldn't leave them.

"Beck is close." Captain E tapped a COM unit in his ear. "They've picked up the cargo and will have plenty of time to get on board."

What cargo was so important? I studied the city again. There were too many vehicles on the ground and in the air. I wouldn't recognize the shuttle until it was right in front of us.

Boots clanked on the ramp, and I turned to the captain. He used to tower over me, but I'd grown and now I didn't have to strain my neck to look up at him. "What's going to happen to the people here?"

"They should be fine. Like Jakaru, the Hatana needs them to keep doing what they're doing. Building things he can use." He too gazed at the city.

"He won't destroy them like Manawa?"

"I don't think so."

"Are you sure Uncle will make it back?" I asked.

"Yes. I promise I won't leave without him."

"I'd rather stay here if they're not going to make it."

The captain sighed and shook his head. "You don't want to be here when the Hatana's fleet arrives."

"You said they wouldn't destroy the planet."

"That doesn't mean they'll let Mirimbia go unpunished for helping us. And if they find refugees..." He didn't need to finish the sentence. All of us had seen vids of the fleet invasions over the last two years. "Beck will drive into the lower cargo hold. Come in so we can seal this door."

I knew I should listen, but my heart pounded, my hands tingled. Everything inside screamed to wait for Uncle. I concentrated on breathing, trying to stave off the growing anxiety.

I heard the fifteen-minute warning. *Atua, let them get here.*

"Eleena." His voice sounded more like a captain's when he said my name. "You must come in."

I'd given up everything else. How could I do it again?

I heard him sigh right before he picked me up and tossed me over his shoulder.

"No! I have to wait for them. Please." My yelling didn't do any good. I kicked and beat my fists against his back. "Put me down!"

"Trust me," Evander grunted as I punched him again, but he continued marching up the loading ramp. One of his men retracted it behind us. He didn't set me down until the doors were sealed.

"Go to the cargo hold and strap in," he ordered.

I tried not to give in to the hysteria. Uncle wasn't here. Iri wasn't here. I glared at Captain E, but couldn't speak around the growing anger and panic.

"Eleena, look at me." He turned my face toward him. "Your uncle will be here. Trust me."

I swallowed, blinking back stupid tears. *Atua?*

There were no words spoken to my mind, but the soft feeling of warmth slipped over me. I recognized it as Atua calming me. The pressure in my lungs eased.

"Fine," I whispered.

Evander smiled. "It's my job to watch out for everyone. If I left you behind, your uncle would take over and turn the ship around. Then we'd all be in hot water."

Captain E headed down one hallway, and I hurried to the upper cargo hold in search of Harper. It was smaller than the main one and consisted mostly of our classmates. I knew them all. A lot of the other kids were orphans like Harper and Iri.

"Leena, over here." Harper waved to me. "Where are Iri and Beck?"

"They're not back yet. Captain E made me come in."

Harper grasped my arm. "What if they get left behind?"

"Captain promised he wouldn't."

"Maybe he just said that to get you inside."

I shook my head. "I don't think so."

Trust. Atua's voice brushed through my mind sending a shiver down my arms.

The lights flashed yellow. Three short whistle bursts followed by one long siren sounded all attention. Out of habit, we looked toward the amplifier in the corner closest to us.

"The *Krahvuus* has begun lift-off procedures. Once she's in orbit, we will follow. Prepare yourself." The speaker fell silent.

"They're not here. What do we do?" Harper's grip hurt my arm.

I pulled down our seats from the wall. "Strap in."

"Eleena?"

"Please." I swallowed the twinge of dismay, trying to hold onto Atua's peace. What would we do if Uncle didn't come back? I shook my head. "They'll be here. We have to believe."

Harper sat down and we strapped ourselves in for take-off along with everyone else. The next thirty minutes stretched endlessly, but everything went smoothly. Captain E had taken advantage of all the upgrades available on Mirimbia. The launch seats along the bulkhead and down the center of the hold were prime examples of that.

It made the process safer for everyone, but it also left my mind free to wander.

It had been almost three years since we left Manawa. I'd gotten used to life as a refugee. All of us had. There was a dull ache when I thought of my parents, but even that wasn't as bad as at first. Uncle Beck, Harper, and even Iri were my family now. If Uncle and Iri weren't on board the ship, everything would change again.

I glanced at Harper. She sat with her head back, eyes closed. I reached over and held her hand.

She turned to me and squeezed back. "It'll be okay."

"I know." *Please let it be okay.*

We waited until the all-clear signal was given before folding the launch seats into their spot on the wall. The seats in the middle of the room receded into the floor, giving us more space to move around.

Some of our classmates started a game of cards. Others read from the datacoms we'd received on Mirimbia. Everyone settled in for the journey.

"Should we try the lower cargo hold?" I asked.

"Yeah. The ship's crew will be busy. It might be our only chance." Harper nodded toward the door.

As soon as we stepped into the hall, I saw Uncle Beck jogging toward us with Iri beside him. All the pent up worry exploded.

"Don't ever leave me again!" I ran to him, punching at his arms and chest.

Uncle simply pulled me closer, holding me tight. I drowned his tunic with my relief.

"I'm sorry, Eleena. I shouldn't have cut it so close, but I knew Evander wouldn't leave without us. I should have made sure you understood that."

I tried to stop crying, really I did, but I couldn't. Not until I heard Iri talking to Harper.

"She didn't use to be such a baby."

Pulling back from Uncle, I stuck my tongue out at him. "Shut up, Iri."

Then I stomped back into the cargo hold. I'd show them. I'd ignore them both. Harper sat beside me, and I found it hard to pretend Uncle's boots weren't right in front of me.

"Eleena, don't be childish," Uncle spoke kindly, and it irritated me even more.

"Then stop treating me like one. You never tell me anything." I swiped my datacom on. "All things considered, I've been more than reasonable the last three years. I'm almost sixteen and will join the work rotation soon, so talk to me already."

Uncle rubbed the back of his head. "We're not sure about that cut off age. You might get to stay in school."

"You're doing it again," I growled.

"What?"

"Deflecting. If you can tell Iri what's going on, you can tell me. He tells Harper anyway, but she's been following your lead of protecting me." I let the anger taint my voice. "I've learned more about this ship and people from my own observations and Atua than you. You're supposed to be my family. Families plan together."

"You're right." Uncle turned to Harper. "Maybe you should talk to her about hormones and women's cycles?"

"Uncle Beck, you're kidding right?" I seriously wanted to scream.

"No, I'm not. This emotional outburst isn't like you. Forget it. What do you want to know?"

I shoved the datacom in my pack, thoroughly embarrassed he'd even hint at something so personal with Iri standing there. However, I did ask him to stop babying me. I sighed and faced him, "What was so important you almost missed launch?"

"These." Uncle held up four bracelets. "They're going to change camp life. We brought back five crates. Enough for everyone on both ships. They'll keep us organized."

All of this because of some bracelets? I groaned my frustration, picked up my pack and stomped to the other side of the hold. For once, I wished Uncle would let Captain E give us our own room. I'd lock them all out for some much needed quiet time.

Stupid bracelets.

21
___

ALONE: AMIRAN

3 **Years After Manawa**
Only five people attended Brindyn's funeral. He'd only been in the fleet a year. Unfortunately, he became another casualty of my existence.

As they pushed his coffin into the launch tube, I vowed to keep my distance from everyone else from there on out. It wasn't fair to them. Every time I selfishly made a friend something bad happened. This was the third man to meet a pointless death.

Their only connection? Me.

As much as I hated being alone, I knew the good men on the ship would be safer if I stayed away from them.

They will respect you for it. The voice of Atua sent a shiver through me.

I glanced around, but only Schirra watched me. His face mostly impassive. However, at the sight of my grief, he let the tiniest of smiles slip from one corner of his lips. His message was clear, even if Atua's was not.

Refocusing on the process in front of me, I sent my silent question into the cosmos. *What do you mean?*

There are many who will follow, but they need to know you are willing to sacrifice to be the leader they need. Atua had never said so much at once. My heart beat strong and steady. The truth of his words settling in.

They need to see me isolate myself?

They need to see you as a leader. Kind, but separate.

Huh. Sadly, this lesson came too late for Brindyn and the others. *He is in my hands.*

That phrase always brought comfort and fear. Atua used it often. Manawa had been in his hands but so were Evander and Eleena. I struggled to put my faith in the eternities, but I wanted safety in the here and now for them.

Atua? I knew he understood my silent plea.

My hands are enough for the deceased and the living.

I sighed. It wasn't the clear promise I hoped for, but it would have to be enough.

Brindyn's casket disappeared into the shoot. The hatch sealed, and someone read off his name, rank, birth planet, and age. He'd only been sixteen, same as Eleena. I clung to Atua's words that the boy was in his hands. It was easier to let his body return to the stars knowing his spirit was with Atua.

My acceptance flowed freely, but it was always tainted with that silent desire. *Please, let Evander and Eleena live.*

That night in my room, I prayed for my friend and his camp. It had been a while since Atua had sent a dream about them, and I needed the comfort. I asked to see them.

Atua sent a short vision. Evander stood on the bridge of his ship giving orders and talking with Eleena's uncle. They appeared excited in a good way. Before the relief could fully settle on me, the view shifted. Down a corridor and into a cargo hold. A couple hundred people crowded in the room, sprawled across blankets. The kids looked at datacoms while adults talked. It took a while before I found her.

Eleena sat propped up against a wall with her two friends. She'd grown since the last time I'd seen her. Even sitting, I could tell she was growing out of that awkward stage. Her hair was longer, and she'd lost the baby fat in her cheeks. She twisted her hands in her lap until Harper reached over and touched them. I hadn't heard anything from Ev, but Atua let me hear the teen's conversation.

"Eleena?" Harper asked.

"Sorry, I'm restless." Eleena sighed, leaned her head against the bulkhead, and closed her eyes.

"Why?" This time it was Iri who asked the question.

Eleena shook her head. "No reason."

"There's always a reason. Did Atua tell you something?" Harper took the lead again.

"Maybe." Eleena ducked her head.

"Tell us." Harper and Iri said at the same time.

"It's not about us. I just felt someone was sad. That's all." Eleena shrugged.

"Lots of people are sad, Leena. What's different about this one?" Harper didn't give up.

Eleena focused on the floor, her cheeks turning pink.

"Is it Am?" Harper sat up straighter. "I thought you'd gotten over your crush."

"Harper!"

The scene faded. Eleena had a crush on me? How did she know I was sad?

Atua?

The sensation I associated with his assurance warmed my chest.

"You tell her of me?" I whispered out loud.

Yes.

I liked the idea she knew something about me but I worried about Harper's words. The rest of my sleep passed in a series of ups and downs. Sometimes pleasant with the relief I wasn't alone, other times I remembered Talrano asking me to protect his daughter. I'm sure he never intended her to think of me as anything other than a friend. Good thing there was little chance of me seeing her in the next three years. There was plenty of time for her to grow out of her infatuation.

A MONTH after Brindyn's death, I was assigned to a ship on refugee duty. Our mission was to find and capture any and all refugee groups from several planets. Schirra didn't want them gathering together and forming any kind of resistance.

The first raid was a nightmare. We approached the camp by night. I hung back, following the others. We'd been told to take prisoners for the mines and factories, but the other men had a loose interpretation of what that meant.

They went in, blasters firing, killing most of the adult men, many boys, and some women and girls in the process. My stomach turned at their obvious enjoyment. It was a game to them.

I helped two officers corral as many men as we could. We got dirty looks from the other soldiers, but they left the ones we'd captured alone. Then the real nightmare started.

They went after the women and girls.

"Don't let them do this," I pressed the CO.

He looked at me with disgust in his eyes. "There's nothing I can do. Schirra told them to take the spoils."

"Schirra's not here. Stop them." My shock quickly burned away with my anger. The man clearly disapproved, and yet he did nothing.

"I wish I could, but others have been replaced for doing less." He turned away. "Schirra's followers outnumber the decent."

"Then let it be on my head." I stormed toward the closest man. Ripped him off the woman he straddled and punched him with all the hatred and futility I'd bottled for the last two years. He didn't get up.

I incapacitated three more before the men in my unit noticed my rampage. Then they fell on me like flies on a dead dinge. I woke up in medical on our ship feeling like I'd been beat on Cassia once more.

My CO stood over me. "Thank you, doctor, you can leave."

The medical officer put down the hypospray he must have used to wake me and left us alone.

"Amiran, I thought you'd learned to keep your head down and blend in." The CO shook his head, but a smile graced his face. "Today was stupid. Don't do it again."

He saluted me and stalked out of the room as if he'd truly been angry.

I sat up with a lot of effort and assessed the damage. Everything was bruised, one arm was in a sling, and I couldn't get a full breath without seeing starbursts out the corner of my eyes.

Useless. Nothing I did made a difference.

You were an example of goodness. That is never useless. Atua soothed my nerves.

Maybe, but I'd prefer to save that which is good.

In time, my son.

22

DERRITUS: ELEENA

3 .2 Years After Manawa—Derritus

UNCLE'S BREATHING SOUNDED WORSE. I clasped his hand in mine. He had fluid on his lungs. Half the camp had succumbed to whatever currently ate away at him. Luckily, Harper, Iri, and I had escaped so far.

"How is he?"

I jumped. Captain E stood inside the tent flap. I'd barely talked to him since he'd dragged me onto the *Vapous* months ago.

"I don't think he's going to get better." My voice caught. Lots of other people had lost everything. I had to stop thinking I was any different.

Evander sat beside me. "Your uncle was a great man. Without his help, we would have fallen apart on Jakaru. He knew what we needed to keep everyone occupied. Did you know the new tent designations were his idea?"

When we arrived on Derritus, Captain E had rearranged the tents. Instead of lots of smaller family tents, we now had large dorm sized tents to house all the kids without parents. Single adults also shared a larger tent. We sewed for weeks, using the smaller tents to create the larger ones. Those dorms now had random numbers in various places all over them.

"I only knew about the school on Jakaru. He was my mom's brother after all. Education is in our blood. And the bracelets of course." I waved my wrist, wondering if he felt that last part as the barb I meant it to be. The bracelets kept time, and once you entered the workforce, listed the assigned rotation for the day.

He chose to ignore my petty jab. "Your teachers say they can't keep up with you. They've run out of lessons."

I shrugged and felt my face grow warm. He wouldn't understand that I studied because I got bored if I didn't. And because my parents would have wanted me to. None of the other kids talked about their parents anymore, but mine were always with me.

"It won't matter in another month. I'll enter the work rotation and they'll be able to relax."

"They like the challenge." Captain E stared at Uncle.

"Is that why you let me stay in school so long?"

"No one thrives there the way you do." He shrugged. "I'm sorry I couldn't find medicine. The Hatana's fleet is everywhere. The Coalition planets are too scared to help." He ran his hand through his hair. "We're going to evacuate again."

"What about the sick?" Panic squeezed my chest, and I crushed Uncle's hand in mine.

"He has to leave us." Uncle's voice sounded like wood being dragged across the ground.

"Uncle Beck." Tears pricked my eyes. He was awake! "You have to get better. It will take a while to load the ships."

Uncle lifted a hand, ever so slowly, and waved at Evander.

Captain E placed a hand on Uncle's arm, the other one rested on my shoulder. "We started preparations last week on Beck's recommendation. The sickness is tied to this place. The damp climate. He thinks we'd be better off on the ships until we find a safer place to live."

I glared at Captain E and then Uncle. "No."

"It's okay." Uncle hadn't opened his eyes, but now he forced them open. He turned to Evander. "Give them the letters and keep your promise."

"I will." The Captain held my uncle's other hand. "For you and Am."

Uncle coughed, the air rattling around his chest. I wiped the sweat from his brow and the spit from his chin.

"Uncle Beck?"

"Leena, so strong," he coughed some more. "The daughter I never had." He closed his eyes again, squeezed my hand, and relaxed. I heard his last breath hiss out in a slow stream.

Fear clutched my heart. I was truly alone now. My breaths came in short bursts as my lungs refused to expand.

Harper and Iri ran into the room.

"Are we too late?" She took one look at Uncle then wrapped her arms around me, holding me together. "Breathe, nice and slow. Beck wouldn't want you to worry."

"I'm sorry for your loss." Captain Evander backed toward the door while Harper continued to soothe me. "Stay here. I'll get the letters."

I nodded, but couldn't say anything. Iri stood on the other side of the bed, all by himself. He didn't touch Uncle Beck, but he stared at him with the same lost look I remembered from three years earlier.

"Are you okay?" Harper asked.

"Yes. I will be." I'd have to be.

She squeezed my arm, then moved to stand by Iri, reaching for his hand. I noticed he didn't pull away. That one little thing eased my breathing another notch, even though she'd left my side. It was a testimony of how much Uncle had affected them both. Iri's anger was gone, replaced by a quiet strength. Harper was still bossy, but now she had a sensitive side Uncle would be proud of.

Captain E returned. "Beck wrote letters for the three of you when he recognized the early stages of the disease." He handed each of us an envelope. "Mourn tonight, but be ready to board the ships tomorrow. Once again, your Uncle will be missed. Without his insights and organizational skills…" Evander shook his head. "I know Beck didn't want preferential treatment, but I can give you a room to share on the ship if you'd like. It'll be tight, but it will give you some privacy."

"Thank you, Captain. We'll talk about it and let you know." Harper answered for all of us.

He nodded and left us to mourn.

It felt strange to unfold the thick paper. We'd made it by hand just so we'd have something to do. It was another of Uncle's suggestions. Stay busy and life wouldn't look so bleak.

Eleena, I'm sorry. By now you know we cannot stay on Derritus. Don't give up hope. One day Evander and the brave men who serve with him will find a safe place to settle. When that time comes, live your life with joy, not regret. Until then, continue as you have thus far. Your mother and father would be proud of you. I am proud of you. In spite of your own fear, you've met each challenge with courage and kindness. Those traits will become even more important as the Hatana's war stretches on.

Harper and Iri need you to be the voice of hope. They don't have happy memories to lean on when things get hard, but they are good and worth every encouraging word you can give. Don't let age be a barrier between you and anyone you come in contact with. Love them. Help them. See the good in them the way your mother always did.

Finally, stay close to Atua. Listen and follow his guidance. I firmly believe I will join your parents. All three of us will watch over and plead your cause before Atua.

Have faith,

Uncle Beck

I brushed away tears. How could I be strong when I felt so lost? I glanced across the room. Harper and Iri sat reading their letters. Both had tears streaming down their faces. They were stronger than me, rarely afraid, and always ready to stand up to the bullies. Harper could hold her own if it came to pushing and shoving, and Iri was the undisputed champion of his age group. I'd never been in a fight. They always jumped in to protect me.

How could I help them? I glanced down. Uncle wanted me to be the voice of hope. Hope for what? A home? Family?

Hope in me. The warmth in Atua's voice melted the rest of my fear.

I had Harper, Iri, and Atua would always be there. And now Uncle had joined my parents. I would hold on to that.

Camp life wasn't easy. It wouldn't get better, not if we had to keep moving over and over. We'd already seen how ugly people could be. I'd make it my job to show them how good we could be too. No matter how scared or hurt I felt, I'd keep the end goal in mind. One day we'd need to build a home somewhere, and I'd make sure everyone remembered how to do it.

23

FURLOUGH: AMIRAN

4 **Years After Manawa**
   It had been four years since I'd tasted freedom. Furlough on
Porobongos wasn't true liberty from Schirra, but it was as close as
I'd get. The space station was deep in Allegiant space. I planned to
meet Llandula, both of us in disguise. The good doctor and I had
crossed paths several times since our initial meeting on the ship to
Cassia.

   A year earlier I'd run into him on a mission to Mirimbia. We'd
been tasked with searching out refugees hidden among the billions
of residents. It had been tedious and depressing when we found
pockets of rebels. Even though I tried to soften the blow, Schirra's
men were brutal. Llandula's ship had also been sent. I found him
ministering to those that had been left alive. He could heal their
bodies, but the haunted look in their eyes soon took residence in
his own.

   Llandula wasn't monitored as closely as I, having been in the
fleet for over twenty years. He made contact with the underground
movement on Mirimbia and retrieved several holoprojectors that
had been calibrated to work as human camouflage. He'd slipped me
one before we left Mirimbia.

   I used it now to change my appearance and walk the space
station unrecognized. The cool vibrations molded to my skin. The
soft tingle wasn't dangerous, not like the vibrocuffs from years
before, but it felt like treading through water.

Meeting the doctor was foolish, but my worry about Eleena drove me to take the risk. Even though Atua sent dreams of Ev as well as Eleena, I hadn't personally spoken to him in four years. Now I needed a favor from him.

The dreams showed that when Eleena grew out of that awkward stage the boys took notice. It shouldn't have been any of my business, but she'd been cornered in the ship's corridor. It started harmless enough. He flirted and tried to kiss her. She'd pushed him away and he'd let her leave. But boys grew up to be men. And men didn't always take no for an answer.

My stomach churned with the things I'd seen on the raids. Many times I woke in medical not sure how I got there. A couple of times others had stood beside me, but they were transferred to other ships soon after. I couldn't stop Schirra's men. Not yet, but I could warn Evander to watch for similar problems in his camp. He could protect Eleena and the other women. Why else would Atua have shown me that vision?

I entered the Quasidigger Lounge and ordered an Azoth Flux. The drink was repulsive, but the distinctive blue liquid and red flower were how Llandula would recognize me with the disguise. I took a sip of the sweet nectar, letting the alcohol burn my throat. Yeah, didn't need to drink much of that.

"That'll darken the moons." A man slid onto the stool beside me.

"And dry the oceans." I gave the reply to the code phrase.

The man smiled but didn't react in any other way. He ordered a drink and we sat a moment in silence. It was nice to sit in the company of a trusted friend. No words needed.

After his drink was downed, Llandula turned to me. "You shouldn't take such risks."

"I know." I reached into my pocket and pulled out a data drive. "If possible, get this to Ev."

He nodded. "How have you been?"

"Fine."

"Lonely?"

I shrugged.

"Word gets around. Loyalties are shifting. Good men recognize your integrity, your willingness to sacrifice for them. To take the beatings trying to help the women." He stood and clapped me on the shoulder. "Hang in there. Two years to go."

"Will it get better when I leave the fleet?"

"What does Atua say?"

I chuckled. "What he always says. Be patient, it's in my hands."

"Yep, that's what I get too. At least we're all on the same page."

"What?" But he was gone before I could get answers.

PART II

24

HOME: AMIRAN

6 Years After Manawa—Amiran

I STOOD on the observation deck, watching the planets in my home system stream by. It had been six years since I'd last stood on Rawiri. Six years since Schirra and my father rendered Manawa uninhabitable. Five years since I left the mines of Cassia. They had been a day excursion compared to the isolation of the fleet. After the first two years, everyone had given me a wide berth. It didn't bother me. We all understood it was for their safety, and I didn't blame them.

I doubted anything would change now that I was returning to the palace.

Movement in the periphery drew my attention. A high ranking officer joined me at the window.

"It's beautiful, isn't it?" he asked, pointing to Rawiri.

"Deceptively so." I didn't offer an explanation.

The man nodded. "Be patient, it's not quite time."

With that parting remark, he hurried from the room. I filed his face, rank, and name away with the ever-growing list in my mind. Others had whispered vague remarks over the years, alluding to the fact I wouldn't be alone when the time came to end the Hatana's rule. Many hinted at hearing or at least feeling Atua with them. It gave me hope when I needed it most.

I sighed. Five years of waiting, observing, planning, and I still didn't know if I'd be successful when I made my move.

Atua, lead me and I will follow. Over the years I'd learned to trust his promptings. Always marking his words. I learned patience and immediate obedience.

Rawiri loomed in the window. It was only a matter of minutes until I could retire my uniform and take my place once more as heir to the empire. A tremor of anxiety increased my heart rate. Would my father finally be proud? If he was, what did that say about me?

After one last look, I headed to the shuttle bay. There were no belongings to collect. It was time to leave the fleet behind while clinging to the lessons I'd learned. The most important being that fear bred weak loyalty.

Only a handful of personnel waited to board the shuttle. I recognized faces but didn't acknowledge anyone other than the mandatory salute to the officers. Others chatted while I leaned against the bulkhead. I was the last to board.

The trip down passed in a fog. My mind tumbled over a thousand different thoughts and memories. Even though I felt like a foreigner, I ached to stand on my homeworld.

It was early evening when I stepped off the shuttle ramp. A misty rain dampened my skin but I refused the transport that waited. I stood, allowing the cool air to wash away the last few years. For the first time in years I stood alone, completely free to do as I wished.

With a sigh, I began the fifteen-kilometer trek to the palace.

At first, the night was peaceful, filled only with the call of birds and water dripping from the trees. The sky cleared as I neared the city, and the sounds and smells became more human. Food from the restaurants, the scent of laundry detergent from one of the houses I passed, music, laughter, traffic. I kept to the side roads, avoiding the more crowded thoroughfares as long as possible. Few people paid much attention. I'd been gone too long and my photo had been absent from the nets for years. It was one of the perks of being in the fleet.

Five kilometers from the palace, guards arrived by transport, exited the vehicle and shadowed me.

I nodded at the nearest. "Protection or guard detail?"

"Protection, Hatana Tama." He saluted and fell into line.

"So it begins." My illusion of freedom set with the sun.

The escort drew more attention than my solitary journey. Many stopped to gawk but no one approached, thanks to the soldiers that now flanked me. Did the people recognize me or simply wonder who needed such an escort? I wasn't even in the palace and felt the noose tightening around my neck.

The palace complex glowed white at the top of the hill. A pang twisted my heart. How could something so beautiful house evil? The lights cast shadows on the intricate carvings around the windows and soffits. I couldn't see the gardens yet, but I remembered their beauty. The courtyards were a place of color and life. They always reminded me of my mother.

We reached the gate. The soldier on guard stepped in front of me, halting my progress.

"Your Highness, Hatana Anaru wishes you to join him in the lower dining room immediately."

"Thank you," I grumbled. Not even an hour to visit my quarters and change? My life had not been my own for years, but it rankled more now that I was home.

I expected the dining hall to be full of high ranking officials. It gave me pleasure to imagine their response to my slightly damp and wilted appearance. However, only my father sat at the massive table. The men who'd followed me disappeared into the background.

"You've finally become a man." Hatana Anaru sat with his hands steepled in front of him. He didn't stand but waved me forward when I remained by the door. "Come, sit, eat with me."

The childish urge to be accepted and approved by him choked me. I pushed it away, knowing I could never be who he wanted me to be. Swallowing my personal pain and anger, I kept my face impassive.

"Your mother used to get that look."

"What?" I asked.

He hadn't mentioned her in years.

"The patient martyr face." He stabbed the chunks of meat with his fork.

"Is that why you sent her away?"

Anaru didn't even glance at me. He simply chewed. Eventually, he swallowed. "Her life wasn't meant to be lived in the palace."

"Then why marry her?" The anger was harder to hold in.

"Mind your business and eat. Tell me about the fleet. What you learned." He took a swig of the drink in front of him. "I'll get Schirra's report when he joins us tomorrow, but tonight I want to hear your thoughts."

I knew what he wanted to know, but could I lie well enough to satisfy him? I picked at the food for the next hour while telling half-truths. By keeping everything to cold facts, I avoided taking a stand on his and Schirra's method for expanding the empire. Anaru nodded but didn't say much otherwise. When I finished he tossed his napkin on the plate and stood.

"Not everything is as you think." He stared at my face as if memorizing it. "Tomorrow you will be anointed as the next Hatana. I'll not have the empire thrown into confusion if anything happens to me. The question will be if you can keep the throne from Schirra after I'm gone."

AFTER MY FATHER left the dining hall, I walked to my suite in confusion. What had he meant by his parting remark? Did he want me to keep Schirra off the throne, and if he didn't trust his general, why hadn't he gotten rid of him? I remembered something the *Itzalak* had said in the mines. Something about Schirra holding the real power.

Atua, I don't know what to think. Is this all a ruse to confuse me? I needed to stamp out my doubts.

I examined my rooms while waiting for Atua's guidance. They were much as I had left them. The only difference was my clothes were gone. What was I supposed to wear to the anointing ceremony?

Atua's voice refocused my thoughts. *The Itzalak are wise. They saw much around the palace and knew your father's true heart. It is something he's kept hidden a long time.*

My father was hiding his true heart? What did that mean?

A knock at the door distracted me further.

"Come in," I called.

Evander's father, Timoti entered. He had aged well. His hair was grayer, but he still moved with strength. Before I could speak, Timoti held a finger to his lips. He closed the door, reached into his pocket, and pulled out an amplifier and flicked the switch.

"Now we can talk freely." Timoti set the small cube on the table by the couch and hugged me. "It's good to see you, Am."

I swallowed the emotion that threatened to overwhelm me. That simple greeting held more warmth than the hour or more I'd spent with Anaru. But now I feared I couldn't trust a lifetime of impressions about my father.

Shaking it off, I pointed to the amplifier. "Jammer?"

"Yes. Sit, tell me everything that's happened to you over the last six years." Timoti sat in one of the armchairs. "Then I can tell you what little I know about Ev."

"Have you been able to stay in touch with him?" I didn't want to talk about my experiences.

Timoti nodded. "It's been hard. Schirra still watches me closely. He suspects I've lied about something, but I don't think he's sure what. You'll have to be careful."

"Do you think he's bugged my suite?" I studied the room, moving from one object to another. Tables, lamps, a flower arrangement, chandeliers hanging from the ceiling, various artwork and sculptures. Any of them could hide a camera or microphone.

"I had them swept this afternoon. It's clean for the time being, but don't say anything important without a jammer on."

"Surely he'll notice that."

"He expects it, I'm sure. Everyone, including Anaru, uses them in their private quarters. That pocket one is for keeping with you outside these rooms. The larger one is in the cabinet over there." He pointed to an antique armoire.

I sighed and relaxed into the couch. "Right now, this moment, I'm glad to be home."

Timoti chuckled. "Good. Are you going to tell me how you've been?"

"No. I'll just say that only by the grace of Atua did I survive with my integrity and mind intact. And that was probably a challenge for him."

"I'm sure it wasn't, and not just because he's God." Timoti leaned forward. "I heard rumors through the underground. That you had become a believer. Is it true?"

I wasn't sure where Timoti stood on the subject, but my instincts suggested he'd always been a believer. "Yes. You don't live through the things I've seen and been required to do without turning to him. Not unless you become like my father and Schirra."

Timoti's head bobbed up and down. "Good. We need our next Hatana to be a believer." He stood as if to leave.

"Wait, what about Ev?"

"Ah, yes. My guess is you know as much as I do. He's moved to several planets over the years. His camp stays just ahead of the fleet. He splits his time between camp and Olea. I just wish I could see him. Am, what is your plan?"

I rested my head in my hands. "It's still the old plan, but Atua says it's not time."

"Not time? How long must we wait?" Timoti gripped the edge of the couch.

Atua? I hoped for a more definitive answer.

Soon.

"He says soon." I met Timoti's gaze and shrugged. "Until then, I need to observe and find the weaknesses here at the palace. "Will you help?"

"Of course. I can tell you many areas that you can use to your advantage."

"We will have to do it carefully. My father and Schirra must think I'm toeing the line. Which brings me to a pressing question." I stood and walked back to the bedroom, Timoti followed. "What am I supposed to wear tomorrow?"

"Don't worry about that. The valet will be here by six to take measurements. You'll have a complete wardrobe including uniforms, casual wear, and formalwear by lunchtime."

Groaning I leaned against the doorframe. "So what you're saying is I should sleep."

"Definitely." Timoti smiled and retreated to the door of my suites. "It is good to have you home, Am."

After he left, I paced a little longer. Truthfully, I was afraid to sleep. Whenever my mind was full of questions or fear, Atua sent dreams of Eleena. They calmed me, but lately, they also left me uncomfortable. I spent too much time thinking, worrying, and wishing for her. It wasn't right, or safe.

Giving in to the exhaustion, I removed my clothes and went to bed. I'd taken to praying each night not to dream.

"Atua, keep them safe. Guide me and let me be your hands."

25

KAHU REFUGEE CAMP: ELEENA

6 .4 Years After Manawa

AFTER A LONG DAY OF TEACHING, I sagged behind the med tent. This spot was the only place dark enough to see the stars. Even here the glow of the spotlights bleached out the potential drama. The stars looked different on Kahu. Of course, they altered with every planet we fled to.

It always made home seem so far away.

Reminded me how far away Am was.

I wished for more dreams. They'd grown farther and fewer over the years. I missed them and the closeness I'd felt to Am.

His years in the fleet changed him. It became harder to read his expressions. The kindness in his eyes disappeared and there was a hardness that didn't sit right on his face. I don't know what I would have done if not for the peace Atua whispered into my heart after some of the dreams. Somehow I knew the kindness was still there, only hidden.

Stop wishing for the impossible. I determined once again to forget about him and try harder to find someone real to obsess over. Boys used to flirt with me. Sadly, there didn't seem to be many left in camp close to my age.

"Eleena? You daydreaming again?" Harper snapped her thin fingers in my face. "Come on, you'll miss dinner."

"Like I'd miss much." I'd grown used to the emptiness in my

stomach. The bristled hair on my head was a different story. I rubbed a hand over it. A week had passed since the camp-wide shaving. The first one we'd ever had. "I hate this."

"You'll get used to it." Harper touched her bald head too. "Way better than the bugs."

"I guess." She didn't know my hair was the one vain thing about me. I caught a whiff of coal. "You worked the mines today?"

Harper nodded and pulled me to my feet. "Come on and stop staring at the stars. There's nothing left to return to."

She was right, and I felt a twinge of desperation. There had to be something for us somewhere. We couldn't stay on Kahu forever. It wasn't anywhere close to the kind of place we could settle for good. We were still too close to the Hatana's empire.

I clenched my fists and followed her to the mess hall, the only permanent building in camp. The line of refugees stretched past the hall and around the school tent. Young, old, tall, short. Some had hair, having just arrived from another camp on the planet. None of them could be called clean or fat. The air reeked of defeat and hope-lessness.

"Bet we don't get much tonight." Harper groaned at the line in front of us. "Tomorrow I'm not looking for you."

"I didn't ask you to take care of me." Everyone in camp thought they had to watch out for me, but I wasn't sure why. They whispered about me though. I'd felt their stares.

The heat of the night embraced me with less intensity than the day, but it was enough that I wished for the coolness of the river. I wiped the sweat from my brow. "How did it go in the mines?"

"Same as always."

Harper was grumpier on the days she worked beneath the ground. I didn't blame her. It was the worst rotation of all. Dark, damp. The dust eating away at your lungs. And for what? A pitiful amount of coal and other minerals. We'd never carve out enough to trade for the celestium we needed to run the ships' engines.

Atua, give us time. Give us luck.

Pushing my worry away with prayer, I inched forward and hoped for a bit of bread to dip in some watered-down broth.

I am with you. His words always brought comfort, even when they couldn't bring a smile.

Atua might be with me, but the people in camp could still make their own decisions. Sometimes they forgot kindness and chose paths to make Atua weep. Like the riots in the last camp.

Our numbers fluctuated with every move. Captain E didn't like to turn anyone away, even when it made rations tight or stretched our other resources. That and his connection to Am were why I stayed with him.

"Think we'll get the celestium before we need to evacuate again?" I watched a young mother with two small children approach from the dorm tents.

"Depends. Maybe they'll smuggle more food in to tide us over until we harvest the crops." She didn't bother pretending we might settle here. The longest we'd stayed in one place had been the two years on Mirimbia. We almost lasted as long on Tobongos.

I nodded, only half listening. The family had to be new. The mother still had hair down to her waist. Ratted and dirty, it covered most of her tunic. She stared at the ground. Her boy, maybe five years old, had tear streaks in the dust of his face. The girl appeared younger, maybe two or three. She stared vacantly in front of her. All three were pale, but the girl showed the signs. Swollen tummy, listless dull eyes.

It wouldn't be long. The breath squeezed out of me.

They stepped into line, and we shuffled forward another foot. I stared at the little girl. How did they get here? What planet did they call home? Had the Hatana's men left it in ruins or simply taken over? The lump that used to be my heart constricted into a tighter ball of stone. It wasn't enough to make me stop caring. My hands clenched, and I tried not to give in to my anxiety and hyperventilate. I'd gotten better at controlling it.

Anyway, I had a promise to keep.

"Leena?" Harper touched my fist. "Don't."

"Don't what?" I shook my hands loose, avoiding her gaze.

"It won't help and you know it."

How did she always know what I was thinking? Maybe my idea wouldn't make a difference, but then again it might. I tried to glimpse the stars for comfort, but they didn't cut through the camp lights.

We finally reached the entrance to the mess hall. I heard a few whispered voices, but mostly the slurps of the hungry filled the air.

"Hi, Eleena. I was afraid you weren't coming tonight." One of my students stood behind the table. She poured a ladle of liquid into a bowl and handed it to me. No bread.

"I wouldn't miss it." I smiled at her, hoping she couldn't see the dark clouds in my heart.

She smiled back until it felt awkward. Harper nudged me to move.

I sniffed the broth. It didn't have a smell, and it wouldn't have a flavor. If we were lucky it would have vitamin supplements. There was no way to know for sure. We might all be dying from lack of nutrients and we wouldn't know until our bodies wasted away. For a moment I gave in to the hopelessness. Even memories of the aroma from Mima's kitchen couldn't survive the stench of so many unwashed bodies crammed into the building.

You forget so easily. Atua's voice gently reprimanded me.

I don't mean to. I guess I just miss them tonight. Sometimes I felt lonely for my family, other times it was for things. Soft clothes, good food, books.

This won't last forever. Hope flooded out the negative thoughts, and Harper's voice called for my attention.

"Looks like tonight's fare is warm water with a bit of carrot." Her sarcasm wafted to me as she trudged to our usual spot in the corner.

"I didn't get the carrot, so count your blessings." I laughed in an effort to lighten both our moods.

The mother and her children passed by us. Thoughts of the Hatana's cruelty sliced at me. What would Atua have me do? He'd have me share his love with those who needed it most. I followed the family to a table near the center of the room.

"Looks like you're new." I crouched beside the little girl and spoke softly. Her mother watched wide-eyed with trembling hands. "We have a tradition. New girls get extra soup their first day."

I poured mine into her bowl. *Please, let there be vitamins in there.*

"Thank you." The small voice belonged to the mother.

I touched the girl's clammy cheek but focused on the woman. The loss written across her face appeared raw and new. "My name's Eleena. If you need anything, you can find me at the school."

The mother barely nodded as I left. Harper shook her head but didn't look angry anymore. I returned the empty bowl to the pile. My hunger didn't matter. Maybe I *had* made a difference.

I headed for the female juvie tent. This would be my last year to enjoy its safety. At least then I'd be with Harper again. She had left for the women's tent two years before. We didn't have beds or cots in the juvie tent like the adults. There were too many of us.

I barely made it to my bedroll before my bracelet lit up. Every time I looked at it, I missed Uncle Beck. My heart rate increased while I watched the numbers count down from five. We had eight work rotations designated by a solid color or combination of stripes. When the bracelet hit zero it flashed before turning deep purple.

The mines. I sighed and lay down.

I'd never actually taken my turn in the mines. Not once in the two plus years since I joined the labor sequence. Part of me was grateful, the other curious. Maybe this time I'd finally see what it was like down there. A few minutes passed before I heard the scratching on the tent wall.

"Eleena?" The loud whisper confirmed I couldn't hide from him.

I flipped over and pushed my head under the side of the tent. My heart warmed at the sight of my second best friend. "Hey, Iri."

The twenty-one-year-old was muscular from years of hard work, most recently in the mines. He sat cross-legged with his bracelet held in front of him. His blue eyes stared at me. I missed his fluffy shock of blond hair that used to fall over his forehead.

"I got sewing. Lots of people will trade school for sewing." He pushed it toward me.

"Why do you do this?" I shook my head. He and Harper still tried to protect me from the harshest parts of camp life. The only consolation was knowing everyone traded jobs. That's how Iri managed to go into the mines every day. On S'klinctic it had been the quarries.

"What do you mean?" His brow wrinkled.

"I should work all the rotations, just like everyone else." I kept my hands hidden inside the tent.

"Harper told me what you did for the new girl."

I rolled my eyes at his topic change. "Was she laughing at me for being stupid?"

"No." He clammed up, and I wondered what he was thinking. He talked more than he had when we were younger, but he was still a man of few words. His eyes met mine again. "Come on, trade."

"We don't need to trade. I already have school."

Iri leaned closer. "You're a horrible liar. Show me your arm."

"No."

He grabbed me by the shoulders and dragged me outside.

"What are you doing?" I screeched, trying not to laugh.

He caught my right hand and looked at the bracelet. "You don't belong in the mines."

There it was again. I snapped, "You let Harper go."

"I help her. She's safe." He reached for my arm again, this time unclasping the bracelet.

"Iri, stop." I tried to sound like I meant it, but my body relaxed as an overwhelming sense of relief claimed me. "You can watch out for me too."

"Take the bracelet. Go to the mess hall and trade for school. That's where we need you." He dropped his bracelet with its red glowing stripe and walked away.

Iri remained a mystery, even though I'd known him for six years. He seemed to understand me as well as Harper, but I never knew what he was thinking.

Atua, what should I do with him? It was a half-hearted plea that I didn't expect an answer to. I was surprised when I got one.

Let him protect you. He's one of mine.

My breath caught. I don't know why. Of course, Iri was one of Atua's children. We all were. However, this felt like something more.

He listens. The voice came again.

Did Iri hear Atua's voice as I did? Obviously, he knew when I tried to lie, and he had a second sense that let him know when I had the mines. He always found me to swap. Harper once told me Iri knew there were enough people scared of teaching that I could trade for school every night. He was right. Even when I didn't look for them, they sought me out.

I don't know if they were scared of kids or afraid of showing how much they didn't know, but I'd never sewn, worked the water pumps, or fed the chickens. My fingernails stayed clean of garden dirt and my lungs free of mine dust.

With a sigh, I picked myself up out of the dirt and headed back to the mess hall. If everyone wanted me to stay out of the mines, I'd gladly comply. I barely entered the hall when a man ran up to me.

"Eleena, I've got school duty tomorrow. Please tell me you have something else, anything else." He had more bristle on his face than his head.

I held up the bracelet. "Sewing?"

He pushed his bracelet toward me. "I'll take it. Thanks."

Before I could even put the bracelet on my arm, he disappeared into the crowd. Did he think I'd change my mind? Suppressing a grin, I hurried back to the tent. Soon the other girls would find their way back from dinner or whatever social activity had been planned. I soaked in the few moments of alone time, trying to reclaim the lost feeling of being an only child.

26

HATANA TO HATANA: AMIRAN

6 .4 Years After Manawa
The palace staff draped the windows and mirrors in black. I imagined they did it out of protocol more than reverence for Hatana Anaru. My father's passing was not likely mourned by anyone. I still felt conflicted about him. There had been moments during the last few months I felt he might like me. Be proud of me. And not for the act I put on for him and Schirra.

Atua never confirmed my suspicions, but I caught more unguarded emotions on the Hatana's face than ever before. Those moments kept me wondering if all I'd known was the mask he wore.

I didn't mourn in a traditional sense, but I felt incomplete. There were too many unanswered questions that I would never find solutions for.

The tension in the palace had increased with my father's illness. It had come on suddenly and progressed swiftly. Everyone had suspicions. General Schirra might be cautious, but the obstacles between himself and the crown were conveniently down to one. Me.

Did my father know? That first day home, he spoke of his death. Had he been trying to tell me something?

"Your Highness?" Timoti entered from a side door.

"Yes?"

"Schirra requested a meeting of all government heads." His shoulders were tense, his jaw clenched.

"Anaru has only been in the ground an hour." I stood and straightened my jacket. There was no point in putting this off. Perhaps Schirra would reveal his intentions if not his hand.

"Would you like me to remain in the conference room?" Timoti followed.

"Yes. I'll watch the military leaders, and you focus on the civil government heads. If we're lucky, we'll be able to discern where their loyalties lie."

"Yes, sir."

We fell silent as we left the royal wing and entered the busier council halls. Many bowed in respect as I passed. None offered condolences.

Only half the room stood when I entered. I noted they were all city leaders. No surprise there. My years in the fleet had taught me most of the captains were loyal to my father and Schirra. It made my goals more difficult. Schirra thrived on war, and he had the manpower to slake his lust for it. He'd never back off. I knew all too well how easy it was for him to make people disappear.

"Please be seated." I took my place at the head of the table. "General Schirra, to what do we owe this pleasure? I'm sure it is of the utmost importance since it could not wait the standard mourning period."

"Of course." Schirra remained standing.

It took all my concentration to remain calm. The general had aged well. Even though he was in his late sixties, he could probably take any man in the room. Of course, my father had been just as healthy four months earlier.

"As Hatana, Anaru set this empire on the course to greatness. We are aware of the rumors regarding his death, and I am personally investigating the possibility it was not a normal illness."

My skin crawled, but I nodded. "Thank you. I'm sure you will leave no stone unturned."

"There is another reason I wished to speak with the council today. It is in regard to your marital status."

A wave of ice hit my gut. I gripped the edge of the table. "My personal life no longer falls under your purview."

"Amiran, as Hatana, your life is not your own. In light of your father's sudden death, the council agrees you need to marry and produce an heir."

"There's time for that. I'm only twenty-five." My mind whirled. I'd never considered marriage. It didn't seem wise to bring an unsuspecting woman, much less innocent children, into the palace under the current circumstances. "Marriage is not a priority while continuing to expand the empire."

"Marriage is imperative. If something happened to you while overseeing a mission, Rawiri would be left without an heir. We'd be thrust into civil war. Your father's efforts to increase our power would be wasted." Schirra didn't smile, but I recognized the gleam in his eye.

"I'll consider it." And every possible motive behind this demand, because I knew without a doubt he would never allow a civil war.

Schirra pressed forward, ignoring my dismissal. "Good. I have invited the daughters from several high ranking families from Allegiant planets to gather at the palace. These eligible women will begin arriving in a month. You'll be able to court them if you wish, but I encourage you to choose quickly."

It took all I had to hold in my shock. He'd already chosen who I could marry? I took a steadying breath. There was no way I would play into his plan without some kind of fight. Think, think, think!

"Thank you for your proactive enthusiasm," I spoke slowly, desperately searching for my own plan. My gaze moved around the room. Some of those present looked as appalled as I. Timoti most of all. *Atua, guide me.*

The warmth of his spirit filled me. I pushed out all other sounds as I waited for his will.

Refugees. Eleena's face flashed through my mind. I quickly pushed it away. Now was not the time to be distracted.

Refugees. Atua asserted again.

How can I use them to buy time? I'd barely thought the question when I found myself speaking once more. "General Schirra, while I appreciate your efforts, I also require women of a marriageable age from the refugee camps."

The collective gasp of the room almost undid me. No one saw that coming. Not even me.

"You can't marry filth." Schirra fisted his hands. "It will pollute the bloodlines."

"On the contrary, some were once the highest ranking families on Coalition planets. Marrying one of them could put an end to the entire refugee problem. Show those who choose to flee that they can be a part of the empire instead." I nodded my head. That's good. Believable even.

One of the soldiers stood. "General Schirra, Amiran might be onto something. Perhaps we should indulge him."

A look passed between the two, and Schirra gave the slightest inclination of his head. "Fine. We'll gather some women from the workhouses."

"No. I want them from off planet. From the camps."

Schirra glared. "Twenty women will be gathered from the next camp we find."

"I want a hundred, and they can't be from the same camp."

This time Schirra growled but nodded his head. "A hundred it is."

"Is there anything else? My father has only been in the ground a short time, and I have a coronation to prepare for." I stepped away from the table.

"We will need to build some kind of barracks to house them. They won't be allowed to roam the palace halls." Schirra visibly pulled himself under control.

"Fine. Get started." I hurried away, Timoti falling in step beside me.

"That was interesting. Refugees?" he asked.

"I don't know what I was thinking." I tried to massage the headache growing between my eyes. Atua had said refugees and I'd let my imagination run away with me.

"Does this have anything to do with Talrano's daughter?" Timoti spoke low, his eyes constantly roaming the hall we walked down.

"No. Heaven forbid the fleet finds their camp." Shame filled me as I realized my efforts to keep my thoughts of Eleena at bay had failed miserably. "How could I have fallen for her?"

Timoti opened the door to my quarters, but he didn't speak until we were inside. "How could you not? Atua has allowed you to watch her grow into a kind young woman. He's made you privy to her girl-hood crush as well as her daily prayers on your behalf. Why are you surprised to find you have feelings for her?"

"She's my teacher's daughter. His child. I promised to protect her, not this." I'd prayed for her safety for years, and lately, I'd prayed that Atua would help me distance my emotions from her. She deserved better. I could only put her in danger.

Timoti rested his hand on my shoulder. "Am, children grow up. However, I see this is not what you want to hear, and as you said, heaven forbid they are found. Come, sit. I'll have dinner sent up."

"Thank you."

"Am, one day you will see her again. Then you'll have to face these feelings. It'll be easier for both of you if you come to a decision before then."

I nodded as he left. The decision was easy. No matter what I felt, for her own safety, Eleena couldn't be pulled into my world.

27

LIVING VS SURVIVING: ELEENA

The education tent smelled of dirt, sunbaked wood and sweat. My group of fifteen-year-olds would join the work rotation at the end of the term. Twenty faces stared at me. Some already looked resigned to their fate. I knew they wouldn't last long if they gave up before they even started. I'd seen it many times.

Like me, most of them didn't have parents in camp. Unlike me, they thought school was something to keep them busy and out of the way until they were old enough to work. It never entered their minds that one day they might be able to use their education for something more fulfilling than merely surviving.

It's time. Atua prompted and I changed plans immediately.

"We're doing something different today." I searched the tent for the education manager. Owasso walked from one group of students to another. He nodded in acknowledgment. "Everyone up. We're having class by the river."

Little sounds of surprise came from them as they glanced at each other. It was always like this. Most people didn't leave the illusion of safety the camp fence provided.

"Come on." I couldn't help but smile as I led them out of the tent.

Shades of brown and tan stretched everywhere. Earth, trash, tents. The once vibrant colors that marked the original tent numbers had faded, almost disappearing all together from the years of sunlight. Even Kahu's sky appeared more brown than blue.

Only the wind moved veils of dust between the empty walkways. My students shuffled, kicking up more dirt. They hesitated at the gate even though it stood wide open. I marched through and continued down the hill. Tall brown grasses waved in the breeze. They were different from the soft blue pastures of Manawa, but they danced and swayed with the same grace.

Thoughts of home equated to thoughts of my parents. It was nice to think of them without hurting, and right now I only felt gratitude. Their guidance had given me something I could share with others—the love of knowledge which led to hope. These kids desperately needed that.

After five minutes following the road, I cut to the field. The grass reached my waist. My fingers trailed over the tops of the rough seedpods topping the blades. A hundred yards and we reached the edge of the hill. Looking down I could see the road as it twisted its way down the switchbacks. I'd take my students down the harder, faster way.

"Spread out and take your time." I beckoned them forward.

They looked at the steep slope, eyes wide. No one moved. With one last look at them, I picked my way down the side. I slid on loose rocks and had to catch myself, scraping my hands. My ankles bent at odd angles in an attempt to find footholds on the nearly vertical surface. Every moment was a dance to stay upright. The physical exertion woke me up. At the bottom, I crossed over the road and waited for my students to join me.

"Okay, once more and we'll reach the river." I paused, waiting. Someone always asked.

"Does the road go to the river?" It was one of the girls with a defeated look.

"Yes, it does."

"Then why are we sliding down the hill?" she asked.

"I'll tell you at the bottom." I turned and moved as fast as I dared.

My heart pounded harder every time I slipped and with each desperate grab for a handhold or steadier footing. It beat stronger. I gasped for air and laughed into the warm morning. The sound of the river mingled with the trills of local birdlife. I hadn't learned their names yet, but I felt their joy all the same.

I didn't wait for the kids at the bottom this time. My legs felt powerful, my lungs moved the oxygen efficiently. They carried me across the road and into the meadow beside the river at top speed. When I reached the rushing water, I fought the urge to leap. Instead, I turned and watched my students while my heart calmed and my breathing slowed to normal.

When the last pupil stood before me, I motioned for them to sit.

"Close your eyes. Look inside yourself." I walked around the scattered groups of kids. "What do you feel?"

"My heart." A boy in the middle pressed his hand to his chest. "It's beating so hard it hurts."

Many nodded.

"I have a pain in my side where I landed on a rock."

"I can't breathe!" someone else gasped.

"I can breathe better than in camp," someone countered.

The answers came faster as more students found words for what they experienced. Eventually, they spoke of the breeze on their skin, the sound of the water and birds. They mentioned the way it felt peaceful.

"This is what it feels like to be alive." I looked each one in the eyes. "Sometimes we forget in the camps. The ship's officers know this. That's why they don't lock the gates during the day."

"I thought it was because everyone is welcome to join us." A boy in the back spoke up.

"That too, but they also understand that we have to remember. Survival is important, but what happens after that?" I could tell they were thinking. "How many of you were in S'klintic? Do you remember the riots?"

Heads nodded, hands raised halfway in the air. Many faces held the fear those memories brought to the surface.

"The riots and cruelty start because people forget." *Atua, help them understand.*

"What do they forget?" The girl who wanted to walk the road looked up at me intently.

"They forget Atua and what it feels like to be alive. Really alive. They let the anger and desperation make them feel what you just felt. And they think it's good." I struggled to push my own memories away. "After feeling nothing for so long they can't let it go. Today we are going to practice feeling things without fear. Without anger. It's part of why learning about history is so important. We can learn from their mistakes, do all we can to prevent it from happening again."

We spent the rest of the day running races through the fields, discovering animal holes and tracks. Someone started a spinning contest. I twirled until I lay dizzy in the grass, laughing with them. Lighter shades of gray floated across the sky. If I closed my eyes, I could almost pretend the sky was a deep blue.

You've done well. Atua's voice floated over the breeze. *Many felt me today.*

If more of the refugees remembered Atua was aware of and loved them, life would be more bearable. The hard work and limited freedoms would be understandable.

"Eleena?" One of my students leaned over me.

"Yes?"

"Should we head back?"

I looked at my bracelet. Rotations ended in twenty minutes. In spite of our dire circumstances, Captain E and the other officers tried to make camp life enjoyable. There were several free hours after mealtime. Sometimes they even had music or old vids for us to watch.

"Yep, let's gather everyone. We can take the road back."

My students walked into camp with a bit more pep in their step. If they forgot everything else I'd tried to teach them about the stars and life before the war, they'd remember this day when they were free. Free to experience the innocence of childhood, even if it was an illusion.

I glanced at my bracelet again. We were only a few minutes past shift end. Harper would be off her med rotation and headed to the field by the mines to wait for Iri. Their friendship had deepened over the years. He was her rock, and Harper had become Iri's sunshine. I headed that direction too, grateful they still let me intrude on their private time together.

Owasso waved at me, so I veered back to the school. "Your students look much happier than this morning."

"They just needed a break." I smiled at the older man. He was probably the oldest man in camp. It felt like he knew everyone by name, and he treated us all like his own grandchildren.

He nodded. "More of the adults need a break like that. The officers will talk to you soon. They've been waiting for you."

"Waiting for what?"

"For you to be old enough to take the adults out on your little trips."

My hand flew to my mouth. "They want me to take the adults?"

"Yes, and I think you're ready." He patted my arm. "We need your kind of determination if anything is to change."

I didn't know what to say. Owasso winked at me.

"Go on now. I'm sure Harper's waiting for you somewhere."

28

REFUGEE BARRACKS: AMIRAN

"You can't deliver messages yourself. Schirra's spies are everywhere." Timoti laid out my clothes for the day.

After a fitful night's sleep, I wasn't in the mood for lectures no matter how well intended. Atua had sent dreams of Eleena spinning in a field by a river with her students, making my declaration to keep her out of my heart even harder. Her hair had been shaved to a prickly fuzz in the dream, driving my need to speak with Ev. What was happening in his camp?

"I don't trust anyone else," I mumbled as I dressed.

"Am…"

"I know, I know, but it has to be done." I glanced at the amplifier to make sure the jammer was on, then found a legitimate reason for doing it that didn't evolve Talrano's daughter. "We need to double our efforts of infiltration."

"It'll be risky."

"Everything is a risk. I need De'truto out of the mines. He could help Ev with strategy."

"That old goat's still alive?" Timoti shook his head and sank into a chair. "How? He's been on Cassia for six years at least."

"It's been more than seven." My thoughts turned to Na'mune. He'd lasted four in the hell I'd only known a year. The Celestium dust had eaten away his lungs. "I don't know how De'truto has survived. It can only be the will of Atua."

"Definitely. How many men are on Olea?"

"There are close to four hundred training on the asteroid. Over a thousand have been successfully integrated into fleet bases and ships over the years. Men like Doctor Llandula have been instrumental in finding others sympathetic to our cause. It's unclear how many we actually have on our side."

"Will it be enough?"

"There's no way to know." I waved my hand in the air. "I'm waiting on this last group to be placed before making our move. Even then, there'll be no opportunity for a fair fight. Not in space or here in the palace. We'll need the strength of Atua. Only then will we succeed."

"I agree, but with your father gone, why can't we simply take out Schirra?" Timoti always came back to that. I didn't blame him, but it wasn't the solution. Atua warned against it.

"He has too many loyal to him in the palace. It would be suicide. We need to bring in more of our men before we try anything."

"We're working on it," Timoti grunted and changed the subject. "If you get through to my son, tell him hello for me."

"I always do."

I finished my preparations for the day then made my rounds in the courts. It was heartbreaking work because I couldn't govern the way I wished. Schirra kept an ever watchful eye, waiting for me to show the weakness he expected.

Be patient a little longer.

By lunchtime, I wanted to beat the general with my own hands. It took all I had to turn my back on him and leave the room. A guard stopped me at the palace entrance. He was young, probably straight out of the academy. There was a good chance he hadn't been brainwashed by Schirra's upper echelons yet since the academy was one place I held the reigns. It had taken four months to swap Schirra's men with mine.

"Your Highness, wait here. I'll get an escort detail for you." The soldier saluted and made to move into the gate office.

"There's no need. I'm not going far. Just to get a bite to eat." I paused and pulled out my handheld holoprojector. It was the same one Llandula had given me on Mirimbia. "I've even brought along a disguise."

"Sir, General Schirra would not approve." He shifted from foot to foot.

"Then don't tell him. I'll be perfectly safe. It'll be our little secret." I winked and selected an image to portray from the holo. "See you in an hour."

He didn't try to stop me again. I turned my mind to the task at hand. There was a short window each day when I could contact Evander.

I hadn't personally spoken to Ev since I'd returned to Rawiri and wasn't sure what planet he was on. He was probably low on supplies, and I'd need coordinates to smuggle rations.

My favorite deli came into view. Hebe, the owner, was another person I trusted. He migrated to Rawiri from Attalea a few months before the fleet attacked. Many from the Coalition planets ran messages through his back rooms.

The mood was festive when I sauntered in. Many glanced my way. They recognized my avatar as a non-threat and continued about their business. I often wondered what they'd do if I strolled in wearing my own face.

"What are you chuckling about Fig?" Hebe waved at me from behind the counter. "Want the usual?"

"Yes, please." I watched him move about, frying meats, chopping vegetables, and slicing the bread he pulled from his ovens. "And I'll take the special with that."

"Thought you might. As soon as it's ready I'll call you back."

"Thanks, Hebe. Anything you need?" I always asked, but he never took me up on the offer.

"Not today, but thanks for asking."

I picked up my sandwich and sat by the window. The city bustled as always. As I watched the people scurry about, I wondered how many would support me if they knew what I really wanted. Did they care about the planets Schirra turned into slaves for my father? What about Manawa and Artemese? They were completely uninhabitable and would be for decades, if not longer.

My food turned to sawdust, and I left it on the plate. I'd visited both planets before my father launched his war to stamp out any and all voices that spoke against him. It had only taken him ten years to bring our quadrant under his control. Two planets destroyed, five others enslaved. And now I wasn't even sure it had been his idea.

Father, I wish you could have been honest with me. Shaking my head, I cleaned my table. *He was exactly who I thought he was.* I had to stop wishing it had been an act for some greater good.

"Fig, you're up," Hebe called out.

I tossed the trash and made my way to a back room. It was encased in metal a foot thick, equipped with jammers, coders and a few devices of Hebe's own creation. Every bit of it was to protect the communications that came in and out of this place. As far as I knew, there had never been a leak.

The room smelled faintly of sweat from the last occupant. I flapped my arms back and forth a few times in an effort to clear the air before locking myself inside. There was a desk, computer, and chair. The air hummed while I waited for the interface to load so I could type in my code and request a connection with Ev.

Time barely moved. Each second stretched endlessly.

When Ev came online I noticed his head had been shaved bald, similar to Eleena's. His skin was deeply tanned, his cheeks a bit more hollow.

"What happened to your hair?" I ran my fingers through mine to tease him, grateful I could ask without mentioning the dream.

"Show off. This camp had bugs. Everyone cut off their hair. Trust me it was worth it. I don't miss it yet." He grinned and dimples appeared in spite of the gauntness in his features.

"Everyone? Even the women?" I pressed because it seemed logical to ask.

"Yep. There may have been more than a few tears from them."

I wondered if Eleena had cried. Somehow I doubted it. She was too strong to let something like that bother her. "You're looking thinner these days."

"We've planted crops, but it'll take a while for them to mature. If you could send rations it would be a huge help."

"I'll do my best. It's getting harder to find smugglers. Schirra's men are working overtime." I cringed, stopping short of telling him I was culpable for that.

"We'll do the best we can. How's dad?"

"Good. He wishes he could talk with you."

Ev nodded. He didn't need to say anything. Instead of dwelling on things out of our control, I dove to the important stuff.

"Anaru died."

"That was sudden." Ev leaned forward in his seat.

"Yes, pretty sure it wasn't natural causes. We've got to move up our timeline."

"I've got several hundred men on Olea and a handful of refurbished firebarges, but we still don't have a battlecruiser. One wouldn't be enough against the fleet anyway."

"We should forget about our own fleet. Keep placing the men on the Hatana's ships. Once they've infiltrated they can take out the crew leadership and cripple or commandeer them for our usage."

"It's going to be hard to coordinate such an effort without Schirra getting suspicious."

"I've faith you can pull it off. You need De'truto."

"He'd be a great help if I can get him to leave."

"Tell him I'm asking."

"Call back in a month and I'll let you know what he says."

"Thanks, Ev. How's everything else?" I tried to stop there, but her name slipped from my lips anyway. "Eleena?"

"We're fine. Eleena moved off the ship and is staying with the other girls her age."

"Why?" She'd be safer in the crew cabins.

"She didn't want preferential treatment."

I didn't like it but nodded anyway. "Just keep an eye on her. Any chance of adding more men to our ranks?"

"I'm grooming the last batch on Kahu. Our numbers have increased, but I don't trust the newer men. Iri continues to weed them out for me."

"Eleena's friend?"

"Yes, he's quiet, dependable, and more determined than most men his age. The others respect him."

"Good." I nodded and glanced at the clock. We only had a few more minutes. "How many in this last group?"

"Only ten. If we had time, I could get maybe twenty more from the schoolboys."

"I doubt I can convince Schirra I've got the potential to be like my father for long. The countdown has started. I only wish I knew the timeline."

Ev rubbed his bald head. "Yeah. I can feel it here too. Everything is falling apart. Tensions are high, as is the dissatisfaction. When this group is ready, I'll take them to Olea. What should I do about the other refugees? I can't trust everyone with our base location."

"If the crops come in, can they stay on Kahu?"

"Yeah. The conditions are livable." His shoulders sagged. "I just hate to leave them behind. They trust me to take care of them."

"If we put an end to Schirra's momentum, you will be taking care of them. We have to keep that in mind." Each conversation was harder than the last. I could see Ev's exhaustion, feel the worry. How many suffered while we dragged our feet? "Our time is up. Whatever you decide, make sure Eleena goes with you."

"I will." Ev rubbed his head again. "Am?"

"Yeah?"

"Eleena has really helped with moral around here. She takes her students on these field trips. Reminds them what it feels like to be alive. She talks about Atua with them."

"I know."

"How?"

"Atua's dreams. I went on a tree climbing excursion with her on S'klinctic, and just last night I watched her talk to students by a river." I smiled at the memory. Eleena had an iron grasp on the concept of living versus surviving. Her trust and faith in Atua, even after losing her parents, was amazing. "I hope to talk to her about it one day."

Ev grinned. "Is that so? She's grown up since you left her with me on Manawa."

There it was. Everyone could see I had feelings for her even though we'd not spoken since she was a child. My transparent emotions would be a weakness Schirra could exploit.

"I've got to go. It's good to see you, Ev. Hang in there." I could get control over it if Atua would stop the dreams. I was sure of it.

"I get it. Not up for discussion." Ev winked.

I sighed. "Just keep her safe."

"Good journey, Am."

"Atua be with you."

"AMIRAN, the building council will meet this afternoon." Timoti met me at the front gate when I returned to the palace.

"How long until they arrive?"

"Three hours. Perhaps we can walk to a site I think would be perfect for the barracks?" He showed me the miniature cube in his pocket.

Recognizing the jammer, I relaxed. "Ev is fine. He looks thin, but we can help with that. I'm supposed to contact him again in a month."

"Good. I'd love to end this so I can see him." He led me across the courtyard and out the east gate.

"Go to Olea, then you'd get a chance to see him for real." We walked down the sloping hill behind the palace that fell to a large meadow. There was plenty of room to build the barracks.

"I can't take that chance. Schirra never fully bought that story you cooked up about Ev's death. There's no way I could leave the planet without a tail."

"Then we need to end this as quickly as possible. So, the meadow?"

"I was thinking we should build the housing into the side of the hill. You could get three or four stories but it would look like less. Put the girls on the bottom floors. The hillside would be a natural barrier for amplifiers. That way it would be harder for him to spy if they talk about things we wouldn't want Schirra to overhear."

"That's good thinking." I hadn't really thought much about these women, but I wanted them to be as safe as possible once they arrived. "Tell the builders. I've got to get back to the council room for the afternoon session."

"Yes, sir."

It bothered me when he called me sir, but there wasn't much I could do about it. I waved goodbye and headed to the palace, entering the council room moments before the doors opened to the public.

Holding court was an antiquated system I wished to get rid of. Schirra enjoyed it though. The high society of Rawiri came to offer gifts and complain of workforce problems. As Hatana, I was expected to mediate in their favor in return for loyalty. I didn't want their gifts. I wanted to take care of the people. All the people.

Schirra waited at the front of the room. "I was beginning to think you would ignore your duties today."

I didn't reply but pulled up the computer console at the center chair.

"Amiran, we need to discuss this ridiculous demand of yours." Schirra sat beside me.

"You will address me as Hatana in the council hall." I made sure to use the voice of command his fleet officers had drilled into me.

"When you've earned the title, I'll use it." Schirra lowered his voice so the others wandering the room couldn't hear. "You are not the man your father was. You don't deserve the honor."

I stood. "Perhaps you should remember where you are."

He stood and hissed low, "And you should remember the fleet is under my command. Not yours. Forget this foolishness with the refugee women."

"Are you worried I'll choose one of them over your hand-picked society women?"

"You'd do it to spite me and your father's legacy."

"General, you overestimate how much thought I give you." My natural tendency was to lash out, but the gentle pressure of Atua reminded me to calm down. "My reasoning stands. Bringing in refugees will help the rebels see we can make a place for them in the empire. Plus, it will ensure your officers do their job. They'll have to locate camps in order to collect women. Your success rate has dropped forty percent since I returned to Rawiri. Forty percent in four months. I'd hate to think I was a better fleet officer than you led me to believe."

Schirra narrowed his eyes. "My fleet is always on the lookout for camps. Our rate has dropped because there are fewer to be found."

"Then you've got your work cut out for you. We've chosen a suitable building site and are awaiting the plans. Once it is complete, I expect you to do as ordered."

"In the meantime, the ladies I've chosen will move into the palace. You will be expected to spend time with them and consider each of their merits to the empire. Make no mistake, this is a political marriage."

"I don't doubt that for a moment."

The doors opened and people streamed into the hall. As they filled the seats, I returned to my designated spot. "Schirra, either sit down or leave. I have work to do."

He scowled but wasn't ready to openly defy me in front of the general public. It seemed he still needed me for something.

29

NO ROTATION: ELEENA

That night my bracelet didn't light up with a new shift rotation. The time function blinked, counted down and then the clock reappeared without a band of color. I tapped it lightly, thinking maybe I'd damaged it on the hill. Nothing happened.

"Weird," I whispered.

"Huh?" one of the younger teens sat at the end of her bedroll searching in her storage box. "Did you say something?"

"No, sorry. Talking to myself." I spun the bracelet around. It looked the same as always—minus my rotation. There was no dirt, no scratches or other issues that might clue me in as to why it malfunctioned. I'd have to find one of the crew managers to see about getting it replaced.

All the managers shared a smaller tent in the center of camp close to the mess hall. They were the first to eat in the morning, and often the last at night. Their tent flap was still open when I reached it.

"Excuse me?" I called inside.

"Yes, can I help you?" Judythia, the manager in charge of the sewing tent walked toward me.

I held my bracelet up for her to see. "I think it's broken."

She lightly tapped it in the same way I had. Nothing happened. She frowned.

"These don't usually wear out. Let's check the duty roster and then we can get you a new bracelet tomorrow." She pulled out a datacom and tapped and swiped her way to the place she wanted. "Name and camp number?"

"Eleena Talrano, 378437." I swallowed. I'd traded bracelets so many times there was no telling who this one belonged to, or where my original was. What would she say?

"Oh!" Her gaze jumped back to my face. "You don't have a rotation tomorrow. The captain requested you join him at O-nine-hundred hours by the *Vapous*."

"Really?" I wasn't in trouble? "Is the bracelet broken?"

"No, you don't have a rotation so it didn't light up." She smiled at me.

"But," I looked at the bracelet. "I don't understand."

Judythia laughed. "We know everyone swaps with you. Each bracelet has a DNA scanner."

"Oh." And they didn't mind? "Do you know what this is about?"

"I'm not sure, but there isn't any need to worry. Just report after you eat."

"Okay, thank you." I nodded and headed for my tent. As I walked, my chest tightened, and my mouth dried up. I recognized the early signs of a panic attack. Change had always been hard on me.

Atua, please help. Don't let the worry take over. Sometimes he helped, sometimes he didn't, but I'd learned asking was always better than not.

Tonight, his spirit soothed me. Whispers of comfort assured me everything would be fine. There were no words, but I didn't need them as my throat relaxed and the weight lifted from my chest.

The next morning, I sat in the mess hall with Harper, the tasteless oatmeal stuck in my throat. I tried to eat it anyway. Harper watched me but took her time eating instead of interrogating me.

"Go ahead and ask." I set the bowl down.

"I figured I should wait until this afternoon. You'll have more to tell." She took another lazy bite and pointed at my bowl. "You should eat all of that."

"I'm too nervous. Nobody gets to see Captain Evander any more."

"Iri does all the time." She shrugged.

"Really? When? Why?" I couldn't think of a reason the captain would meet with Iri. He was a good worker, but it wasn't like he'd be able to learn how to fly the ships or anything.

Harper shrugged. "He doesn't say much. One time he let it slip that Captain E goes somewhere else."

"What do you mean?"

"There are times he leaves Kahu. Sounded like he's done it on other planets too. Maybe that's why we don't see him as often. He just isn't here."

"But where would he go? Do you think he's out looking for rations?"

"Maybe." Harper kept eating.

I wanted to scream. How could she be so calm? This was huge. I hadn't thought about the captain leaving us since Derritus. He'd left in search of medicine then, but we hadn't been that desperate since.

I could feel Atua's presence. It calmed me, but it didn't remove my curiosity.

"We should ask him what they're doing."

"I don't care what they're doing. I know if something important comes up, Iri will watch out for us. That's all that matters." Harper ran her finger around the inside of her bowl and licked the last bits of oatmeal from it. "I'm more interested in why they're calling you in."

My nerves zinged again, even while I tried to give her the most logical reason. "It's probably something to do with school. Did you know our bracelets have DNA trackers? They've known all along we trade jobs."

"They shouldn't care about that. If they did, they would have put a stop to it a long time ago."

"That's true. Oh, and Owasso said the officers wanted me to take the adults to the river."

"Maybe that's it." She pointed at my full bowl. "Leena, eat your food."

I managed two more bites. "I can't."

"Whatever. Find me as soon as rotation is over. I'm in the garden today."

I nodded and headed out the door. It had been at least six months since I'd last seen Captain E. I hadn't been on his ship during the last evacuation, and after we landed on Kahu he had stayed on board the *Vapous*. That was a new development. He used to walk the camp regularly. I remembered him visiting everyone before Uncle died. Over the years he'd become busier and visited less often. But if what Harper said was true, he may not have been on the ship either.

Riggs, one of the junior officers waited for me at the top of the ramp. How did the captain leave without us knowing?

"Eleena?" He gave a short nod and then waved me up. "Captain

Evander is waiting for you in the mess off the bridge. Do you know where it is?"

"Yes, thank you." I stepped through the opening and took three steps before the cooling system became strong enough to push the mugginess of Kahu away. In the few short months we'd been here, I'd forgotten how it felt to be cool. The air dried my sweat, and by the time I reached the mess hall, I was shivering.

"Miss Talrano?" Evander stood by a table with several other men.

I studied him carefully. He didn't look more than ten years older than me, but he had to be much older to have three large ships. Maybe he had a lighter personal cruiser he used for his off-planet trips?

The questions kept distracting me. I pushed them away, determined to focus, and maybe gather clues as well. "Good morning. You asked to see me?"

He smiled and held out his hand. "Are you cold or just nervous?"

"A little of both?" my shoulders shrugged of their own will.

Evander laughed. "I forgot how honestly you speak your mind. I'm glad that hasn't changed. Here, have a seat." He indicated a chair at the table and turned to another man, much older. "Mynor, would you please grab a blanket."

The man slipped out of the room, and I discovered my body odor. In camp, it didn't matter. We all stunk, but the officers were clean. My face heated uncomfortably. I wished I had taken the time to wash up but quickly pushed the thought away. There was nowhere to do that other than the swift flowing river. If I had cleaned, I would have been covered in sweat and dirt before reaching the ship anyway. Captain E sat beside me, bringing my attention back to him.

I shrunk inward, keeping my arms pressed against the sides of my body. His eyes never left my face. I stared back, grateful he looked calm and not like he smelled something dead. Mynor returned and wrapped a blanket around my shoulders. It smelled like fresh soap and the fibers were much softer than the thin sheet I lay on every night. I buried my head in it and breathed deep.

"I've missed that smell!" My head jerked up. "I'm sorry, I didn't mean to say that out loud."

"It's perfectly okay. Owasso tells me you still know how to enjoy the little things. Like the smell of soap." Evander tilted his head to the side. "It's been a while since we've talked."

I nodded. "You've got a lot to take care of."

"Yes, but I promised I'd watch out for you." He continued to stare at me as if he'd never seen me before.

"Uncle would understand." I shrugged again.

"He's not the only one I have to answer to." Captain E smiled. It made him look younger. "We've been watching to see how like your parents and uncle you might be. You definitely have their clarity of thought, as well as their ability to love everyone around you. They'd be proud."

"Thank you, but why are you keeping tabs on me?"

"We need strong leaders, Eleena. We've simply been waiting for you to grow up."

I frowned. "I grew up the day I left Manawa."

A haunted look crossed his face. "Yes. We all did. However, we're a mixed camp now and not everyone can look past something as insignificant as age. Trust me, I know. However, you'll be leaving the juvie tent and joining the adults soon. I need your help. Owasso told me about your nature walks. He said you've done it for the last four years."

"Yes, Sir."

"I've talked to several people in camp. Ones that went on these trips with you."

"Oh?" I sat a little straighter in the chair.

"They might have taken the walk on different planets, but they all said the same thing. You taught them to wish for something better. Something we don't have in the camps." He wasn't smiling now, but his eyes stayed riveted to my face. "You reminded them what it felt like to be free."

My heart sank a little. If I bred dissension he'd never let me continue, no matter what Owasso thought. "I'm sorry, Captain. I didn't mean for them to feel dissatisfied."

"But they don't. Not at all. After being outside the gates, they were more determined to help us succeed. Each one has high commendations on their service record, and none have caused problems." Evander stood and walked around the table. "We need to build morale. Things are going to get harder before they get better. Our supplies are low. Rationing will be stringent as more and more refugees join us. However, the other camps on Kahu are worse off than we are. We can't afford to help them, but how do we turn them away?"

All the men in the room watched me, but Evander was the only one who spoke.

"The only way to prevent riots like S'klinctic is to remind people we aren't the enemy." He waved at the men in the room. "You have a talent for giving people hope through your day trips. We believe it can help everyone."

I dropped the blanket and stood too. "It will. A lot of people have stopped feeling anything, but if they remember why they wanted to escape the Hatana in the first place, they won't be as quick to anger. We should start immediately." Evander's eyes widened just a bit. Perhaps my voice had been too loud. Or maybe he wasn't used to someone telling him what to do. But I hadn't said anything he didn't already know. "Sir, this is a good camp, but it's still a camp. To survive is human nature, but it isn't living. I didn't mean to be disrespectful with my outburst. Hopefully, Owasso told you I tend to speak my mind."

"He might have mentioned something to that effect, but I know that well enough myself. Do you remember telling me we needed to know the truth to make correct decisions?"

"Yes, sir." There had been many times I wondered what my life would be like if I didn't know what had happened to my planet. To my parents.

"I haven't forgotten that lesson. Most of the adults in camp haven't worked out the difference between survival and living. They know life has changed for the worst, but they can't pinpoint why. They still have shelter of a sort, food, family units, work, but even our attempts at free time and social activities are lacking." Captain E finished his circuit of the room and returned to the seat in front of me. "Please sit down. When will you turn nineteen?"

I sat. "With the change in day lengths and year cycles I'm no longer sure. Math isn't my best subject. I think next month."

He laughed. Several other men chuckled. Their continued silence seemed strange, but then again, Captain E was in charge. Maybe they didn't feel the need to interrupt?

"Miss Talrano, if you're that close, we will grant you adult status so you can move sleeping quarters. We need your help here, and very soon we may need you to go—"

"Sir?" A stocky man across the table interrupted. "She's still young. Perhaps you should wait on that next part?"

"She's the same age Am was when we started." The captain sighed and placed his clasped hands on the table. "We can't wait much longer."

I looked from one to the other. Harper was right. The officers had secrets.

"We'll move you into the crew manager's tent today. I want you to develop the program with Owasso. You'll have to work out the schedule with the other managers in order to tweak the rotation system." Captain Evander relaxed into his chair. "Finish this school cycle before starting with the adults. Your students still need you."

"Okay. I mean, yes, sir." I wondered if that was it. After an awkward, moment I stood. "Am I free to go?"

"Yes, yes. Sorry." Evander once again studied my face. "How are you really doing? Am asks about you."

"He does?" Something warm lodged in my chest. "You've talked to him? Is he out of the fleet yet?"

"Yes, he returned home four months ago. Now he's the—"

"Sir!" Another man jumped up. "I know you trust her, but not with that."

Captain E scowled at him. "She wouldn't expose his connection to us."

"Maybe not, but think of her safety. If we're captured, it won't help her to know."

I watched them glare at each other and wondered who Am could be. Obviously, he was important, but I'd always known that.

"Captain," I touched his arm, "you don't need to tell me. It's enough to know Atua is with him."

"What?" The same man that didn't want me to know who Am was moved toward me. "How can you know that?"

I glanced at the captain to see him nod. Taking a deep breath, I told the truth. "Atua wanted Am to live more than my parents. I knew that the day we left Manawa, and Atua has sent dreams of Am off and on ever since. I've seen some of his struggles and how they've made him stronger. Am is a good man and that's all I need to know."

The room was eerily silent to match the shocked looks on their faces. I could hear the air seeping through the vents and Captain E's low chuckle.

"That will give you lots to think about." Captain E placed his hand on my elbow and led me toward the door. "I'll explain more of Miss Talrano's gift after I walk her out."

He closed the door as they began to protest.

"What will they think?" I pointed back toward the conference room.

"They'll be fine. You surprised them is all."

"You still believe me?" We walked through the corridor quickly.

"Yes." He paused at the open gangway. "I forgot that you'd dreamed about Am in the mines, but I remember now. He can hear Atua too. The last few years were not easy for him in spite of who he is. One day you'll know everything, and I want you to remember he's had to pay a price as well."

"I'll remember, but why is this important?"

"It's complicated. I've never heard Atua's voice, but at times I think he's nudged me in the right direction. Right now, I feel the need to tell you that Am isn't just good. He's a great man. Someone the empire is watching closely for one reason or another. He's fighting for us the best he can, and he always asks about you when we talk."

There was that feeling again. All warm and cozy. It was more than nice to think Am thought of me regularly. Although, the knowledge would make it that much harder to let go of my child-hood crush.

"Captain," I paused not sure exactly what I wanted to say or ask. There had been glimpses and vague impressions of Am's life over the years. Finally, I settled on the one thing that bothered me the most. "He seems lonely."

Evander nodded. "It's part of his trial. Never knowing who he can trust and knowing that anyone he cares for can be taken from him at any moment."

My heart ached for Am. The sadness in his eyes now made sense. His life was as precarious as ours. At least I had Harper and Iri.

"The next time you talk to Am, tell him I'm praying for him." I touched the captain's sleeve, hoping he understood all that I couldn't say because of the tangle of emotions running through me.

He smiled. "Go and move your things to the manager's tent. I'll let them know you're coming. I meant it when I said your parents would be proud of you."

I nodded. "I'll always miss them and Uncle, but we can't change the past."

"You do well to look forward, not back. Teach the others to do the same."

My mind jumped to the people I loved in camp. I glanced at my bracelet. "Why do you allow us to trade rotations?"

Captain E laughed, rubbing the back of his neck. "As long as the work is done and people aren't complaining, we don't care where you work. It's one way we can offer free choice. Plus, people eventually gravitate toward the jobs they enjoy."

"I've noticed that, but there are fewer men in camp now than in the beginning. It's going to slow us down in the mines."

A far away look crossed his features. "True. Maybe you can ask Atua to send us strong men to help?"

I wasn't sure if he was serious or not. His distracted expression didn't fade. Perhaps he was having one of the moments when he felt Atua's guiding influence? I left him standing alone on the ramp, gazing off at nothing.

30

MARRIAGE MATERIAL: AMIRAN

The contractors designed the compound and started construction. I received a message that Ev successfully extracted De'truto. Things sped up after that.

While I waited for an opportunity to contact my friend, I watched the frame for the barracks go up and then the two lower dorm floors. The designers added several rooms on the ground level, which was also the third floor, for the intake process. Classrooms and a medical clinic were added to the top two floors. Looking at the empty building added extra weight to every thought. Filling it would make the refugee's plight real again.

Schirra required me to be present as each of his candidates stepped foot on Rawiri. They came separately, on their own private glorywinger class ships, and were exactly what I feared they would be—rich, pampered, not a care in the world.

I traveled to the spaceport for each arrival only to be disappointed once again. They were all beautiful, but I couldn't see any substance to them.

"There are only five women left. Once they arrive we'll have a ball to officially kick off your courtship. My staff will organize meetings, dinners, and outings with all of them." Schirra rubbed his hands together. "See, I'm willing to let you choose someone you find appealing. Just make sure it's one of these."

"We will not discuss this with guests arriving." I nodded at the woman descending from another luxury ship.

She looked like all the others. Perfectly designed clothes, hair, makeup. Her blonde curls draped over her shoulders like a cape. I put on the expected smile and reached for her hand as she stepped to the ground.

"Welcome to Rawiri. I am Hatana Amiran. I hope your stay is a pleasant one." It was the same greeting I'd offered each of the women. I waited for her version of the flirty response.

She simply said, "Thank you."

I looked at her more closely. Her features were as soft and delicate as the other women. However, there was something different about her eyes. I couldn't put my finger on it. She also had an air of familiarity about her that didn't make sense.

Don't ask. Atua's warning came just before I spoke the forbidden question causing me to swallow it with a cough.

Schirra stepped in. "Miss Masaki, you've grown up since the last time I visited your father. I don't think I would have recognized you if not for our arrival schedule."

Miss Masaki blushed and stared at the ground for a moment before meeting his gaze. "I'll take that as a compliment since I was an awkward child."

"Hmm, yes." Schirra continued to stare at her, his brow wrinkled in thought.

Get things moving again. Atua's second command only increased my curiosity. Who was this woman?

I offered my arm. "Miss Masaki, may I escort you to the palace? Another vehicle will collect your luggage and deliver it to your rooms. In the meantime, lunch is waiting."

She took it hesitantly, unlike the others before her. It wasn't that she appeared scared or even timid. It felt more like she didn't want to touch me. For some reason, that relaxed me. If things became desperate, there was at least one woman on Schirra's list that didn't want to marry me.

"Hatana, thank you for this invitation. I've always wanted to visit Rawiri." She looked at everything but me.

"Miss Masaki, I'm sure the Hatana will show you many of our wonders while you're here." Schirra acted as if I couldn't hold up my end of the conversation.

"Please, call me Corvey." She shot me a quick look before staring at the horizon again.

The name stirred a memory from long ago of a giggly girl in braids. A friend of Eleena's. I struggled not to react or stare outright. It couldn't be!

"Corvey?" the general halted our progress to glare at the woman.

Corvey blushed. "It's a childhood nickname. I'm afraid I'm not used to being called by my given name. It would be embarrassing to have the Hatana speak to me and I not know it."

Help her.

I responded immediately. "Corvey it is then. Schirra doesn't know what to do when he's caught off guard. Come, you can meet the other women before lunch is served if we hurry."

Yes, Corvey Masaki was a pleasant surprise. Atua obviously approved of her, she didn't fall all over me, and she aggravated Schirra.

However, how would I answer the burning question? Had we met before at Eleena's house?

31

TENSION IN CAMP: ELEENA

The days flew by. I moved into the new tent and started getting to know the crew supervisors. It was strange to have men and women in the same place, but no one else seemed to mind. The women slept at the back of the tent, and the men up front. A work area sat between with tables, chairs and several computer terminals we used to organize the work rotations.

I expected to feel different now that I was officially considered an adult in camp, but I didn't. The only real change other than where I slept was my bracelet didn't rotate anymore. Instead, it stayed orange, indicating a position of leadership.

Owasso and I taught in the school every day, then discussed how to work all the adults through the program without disrupting the other rotations essential to camp. It didn't leave much time to be with Harper and Iri, but I made sure to join them for breakfast and dinner every day.

Harper was happy for me, and Iri didn't act surprised. I wondered how many of the captain's secrets he was privy to. After all, he'd hung around Uncle and Captain E since the beginning.

By day two in the manager's tent, I found proof men and boys were disappearing from camp. With my new clearance level, I could access reports of when and how many men joined us. Several hobbled in from other camps as their food ran out. However, the number of men didn't increase. I noted familiar names and when they'd been taken off rotation, but there was no record of where they had gone.

"Judythia, can you explain this?" I pointed to the screen that showed ten men that had been removed from the list right after we arrived on Kahu. "Was there an accident in the mines?"

She leaned over my shoulder to read the screen. "No. You don't have clearance for this yet. Be patient."

I twisted around to meet her gaze. "What happened to them?"

"Eleena, I can't discuss it." The determined look on her face confirmed she wasn't going to budge. I turned back to the screen and sent up a silent prayer. *Atua, what's going on?*

My plan. There was nothing else, but I'd learned to accept his word at face value. Wherever the men were, they were doing what Atua needed them to do. That would have to be enough for now. All the mysteries kept me anxious though.

I sighed and shut everything down. Maybe dinner with Harper would be what I needed to calm down. She waited for me outside the mess hall.

"About time you showed up. Thought I was going to have to look for you." She grinned and we stepped through the line.

"Got carried away with work." I shrugged. We had soup again, but this time there was a protein disk in each bowl.

"That doesn't surprise me. Iri said Captain E is excited about your new program. I got the impression he's been waiting to put you to real work."

"Sure." My attention drifted to a table near the back of the hall. Where was the little girl?

Her mother and brother sat at the table. Both had newly shaved heads. There was no sign her. I didn't have to ask what happened. The kick to my gut felt as real as any physical blow.

"What is it?" Harper turned at the sound of my gasp.

"It's too late."

"*Teina*, what are you talking about?" Harper only used the old slang words when she was frustrated. *Teina* meant "please" and sometimes "dear god." Usually, Harper meant it the second way. However, she used it more like an expletive than a prayer.

"The protein." I pointed toward the family that was now one member smaller.

Harper nodded and stared at her bowl. Her shoulders slumped. "I'm sorry Leena. I wish it was different, but you can't take it person-ally. At least you tried."

Ignoring her last comment, I concentrated on my personal guilt or lack thereof. "I know it's not my fault. I blame the Hatana. He doesn't care who he hurts."

I pushed my way past her and went to our regular eating spot.

Harper followed. "He doesn't know who he hurts."

"Where's Iri?" I needed to change the subject in order to keep my soup down.

"He's with Captain E now. Iri told me about the supply shipment earlier and how it made it through the fleet's scouts."

"Iri knew about the supplies because he's hanging out with Captain Evander?"

"Yeah." Harper tipped her bowl and took several swallows. She wiped the drips from the edge of her mouth. "That's not all. The smugglers told Captain E the fleet is headed this way. We have a month. Maybe less."

My bowl wobbled, but I managed not to drop it. I sat it on the table and clenched my shaking hands in my lap. "What are the officers doing about it?"

"They're stripping down two of the freighters for parts. They'll try and sell them in the towns. If they get lucky they might earn enough credits to buy celestium for the *Vapaus*."

"There are too many of us to fit on one ship." A sinking feeling pushed my dinner back up. I swallowed hard to keep it from spilling out. Why hadn't I heard about any of this? Did the other crew managers know?

As afraid as I'd been in the past, I never doubted Captain Evander.

Don't worry. I almost jumped at Atua's voice.

Sighing, I tried to push the doubt away. Captain E said he felt Atua's guidance. I could be sure he endeavored to do what was right. What was best for the camp. My eyes scanned the room. New faces mixed in with those I'd known for years. There had to be four or five hundred people crammed in the mess hall, and that was only half of us. Who would escape? Who would be left behind?

Trust.

In spite of Atua's admonition, my gaze settled on the newest group of refugees. They looked rough. Their eyes cold. Everything about them made my skin crawl.

"Do you think Captain E will take them before he takes those of us who've been with him for years?" I pointed them out to Harper.

She shivered. "*Teina*, I hope not."

I stood, knowing I couldn't finish my soup if I tried. "I'm going to find the captain."

"Now?"

"Yes." I fished out the protein disk from my bowl. It melted on my tongue, while I poured the broth into Harper's bowl.

"But he's busy."

"They shouldn't keep this from everyone. We deserve to know." I turned and walked away.

I heard the whisperings of Atua's spirit, but couldn't focus on what he tried to tell me. Instead of comfort, one of my anxiety spells built deep in my chest. It was often harder to hear him when I was angry. Hopefully, I'd understand the message after I calmed down.

The world quieted as soon as I left the mess hall. A deep breath of air, free from the smell of sweat in the hall, cleared my mind, but I still felt uneasy.

Atua, does Captain Evander have a plan? He'll be fair. I have to have faith in that. Feeling slightly better, I headed for the *Vapous*.

The sound of scuffling feet finally registered. Harper stomped but never scuffled. Three men I didn't recognize approached. Their clothes were worn thin. The smell of oil hung heavy around them. My gaze darted around, but no one else was in sight.

Run, Eleena. The command had the opposite effect than desired. I froze.

Their eyes glinted in the light. A crawling sensation traveled through me and lodged in my chest. I wrapped my arms around my body.

"Can I help you?" I found my voice, and the ability to move, but it was too late. They had surrounded me.

The oldest of the men pointed to my bracelet. "She's in the work sequence."

"Mean's she's old enough." Another one licked his lips.

"Old enough for what?" My heart raced. I turned side to side, trying to keep them in sight. The long side of two tents blocked escape on both sides. I couldn't go forward or back.

Scream, Eleena.

This time I obeyed immediately. As soon as I did, the oldest one grabbed my arm. Another covered my mouth, sliding around to hold me from behind. His foul scent made me gag.

Atua, help! I struggled. Kicked. Twisted. But they dragged me towards the shadows at the edge of the camp.

I bit down on my captor's hand. He swore and released my

mouth. I screamed again. One of them slapped me hard. My head snapped to the side from the force of the strike.

Don't give up. Atua had not left me.

My ears stopped ringing from the blow, allowing me to think again. I threw my head back, connecting with someone's nose.

"*Po'tash!*" The man swore. He slammed me to the ground. "Don't fight and you won't get hurt."

My vision blurred as the pain radiated through my head. I heard the slap of running feet, but it sounded far away.

"Stop!" A man's voice called out. "What are you doing?"

"None of your concern." The ringleader sneered and pressed my face harder into the dirt.

Something warm trickled from my forehead and down the side of my nose. Iri and Harper pushed their way to the front of the group of people gathering. She looked frightened, but Iri's glare would have cut holes through the hardest steel. I sobbed with relief at the sight of them.

One of the camp medics stood with his hands on his hips. "I don't know how things worked in your camp, but we don't take women against their will."

"Fine." The man pulled me to my feet by my ear. I bit my tongue to keep from crying out. His nails dug into the skin of my neck and one arm, then he shoved me toward the growing crowd. "She's not worth this much trouble."

Two stumbling steps and I fell into Harper's arms. She hugged me tightly, breathing as raggedly as me.

Iri didn't turn from the men. "Our women are protected. If you can't keep our rules, you leave."

The men didn't answer but slunk into the shadows.

"Someone keep an eye on them." The medic probed the side of my face. "You've got a cut and will probably have a nasty bruise by morning."

He pulled open a kit, cleaned my face, and placed bandages on my wounds. "How many fingers am I holding up?"

"Two."

"And now?"

"Four."

"Good. You may feel sore tomorrow, but you'll be fine." He pressed a hypospray to my neck before he packed up. "I'm going to speak with the captain about this."

I nodded but felt numb. The soft sound of whispering bounced off my skin. My nerves thrummed, every muscle tensed to run, but I was afraid to move.

"Eleena," Owasso appeared at my side and pulled me into his arms, "are you all right?"

"I'm okay," I mumbled into his shoulder before I started shaking. *I'm okay, I'm okay. I'll be okay.*

After releasing me, Owasso stared into my eyes. "I'll speak with Evander. It's time we closed our doors and protected our own."

"What about the children?" I reached for him but quickly pulled back. There already wasn't enough room on the *Vapaus*. Bringing in more children would make the choice about who left and who stayed harder, but Evander couldn't turn away the children. He just couldn't.

Owasso smiled. "I knew those men couldn't destroy your spirit." He turned to the crowd and pointed to me. "Did you hear? She's more worried about the children than herself."

Embarrassment burned my face and I mumbled, "I'm plenty worried about me too."

Everyone chuckled, but it held the awkwardness of people trying too hard. Then silence fell around me as people dispersed in groups. No one wanted to be alone.

Finally, only Harper, Iri, and Owasso remained.

"You two, take care of her." He shuffled a few steps away before stopping. "Come to think of it, don't hang out here yourselves. Follow me back to safety."

Owasso didn't speak again until we reached our tent. "Iri, come with me. Harper, stay here until we return."

We sat at a table, the other crew leaders huddled around us. Everyone had an opinion on what should happen to the men that attacked me.

"The officers will find them and kick them out." Harper was sure of it.

"There will be others though." The man in charge of the gardens rubbed his chin. "We need a police force to keep everyone safe."

They discussed options, and I tried to listen. It helped take my mind off the oily smell that lingered in my nose, but it was hard to focus. Eventually, Iri and Owasso returned with Captain E.

The captain looked at the bandages on my head and gingerly probed the finger-sized bruises developing on my arm and neck. "We've got men looking for the guys who did this."

I nodded. Somewhere in the last thirty minutes exhaustion had set in with the numbness.

"Try to rest. Guards will be posted at all the women's tents, including this one. They won't hurt anyone else." Captain E gripped my hand.

"Thank you." I squeezed back.

"Would you consider moving to the ship?" he asked.

I shook my head. As scared as I was, I didn't want special treatment.

The captain sighed. "I was afraid of that. Please, stay with people you trust. Don't be alone." He turned and spoke a few minutes with the men near the doorway before disappearing.

"I'm going back to my tent so you can sleep." Harper led me toward my cot. "We'll meet for breakfast like normal, okay?"

"Uh huh." I sat but clung to her hand. "Will you be safe?"

"I'll make sure of it." Iri glanced at Harper with something tender and real. There was no doubt in my mind he'd protect her. "Don't worry Eleena."

Atua? I needed to know he was there. He didn't speak, but the warm comfort I needed enveloped me as I drifted to sleep.

I dreamed of Am for the first time on Kahu. His hair had grown out. It brushed the edges of his collar, curling around his ear. I couldn't see much of his surroundings in the dark. He stared off into the distance, no expression on his face.

Atua, how does he feel? I craved those days when Atua had let me know Am was happy or sad. If he felt safe wherever he was now, maybe I could feel safe for a while too.

A warmth moved through my chest. Pleasant and yet heavy. I felt love, but it was tainted with worry.

Who is this for? I asked.

Atua let me hear Am's thoughts for just a moment. It was strange to hear his voice without his lips moving.

"Atua, be with Eleena and Ev. Help me do what's right." He sighed and ran a hand through his hair.

I felt another twinge of that heavy warmth that so closely echoed the ache I felt when I thought of him.

Atua?

The vision faded. *All in time, Eleena.*

32

SECRETS: AMIRAN

Several days passed before I found an opportunity to speak with Miss Masaki alone. She was walking through the courtyard garden shortly after lunch.

"Are you bored already?" I asked as I fell into step with her.

"Of course not, Your Highness." She glanced at me, and before she turned away I caught a glimpse of fear.

We approached a bench off the path near a plot of yellow and purple flowers.

"Please, sit for a moment?" I indicated the intricately carved stone seat.

She sat with a slight nod of her head. It interested me that she rarely made eye contact.

"Miss Masaki, may I call you Corvey?"

"Of course." She twisted her hands in her lap. As I watched, she took a deep breath and relaxed.

"I met a Corvey once, many years ago." I watched her face.

Her eyes shifted my direction even though she didn't turn her head. "Oh?"

"She was quite a bit younger than me, so she might not remember. That Corvey was visiting a school friend. A daughter of someone I greatly respected."

Corvey blinked rapidly. Her chest rose and fell as she tried to regulate her breathing.

I reached out to touch her arm. "Are you okay?"

She turned to me then, and I saw the truth in her eyes with the unshed tears. It was Eleena's friend. But how?

Her eyes widened. She pulled away and stood. "I should return to my rooms."

"Wait." I stood to block her retreat. "We need to talk. You should know—"

"Hatana," a courtier strode down the path toward us, "General Schirra is waiting for you in the council rooms."

"Reigna." I stepped farther away from Corvey. "I'm on my way. Until next time, Miss Masaki."

33

RIOT: ELEENA

For the first time ever, I didn't want to go to the mess hall. Or school. I didn't want to leave my tent at all.

The skin on my face and arms felt like someone had scoured it with sandpaper, but it was the dull thudding behind my eyes that bothered me the most. Even my neck protested when I tried to turn it. In addition to a black eye, there were bruises on my arms, shoulders, and one hip from when I hit the ground.

"Eleena, there's a group of girls outside." One of the other female managers gently touched my arm. "They're going to walk you to breakfast."

"Thank you." I moved in slow motion.

Several girls waited outside the tent flap. I recognized the one in the middle. She was a year younger than me, and used to have brown hair she kept in braids.

"I'm glad you're coming with us," she said.

The jitters in my stomach hadn't settled, but I couldn't hide all day. Even though I didn't know her well, she'd always been one of the steady ones.

"What's your name?" I asked.

"Ulla."

I tried to smile, but it felt fake so I dropped it. "Let's go."

The girls talked in hushed tones. I listened half-heartedly while my gaze darted to every person that appeared from a tent or around a corner. My body tried to relax when I recognized them, but then

another motion to the side would have me hyper-vigilant
once more.

A strange energy weighed down the air inside the mess hall.
Things looked normal, but it was too quiet. People glared at each
other instead of talking. The sound of chewing was ominously
absent.

"Morning, Eleena." One of my former students stood behind the
serving table. The food bin contained protein bars. They'd been cut
in half. "Take two halves. One's for breakfast, the other for the
midday meal."

Rationing had escalated more quickly than anticipated.

Harper and Iri waved to me from the back wall. I pushed both
bars into a pocket and hurried over.

Harper hugged me. "You look rough this morning. Did you sleep
at all?" she whispered as if she were afraid to disturb the eerie
silence in the hall.

My hand flew to my face, but I made an effort to drop it midway.
"Enough."

Iri watched the growing crowd. I felt his shoulders tense when
the group of men came in. The three that had attacked me were
accompanied by six others.

"The officers didn't find them," I trembled.

"I'll get them." Iri took a step forward before stopping to really
look at the group.

They pushed their way to the protein bins, shoving others out of
the way as they went. All eyes followed them.

The leader spoke loud enough for everyone to hear, "Load up."

The men surrounded the bins and shoved bars into ratty
cloth bags.

The girl who stood there yelled, "You only get two a piece!"

One of the men slapped her and she fell. That's when everything
exploded. Men rushed the bins. Women screamed. Some dragged
children toward the door, others tried to join the melee for food. Iri
pushed open the window.

"Harper, Eleena, get out now." Iri shoved Harper halfway through
the opening. "I'll get Captain E, but you can't stay here."

Harper climbed out, Iri right behind her, but I couldn't take my
eyes off the fight.

"Leena! Come on." Harper grasped at my tunic to get my attention. "Now."

A woman stumbled back from the mob. Her face covered in

blood. She clasped several bars close to her chest. She didn't make it two steps before three other people were on her, kicking, hitting, clawing the food from her hands.

These were people I knew. People I'd worked beside. The light had gone out of their eyes, replaced by the crazed look of wounded animals.

Harper dragged me to the window. This time she pushed me through before she followed. Iri was nowhere in sight.

"It'll be safer by the ships." Harper tugged on my sleeve until I ran.

A few women with children cowered around the landing gear of the *Vapaus*. Evander and what appeared to be a small army of thirty men with weapons marched toward the center of camp.

"Is Iri with them?" I asked Harper.

"Probably." She sounded calmer than I felt.

"Aren't you worried about him?"

"Always, but I'd rather he be on the captain's side than in the mess hall." Harper's eyes shone with pride.

"Me too," I whispered and huddled closer.

The noises were muffled and distant, but every once in a while I heard the whine of a sonic blaster. Harper gripped my hand in hers. We didn't speak.

After ten minutes, the line of soldiers marched back to the ships. They dragged four of the nine men who started the riot stopping short of the front gate. The older man who attacked me wasn't one of them. In fact, I didn't see any of the men from the night before.

Captain Evander's uniform was mussed and he squinted through one eye. I watched him order his men about. He sent extra guards to the med tent, crews to clean the mess hall, and finally, he stood before the prisoners.

"We offered you refuge among us. All we asked was you obey our rules and contribute to the camp. Instead, you've stolen food and attacked our women. Your actions have caused fear and riot." Evander ran a hand through his stubbled hair. "I can't allow you to stay. I can't let you leave."

I clenched Harper's hand.

"These are my people to protect. I will do all within my power to keep them safe from the fleet and men like you. May Atua forgive me for my judgment." Evander nodded his head and the soldiers led the men through the gate and down the road out of sight.

Captain E stood by the boarding ramp. When the sound of

blaster fire drifted up the hill, he nodded once before heading inside. I caught a glimpse of his face as he entered the *Vapaus*. Determined.

"*Teina*, I didn't think he'd do it," I whispered.

"We should see if they need help in medical." Harper's voice remained soft too. "Here comes Iri. He'll tell us if it's safe to go back."

"Thank Atua you guys got out. The med tent is full of injured women and children." Iri shook his head in disgust.

"I didn't see my attackers with the prisoners." I needed to know where they were, especially the leader. His face had haunted me all night.

"Those three wouldn't surrender. They won't hurt anyone else." Iri patted my arm, and I almost collapsed into Harper.

"Thank you." I quickly pulled myself together. There wasn't time to fall apart. "What can we do?"

"Harper should go to the med tent. Why don't you go to the school tent? They've set up a temporary pediatric ward there. You'll be more comfortable with the younger kids, and I know they'll be happy to see you."

Iri had always let Harper speak for both of them when we were together. As he took charge now, I recognized a strength I'd missed before. I felt a surge of pride for him but also noticed how Harper gazed at him. My mother used to look at my father the same way. In the midst of so much ugliness, they'd found something wonderful together. If only I could find the same. Am's face flashed through my mind but I pushed it away.

Shaking my head, I got back to the task at hand. "Will things go back to normal?"

"No. Captain E will post guards around camp." Iri nodded toward the soldiers coming through the gates. "I've got to go. Talk to you tonight."

IRI LOOKED ESPECIALLY dirty the next morning as if he'd just come up from the mines.

"What happened to you?" I asked.

"We struck a vein of celestium last night." His smile almost made the grime on his face disappear. "They'll announce it soon."

My heart leapt. Celestium! I hugged Harper and swallowed the now too thick food in my mouth. We were going to make it. We'd be able to leave before the fleet arrived.

Mind racing with questions, I hugged Iri too. The dust all over him made me sneeze. "Wait, why were you in the mines last night?"

"After yesterday's riot, Captain E was angrier than I've ever seen him. He told us he wasn't going to give up. Not until he had too. He asked for volunteers to go into the mines. I went."

"Tell her what he said about incoming refugees." Harper squeezed my arm.

"He said women, children and only men that were part of those families could join our camp. No single men. And everyone has to be interviewed by the officers."

For some reason, my eyes misted over. Stupid! I couldn't help it. The fact Evander wanted to keep families together made me happy.

I studied Iri. His face was so dirty his teeth almost glowed, but his eyes were red-rimmed. "You haven't slept have you?"

"No. I might get some sleep before my next rotation."

"What do you mean?" Surely, they wouldn't send him down today?

"Everyone will rotate through the mines. Three hours per interval down the hole. So we stay strong and keep working fast."

With around the clock mining, we'd make it. I must have stopped breathing because Harper squeezed my hand again.

"Breathe, Leena." She looked worried for half a moment before smiling at me. "It's not that bad down there."

"It's not that. I'm glad we can all escape." And I was. "Anyway, I know what it's like in the mines from my dreams."

"I forgot about that." Harper nodded.

Iri scowled. "Only two of the three ships are spaceworthy. It's going to be cramped."

"It'll be better than one ship though." Subconsciously, I crossed my fingers. Tight quarters caused problems of their own.

"Not without stores of food on board." Harper held up half of a protein bar as proof. "There's hardly anything left."

She was right. Again. The thin hope I'd grasped slipped from my fingers. If we stayed, the Hatana's men would slaughter us. If we got off the planet in time, the conditions on the ship would be worse than here.

People would die no matter what.

"There has to be a better way. We can't keep running." I sagged against the wall.

Harper and Iri had chosen the same spot near the window. My

breathing eased just a bit with the fresh air flowing in, but my nerves jittered as the crowd grew more impatient.

Out of the corner of my eye, I caught Iri glance at his bracelet. His eyes rounded, then his gaze jerked up to the ceiling.

He grabbed Harper's arm and tugged her toward the window for the second day in a row. "Out now!"

Iri pulled Harper through the opening and reached for me. I didn't argue this time.

"What is it?" I asked. There was nothing unusual that I could see.

"Ships." He pointed to the gray sky.

A low rumble like distant thunder. It was high up, but growing louder every moment. Clouds painted the sky shades of dirty brown as they rolled in waves like the ocean. Even they couldn't flee from the impending destruction. There was no mistaking that sound for a supply ship.

The ground started to vibrate. Softly at first. Only disturbing the finest dust. It tickled my feet, but as it grew stronger it crept up my legs.

"What do we do?" Harper's voice trembled.

"How did you know?" Sweat broke out on my nose. My hands shook. The only thing that kept me standing was Harper's arms wrapped around me as we clung to each other.

"Get out of camp." Iri tugged Harper, and I followed. "We have to get to Captain E."

"At the ship?" I asked.

"No, the hiding place." He tapped his bracelet. "Evacuation message."

"Hiding? Evacuation?" I gasped. "My bracelet didn't do anything. What are you talking about?"

"No time." He jogged toward the front entrance. "We need to reach him."

"Won't he help everyone?"

"He needs to survive."

"We all need to survive!" How could the captain leave us to fend for ourselves? *Atua, I don't understand*!

"There are things you don't know—more important than all of us." Iri dragged us farther down the path.

"What do you mean?"

"No time, just go." Iri dragged us along.

By now others had noticed the sound, felt the pulse of the

ground reaching up to meet the ships. Screams filled the air as people crowded into the pathways.

Someone shouted, "Hide in the mines!"

"Run to the ships!" another voice called.

People scattered. Pushing, crying. I clutched Harper and she never let go of Iri. We were knocked and shoved, but we had almost reached the gate.

"Iri, where," I found my voice, "are we going?"

He looked me square in the eye, and I saw his fear for the first time. "I don't know if we have time to reach the captain."

"Where should we go then?" Harper asked.

"Not the ships. We could try for the captain's hiding place." He sounded uncertain, and it made me uneasy.

"You said there wasn't time." I tried to think of an alternative, but I hadn't been anywhere other than camp or the river since coming to Kahu.

"There isn't, but I don't know. Wasting time." He pointed upriver and to the south. "That way!"

We ran through the open gates and cut across the road. The plateau the camp had been set on ran for a couple of miles to the south.

Not safe. Atua's voice rang loud and clear in my head, causing me to stumble.

"Wait!" I cried. The fleet ships were getting closer, growing louder. It was hard to concentrate with the fear pumping through me.

"We can't stop." Harper tugged on me.

"Atua says this isn't safe." I gasped. They both paused. "Give me a second."

I prayed and listened harder than ever, but it wasn't necessary. My answer came almost immediately.

River.

"To the river!" I yelled and we all ran for our lives.

34

PARADE OF WOMEN: AMIRAN

Other than the chance meeting with Corvey in the garden, I avoided Schirra's women until they all arrived. That time came to an end with the ball. I had to pretend to search for a wife.

"Is there any way to get out of this?" I asked Timoti.

"Afraid not." He finished dusting off my dress uniform.

The stiff fabric didn't allow me to relax. The crisp collar stood straight up, the royal ribbons and medals draped around my neck and sat heavily upon my chest. At least it had been tailored for a comfortable fit. My neck would just itch all night.

"Schirra will be watching. Play your part. He's pleased with the women he's brought in. They've been making the staff miserable since day one." Timoti ran a soft cloth down the length of the decorative sword before replacing it in the scabbard. He handed the belt to me. "Wish I could give you a blaster to hide in your waistcoat."

"I'd be tempted to use it and hang the plan." I attached the last accouterments to my wardrobe. "At least I won't have to carry on much conversation. Small talk will work fine for dancing."

"True." Timoti stood, at a loss for what else to do.

"Go to Hebe's. It's worth the chance."

The older man nodded. The fact he would go was a testament to his concern. He never went himself out of fear spies would follow. However, no one had heard from Ev since he retrieved De'truto from Cassia.

"Careful." I left Timoti in my quarters and took the grand staircase down to the ballroom.

Music filled the lower levels of the palace. Dignitaries and the military elite danced and mingled. There was no fanfare. No announcement of my arrival. And I was glad. I didn't want to be there anyway. I cut my way around the room, hoping to find a shadowed corner to hide in.

"Hatana." Schirra's voice dripped with derision. "Glad you could join us. Let me introduce your first dance."

Corvey stood beside him, her golden hair in ringlets. She was almost as tall as me in the heels she wore. Her blue eyes twinkled in the lighting.

"Corvey Masaki from Birilu." Schirra pressed her hand into mine. "Dance. Choose."

He left us and Corvey blushed. "He's rather blunt, isn't he?"

"You've no idea. Come." I led her to the dance floor. "We never did get to the important things in the garden."

"It's best if we don't." She avoided my eyes as she moved gracefully, clearly used to dancing.

"Corvey, what do you remember about me?"

She blushed, but when she finally looked at me, her smile was sad. "Leena talked about you a lot. She…" Corvey shifted her gaze over my shoulder. "I wish her father had sent her with me."

"Her family meant as much to me as they did to you." I wanted to tell her, but not in the middle of a crowded room full of listeners.

Corvey's lips pressed into a hard line, and she kept her thoughts to herself.

The song ended and Schirra appeared with another woman. Corvey slipped away.

Turning to the new partner, I asked, "Why are you here?"

"Because I was invited. My father does a lot of business with the general."

"What kind of business is your father in?" I tried not to sound too interested, but any information about Schirra's contacts could come in handy later.

"He builds laser cannons for the fleet."

Of course.

The woman's brow creased. "You don't like to think about war while dancing?"

"No." I certainly didn't want to talk about it with her. She was exactly what I thought Schirra's candidates would be. A pampered daughter of someone who had grown rich off of other's tragedies. How had Corvey passed his inspection?

"What shall we speak of?" Her smile turned seductive.

Luckily, the music ended. I released her and bowed. "Sadly, our time is spent. I must dance with everyone in attendance. Enjoy your stay."

Determined to get it over with, I turned on my heel and strolled to another young woman before Schirra could continue handing them off to me. I wanted some control over my evening. The third dancer was a giggler. It was going to be a long night.

Schirra's twenty women were all from Allegiant planets. Other than Corvey, they were all spoiled and connected to various businesses that supplied the fleet. Some were more bold with their hope of becoming queen. The hours of false flattery dragged by. I feared I'd grind my teeth down to nubs.

Miss Masaki often drifted in my wake. I caught her studying me as if she were working out a puzzle. After meeting the other women, she had become even more of a mystery herself. I knew she was from Manawa, but there was no way Schirra would have invited her if that was common knowledge. Unless she replaced someone that had been invited.

Patience, Amiran. Tonight is not the time. Atua's voice slipped through the sounds of the orchestra, muted conversations, and laughter from those around me.

I swallowed my momentary frustration. It was never the right time to get my answers. *How much longer, Atua? People are suffering.*

My plan is in motion. Your part will come soon.

Heart beating fast, I tried to exude a calmness I didn't feel. Small talk grew harder as I imagined a clock ticking down to an unknown end in my head. I retreated to my quarters as soon as I could. Timoti waited just inside the suite doors, jammer in hand.

His cheeks had sunk in over the last week. His eyes had lost all spark. I hated what Ev's absence was doing to him, and I had never been more aware that I wasn't his son. It hit me hard. If I could, I would have switched places with Evander.

"Anything?" I asked.

"No."

"Maybe they're having communication problems." I searched for a logical explanation that didn't lead to Ev's death. "Could be a loss of power."

"Thanks for trying, but we have to face the possibility it's more critical than a power failure. Schirra has increased his patrols. And accidents happen in space all the time."

"He said he'd only been planet-side a couple months. I don't think he'd need to evacuate so soon." I refused to think about the worst-case scenarios.

"Maybe they didn't get the supplies we sent? Starvation could have caused another riot." Timoti continued to worry. "Or something happened on the way to Olea."

"Let's hope not."

Timoti didn't say anything else. He set the jammer down on his desk. Many staff had given me grief over that desk in my rooms. They felt he should have to stay in the offices with the rest of them. I didn't care what they thought. He was more comfortable here, and I knew he was safer.

"I hate this." I flopped into a chair. "Ev is out there taking all the risks, and I'm stuck here."

"You're taking risks too." Timoti rallied and stepped up to my defense.

"Attending dinners and banquets doesn't seem like much of a risk."

"Being on the same planet with Schirra is a risk, much less having to occupy the same room for hours on end. My two boys are simply taking different kinds of risks."

"I can't help but think he's making more of a difference in people's lives. I'm still playing games. What if my life doesn't matter? What if I can't stop Schirra? Maybe someone else will have to do it."

"Stop moping and get out of here. Walk by the river. Speak with Atua, but take some soldiers with you. Here's a list of the newer ones that haven't been around Schirra enough to be a true follower." He handed me a paper.

"You can keep these on the datacom, you know."

"Nope. Nothing is safe on those things."

35

THE HATANA'S FLEET: ELEENA

W e didn't take the road. Instead, we slid and crashed down the side of the hill toward the water. My heart raced like it had the week before. But not because I felt alive. Others followed at first but soon split off toward the nearest city. Some turned toward the mountains and the camps hidden up there.

"They'll never make it." Iri pushed us to the second hillside and final drop to the river.

"Leena!" Harper tripped and slid past me.

I reached out and caught her by the arm. The weight of her body almost jerked me off my feet.

"Hold on, I've got you." My shoulder throbbed.

"Go! They're almost here." Iri dragged Harper to her feet and pointed to the sky.

Four ships emerged from the cloud cover. They were sleeker than the smuggler's ships but still pocked with black soot from entering the atmosphere.

"Stop staring and run!" Iri nudged both of us.

We obeyed, but my mind tried to place the ships. They looked like the troop carriers I'd seen on the vids. Each carried a hundred or so well-trained soldiers. They didn't need to overwhelm us with numbers. Not with the firepower they had at their fingertips.

The ships separated. One hovered directly over our camp, raining down plasma bursts on our ships. The first explosion knocked us to the ground. The rest of the carriers headed to the neighboring camps, one to the mountains, and the last one to the nearest town.

Iri pulled us to our feet. "Get up and run!"

"River." I clung to Atua's one word. My breathing came out ragged, and my voice sounded small next to the shrieking and thumping of the ship setting down at the top of the hill.

My ankle twisted and I rolled down the last five feet of the incline. When the world stopped spinning, it felt oddly quiet.

Harper appeared above me. "They've landed."

"We've got to go." When I put pressure on my food, sparks erupted behind my eyes. "*Po'hehe!*"

How could this happen? I was doing what Atua told me to. Harper wrapped her arm around one side, Iri did the same on the other.

"Keep moving." He dragged us parallel to the water but nowhere near it.

"I'll never be able to run. The river is our only chance." I tried to hide my grimace as another spike of pain shot up my leg.

"I can't swim. Neither can Iri." Harper sobbed.

"All you have to do is float. The river will do the rest."
This is my will.

I gasped. "Atua says it's his will."

"Then we'll do it." Iri directed us toward the water.

Gritting my teeth I pushed them a little off me so we could move faster. "Don't let go, just give me enough room to move."

Tears streamed down my face from the pain. My heavy breathing almost drowned out the screams and the sound of blasters from camp. Almost. Were the officers fighting back, or had Captain E really hidden?

We reached the river. Iri let go of me and I collapsed. He pulled Harper close. I'd never seen them kiss. For some reason it made me want to cry even more. It wasn't possessive, but gentle. It reminded me of my parents.

"*Teina*, don't you say goodbye." Tears flowed from Harper's eyes.

"Live a good *te'ora* for me, Harper." He held her face in his hands.

"Iri, please," she sobbed.

"Remember the good times and that I fought to save you." He let her go and pulled me to my feet. After standing me next to Harper he continued. "Ev's building a secret army. That's why he can't be caught. Trust him. After the soldiers leave, go upstream to the edge of the second plateau." Iri pointed, then pushed us in the river.

The cool water slammed the breath and all other thought out of me. I let go of Harper, but she clung to me making it harder to fight my way toward the surface. I tried to push her to arm's length once we gasped for air. The strong current carried us downstream.

Iri didn't jump.

Harper thrashed, her legs kicking mine before tangling with them. I barely registered the pain of her hitting my foot before we started to sink. Working my arms free, I fought my way toward the surface, dragging her with me.

"Stop fighting me!" I screamed. She tugged me down again. Once more I pulled with all my might and came up sputtering. Every muscle hurt. Tears flowed freely. I didn't think I could do it again. "You're going to kill us."

Harper finally listened but she kept twisting her head around. Each time she'd dip under the water a little.

"Be still!" I screamed.

"Where's Iri?"

"He didn't jump." I tried to keep us both above the water.

If Captain E had an army, where were they? We needed them.

Focus on the now. Atua's voice pulled me from my thoughts.

The current kept us moving. The bank rose four or five feet, a wall of dirt. There were no tree roots to grab hold of. I hoped the river contained some natural beaches or we'd be in trouble.

The water slowed as the river widened. I still couldn't touch the bottom. A high-pitched sound registered in my brain.

"What's that?" Harper panicked and slipped beneath the water. It felt like a long time before she came back up.

"Harper!" I yelled.

The bank hid the meadow, but something was coming. The sound grew louder. I concentrated on moving closer to Harper. If she could see me, we'd be fine.

Atua, protect us!

She disappeared under the water again.

One, two, three, four, five…twenty-three, twenty-four…

"Harper!" My tears mingled with the river. "Harper!"

Had Atua abandoned us?

Harper appeared to my right, then slipped away again. There was motion on the shore. Several men ran along side our position.

"There's one in the river!" One waved toward us with some kind of weapon.

My mind barely registered them. *Harper!*

I dove. Stretching. Reaching. A few feet down I saw her shadowy form reach back. My fingers slipped against hers, but the current tugged me away. Another determined kick and I had her. We broke the surface together, gasping.

Water clouded my vision, but shouts sounded all around. Men ran along the bank pointing and yelling and a couple of them jumped into the river. Harper scrambled away from the approaching men, pulling her hands from mine. She immediately dipped back under the water.

The men swam our way. My stomach flipped. This was it. They didn't matter. I had to help Harper.

Another quick gasp of air from the surface and I dove again.

Her eyes were shut, but she was drifting toward the surface. I almost had her.

Arms wrapped around my waist and jerked me upward. They held me up when all I wanted was to swim to my friend. I gasped for air, the fight momentarily gone.

"Be still." He yelled the next words to shore. "This one's a woman."

"Save her! Let me go and save her!" The fight returned. I flailed and kicked, but he held me tighter, dragging me to the bank.

I could see the black and red of his uniformed sleeve. A fleet soldier. Another one surfaced behind us dragging Harper's limp body behind him. I noticed he had some kind of motor on his back that propelled him toward us and the bank without getting carried farther downstream.

The current tugged at me, but the soldier was stronger. Since we were no longer drifting, I figured he must have a pack too. He turned me toward the bank. It wasn't as tall here but still rose three feet above my head. Another soldier scowled down at me.

"Why are all their heads shaved?" He asked.

"We probably don't want to know." My captor answered while nudging me closer to the wall of dirt. "Take her."

The man bent down, extending his arms toward me. I didn't lift mine. They were too heavy, and even if they hadn't been, there was no way I could reach him.

The churning of a motor kicked into a higher gear, the sound of water gushing out of something, and I shot forward.

My hands automatically reached for the man above me. He pulled me the rest of the way up, dragging me across the ground several feet from the water.

"Don't move." He pointed at three soldiers jogging from upstream. "Watch her while I help with the other one."

My arms and legs quivered as the muscles tried to relax. There was no sign of Iri anywhere.

An explosion drew my attention toward camp. A pillar of dark black smoke rose into the air where the ships rested. I couldn't think about it, the others in camp, or Iri. All that mattered was what would happen to me and Harper.

They dragged her body over to me. I crawled closer, trying to ignore the pain in my foot. She wasn't breathing.

"*Teina*, help her. She's all I have." I sobbed.

One soldier pushed me aside and breathed into her mouth. I watched her chest rise and fall. She'd kill me when she learned I let a soldier save her. But I didn't care. I held her hand and prayed.

Atua, please let me keep Harper.

After six breaths, she coughed. The man turned her to the side, and she threw up river water all over me.

"Iri?" she croaked.

I shook my head.

"Two more for the Hatana. Take them to camp." The man who'd saved her motioned to the others. There were eight men in total.

We were pulled to our feet. I gasped when I put pressure on my foot. The cold water had numbed it for a while, but the pain was increasing.

"This one's hurt." The soldier gripped my arm, stopping the forward motion I'd barely started. "Maybe we should throw her back in?"

His partner laughed. The first guy looked me over from head to toe. His gaze had the same dirty feel of the men that attacked me. "Maybe later."

A third soldier punched him in the shoulder with a small box. "You know the rules. Set her down."

They let me fall to the ground. This new man was older than the others. Maybe in his fifties, but just as fit. He had a red medical patch on his uniform, but his eyes looked more haunted than hungry.

"Which foot?" he asked.

I pointed. He took off my boot, causing more paint to shoot up my leg. Clumps of grass came out of the ground where I dug my hands into it. The man poked and prodded. My eyes teared up, but I focused on Harper instead of crying out. She stood searched the field and I knew she looked for Iri.

The medic injected something into my foot.

"Ow!" The warmth of the liquid soon changed to an icy chill encasing my shin, ankle, and all the way down to my toes. "What was that?"

"It'll help the swelling and boost cellular repair. In the meantime, the bioshield will allow you to walk." He packed the equipment back into the box. "Okay, load them up."

The officer watched the men taking off their water packs. "What did you do with the body?"

"Body?" Harper's eyes focused on him with a crazed look. Then she screamed and jerked against those holding her. She screamed and screamed, even when she could no longer fight against her captors.

"Shut her up!" The leader of the group stomped toward us from the row of machines. "I'm so sick of hysterical women."

He slapped Harper.

For a moment her head hung down, and I was afraid he'd knocked her out. She slowly lifted her face to look him in the eye.

"What body?" she asked.

The officer turned to one of the men who answered. "I threw the man's body in the river."

Harper's voice was liquid steel. "You'll all burn in *reinga*." Then her bravado disintegrated and she cried as I'd never seen before. Not even when we watched Manawa burn.

"Take them to the treadwheel." The officer shook his head and growled. "I want a real assignment after this one. No more emotional females damning me to hell!"

The other soldiers laughed. My two guards hauled me to my feet. I gingerly put weight on the sore foot and found I could handle the dull ache that had replaced the sharp pain. I limped toward the machines.

"What's going to happen to us?" I felt like my emotions had floated down the river with Iri.

"Some of you will be protected, fed and sent to Rawiri."

Some? Rawiri, home of the Hatana? The shudder that moved through me brought all my fears back and pushed them out my lips. "*Teina*, anywhere but Rawiri."

"Why are these women scared of Rawiri? Don't they know they'll be better off?" The leader waved his hand toward camp. "You'll trade this dump for a palace."

"What do you expect from uneducated filth." Another man shook his head.

Uneducated filth? Anger burned my fear away.

We reached the machines they'd called a treadwheel. It had seats for four and two large tires with jagged edges. The blade-like wheels appeared more than capable of digging into any kind of ground for traction. Harper was shoved into a back seat, and a soldier nudged me toward the seat beside her.

"Don't push." I thrust the soldier's hand away.

"Better watch out. One of these could end up as your queen." The leader tapped the guy on the shoulder. "This one has no fear and already commands with the best of them."

"What are the chances?" They all laughed again.

Ug! Stupid soldiers. I wanted to make them stop laughing. Wait, queen? *Atua, what's going on?*

There was no answer. The treadwheel jerked forward, flinging the questions out of my head. I clung to Harper as it cut through the grass toward the road. Her eyes remained on the river.

"Harper, he's gone." I whispered through the ache in my heart. Why did Atua let the Hatana keep taking my family from me?

The line of machines clawed their way up the hillside, forcing Harper to turn away from the river. She leaned back and closed her eyes. A single tear etched its way down her cheek.

"I know." She squeezed my hand. "I knew the moment he pushed us in."

We hit a bump and I grasped the sides of the machine. It jerked and tossed us around as we climbed straight up. We reached the road and turned toward camp.

We rounded the last curve and approached the camp gates. There were three blackened craters full of twisted metal where the ships had stood. Farther in, the tents were shredded and burning. The Hatana's men had reduced the mess hall to smoldering ash. The air was full of smoke. The accompanying smells testified of a variety of materials and organics fueling the flames. Soldiers walked the pathways herding women and children. The treadwheel drove around it all until we reached a gathering place near the mines.

We stopped in front of two makeshift corrals. Older women with little girls huddled on one side, teens and younger women on the other. There were no men or boys as far as I could see.

Soldiers wandered the camp, dragging bodies toward the field and another smoking heap.

"Move." Our soldier waved toward the wire fencing. "It's your lucky day. Enter the one on the right."

We climbed out of the vehicle and shuffled to the paddock. It was basic in design—a square of dirt the soldiers had surrounded with mesh fencing. As I walked through the gateway, the hairs on my arms rose.

"Don't touch the fence," I whispered to Harper.

36

WAKING NIGHTMARE: ELEENA

Thirty or so other shared our corral. I'd guess the age range to be seventeen to mid-twenties.

"I need to sit." My foot throbbed, even though the medicine had helped.

Harper didn't speak. She lay down and rested her head in my lap. My fingers absently brushed through the inch of hair covering her head. The new hair had changed from bristly to soft. The feel of it comforted me, and the motion must have soothed Harper because she closed her eyes.

None of the soldiers spoke to us after we entered the holding pen. I watched them as they tossed scraps of tent and belongings into a central bonfire. Their eyes often strayed to the women inside the electric fences. The smoke thickened on the breeze.

"Eleena, what do you think they'll do to us?" Ulla sat beside me.

"I don't know. The soldier at the river said they wouldn't hurt us." I answered.

"Do you believe them?" Another girl joined us.

I chewed on my bottom lip. The soldier had said *some* would be protected. "We can't trust anything they say."

The second girl wiped at tears. "I didn't think so. They killed all the men. The boys too." She sank to the ground and sobbed. "My brother was only three."

Tears pricked my own eyes, and I squeezed her hand. "Tell us."

"I stayed in the daycare tent. We thought they'd spare the little ones. They killed the men first, then ripped the boys from our arms.

186

Soldiers broke their necks and tossed them to the side like trash," she sobbed.

I clutched Harper's hand tight and allowed my tears to flow freely. It seemed I would never dry out.

The girl leaned against Ulla for support. "One woman wouldn't let go of her son. They shot them both."

I sucked in a ragged breath. Everyone fell silent and time passed. The fires died down, but the sun burned brightly overhead. My sweat pooled behind bent knees and slithered down my back. The turmoil of thoughts died, and I found I'd gone numb again.

Late in the afternoon, soldiers gathered around the paddocks. They had that hungry look.

"Harper." I shook her from sleep. She moaned and sat up.

She looked around as more soldiers arrived. Her back stiffened, and she jumped to her feet. "Leena, I'm sorry. Really sorry."

"It's not your fault." I grasped her hand, standing up with her.

"Death would have been better," she whispered.

Time stood still. We waited for the worst.

A voice boomed over the area. "The women in the east paddock are for the Hatana, and the Hatana only. If you touch them you will be put to death. You can do as you wish with the others."

Men surged forward. I clenched my eyes and clung to Harper. My scream was quickly drowned out by other screams, but no one jerked me away from Harper.

Her own screams ceased, and she sobbed into my shoulder. "We're the east, we're the east."

I turned to the fencing separating us from the older women. Their outer fence had been ripped down. Men chased them. When they were caught, they were carried off or thrown straight to the ground. Two men fought over the same woman. I saw her fear turn to pain as her arm was wrenched behind her while being pushed to the ground by one of the men. The second man jumped on both of them, breaking her arm.

"Atua help us!" I screamed and ran a few steps closer to the fence. Another man straddled a woman he'd stripped half-naked. "Don't touch her!"

The man turned and grinned at me. "Why don't you stop me."

Rational thought fled. All I could see was that evil grin. Hear the taunting voice. Stop me. You can't stop me. No one can stop me.

I launched myself at him.

Time stopped. The image of wrapping my hands around his neck was shocked out of me. It felt as if I was glued to the fence for minutes instead of seconds. However, the oscillating current released me and I jolted backward.

I don't remember hitting the ground or losing consciousness, but I woke to Harper beating on my chest.

"Don't you die on me too!" she whacked me again.

"Stop." The word was a whimper. My heart sludged back to a normal rhythm. Muscles slowly relaxed from the rigor that had claimed them. I stared at the ugly gray sky. My hands stung, and the sounds of the camp had been replaced with ringing. I still couldn't get any air.

"Leena!" Harper's face hovered above me. "Breathe."

I sucked in great sobs. My arm felt heavy as I lifted it to hide my face.

Useless. I couldn't help anyone.

"Leena, shhh, hold on. It'll be okay." Harper pulled me into a hug, burying my face in her shoulder. She rocked me back and forth.

It'll never be okay. I wanted to yell and swear. Rip something or someone apart. I wanted to hide. Do anything to block out the sounds of crying women and grunting men. How could Atua allow it?

"Leena, stay with us." Harper tried to calm me.

I'd never felt so broken. Not even after my own brush with this ugliness. The pain and fear permeating the camp were too much, multiplying my agony.

Harper's words echoed in my mind. Death would be better.

37

UNEASE: AMIRAN

M y walk by the river did nothing to calm my nerves. In fact, listening to the rushing water seemed to kick it up a notch. Although I rarely spoke to Ev myself, he was always in contact with someone. The fact no one had heard from him in a week was a major concern.

Atua, is he safe?

I waited, but the wind only blew harder.

"Hatana, you should return to the palace," one of the guards interrupted my thoughts. "It's almost three in the morning."

"Sorry, I hadn't realized how late it was." I turned around. The palace glowed in the distance. If the man had not said something, I would have walked until morning.

Several minutes later, the man spoke again. "Is everything alright?"

"Yes, thank you. Just restless." Why hadn't Atua answered my question? His presence had been close since the mines. His absence now rang through my soul like a gong. Something was wrong.

I looked at the young soldier. He couldn't be more than seventeen or eighteen years old. At first it bothered me Schirra didn't deem my safety important enough for more seasoned soldiers, but now I was relieved. Even if he couldn't protect me, I felt safer with him than any of Schirra's trusted men.

"Why do you ask?" I hoped the conversation would take my mind off my worries.

He shrugged. "There's a weight around you. I know you have a lot to worry about, but I thought after a night of dancing with beautiful women you'd be happier."

I laughed. "You would think so." After several minutes I continued. "I wish I could live in the moment. However, until everyone enjoys the same privilege I won't either. There's too much suffering that can be, no, should be stopped."

"Your Highness?"

I waved him away. "Forget I said anything."

We finished the trek in silence. He left me at the door to my suite. Timoti had left long before, and the quiet of my rooms only deepened the pressure around my heart.

Kneeling by my bed I prayed to know what was happening to Ev and Eleena. When I finally slept, I dreamed, but my dreams didn't shed any light on my concerns.

I wandered across a vast field in the dark. Warm wind howled around me and clouds blocked the stars from view. There was no other sound, no moon for light. Only grass rubbing against each other in the night. I stood in place as wave upon wave of emotion coursed through me.

Anger, despair, guilt so strong I wanted to fight and break things with my bare hands.

The wind shifted, turned cold. Fear, pain, sorrow, so deep I felt dampness on my cheek.

Atua, what does it mean?

The sensations dissipated and the wind stilled. *Prepare, my son.*

38

ACCOMODATIONS: ELEENA

By the time the sun set, the sounds subsided to quiet whimpering. Soldiers carried off the last of the women. They didn't come back.

The giant spotlights had all been shot out and silence fell with the shroud of darkness. Even though the heat barely let up, we stayed huddled together.

"We should take turns sleeping," Harper whispered.

"Good idea." Someone agreed.

"I'll take first watch." Harper stood. "When I get tired I'll wake someone else. They can do the same until the sun comes up."

"Harper," I touched her elbow, "our bracelets still work. Tell everyone not to take more than a two-hour shift. After a day like this, they could fall asleep too easily."

Harper nodded. "You're right. Why don't you try to sleep?"

"I doubt I'll be able to."

"Your body needs rest to heal. Who knows what tomorrow will bring."

I swallowed the lump in my throat but nodded.

Grateful Harper had taken charge, I lay my head across my arm. The dirt smelled better than the smoke in the air. At least it was natural. My foot had stopped aching, but I'd gladly deal with that pain if I could lose the memories burned in my mind.

Secret army or not, how could Captain E abandon us? I curled up and tried not to cry again.

The next thing I knew, Harper was shaking me awake. "Leena. Suns up. Another ship is coming down."

"What?" My arm tingled as the blood rushed into it. "Another ship?"

"Last night most of the soldiers left on the attack vessel. Maybe they're coming back?" She pointed to the south.

It wasn't a carrier though. A smaller ship flew low over the hills. As I watched, I heard clicking noises followed by silence. The energy field had been turned off. Five soldiers entered the paddock. The same officer that had been in charge of the river group led the way.

"Your transport has arrived." He pointed to the ship kicking up dust as it settled by the front gate. "Captain Meir will take you to Rawiri. Accommodations and food. Guess you have no idea how lucky you are."

We knew. But how long would it last? The soldiers took up position around us. No one spoke, but we clustered together.

"None of us will touch you. Hatana's orders. Don't know how well Meir obeys though." He turned on his heel and led the way out the gate. "Bring them."

I am with you. The voice of Atua sent a shiver through me. *Lead. Don't let them see your fear.*

Raising my chin higher, I grabbed Harper's hand and stepped forward. The others followed and we moved through the remains of the camp. It was better than having the soldier's pushing and shoving us.

The camp had transformed overnight. All the bodies and trash had been moved to the fire, leaving little trace we had ever been here. Only a few scuffed footprints marred the dusty ground.

I didn't see any other women or children.

Atua?

They are with me.

It was strange how sorrow and joy hit me at once. Both emotions threatened waterworks, but I brushed one stray tear before resuming my mask of indifference.

Harper squeezed my hand and whispered, "What?"

I shook my head and mouthed, "Tell you later."

We reached the ship before the hatch opened. Steam spewed from the hydraulics, and the clicks and groans of a ship cooling from reentry filled the air. We didn't speak but listened to the chatter of the men around us.

"What do you think of the Hatana asking for women from the raids?" one soldier asked another.

"Who cares? It's not like it will affect us," another replied.

"True. Think he'd actually marry one of them?"

"He just wants a harem like his father. They don't have to be pretty to fill a need."

They laughed and wandered off. Another group of guys kept closer tabs on us. Their eyes never strayed from our position.

One of them muttered, "He gets all the prime cuts." It was one of the hungry ones.

"Shut it, Noe. You heard what captain said. If we touch them we bite it."

"Yeah, but who's going to keep Meir's crew off them. It's a bloody waste to me. His men will have them."

"Then they'll be the ones to face the Hatana's wrath."

"Like anyone would know."

Harper's death-like grip confirmed she'd heard as well.

"We have to think of something," I whispered.

"I know you will."

I felt like that twelve-year-old leaving Manawa. Only this time Uncle wasn't there to protect me. There was no kind man to put me on the safest shuttle. I sent my worries heavenward.

Atua, give me courage. Give me the strength to keep my friends safe until we reach Rawiri. Then…

Then what? What was the best we could hope for on the Hatana's homeworld?

Help us survive, one step at a time. That's really all I could ask.

Trust in me. The answer was immediate.

I swallowed. My faith was as strong as before, but now I understood my idea of safe didn't always match Atua's. Iri was gone. Those women were gone. I wanted to live, unharmed. Not return to be with my parents. Not yet anyway.

The airlock opened and one man joined the soldiers. He was in his mid-forties, bald, and sporting a round belly. Food obviously wasn't a problem for him. He shook hands with the officer and waved toward the ship.

The Hatana's men herded us up the ramp. Metallic air tainted with the smell of pungent sweat assaulted us in the main corridor. It was narrower than our ship's walkways. I couldn't stay beside Harper but stepped ahead while keeping her hand in mine. The dirty gray walls were full of hatches and wires. The metal floor rattled as we moved. The air was only slightly cooler than outside.

"In there." The man pointed to the left.

Our new accommodations were the ship's cargo hold. At least we were used to that. This one was two stories tall, with a gangway around the second story area. There were no steps or ladders to get up there that I could see, but men lined the room, leaning against the rail, watching our entry.

The hold was crowded with crates, leaving a small area carved out in the middle for us. There was a pile of blankets and several lidded containers bolted down along the back wall. Their purpose was painfully clear by the smell emanating from them.

Who used them before us?

"Welcome to the *Keefer* ladies! We are happy to take you to your destination." The fat man winked at us.

"Meir, remember the rules," the officer half-heartedly reprimanded the captain.

"Of course, of course. No need to worry." He patted the guy on the back. "Now, I think you and your men are needed farther east. Leave them to us and be off with you."

"It's your head." The soldier saluted and disappeared.

"First things first men," he addressed the crew staring down from the railings. "Let's get this bucket into space."

The men along the gangway grumbled but wandered off to do their captain's bidding. It was only a matter of time until they came back.

"This is supposed to be better than camp?" Harper backed away from the make-shift toilets. "There's no privacy."

"I don't think that matters to them." Ulla hovered close by.

"Harper, any ideas?" I watched her closely, knowing she wouldn't lie to me on purpose, but sometimes she held back. Years ago I'd learned to watch her body language for the whole truth.

"No." Her shoulders sagged. There was no fight in her, but I couldn't be sure if that was because of our situation or the loss of Iri. "We're at their mercy."

The engines fired up. Vibrations shook the ship as clarion bells and hissing filled the air. The floor tilted, knocking several girls to the floor. Harper and I held on to each other. One of the smaller crates broke from its tether, sliding across the floor until it rammed one of the buckets. It too broke loose and clattered against the bulkhead before rolling away from the others, leaving a line of filth trailing behind.

"Gross!" A girl scrambled away from the stench.

"Everyone, sit down," Harper yelled. "Hold onto something if you can."

"We've got to secure that crate or one of us could be next." I stumbled toward it, hands outstretched in case it decided to move again. The ship lurched once more and the box shimmied my direction. "Grab it."

Harper, Ulla, and two other women helped me direct the crate back to its original spot. They held it in place while I used the cords to tie it down.

"Okay, now hold on." I waved them away.

We scattered around the room. I wrapped one arm through a tie-down near the floor and held tight. The rumbling grew louder, the shaking more pronounced as we sped up to break free from the planet's gravity.

Teina, don't let us break apart!

The next ten minutes tested all my strength. The force of takeoff pressed me into the floor. The ship rattled and convulsed. It was much worse than Evander's, and I missed our launch seats. The takeoff drained me of all energy. By the time the engines throttled down, I could barely stand.

"Leena?" Harper stumbled to me. "We've got to get up. Maybe if we stand together we can fight the men off."

"They have weapons. How will we fight them off for weeks?" I pulled myself up. My knees wobbled and my arms shook. "We've got to be smart about this."

The other girls crawled or walked over. All eyes on me.

Atua, be with me. Be with us.

39

APPEARANCES: AMIRAN

The barracks remained empty. I was starting to doubt Schirra would keep his end of the bargain and bring in refugees. Mornings were spent in the council room, the afternoons with the potential brides. My patience wore thin with my growing anxiousness.

"Amiran," Schirra called as I walked the halls.

He hadn't addressed me as Hatana since the dance. I ignored him and continued my journey away from the council room.

"Hatana Amiran." His voice dripped derision but at least he used my title.

I turned and dropped his title when I addressed him. "Schirra?"

He scowled. "I wanted to inform you four ships of refugee women have been collected. However, they should be sent straight to the factories on Attalea."

"That wasn't our agreement."

"The queen cannot be chosen from among them." A vein twitched at the side of his temple. "I won't permit it."

I allowed myself a smile. "I never thought you would. This is all for public appearances. In fact, I've been narrowing down the women you've brought in."

A look of surprise passed over his features before his normal look of suspicion returned. "Is that so?"

"Out of the twenty, there are four you can send home immediately. I will continue to visit with the others." I resumed my exit.

Schirra's parting remark almost knocked me to my knees. "We found the camp that's eluded us all these years."

I turned slowly, desperately hoping my face didn't show my fear. It took all I had not to fist my hands. "Good job, General."

"Some of the survivors will be with the women you requested." He chuckled as he strode past me.

I hurried the other direction. When I reached my quarters, I collapsed on the couch. Timoti wasn't around. How could I tell him Schirra might have found Evander's camp?

This must be why Atua had not answered my questions or sent visions of Ev and Eleena.

"Atua?" Agony stopped the rest of my words as I recalled what I'd seen from fleet soldiers in my years with them. I couldn't verbalize the fear. Instead, I felt the silent plea. *Are they captured?*

That feeling of comfort entered my chest, but my mind needed more this time. So much more. The uncertainty was too much. We were so close. To lose them now shook my faith more than anything else had before.

Amiran.

I jerked in my seat at Atua's commanding tone.

Yes?

Be at peace.

A vision opened before me. Evander and his men were crammed into the glorywinger they used for trips to Olea. They were haggard but otherwise untouched.

"Captain," Mynor addressed him, "how long should we wait?"

"At least a week. We need to be sure the fleet has left Kahu before we make a run for Olea." Ev's eyes were red with dark circles lining them. The scene faded, but I knew Ev was alive and safe.

Eleena?

Another ship came into my view. A group of women huddled together. Eleena stood in the grasp of a man, her chin held high. Bile rose in my throat as he yanked her closer.

His body pressed against hers as he hissed in her ear. "What's to stop me from enjoying you then tossing you out the airlock."

Atua. I can't lose her! A stabbing pain gripped my heart.

Harper stepped forward. "Because we would tell him about that too."

"I could toss you all out the airlock," he yelled.

"But you won't. How will you explain an entire shipment of women lost en-route?" Eleena's voice remained calm.

"Captain, you have a choice to make. Keep your ship and your life or take a chance on losing both." Harper crossed her arms. "We stand together. It's all or nothing."

The man shoved Eleena away. "I'll check your story. Trust me, you'll regret your lies when I learn the truth."

The captain waved his men toward the door. As soon as they left, Eleena collapsed. Harper was there to catch her. The fear she'd hidden from him now plain to see, but only for a moment. She quickly gathered herself again and faced the women.

The tightness in my chest eased. I wished to see her better and the vision zoomed in. She was dirty and thin like the others, but still beautiful. The light of Atua shone through her eyes.

I didn't know how long Atua would let me watch, so I tried to memorize every aspect of her face. Her brown eyes, the curve of her brow and cheeks. The dip in her upper lip, the full bottom one.

She was alive, but definitely not safe. I had to make sure the captain's inquiries made the consequences of harming those women in any way very clear.

The vision faded. Eleena was coming to me!

My joy was short lived as reality set in. As much as I wanted to see her, talk to her, I couldn't take that chance. Schirra must never know of our connection, or how I felt about her.

40

STRENGTH IN UNITY: ELEENA

The hours dragged by after Captain Meir left. We rigged two of the blankets up around the toilets. It wasn't perfect, but it gave us some privacy from the men who occasionally appeared on the walkway above to stare at us. They never spoke. Didn't bother to taunt us. They just watched and waited.

The lights went out, but the captain hadn't returned. It wasn't pitch black in the hold, but the red emergency lights around the perimeter added a sinister air.

"Leena, what's going on?" Ulla asked.

"It could be the ship's sleep cycle." I sighed, wishing they would turn to one of the older women for comfort. "Or it could be a trap."

Harper herded everyone toward the blankets. "We should sleep in shifts. Take turns keeping watch like last night."

"Without our bracelets to keep track of time that might be hard." I considered it though. Maybe fear was enough to keep us alert.

"I'll take the first watch. I'm not tired." Harper moved to the edge of our sleeping area.

The dull throb had returned to my ankle, and I still had that weighted feel from hitting the fence. Even my fear wouldn't be enough to keep me awake.

"Okay, if you're sure you won't fall asleep."

"Ulla and I'll sit up together. That'll help."

The rest of us found a spot to lay down. Women snuggled close on both sides, keeping me warm. The air was full of the sound of breathing and not much else.

I thought I'd fall asleep quickly, but my brain wouldn't give me the rest I needed.

Where was Captain Meir? Had he tried to contact Rawiri to learn why we'd been collected? What would happen to us when we reached the Hatana's homeworld? Where was Captain E?

Too many questions.

"Harper?" Ulla's voice broke the silence.

"Yeah?"

"How well do you know Eleena?"

I twisted around on my blanket to get a better look at them. They both leaned against the wall adjacent to the door. Neither looked my direction.

"About as well as you can know someone after seven years in camp. Why?" Harper whispered, but she'd never been good at it. I heard both of them clearly.

"Why's she different?"

I sat up, then quickly sunk down before they noticed me.

"I've thought about that a lot over the years." Harper thought I was different too? "Somehow none of this has shaken her belief in Atua."

"Yeah."

They were silent for a while, but as I drifted toward sleep, I heard Harper speak, "We have to keep her safe, no matter what happens to the rest of us."

The lights snapped on. Rubbing my eyes I sat up. Harper and Ulla were both asleep several blankets away. Two girls I didn't know stood watch.

After testing my ankle, I made my way to the toilet to do my business. The medicine had done its job, and the foot had almost healed. Only the dull ache remained. When I came out of the curtain, all the blankets had been folded.

The clank of boots on metal echoed around the room. All eyes looked up. Captain Meir stood on the walkway. His fisted hands rested on his hips. He glared down on us.

I asked, "What did you learn, Captain?"

"You will be taken straight to the palace." He moved to grip the rail. "Don't think this means the next three weeks will be a vacation." He turned and stomped his way out of sight.

The tension immediately fled my body. Three weeks! We were safe for another three weeks. Thanks to Atua. My thought was echoed behind me by the other women.

41

SPACE TRAVEL: ELEENA

The days passed slowly. Men walked the railing constantly. We stuck close to each other unless we needed to use the bathroom. Whenever someone made their way to the curtained off area the number of men lining the walkway doubled.

"No need to hide, girlie."

"Why don't you drop that blanket."

They became louder and bolder as time passed. If they weren't taunting us, they watched in absolute silence. Those moments were worse than the noisy ones. We could feel their gaze with that eerie pressure that left us feeling dirtier than normal.

Our most immediate problem was hunger and boredom. They didn't give us food or water. That made the hours of idleness more pronounced. For years we'd been busy. We had a purpose. A way to contribute to our own safety and well being. Now we simply sat or paced the cargo hold with men staring at us all hours of the day and night.

They punished us in other ways too. I tried to tell stories during the day but the men made a game out yelling and banging things on the walkway. I had to yell to be heard over them until my voice gave out.

Once we tried to sleep all day and stay up during the night cycle. We thought we could have peace then, but the captain wouldn't allow that. He blared a siren all night. They chose the next day to feed us.

It was the first time in four sleep cycles. They lined the walkway and threw food at us. Chunks of hard bread and uncooked vegetables pelted us from above. Some slung hot broth at us. They dragged it out while we huddled together to protect our faces. We reached new levels of grime on our skin, clothes, and in our hair.

The only way to clean our hair was to let the food dry then brush out as much as we could with our fingers. I almost wished to be bald again, but my hair was growing in thicker every day. We now looked like a bunch of boys who needed haircuts.

It was humiliating, but we scraped bits of food from our clothes and the floor. It was bland. The bread dry and salty. They didn't give us water that day, and I couldn't help but wonder if the salty bread was on purpose. The men laughed as we tried to get some sustenance out of the mess they'd lobbed at us.

Days passed between feedings. Every meal was delivered the same way. The floor became slippery and sticky at turns. Our clothes grew stiff and itchy as did our hair. The smell of fermenting food slowly overtook the smell of the latrine.

We learned not to gather the food until they stopped throwing it and yelling at us. The torment ended faster if we didn't react. During meal times, the captain joined his men to berate us.

"When you get to Rawiri, the Hatana will give you to his soldiers first. He'll watch to assess your skills at giving pleasure. If you don't meet his requirements he won't bother keeping you around. You'll be lucky to be sent to the mines where you'll never see daylight again."

Sometimes he'd point to one or the other of us and tell us we were too ugly for the Hatana. Promised us we'd be better off leaving the hold to join their company. In trade for our bodies, he offered better food, more food, clean clothes, and a shower. As the weeks dragged on, they threw less food.

Their efforts wore some down.

"Don't do it," I begged one of the younger girls near the end of the second week. "It won't be just one of them. They'll all abuse you. Who's to say they'll keep their promise and give you the food?"

"I'm so hungry. He said he'd be gentle." She cried and I knew she didn't want to do it.

"We can make it another week." I hugged her. "Next time they bring food you can have everything I gather."

Several times I gave half or all of my portion away. Harper would fuss at me and try to give me hers.

"I'll be okay. I'm used to hunger." I waved her away.

"Leena, this is different. You need to keep up your strength. What if Meir changes his mind? You're the one he'll go for. Just to make you pay."

"He wouldn't dare. That has nothing to do with my eating either."

In the end, we'd share what little she had. Sometimes Ulla slip me food. It shouldn't have irritated me, but I kept thinking of their whispered conversation. I didn't deserve anything more than anyone else.

The smell of rotting food and the toilets got worse as time passed. It worked it's way into our clothes, into our hair. It was everywhere. Instead of getting used to it, we found it harder to bear. The only consolation was that with less food, we needed the toilets less frequently.

By the end of three weeks, we'd lost weight, were weak, and I doubted we'd last much longer.

42

WAITING: AMIRAN

Each day felt like a lifetime as I waited for Eleena to arrive. During the day I fulfilled my duties as Hatana. In the evenings I survived social activities set up by Schirra with his women, and at night I dreamed of Eleena. She was alive. The captain had not followed through on his threat to dump the women from the airlock, but he was as cruel as he could be otherwise.

It hurt to watch Eleena grow thinner. I was surrounded by luxury while she scraped food from her clothes and body. More often than not, she gave what she collected to someone else. Her selflessness astonished me.

How can she be so good with all she's seen? I asked Atua one night.

Because she is mine. She knows the only way to survive the fear is to embrace the light.

I pondered the words. Over the years I'd learned to trust Atua, to seek his guidance, but had I truly embraced him as the only hope? Part of me still thought I would be the one to end Schirra's reign.

It was clear the general had been the driving force behind my father because nothing changed with Anaru's death. Not even a hiccup of doubt in the way the fleet would be run or the empire expanded.

Atua, when will we stop this?

Soon.

How soon? My impatience had been augmented by anxiety and sorrow at Eleena's living conditions.

Let her reach Rawiri.

My heart pounded. She would be here in a week, two at the most. Had I placed the right people at the barracks to protect her? To help her after all she'd been through? I paced my suite, moving from room to room. She would need more than a bed and food.

I found my datacom. Since returning to the palace, I'd reconnected with another childhood friend and discovered an ally. She had as much reason to hate her father as I did, and I knew she would help. I sent a quick message.

MEET ME IN THE BASEMENT CONFERENCE ROOM AT 1 AM. URGENT.

It only took a minute to get the reply.

OKAY.

We had a few days to change the program we'd set up for the refugees, but with Atua's help, it would be enough. Valeria would know who we could trust. Then we'd bring Schirra down.

PART III

43

RAWIRI: ELEENA

A fourth week on Meir's ship dragged by, and I wondered if he lied about the duration of our stay. Finally, we felt the shuttering pressure as the ship descended into a planet's atmosphere. The room heated up more than I thought it should. Once more we clung to the tie-downs and anything else we could to keep from being thrown around.

When the engines cut off, a new kind of quiet took over. The stillness reached into our bones. No more vibrations rumbled beneath us.

I was so tired and thirsty I barely cared that we were on Rawiri.

"I guess this is it." Harper pulled me to my feet.

We were a sorry lot. Our hair had grown another two to three inches, just enough to look bad from lack of cleaning. Our clothes were stained with food smudges. We had dirt under our nails and reeked of body odor and spoiled food.

I started to laugh. I couldn't help it.

"What's so funny?" Harper smiled too.

"We're so filthy the Hatana won't want any of us."

Wide-eyes stared back at me for a second before everyone else joined in the laughter. Whatever happened next, we'd survived the trip. Rawiri couldn't be worse than where we'd been the last month.

"I'm glad you're so happy to be on Rawiri." Captain Meir stood above with his men on the walkway. "We can't have you meeting the Hatana looking like the garbage you are."

He flicked his hand to one side and then the other. Men lifted hoses to the top of the rail. Before I could register their intentions, icy water blasted me. It went down my nose, my throat, burned my eyes. The power of it knocked me off my feet and stung my skin everywhere it touched.

I couldn't get away from it. Bodies bumped against me as we were tossed like rag dolls. We were at the mercy of the spray, our clothes flapping against the onslaught, our bodies bruising as we were pressed into the bulkhead until the onslaught of water stopped.

Blinking, I looked around. We were soaked and piled in a heap against the door. Our clothes clung to us while we shivered.

"Much better. As soon as you dry we'll get you on your way." The captain nodded and the men disappeared. "I hope you found the accommodations to your liking."

His laughter added another layer of cold to our situation. How could there be so many mean-spirited men in one galaxy?

Another look around the room and I knew I had to say something to get us back to the relieved state we'd enjoyed only minutes before. "At least we're clean."

And we were. Sort of. I knew it would feel good once we warmed up. In fact, I'd never been so anxious to get out into the heat of the day.

If it was daytime on Rawiri.

It bothered me that I didn't know.

I shook my head and picked up a blanket. A sniff confirmed it wouldn't make an ideal towel, but it was the only option. "Dry off so we can get out of here faster."

We rubbed vigorously before tossing the sodden fabric to the side. At least we wouldn't have to clean up the mess. The thought made me smile more.

My clothes were mostly dry when the hatch opened and the captain ushered us down the corridor to the gangway and outside. I held up my hand to block the sunlight but still couldn't fully open my eyes. Its warmth was tempered by a slight breeze.

Atua, I'm on Rawiri. Are you here too?

His spirit had been absent for days, but when I asked, his warmth steam-rolled me. My breath caught in my throat.

"Breathe, Leena." Harper held my hand, and we followed the line of women down the ramp.

The Hatana's homeworld wasn't unlike my memories of Manawa. The blue dome of sky stretched forever, dotted by brilliant white clouds. Trees grew tall and straight. A cityscape loomed in the distance. I heard vehicles, birds calling, the wind in the leaves. A slight dusty smell filled the air. Before I could get a good feel for this new planet, the ship's crew pushed me toward a large covered vehicle.

Soldiers waited to take over as Meir and his men retreated. These new ones barely glanced at us. They only watched close enough to make sure we did as ordered and climbed into the transport.

Harper and I sat in the middle of the row on one side. Our light-hearted camaraderie had evaporated with the sun's light. The air inside the truck pressed me down. The dark heat held none of the hope from outside.

"Leena, if we get split up—" Harper clutched my hand until it hurt.

"We're not getting split up. Why would you say that?"

"You don't know what they really want us for. I'm just saying if we get split up,"

"Stop. The soldiers said the Hatana needs a wife. It won't be either of us so we'll be fine." I squeezed her hand but stared straight ahead. I refused to think about what happened if we weren't chosen.

"*Teina*, listen to me. You have to remember who you are. You can hear Atua. Whatever they do to you, don't forget that. Don't let them change you inside."

The vehicle hit a bump and we tumbled off the bench. I climbed back onto the seat, reluctant to think about her words. I'd seen the worst of what men could do. What it seemed they all wanted to do. I shook my head. Father hadn't been like that. Neither had Iri or most of the men in Evander's camp. They had been good. I'd cling to that.

Mother used to call me stubborn. That's what I'd be now. I'd keep Harper with me. We would keep each other safe just like we always had.

The transport swayed, turned and slowed. We stopped a moment before lurching forward again. The sounds of a busy city filtered through the walls around us. I wished there were windows. Even now, my curiosity was hard to ignore.

"Leena?" Harper insisted I give her some kind of answer.

"I won't change, but we're in this together. Iri would want us to stay together."

"We don't always get what we want." The pain in her voice poked holes in my stubborn confidence.

The truck jerked to a stop again. This time the engine shut off and the back doors opened.

"Step down and form a line." A soldier waved us out.

We ended up in the middle of the crowd again. The women from our ship, and some from two other transports, lined up in front of four gateways to a large courtyard.

A sparkling white building surrounded the open area standing four stories high, lined with arched balconies. Soft fabric drifted in the breeze from most of the porches. Brightly colored flowers and plants overflowed from baskets and flowerbeds. It was beautiful. So full of life.

"Where are we?" I whispered.

One of the soldiers answered, "The Hatana's palace."

I grabbed Harper's arm, entwining myself in her embrace. How could he live in a place so beautiful? My heart beat a war drum in my head.

"Leena, breathe." She held me just as tight. "You knew we were coming."

"What if he's here right now?"

"We probably won't see him today. Maybe never." Harper nudged me forward.

The line moved quickly. Women stepped through and continued down a path lined with soldiers through a garden. Every once in a while, a soldier separated a woman and sent them down a different trail.

"What do you think is going on?" I pointed as another woman went down the shorter path to a building.

"I don't know. It's your turn."

I stepped through the archway. A soldier in front of me held up his hand.

"Wait." He watched a datacom then flicked his hand down the long path. "Keep to the right."

After a few steps, I waited for Harper. She paused, but the soldier didn't wave her through. After a moment he nodded to another guard.

"We've got another one." He turned back to Harper. "Step to the left."

"What?" I screeched. "We stay together."

"You can't. Move on." He waved me down the path and turned to the next woman at the gate.

"No!" I ran and latched onto Harper. "You can't split us up."

More soldiers surrounded us. One grabbed Harper, another tried to wrench us apart. I held on with both hands.

"Don't let go," I begged.

Harper looked into my eyes. "Leena, it's okay. Stop fighting before you get hurt."

"You're all I have left." My heart hurt, it grew harder to breathe. First Iri, now Harper.

Atua, help!

"Breathe, and wish me peace, Leena." Harper squeezed my hand and let go. The soldier led her away, while another one dragged me the other direction. "Wish me peace."

There was no help from above. I yelled as my heart broke yet again. "Peace on your path, Harper! Peace on your path!"

"Burn a light to guide me home."

I never thought we'd say those words to each other.

44

HOPE: AMIRAN

"Sir, the last ships with refugee women have arrived." Timoti bowed and pointed toward the window.

"Hand me the oculars." I stepped to the window overlooking the balcony.

The women had started arriving a week ago. Timoti and I watched each group walk through the courtyard, waiting for Eleena. He'd taken the news of Evander's camp in stride, but only because he had faith in my visions. Faith was one thing, knowing was another. We needed to be sure they were both alive.

The long line of girls and women streamed through the garden below. They were all dirty and thin, but most of them had long hair. Evander's group wasn't among them.

"It's not them." I lowered the oculars. Before I turned away, a skirmish erupted near the gates. "Timoti, the amplifier."

I zoomed in on two women clinging to each other. Soldiers struggled to separate them. They had short hair. One looked like Eleena's friend, but the other had her back to me. I tried to get a better angle as Timoti focused the amplifier on them. Their voices echoed around my chambers.

"Don't let go." The one facing away from me cried out. Her voice sounded shaky, but it was as familiar as my own, thanks to Atua's dreams.

"Leena, it's okay. Stop fighting before you get hurt."

I almost dropped the oculars. "It's her."

"You're all I have left," Eleena pleaded.

"Wish me peace, Leena." Harper appeared to hold on simply to say goodbye. There was clearly no fight in her.

"No, no, no!" Eleena continued to kick and thrash while clinging to her friend. The soldiers pulled them apart.

"Wish me peace, Leena!"

"Peace on your path, Harper! Peace on your path!" Eleena tried to stand her ground, but the soldier pulled her farther away.

I was so busy wishing the soldier would be gentle with her that I almost missed Harper response. "Burn a light to guide me home."

"Hurry and collect Harper," I turned to Timoti.

"Right away." He clicked his heels together and left the room.

I shook my head, hating his formality. Turning back to the window, I tried to get another glimpse of Eleena. She was here. So close, and yet I couldn't decide if she was safer with me, or if it would have been better for her to stay with Ev.

Only time would tell.

Atua, give me patience.

45

NEW QUARTERS: ELEENA

"Why can't we stay together?" The guard dragged me away from Harper.

"She's not worthy of the Hatana."

"She's one of the best people I know."

"That's not what I mean." He nudged me forward. "I don't have time for this. Keep walking."

The beautiful courtyard mocked me. Its sweet scents contrasted everything I'd known the last few years. We traveled its length and turned right at a covered walkway. Arches lined the corridor until we stepped out of it and headed down a gentle slope. The other women walked single file around the side of a long white building set into the side of the hill. Rows of window wells marked the side of it.

"You should bring her back. She's strong and smart." I tried again.

"She's already been used. She ranked C on the scale which means she's pregnant too."

I stopped dead in my tracks. It couldn't be true. She would have told me.

"Keep moving." This time he shoved. I stumbled and hit the ground, landing on my elbow. "Ow! Why do you guys have to push so much?"

"Because we're stuck babysitting a bunch of camp rats. Schirra will never let him pick one of you anyway. It's a waste of my time." He dragged me to my feet and pulled me the rest of the way down the hill, past other women, to a sidewalk near the building. "Stay here and do what you're told."

The line came to a halt as we queued up at a door. Others fell into place behind me. I'd been mixed up with the women from the other ship. I didn't know anyone. More than anything I wanted to find Ulla. Did she know about Harper?

My arm hurt. Tiny pinpricks of blood dotted the skin from sliding across the grass. I didn't bother to wipe them away. At the door, another soldier asked my name and the camp I'd come from. Then he waved a digital recorder over my body.

"Eleena from Kahu," I mumbled.

"You're clear. Step inside."

I wanted to ask questions, but he'd already turned to the woman behind me. I entered a well-lit hallway. Doors lined both sides and stretched the length of the building. Everything looked new and clean. I took a deep breath through my nose. There was the slight smell of paint in the air. Definitely new.

"Eleena from Kahu. This way." An older woman dressed in a drab grey tunic waved me over. She held a datacom, where I assumed she read my name. "Shower, move on for your clothes and then to the waiting area. We'll talk to everyone after they've received vaccinations and a full medical workup."

"Medical workup?" I asked.

"Nothing to worry about, now go on." She too pushed me toward the next door.

Seriously, if I ever got the chance to give the Hatana a piece of my mind, pushing was definitely coming up. I shook my head at the stupid thought. Pushing was the least of his or his people's crimes.

My head ached, and my heart felt empty. What would happen to Harper and the baby?

"Take off your clothes and throw them in the bin. There's soap and shampoo on the shelves." Another woman directed me toward a long row of shower heads. "Quickly now."

Several of the other refugees huddled under the spray of water, carefully keeping their backs to the rest of the room. We hadn't had communal showers at camp in years. Water was too precious to waste. I quickly slipped out of my threadbare tunic and tossed it in the bin. A quick look around and my undergarments joined it.

I hurried to an open spot and twisted the handle. Much to my surprise, warm water sluiced over my head and shoulders. It was heavenly. The shampoo smelled like flowers. The soap made my skin tingle, especially around my scraped elbow. I could have stood there for hours.

"Move along. Others are waiting, and we don't have all day." The voice chided, and I knew it was directed at me.

Reluctantly, I turned off the water. There was nothing to dry or cover myself up with.

"Excuse me?" I tried to get the woman's attention.

"Go that way. There will be clean clothes in the next room." She pointed to another door.

I followed the others, trying to cover my body as best as I could with my arms. Warm air blasted me from all sides when I stepped through the doorway. It didn't quite dry me, but it was better than continuing to drip my way forward.

More women in grey stood behind tables handing out garments and new tunics. After grabbing some, I moved to the far side of the room to dress. The underthings were so clean and white I was afraid to use them. I hadn't seen anything so nice in a long time. They were soft on my skin; a direct contrast to our old items. The tunic was a pale blue fabric that folded around my boyish curves, moving with me instead of fighting to hold a shape at odds with my own.

I hated to admit it, but the soldier at the river had been partially right. This was much better than camp. Warm water, soft clothes. If only that could erase seven years of hardship, my memories of fleet soldiers, and the last month of *reinga*.

The woman beside me caught my eye. "Looks like you're having the same struggle I am. Is this heaven or hell?"

"Right now I'm voting a bit of both." I nodded.

"We'll see." She was several years older than me. Possibly one of the oldest in the room. "I'm not going to hold my breath."

"Me either." I followed her through the next set of doors and was surrounded by a mouthwatering scent. Long tables filled this room. Women moved quickly to a seat and servants brought food. "Wow."

"Well, don't stand there, it has to be better than the mess we were fed on the way here."

I wondered if her trip had been different than mine. Had she been scared of the men on board? Had they fed them like human beings rather than animals? I sat down and a plate was put in front of me, and I didn't care about anything else.

A large helping of brown meat smothered in some kind of white gravy took up one section of the divided plate. Vegetables and the softest roll I'd seen in years took up the other two. Someone handed me a pitcher of ice water before I could take a bite.

Ice, real ice! I poured, thrilling at the sound of an ice cube hitting the side of the glass.

Some women ate like they hadn't eaten in months. I'd had so little food over the last six months I'd lost my appetite, but I wanted to savor a bite of everything. The meat melted in my mouth. Nothing had ever tasted so good. The vegetables were soft crisp with a light seasoning, leaving the natural goodness to shine through. I took a bite of one, then the other. My stomach twisted at the strangeness of real food filling the emptiness.

"Are you going to eat the rest of that?" A woman across from me asked.

"No, I'm full." I passed her my plate, glad it wouldn't go to waste. "What's your name?"

"Tryla. How about you?"

"Eleena."

"You were on the other ship, right? What camp did you come from?"

"We were last on Kahu."

She nodded her head. "Never been there. How long you been running?"

A little thought wiggled into my mind. Something Harper had said about questions and giving out too much information. For the first time, I really looked at the woman. Her hair fell below her shoulders, leaving a wet mark on her tunic. Then there were her cheeks. They were nice and full. Maybe I was overreacting, but I didn't want to share anything else with her.

"It's hard to keep up with time." I shrugged. "How about you?"

She looked at me over the fork as she took another bite. Then mumbled, "Two years. We were on Jakaru."

I almost spit out my drink. There was no way she'd been on Jakaru. I still remembered the government sending us off the planet when the Hatana threatened retribution for harboring us. It was doubtful they'd changed their minds. And there was no way she'd been a refugee for two years. She still had dimples at her elbows. That uneasy feeling grew and I wished Harper was with me. She was good at knowing what to do in situations like this. Not that we'd ever been in this kind of position before.

Atua?

He remained silent, and I felt even more alone.

"Ladies, please turn your chairs this way and we will get started." Another woman stood at the front of the room.

She was by far the youngest I'd seen that day. Her auburn hair lay in waves around her, and she didn't wear the drab grey clothes the others did. She was very pretty. Of course, it could have been the smile she gave us. It was warm, kind.

Chairs scraped and moved. Grateful for the excuse to end the conversation with Tryla, I moved as well.

"We have a few things to do before we take you to your rooms. When we call your name, come forward." She turned and waved to her left. "You will go through here in groups of four. You will have a quick physical to assess any nutritional or medical needs we should address. There is nothing to worry about. Then you'll get vaccinated for a wide range of diseases you may be susceptible to as new residents of Rawiri."

One of the sour-faced women took over. She called groups of four and waited for them to leave before calling the next four. My name came up in the fourth round. Ulla and two others from my ship were in the same group. We gripped hands and went through together. Four men stood by four exam tables.

"One per table, quickly." The soldier at the door barked at us.

We scattered. I sat on the edge of a table. The man assigned to me looked in my ears, eyes, my throat. He listened to my heart and breathing. Everything was very basic and I relaxed.

"Good. Lie down," he ordered.

I lay down and squeezed my eyes shut.

"Relax." His voice softened. "I'm getting your weight and this scanner will type your blood and test it for a variety of vitamin deficiencies." There was a soft beep and a prick on my finger. "Okay, you're done."

He ripped a sheet of paper from the side of the table and handed it to me. There were no words, just a barcode. I took it and noticed the other three were finished as well. We walked through the next door. The line was backed up here.

"Where's Harper?" Ulla whispered.

I shook my head. "I don't know. They took her away. The soldier said she was pregnant."

"Oh! I'm sorry, Leena. Did you know?"

"No. I don't know if she did."

"She probably did after a month on the ship."

I nodded. We'd all learned about women's reproductive cycles but a lot of us had never bled. Harper had a couple of times, but never regularly. She asked lots of questions about it when she worked in the med tent. That had always been her favorite rotation. When I worried that I'd never had a cycle, she explained it was probably because of low body fat, poor nutrition, and high stress.

We moved forward until it was Ulla's turn. She left me lost in my thoughts. Harper had never kept secrets from me. Well, I guess that wasn't true. She and Iri had obviously shared more than kisses. I suspected but never asked.

"Next."

I stepped forward and handed the man my slip of paper. He scanned it and waited for something to come up on the screen. Then he turned to a drawer and pulled out several vials.

"A few good meals and you'll be as healthy as any woman your age from Rawiri." He pressed the hypo to my shoulder. A hiss and sting and he sent me on my way with a new paper.

The next door led to a stairwell.

"Take your paper to the first floor. They'll show you to a room, then to the auditorium." The red-head directed traffic. "We have so many good things planned for you."

"Thank you." I hurried down the steps, hoping to catch up with Ulla. She was nowhere to be seen.

Instead, another soldier took my slip of paper and led me to a room several doors down the hall. He put the paper in a little card holder by the door where it was scanned again. Once the blue light finished its journey down the paper, a screen lit up in the middle of the door with my name on it.

"This is your room. After orientation, return here until further instructions. Go up the stairs in the middle of the hall to the third floor and you'll reach the auditorium."

46

PASSING THE TORCH: AMIRAN

Harper stared at the wall, barely glancing at me when I entered the room. She appeared to be in her early to mid-twenties, short blonde hair, and blue eyes devoid of expression.

Atua, guide me. Let me know what's safe to say.

"Do you need anything?" I asked.

She shook her head but didn't speak.

I sat in a chair across from her. "Do you know why they separated you from the others?"

Harper nodded. "I'm pregnant."

"Was it one of the men from the ship that brought you here?"

"No, Leena made sure none of them touched us." She finally met my gaze. "What will happen to her?"

"Aren't you more worried about what will happen to you?" I leaned forward to study her reaction. She'd been with Eleena in almost all the dreams. This woman knew her better than anyone else, and I wanted to know how she saw Eleena.

"My life doesn't matter. Hers does." She looked me in the eye confirming she believed those words.

I relaxed. Atua didn't speak, but his presence testified that her love for Eleena was real, not just an act. I wanted to hug her, thank her for taking care of Eleena all these years, but I couldn't. I had to play the game.

"You said she kept the men from touching you. How did she do that?"

Harper smiled for the first time. It softened her features, making her almost pretty. "Leena knows how to present the facts in a way even the stupidest man can understand. She simply pointed out that if any of us had been defiled, they would have had to kill all of us to keep us silent. How would they explain that?"

This was the dream Atua had sent after their capture. I struggled to hide my own pride as I remembered how Eleena had stood up to the man that manhandled her. Instead, I tried to continue the conversation as if I knew nothing about the event itself. "They honored the threat?"

"It helped that we stood behind her and never left her alone." She picked at a thread on her tunic. "Leena is different than the rest of us. My only regret is I can't protect her anymore." A sob escaped before she choked the rest down.

I reached for her hand, but she pulled it away. "What if I promised to watch her for you?"

"I don't know you, but I've learned not to trust the words of men."

I pointed to her stomach, "Your child's father?"

"Iri was everything. Thanks to the Hatana he'll never know this child." She wiped a tear but held on to her composure. "I should have made him leave. The captain asked him to go, but he wouldn't leave me and Leena. Said he promised Beck."

Iri. Evander had spoken of him often. Right now I wished more than anything Iri was safe on Olea, but her words confirmed he wasn't. The knowledge of how much loss these two women had endured in such a short time added more weight to my shoulders.

"Harper, I know you don't trust me, but I'll do everything I can to keep Eleena safe."

Her gaze jerked to my face. "I never said Eleena. How did you know?" She twisted her fingers into knots, all the while studying me. "How do you know my name?"

I could lie, say it was a guess, but the fear in her eyes was too much. *Atua?*

Give her hope.

"Evander is my friend. I've been sending him supplies as often as I could. It's not been easy, but I never wanted him or anyone from his camp captured."

Her eyes widened. "And Eleena?"

"I'm the one that put her on Evander's ship on Manawa."

She gasped, her hand flying to her mouth. "You're the one she used to talk about. What are you doing here?"

"I can't tell you, and you have to promise not to mention any of this after you leave. It's the only way we can keep her safe." I touched her hand, and this time she didn't pull away. "I'm truly sorry about Iri. Evander had great respect for him. This wasn't supposed to happen."

"A lot of things happen that shouldn't. The soldiers," she looked away, swiping at tears.

She didn't have to say it. I'd seen the worst with my own eyes. Two lists lived inside my head. Those I could trust, and those I desperately wanted to bring to justice.

"I'm sorry. One day they will be judged."

"But we will live with the memory."

"Wait here." I moved to the door beckoning Timoti inside. "This is Evander's father. He will set you up in a house close to the palace."

"Why?" she asked.

"Because you're Eleena's friend. She would want to know you're being taken care of."

Timoti stepped close enough to help Harper from her seat. "What do I say if Schirra hears of this?"

"Let him believe I've started my own harem. That's something Anaru would have done." I spit the words out, sick of pretending to be anything like my father.

"You know it's not." Timoti shook his head.

I sighed. "You're right."

"Anaru? Hatana Anaru?" Harper's eyes rounded again.

Tell her.

I sighed. "He was my father."

"Was?"

"He died months ago."

"You're the Hatana?" Harper moved to sit back down. "This is not what we expected."

"You and Eleena?"

She nodded. "How…why haven't." Harper struggled to find the words. She settled with, "You're the Hatana. Surely you can do as you wish. End all of this."

"It's not that simple. Hatana is simply a title. The real power currently resides elsewhere."

"Then how can you keep her safe?" Her eyes sparked with a renewed fire.

"By staying away from her until we reach the end of this." I waved at Timoti again. "You need to go as well, and have faith in Atua's plan."

Harper stood. "For Eleena's sake, I hope Atua is with you. If not, we're all lost."

47

SCHIRRA'S THREAT: ELEENA

The auditorium was decorated in deep reds. Several rows of chairs on a sloping floor faced a stage. The women that arrived before me sat scattered around the room. I found Ulla toward the front.

"Hey." I sat beside her.

"Do you think one of us could marry the Hatana?" Ulla leaned back in the seat, scrunched down, and rested her head on the back.

"No. One of the soldiers said some man named Schirra would never let it happen."

We sat quietly until the last of the women took seats. The silence taught me all I needed to know about Ulla. She was a lot like Harper. Strong, practical. She wouldn't waste time and energy worrying about what she couldn't change. It was nice not to have to console each other. Whatever happened would happen.

Everyone quit talking when a tall man in full uniform stomped from a side door and onto the stand. It was hard to tell his age because his head had been shaved. The lights reflected off the smoothness of it. He was in impeccable shape, all muscle. His most noticeable feature was his eyes. Coal black, they burned their way across the room.

The red-headed woman followed him in. She looked pale, wilted. The folder in her hand was slowly being crimped in the corners as she worked it with her fingers. She looked from the man on stage to us and back.

His lip curled. "I am General Schirra. All of you are here because of me in one way or another. And I do not mean that I authorized you to be taken from the refugee camps and brought here. If I'd had my way you would have all died in the filth you left behind.

"I am responsible for the siege of each of your homeworlds. It has been my pleasure to carry out the Hatana's war for him. You are here because I have the power to take away everything you hold dear. Don't forget that."

My stomach lurched and the red-head dropped the folder. She scrambled to pick up the scattered papers while I struggled to keep my food down. He attacked Manawa? Was he there, or did he just order it? It became hard to breathe.

Schirra glared at the woman on stage and continued, "Valeria thought the job she'd been given was real. I do not want you to be under the same delusion. None of you will meet the Hatana. It is not possible for him to marry one of such low birth."

My vision blurred. My head pounded. Ulla reached over and held my hand.

She whispered, "Breathe, Eleena."

The man continued. "Enjoy this luxury while it lasts. Once the Hatana chooses his bride you will officially be under my jurisdiction as war fugitives."

Schirra turned to the red-head and grabbed her by the elbow. He dragged her toward the door, but she dug in her heels.

"Let me go," she hissed.

The man rounded on her. "Defy me, Valeria, and I won't show mercy because of our connection."

Valeria raised her chin. "I am following the Hatana's orders. Would you have me defy him?"

"Yes. Soon you'll have to choose a side." Schirra shoved her, knocking her belongings to the floor once more before stalking out the same door he'd entered.

The slamming of it vibrated across the room. Valeria stood with one hand on her forehead, the other hanging limply by her side. When she turned to face us, she looked confused. Her gaze traveled over the room. She stood straighter, her hands stopped shaking, and the smile from earlier returned.

"I'm sorry for the rough start today. You should go to your quarters." She bent and retrieved the papers, sliding them back into the folder. No one moved. "Please, don't worry. I'll speak with the Hatana, and we'll try this again tomorrow."

Instead of following the man out the door beside the stage, she stepped off and walked up the aisle. I could hear her telling women it would be okay. Slowly, they dispersed.

"What do you think he meant?" My mind churned.

Ulla stared at me. "I thought he was pretty clear. He's going to make our life a living *reinga* as soon as he can."

"No. He told her," I pointed at Valeria as she reached the top of the room, "she'd have to choose between him and the Hatana."

"Oh. I don't know. Come on, Leena." Ulla stood and worked her way to the aisle. "There's no point in staying here."

I followed, my hands still shaking from the anger and fear that surged through me. "We have to do something."

"What? There's nowhere to go but our rooms. I, for one, am ready for a good night's sleep."

"But it's still day."

Ulla chuckled. "Are you always so literal? Come on, at least check out where we're going to be. Rest. Do whatever you want. Do nothing. Who knows how long we have until he gets his hands on us."

She was right. We drifted into the hall with several other women. Five soldiers lined the way encouraging us to go to our own rooms.

"Can we visit with each other?" I asked one of them.

"You are to go to your quarters. General's orders." He didn't bother to look at me.

Ulla's room was across the hall from mine. We waved goodbye and opened our individual doors.

My room was decorated mostly in whites and creams like everything else, but the blanket was the same soft blue as my tunic. A bed rested against the left wall. Three feet from the bed was the right wall. It held a little sink, a shower stall barely big enough for me to fit in, and a toilet. I pushed the button on top of the toilet and was relieved to see it flush. I hadn't had that luxury since Mirimbia.

A tiny window sat on the back wall at shoulder level. After a quick inspection, I confirmed it didn't open, but at least I could look out at the green grass leading up to the palace. It was beautiful, even from the back. I couldn't see the garden courtyard, but the architecture was art itself. The smooth white stone glittered in the sunlight. Balconies with fluttering white curtains made the building feel alive, and decorative boxes overflowing with bright red, purple and yellow flowers broke up the vast white surface. Arches were carved above each window with intricate designs. From this distance and angle, I couldn't tell what those were. Flowers? Symbols?

I turned back to the room. There was nothing to do. No datacom, no books. I didn't have paper or a pen. It seemed the only thing left was to sit on the bed and wait.

For the first time in a month, I found myself completely alone. The silence pressed all around. I studied everything in the room, trying desperately not to think, but it was no use.

Harper was gone.

Iri was dead.

All the fear and pain of the fleet's arrival hit me at once. The memories turned me inside out. Ice flowed through my veins causing me to shiver and gasp for air. My stomach churned and my heart raced. I curled into a ball on the bed, hugging my knees to my chest.

"*Teina*, help me." I couldn't breathe. My vision blurred.

Let it go. Atua whispered. *Give me your fear*.

How? I could feel the acid burning up my throat. I stumbled to the toilet and heaved my lunch. The tears ran down my cheeks as I rinsed my mouth at the sink.

It's okay to cry.

The sob broke free. I collapsed on the bed, holding the pillow tight, and cried for everything I'd lost.

48

REVELATIONS: AMIRAN

I needed a distraction from the barracks. My thoughts had been on Eleena all day, wondering what she was thinking, if she was worried about Harper. It had taken every ounce of discipline not to pull up the video feeds from the intake process. Knowing I could access the mess hall, auditorium, hallways, and even the rooms made keeping my distance harder. To keep from giving in, I moved along in Schirra's game.

"You're dressed up." Timoti entered and set papers down on his desk.

"Yeah, another evening of courting."

"Who is it tonight?"

I dusted off my jacket even though it was impeccable before putting it on. "I pulled some strings and moved Miss Masaki up. It's time I learned how she got passed Schirra."

"These women are vultures. Who knows what she did to get here in the hopes of becoming queen."

"I don't think she's like that. The last two times she spoke to me, it was about the refugees. There's more to her than being one of Schirra's puppets."

"Maybe she just plays the game better than the others. She could be a spy and not a puppet at all."

"Point taken." I slipped a jammer in my pocket and headed to the foyer where we were to meet.

If Corvey was a spy, she played it well. She carried herself like the other ladies, had their manners and occasional cattiness, but there was a depth to her the others lacked. She knew sorrow. She'd lost Manawa like Eleena and I.

Schirra stopped me at the bottom of the stairs. "I see you're finally taking some initiative. Miss Masaki is an excellent choice. Her father is loyal to the empire, and his wealth is unparalleled on Birilu."

I tried not to fist my hands. "Good to know." He grabbed my arm when I tried to move past him. "Is there something else?"

"You don't need the refugees. Let me deal with them." He sneered.

"They stay until I choose my bride. In case you missed the latest intel, two camps surrendered as soon as the first refugees arrived at the palace last week."

"We'd already located both camps. They only surrendered before we hit to avoid death." Schirra dismissed them with a wave of the hand.

"I'm sure many died anyway. Or wish they had." I pulled away. "Now, if you'll excuse me, I mustn't keep the lady waiting."

Corvey stood by a portrait of Hatana Anaru and my mother. It was the only one in the entire palace with my mother in it. I joined her and looked up at my parents.

Corvey pointed to them. "They don't look like a match but look in his eyes. He loved her."

"No." I turned away. "He never loved anyone."

"I think you're wrong, but I won't argue." She followed, leaving the painting behind. "Forget I said anything if you wish."

I nodded and led her through the doors to the courtyard gardens. The gates had already been removed from the refugees' arrival. It was still day out, and the sunlight highlighted the flowers at their best. The warm air was heavy with their scent and the sound of insects. Unfortunately, the gardens did not allow me to forget my mother or Miss Masaki's comment. I slipped my hand into my pocket and switched on the jammer.

"You know the artist is responsible for anything you think you saw in that painting. There was nothing kind about my father." Not that anyone could prove anyway.

Corvey glanced around before whispering. "You don't know everything."

"Care to enlighten me?"

"I, um. I shouldn't have said anything." She picked up her pace, walking to the end of the garden.

"Miss Masaki," I touched her shoulder to get her attention before showing her the jammer. "It's safe."

"It's never safe." She barely whispered.

"True, but if you know something that can help me, I'd appreciate you taking a chance."

"Can we walk toward the barracks?" She looked down the hill, twisting her hands in front of her.

"Sure. Why are you so fascinated with them?"

She didn't speak until we'd moved away from the palace walls. "You know why. I should have been one of them."

We walked slower. "Tell me what happened after you left home."

Corvey took a shaky breath. "Father sent my mother and me to Birilu. He said we would be safe there with mother's cousin." She paused, looked behind us, all around, then finally faced me. "That's where I met your mother."

All the heat drained from my body. The breeze turned cold and my head fuzzy. "What?"

"You know I'm not Masaki's daughter. He is my mother's cousin. When Schirra requested his daughter, she begged not to be sent. She's already engaged. Your mother suggested I come instead." She talked quickly now. "She wanted you to know your father sent her to Birilu to save her life. That's why I think he loved her. He loved you too, but he couldn't let Schirra know."

"Stop." I gripped my head with both hands. Could my doubts about my father have a foundation in truth? And my mother! *Atua, is this true? Is my mother alive?*

Yes.

The whisper almost knocked me to my knees. Warmth returned to my extremities as did awareness of the world around me. My mother lived.

"Hatana? I know there's no reason to believe me, but it's true." Corvey wrapped her arms around her waist, shrinking in on herself.

"I believe you."

"You do?"

"Atua confirms it."

"You hear the voice of Atua?" A tear escaped and trailed down her cheek. "*Teina*, there's hope."

"Is she safe on Birilu?" I asked.

"Yes. You can't visit her or she won't be. We don't think Schirra knows she's there or he wouldn't have asked for one of Masaki's daughters."

"Why? Why did she have to be sent away?" There were so many questions clogging my brain. Could my father have loved her? It seemed impossible.

"You'll have to get the story from her. I just had to tell you." She swallowed and wiped the streak from her face. "And there's something else."

"What?"

"Please don't pick me. I love someone else." The tears spilled again. "He's a good man from my homeworld."

I reached out and squeezed her hand. "Don't worry. I didn't plan on choosing one of Schirra's women simply because they were his."

Corvey laughed and wiped the tears with her sleeve. "I didn't think you would, but I wanted to be sure."

"Corvey, I need to tell you some of the refugee women are also from Manawa."

"Oh!" She clutched my hand so tight, I was surprised by her strength. "Could I see them? Help them in some way?"

"I'm sorry, but no one must know any of you are from Manawa. Schirra has hunted you down with a vengeance. Do you understand?"

"Yes." She stared at the building as we passed it on our way to the river. "Hatana, do you know if—"

"Yes, she did."

Corvey gasped and covered her mouth with one hand. She cried softly. "What happened to her? Is she here now?"

"I can't tell you. It's too dangerous. We have to play this game until the end and the less you know the safer you'll be. The safer she'll be. Can you accept that?"

"Yes." She turned back to the barracks for a moment until I pulled her forward again.

"Good. I may need your help in time."

"Anything."

ALTHOUGH THE EVENING with Corvey passed quickly, it didn't put an end to the need growing inside. I had to see Eleena.

Later that night, I pulled up the files on the refugees. Eleena's room butted against the hillside facing the palace. I resisted pulling up the video feeds. Until I couldn't.

It didn't take long to find the initial room entry. She walked around, looked out the window, then curled up on the bed. After a moment she lunged for the toilet and threw up. I watched her huddle there crying for a long time.

I'm sorry, Eleena. I hated she was alone, sad, scared, and there was nothing I could do about it. Hitting the live button, I hoped to see some of the strength I'd learned to expect from her in the visions.

She sat curled up by the small window. Her face turned up to the sky. Every once in a while she'd wipe away a stray tear, but she no longer sobbed uncontrollably.

"Sir, what are you going to do?" Timoti sat beside me.

"I don't know." I only knew what I wanted to do. Comfort her.

"This is bordering on obsessive." He pointed to the clock. It was after midnight.

"You're right. I should go to her."

"Is that wise?"

Probably not, but how could I explain the energy drawing me to her? "I have to."

As I watched, she left the window and the lights went out. If I wanted to speak with her I needed to hurry.

"Have her brought here. There's no reason to sneak around," Timoti said.

I rubbed the back of my neck. "No one can know I've spoken with her."

Timoti shook his head. "Okay, but you must make it quick. I'll keep watch."

After looking at the barrack blueprints to figure out which window belonged to her, we made our way out of the palace. I counted windows along the length of the building until I reached hers. Timoti stayed several feet behind.

Why did I have to make things complicated? It would have been easy to order her brought to me. Or I could have simply inspected the barracks and met her that way. The truth dawned on me the moment I tapped on her window. I didn't want her to know who I was. Not yet.

Her light glared on. Eleena blinked. I tapped the window again. Her gaze darted my way as she wrapped the blanket around her shoulders.

"Who's there?" She approached cautiously.

Emotions flickered across her face. Fear and curiosity. Her brown eyes sparkled with life. I wondered if she could see me. Would she remember me?

"Eleena?" I kept my voice quiet.

She hesitated, then replied. "Yes?"

"Harper is safe."

Eleena pressed close to the glass. Her eyes filled with tears but they didn't fall. "You promise?"

I leaned farther into the shadows. "Yes. She's been given a place to live."

"Why? That doesn't sound like the Hatana. He doesn't care who he hurts." Her eyes widened and she clapped a hand over her mouth. Her next words came out muffled. "*Teina*, don't tell on me. Harper would be so mad."

I tried not to laugh. She was real, and she had the same impulsive honesty I'd seen in the dreams. It felt like someone had finally opened the windows of my life. First, Corvey told me about my mother, now Eleena was only a few feet away. The joy was tempered with fear. Her honesty would put her in danger.

"Why would Harper be angry?" I asked.

"Because if they knew how much I hated him they'd kill me." She planted her head in her hands. "She always said I was a bad liar."

Eleena hated the Hatana? I never suspected that from any of the dreams. Would she hate me if she knew I was the Hatana? I fidgeted next to the window.

Atua, what should I do?

Talk.

My silence must have made her uncomfortable. She pressed against the window, probably trying to see me better. "Who are you? Why are you here?"

"I wanted to ask you a question."

Her head turned to the side, her chin jutting forward. "If I answer will you tell me your name?"

"Does it matter?"

"Probably not, but will you come closer? Out of the shadows?" Eleena's hand rested against the glass, her nose almost touching the pane.

"Why?"

She let out a frustrated growl. "Forget it." She jumped from the chair she'd been standing on.

"Wait."

She stopped, her back to me. My heart pounded. I couldn't tell her my name, but I didn't want to lie.

"My friends call me Am."

She spun around, running the few steps to the window and hopped back on the chair. "Please, let me see your face." Both hands now pressed into the window.

I moved forward until the light from her window hit my face.

"It's you," she sighed.

I read her lips more than heard the words. She remembered. I placed my palm against hers. Only the glass separated us.

"You can't tell anyone. It isn't safe." All my feelings for her welled up. I wanted to touch her, hold her. But more than that, I needed to protect her. I looked at our hands, squeezing the window between us. Hers was small next to mine.

"Are you real?" Her voice pulled my gaze back to her eyes.

"I didn't know if you'd recognize me. It's been so long."

"How did you know it was me?" Her brow wrinkled.

How could I not know her? I'd memorized every line of her face, every expression over the years.

Tell her. Atua prompted.

"Atua sent dreams." I blurted it out before I could change my mind.

"He did?" A smile filled her face, and I thought the sun had risen. "Captain E said you could hear Atua, but I never thought he'd send you dreams. I should have known. He sent me dreams too." The wrinkle reappeared. "It scared me all those years you wore a fleet uniform."

"Sir," Timoti whispered from nearby. "The guards will be doing rounds in five minutes."

"Thanks," I answered him, then turned back to Eleena. "I can't stay. I'll tell you about the fleet another time. Are they treating you well?"

"They fed us, gave us clean clothes." She pointed at the bed, "I haven't slept on anything so nice in a long time. I'm just not used to being alone."

"Is that why you're sad?" I knew it had more to do with Harper and Iri than loneliness, but I wanted her to confide in me.

"No, but it helps to know Harper's alright. I wish I could be with her. I wish Iri was with her. I wish I hadn't seen the things I've seen, better yet, that they'd never happened. I wish I could choose for myself what I do, where I go, and who I spend my time with." She placed her other hand against the glass. "Most of all, I'm tired of wishing. Wishing and pretending."

"What are you pretending, Eleena?" I lined both my hands up with hers.

She choked on a sob. "To be happy because everyone needs me to be the strong one. Pretending that I know what to do. Why do they all think I should know? I'm stuck in the same situation they are. Why did the Hatana take everything away?"

"I don't have the answers. The more I learn, the more questions I have. All I can do is hope Atua has a bigger plan. One I can't see yet, but that will lead us to something better."

Eleena swiped at her eyes but put her hand right back beside mine, curling her fingers as if she could get through the glass to entwine them with mine.

"Me too. Thanks for letting me talk. I think I needed to get it out of my system."

"Sir!" Timoti hissed.

I nodded. "I have to go. Remember, don't tell anyone you saw me." I pushed away from the window, then bent down one more time. "Keep the faith."

"I will. Be careful, Am." She returned to the bed and flicked off the light, disappearing into the darkness.

"Good night, Eleena." I wanted to stay, instead, I hurried to Timoti. "Thanks for the warning."

"Did you ask her about Ev?" He led the way up the hill toward the palace.

"No."

Timoti glanced at me. "I thought that was the purpose of this visit."

"You can ask when you see her tomorrow."

"Why will I see her?" he asked.

"Because I forgot to tell her not to reveal her home planet. I need you to do that for me. While you're there, you can get information about Ev."

Atua, how will I keep her safe?

Go to Olea. Bring your men to Rawiri.

I almost stumbled on the path and gripped Timoti's arm. It was the clearest message Atua had given. My heart beat a steady march.

"What is it?" he asked.

"Atua says it's time. I'm to go to Olea."

"You can't risk it."

"It's Atua's will."

Timoti squeezed my arm. "I'm going to lose you both."

"We have to trust Atua's hand will save us." I knew Timoti was scared, but we needed to move forward. "You know how bad the fleet years were for me. I hated following Schirra's orders. Memories are branded in my mind. So many people that didn't deserve to die. Do you know how many times a day I wished Schirra had killed me instead?"

"I try not to think about what you lived through. You're not that kind of person, and…"

"And what? I chose my life over theirs. That's what it comes down to. I'm sick of pretending." Just like Eleena. "We have to do our part, and it's time."

"How will you get away without a tail?" Timoti's brow furrowed.

"I've got a plan."

"What if it brings Schirra down on the entire operation?"

I sighed. Usually, he had more faith than this. "Timoti, I need your faith."

Tears filled his eyes. "May the heavens be with us."

49

DAY 2: ELEENA

I t was hard to fall asleep after Am left. I snuggled deeper into the blanket, thinking about him. His voice had a lovely warmth to it that was even better than my memory. And his eyes. They hadn't looked haunted or cold, although near the end he'd been nervous. Did the Hatana's soldiers have things to fear?

Of course, he hadn't been wearing the fleet uniform. He'd been dressed nice, making me wonder what he did around the palace. I rolled over with a sigh. Maybe it had been a dream after all. If so, it was the best one I'd had yet.

I liked the way he'd placed his hand next to mine. They were good hands, and I imagined they would have been warm if I could have touched them.

He looked at me the way Iri looked at Harper.

The way Iri used to look at Harper.

"I'm sorry, Harper," I whispered as sleep finally claimed me.

A ringing bell and full bladder woke me the next morning. After taking care of business, I washed my hands and face. There was a little mirror above the sink. My skin looked pale after weeks on the ship, but there were no dark smudges under my eyes. Sleeping in a soft bed agreed with me.

My tunic was wrinkled and my hair had been smashed every which way.

Ug! I'm so ugly without long hair.

Of course, I didn't know what I looked like with it long. We didn't have mirrors in camp. Those things weren't important. I dipped my head under the faucet and wet my hair. It dripped water on my shoulders, but I was able to comb my fingers through it and slick it back. Gross.

The door opened and a woman with a cart stood there. She handed me a covered tray with my name on it before moving to the next door. I sat on the floor with my back against the bed and uncovered the tray. Fluffy eggs, shredded potatoes, and meat patties steamed on a plate. There was a little carton of fruit juice and a small cup with two pills in it.

The smell of the food sent my stomach tumbling. It acted as if it could gobble up the food without waiting for my mouth to do the work. I knew it was a good sign to be hungry. Still, I did my best to eat slowly and enjoy it. I was only able to eat half of it.

When I finished, I stared at the pills for a long time. What were they for? In the end, I took the cup and set it on the sink—pills untaken. Maybe I'd get a chance to ask someone about them.

Another bell sounded and the door opened again. No one stood outside, but a voice came through a speaker in my ceiling.

"Return to the auditorium."

Ulla met me in the hall.

"How did you sleep?" I asked.

"It took a while, but really good once I allowed myself to do it," she answered.

"Same here. It was hard to sit still after not working all day. You'd think we'd be used to it after the trip here." I didn't mention Am's visit.

"Yeah, but we were on constant alert on the ship." She grabbed seats in the middle this time. "This place has me so confused. It's wonderful, but how can it be? Schirra told us this is all for nothing."

"Part of me says to enjoy it, and the other part thinks this will be another twisted form of torture."

"What do you mean?" she asked

"When they take it all away. Can you imagine going back to camp after this? It'll make whatever comes next all that more horrible."

Ulla's eyes rounded.

"I'm sorry, I shouldn't have said that." I reached for her hand.

"It's okay. Do you wish we'd died there with the others?"

"No." And I didn't. Especially now. I pushed away the happiness that bubbled inside. Am might be close, but I was still a prisoner. There was little chance we'd get to visit with each other, much less anything else.

Ulla's next question brought me back to reality. "Do you believe Atua accepted them home?"

"Yes." I didn't hesitate. "I think he welcomes everyone back. We are his."

"I wish I believed the way you do, but why would he let the Hatana conquer and destroy so many worlds?" She whispered the last, frantically checking the room for soldiers.

"I don't think he let him. The Hatana just did it. We get to make our own choices. Atua won't force us to do his will."

Ulla nodded.

The red-head,Valeria, entered the room from the same side door she had before. Schirra wasn't with her and we all sighed in relief. She looked more comfortable today. Her hair was swept up and rolled in a twist. She wore a pale yellow tunic with tiny pink flowers on it.

"Good morning, I hope you slept well and enjoyed your breakfast. We will serve meals in your rooms until all vitamin deficiencies are corrected. Then you will be allowed to eat in the common mess hall upstairs. Please take the supplements provided with each meal." She tapped a spot on the floor and a podium rose in front of her. After setting her binder on it she looked over the hall. "I know this has been strange. General Schirra made a hard situation worse with his threats."

Valeria stepped off the stage, closer to the front row. "We are not all like him. Many of us know how wrong this war is. However, we are at the mercy of our own military. And that is led by Schirra, the late Hatana Anaru's general."

Late? The Hatana was dead? Then why were we here? If there were people who knew the war was wrong, why was it still raging across our galaxy?

"You probably didn't know Anaru died six months ago. His son is now the Hatana. He is the one responsible for your presence here in spite of what the general would have you believe. Hatana Amiran is the people's ruler and will protect you."

A chill ran down my back and goosebumps rose on my arms. The new Hatana was named Amiran? It was a common name. One often shortened to Am.

Atua? There was no answer, no feeling one way or the other. Instead, memories of things Captain E had said surfaced in my mind. Because of who he is…fighting for us the best he can…a great man.

Teina, could it be?

Valeria continued, "Over the next week, we will assess your level of education and create individualized programs to provide you with the education you need to re-enter society. You will be provided with clothing, food, and anything else you desire, within reason. Sadly, we can not set you free yet. As you saw yesterday, there are many like Schirra who would do you harm. You are safer here than out there."

I immediately thought of Harper. Am promised she was safe, but was she? If he was the Hatana, she might be in more danger now than before. Especially if he was fighting against a man like Schirra. Another shiver had me gripping the arms of my seat.

Valeria wrapped up her speech, "If you have questions, feel free to ask during your testing. Someone will come for you when it's your turn. Until then, enjoy the safety of your rooms."

She looked pleased with herself. Did she have any idea how crazy we would go with nothing to do? Especially now that I had questions I couldn't ask for fear of exposing him. Maybe there was another way to gather the information.

"Excuse me." I stood and tried to get Valeria's attention. "Can we have access to datacoms?"

She paused by the door. "After you've been tested you will receive datacoms with your educational programs installed."

And she was gone.

"Eleena, come on. The others are leaving." Ulla tugged at my arm.

"Ulla, I'll go nuts with nothing to do, no way to learn about this place and the world we've been dropped into."

She rubbed her arm up and down my back. "Maybe you'll be lucky and get tested today?"

"One can hope."

50

HARPER: AMIRAN

I went through the motions of my day, but it was hard to concentrate on anything. Schirra's top ten wife choices joined me for breakfast. They chattered and asked questions, barely touching their food. Even though they'd been in the palace for almost two months, I didn't know any of their names other than Corvey. They were all the same. And completely different from Eleena.

When breakfast ended, I had an hour before the first court session. I retrieved my holoprojector and left the palace grounds under disguise. Timoti had set Harper up in a row of houses a couple streets over. The servant I'd assigned to watch over her opened the door.

"May I help you?" she asked.

"Yes, I'd like to visit with your charge." I passed her a slip of paper with the Hatana's seal on it. She glanced down, then let me pass. "How is she doing?"

"Physically, she'll be fine with time, but emotionally she's despondent." The woman waved to a chair. "Wait here and I'll get her."

The apartment was devoid of any personality. It didn't look like a good place to begin a new life. Harper shuffled in. She was clean, but dark circles highlighted her eyes.

I stood. "Harper, please, sit."

"Who are you, and what do you want?" She didn't glare, but it was clear she didn't appreciate the company.

I turned off the holoprojector.

"Hatana." The woman gasped and folded herself into a bow of submission.

"Clever." Harper's eyes narrowed.

I ignored her for the moment and turned to the servant. "Please, don't. Can I trust you?"

She nodded her head. "Yes, sir."

"Good. You must never tell anyone I was here."

"Can I ask a favor in return?" Her hands trembled, but she kept eye contact. She didn't look like the kind to threaten me, so I nodded as well. "My son, he's been conscripted to the fleet."

Understanding dawned immediately. "How long?"

"It's been two years with no word."

I paced. Two years might have been enough time for him to become a follower of Schirra. But maybe not. "I'll look into it. If I can get him reassigned to Rawiri, I will."

"Thank you." She clasped her hands in front of her and did a little bounce that made her appear years younger. "I'll give you some privacy. Miss, if you need me, I'll be in the back room." With that said, she left us.

"Please, have a seat." I pointed to the couch.

"Are you going to visit every day?" she asked.

"No. I spoke to Eleena last night."

Harper jumped up, her lips pressed into a tight line. "You said you'd stay away from her. She can't lie to save her life."

I couldn't help it, I laughed. "The first thing she told me was she hated the Hatana and you'd be mad at her for saying it."

"This isn't funny."

She was right.

"She doesn't know I'm the Hatana, but she recognized me."

"From her dreams." Harper paced.

"You knew about the dreams? Please sit down." I waited until she sat. "I'd like you to tell me what you know, but first, Atua sent me dreams too. I watched her grow up over the years. I feel like I know her."

Harper squinted at me then sunk into the couch, covering her face with her hands. "*Teina*, you're in love with her."

Her shoulders shook, but I couldn't tell if she was laughing or crying.

"Would that be so bad?" I asked.

She jerked up and her gaze was like daggers. "Yes. You'll get her killed."

"Help me protect her then. It's time to end this war."

A tear did escape this time. "What are you going to do?"

"First, I need to know what happened to Ev. We haven't been able to communicate with him."

"Ev? Captain Evander?" she asked.

"Yes. I need to know what happened when the fleet arrived."

Harper sunk into the couch and closed her eyes. She'd turned pale again. "I can't tell you everything. It's too horrible to speak aloud."

"Give me a brief recap."

"Okay." She took a deep breath but didn't open her eyes. "We were waiting for a meeting in the mess hall because we'd struck celestium the night before. Things were finally looking up, you know? Captain E had taken care of the troublemakers, and we were going to get the ships back in the air. Then Iri got some kind of message on his bracelet."

Troublemakers? My curiosity wanted to know everything, but it didn't matter anymore so I kept quiet. "What did Iri do?"

"He told us we had to get out. Get to the captain." she placed her hand over her face a moment. Then she sat up and glared at me. "They killed him you know. No questions asked. Just cut him down."

"I'm sorry, truly I am." I tried to keep her focused. "Where was Ev?"

"I don't know. Iri said he would hide from the fleet, somewhere with a way to escape. Said there were things more important than us."

I stood and paced. "So, you didn't see him during the attack?" She shook her head.

"Did you try to reach Evander?"

"That's where Iri wanted to go, but Eleena said Atua wanted us to go to the river. But," she paused again, twisting her hands in her lap. "Iri and I couldn't swim. He didn't jump in, not that it would have mattered."

"How did you get caught?"

"The soldiers came in after us. I don't really remember getting caught. Just them saying they tossed the body in the river. They implied that's what the Hatana prescribed for rebel boys."

"Please believe me that I never wanted this." It made me sick, and saying sorry didn't feel like enough.

"Why would Atua let him die?" she asked as if I had the answer.

"Why would he let Schirra destroy an entire planet?" I countered.

Harper shuddered before taking a deep breath. "Eleena says he didn't. That men do what they want, but there has to be some justice."

"Maybe there is in the next life? I don't claim to understand it, but I know Atua doesn't like the suffering."

"Do you know what they did to the women?" She started to shake.

Ice moved through my veins. I knew the depravity Schirra allowed his men to get away with. How many times had I tried to stop it and failed?

"I've never sanctioned such acts. I'll do all I can to bring them to justice once Schirra is out of the way."

She stared at me, both of us knowing words were cheap. Both knowing nothing would erase what had been done.

Finally, she turned away. "Keep Eleena safe. Whatever your plans are, don't let her get caught up in them."

I wanted to make that promise, but something held me back. Eleena was important. Atua had shared her life with me, protected her, and brought her to me. She was already part of everything I did.

"Harper, I have to leave Rawiri. I want you to come with me. You'll go as a maidservant to a woman who is visiting. I have to say I'm going to marry her in order for all of us to leave safely. Can you go along with this?"

"I'll need to know more before I can answer that."

"You will, but I can't tell you until after we leave."

Harper sat quietly, her eyes closed. Then she nodded. "Okay. You can count on me."

I stood to leave. "Timoti will come for you tonight or tomorrow and set you up in the servants quarters. He'll have papers with a new identity, so you can't tell anyone you were a refugee, or that you've ever been to Manawa. Understand?"

"Yes. Will I see Eleena?"

"Not until we return. It's safer for her that way."

"Can you stay away from her until then?" she studied my face.

"I have to."

51

ASSESSMENTS: ELEENA

I dozed most of the day. My body ached from sitting for so long, and my mind felt numb. Every once in a while I'd stand and swing my arms around. Or I'd sit and stretch in the small floor space. Pacing became the main pastime, with intermittent napping. I tried leaving my room to sit with Ulla, but the door remained locked.

A couple of hours after lunch I'd had enough. I decided to bang on the door until someone let me out, but it opened before I started. A man with gray hair and blue eyes stood only a few inches taller than me. Something about him looked familiar, but I couldn't place him.

"Eleena from Kahu?" He stood relaxed. In fact, he didn't try to intimidate me at all. He wasn't dressed in a uniform, but a simple black and gray tunic.

"Yes?"

"My name is Timoti and I'll be assessing you today. Come with me, please." He moved to the side and waited for me to leave the room.

Thank Atua!

I hurried through the door and followed him to the stairwell I'd come down the day before. We climbed the flights of stairs. I was grateful for the activity even though my thighs burned by the time we reached the top. The older man didn't look troubled at all by the exercise. A month of sitting on Meir's ship had made me soft.

Timoti entered a room and closed the door behind me. "Please have a seat. I have a few questions before you start the exam."

I sat. He took the seat across from me and pulled out a square box. After flipping some switches he set it on the table between us.

"Now, it will be safe to talk. Am sent me to make sure you have everything you need." He leaned forward and smiled.

"Is that a jammer?" I asked, my mind focusing on the fact Am sent someone to me. He couldn't be just a soldier.

"Yes. The guards see the amplifier, but I've hidden a jammer within. We won't have a lot of time though."

"Sure." *Atua, can I ask him about Am?*

Timoti nodded his head. "First, you must never tell anyone where you are from. Your life will be in great danger if you do."

"Why?" I swallowed the lump that had grown in my throat. There was no answer from Atua.

"No time to explain, but trust me." His steady gaze moved over my face. "There are only moments before I have to turn this off. You were part of Evander's camp, do you know if he was killed by the fleet?"

I stared at the man and recognized an older version of Evander's eyes, the dimple in the chin. "Are you related?"

"Please, what do you know?" He glanced at the cube screen.

"Nothing. By the time the soldiers brought me back to camp there were no men left. I didn't see him at all." I watched his face fall. He had to be family. "Iri said Evander would hide." Even though the thought still gave me pain, I knew it might give this man hope.

Timoti nodded. "Thank you. Am said my son is alive, but I hoped you would know for sure."

His son. Am and Evander's father worked at the Hatana's palace.

"Now," he touched a button on the jammer and handed me a tablet. "Use this datacom and start the test that pops up. When you're finished, another staff member will take you back to your room."

He stood to leave. I wanted to ask him if Am was the Hatana.

"Wait." I stood, but he shook his head at me, then pointed around the room and back to his ear.

"Start the test." He quickly ducked out the door, taking all the air with him.

It was a revelation that I hated being alone. The walls pressed close, even though sunlight drifted through a window. The palace wasn't in view from this side of the building. Instead, I looked down a long meadow toward a line of trees.

I sat and turned on the datacom. There was no way to turn off the test screen and access news or historical databases without a passcode. I couldn't look up any records about the current Hatana.

"Arrg!" I fought the urge to throw the datacom. "Take the test."

Two hours later I reached the end. Testing my knowledge of literature, mathematics, physics, astronomy, and history had stimulated my mind and distracted me from my questions. As soon as I set the datacom on the table, Valeria entered the room. Her hair had fallen from its twist and was now in a ponytail.

"You did amazing! No one else has reached the end. The program was tested to its limits. Tell me, where are you from? Derritus? Mirimbia? Maybe Cortiva? They were the last conquests, and your level of education could only be explained by attending the university."

I shook my head, wondering how to answer. "No, I've not been to those planets recently."

"Then how did you score so high?"

"I don't know?" I shrugged. "Maybe it's because we had school in our camp. When I finished I became a teacher. It made it easy to continue learning."

"A teacher? Schools in refugee camps? I never knew, but that explains it I guess. Well, we won't have much to offer you in the way of education. We thought we'd be bringing you up to a level where you could hold down an entry-level job."

"But there's so much more I could learn. Surely there's something I can study? It's been at least two years since we updated the school databases." I'd be bored to death in that room without something to do.

"Why would you need more education than you have?"

"What will I do? Can I teach some of the others?"

"I don't think that would be allowed. Just relax…" Her eyes popped open wide as I jumped up and slapped the table.

"Why does everyone keep telling me to relax?" I yelled and paced behind my side of the table. "I've had to work to survive for years. Sitting still with nothing to do is driving me crazy."

"Calm down, please have a seat." She waved her hand at the chair I'd vacated. "I didn't think of this. We didn't think of this. You're bored? You want to work?"

"Work, read, study. Something, anything. You have to understand

I've not even been alone for a long time. When you live in camp you're always surrounded by people. Having my own room is strange. Lonely. Not having a purpose is even worse." I reluctantly sat down. "Are the other women having trouble with this?"

"Not that I've noticed, but maybe they're too scared to say something. I'll check with the Hatana and see what we can do." She took the datacom off the table and swiped and typed until she was satisfied. "I've put my entire reading library on this so you'll have something to do."

"Thank you. What about local news?"

"I'll have to ask about that."

"History or other college-level classes?" I changed tactics.

"There may be some things in the database." Her brow wrinkled as if trying to remember, then she shook her head as she gave up.

"Can I ask another question?"

"Of course." She handed me the datacom.

"How long will we be here?"

"I don't know. You'll have to stay until the Hatana chooses a bride. After that, we'll try and find jobs and homes for you in cities around the planet. You'll have security requirements placed on you for the first few years, but eventually, you'll be free to live a normal life."

"That's not what Schirra said." I met her gaze head-on. Backing down was not an option. Plus, being outspoken had gained access to a datacom.

Valeria paled. "Hopefully, Schirra won't…" She swallowed. "Well, you need to get back to your room. We need this one for the next test. I'll lead you back."

52

VALERIA: AMIRAN

Two days after visiting with Harper, I slipped away to meet Valeria in one of the smaller conference rooms in the basement of the palace. The jammer was set up, and I had one of my guys watching the security feeds.

"Anyone see you?" I asked.

"I don't think so, but I shouldn't stay long." She brushed a lock of hair from her forehead and pulled a thumb drive from a pocket. "I've put a more detailed report on here."

"Thanks. Give me your first impressions."

"Most of the women are scared. Schirra's visit didn't help."

"I'm sure. I'll try to keep him away."

Valeria twisted her hands in front of her. "The women are responding well to the educational materials. We can help a lot of them, but there were several with high scores. All from Kahu."

"Good." I slid the drive into my pocket, smiled, and changed the subject. "I read the health report. Looks like most suffered from malnutrition but not much else."

"Yes. In a couple more days they will be able to eat in the community mess hall." Valeria paced in front of me.

"What's bothering you?"

"These women from Kahu. One of them." She paused and sunk into a chair. "There's at least one that we couldn't help because she's got the equivalent of a university education. She's miserable. Lonely. Bored."

"What's her name?" I asked though I already knew.

"Eleena."

I'd avoided the barracks as fastidiously as I had Schirra's women that first month, but Eleena had often been in my thoughts. I hated knowing she wasn't happy.

"Can't we find something for her?" I asked.

"I gave her a datacom with my personal library on it. I'm ashamed I assumed they'd all be uneducated, but none of the recently conquered planets had the level of education she has. That's why it was so easy for Schirra to enslave them."

"Valeria, we have to keep this quiet. I understand your concerns, but it's important others don't seek the answer to your question." I grabbed both of her hands and gave them a squeeze. "Do you understand?"

She nodded slowly. "You know more than you're telling me?"

"Yes."

"Will you tell me?"

"Valeria, when it's safe, everyone will know. But I promise to tell you first."

"Okay." She pulled her hands free and picked up her things. "I'd better get back before Schirra notices I'm gone."

"Thank you for everything. Do what you can for them, but be careful. We both know Schirra won't spare you if he deems you a threat."

"Blood means nothing to him unless spilt." She turned away, probably hoping I couldn't see her sadness.

"I wish life had been different."

Valeria shrugged. "We can't change it. Just end this before he decides to marry *me* off." She shuddered. "I'll go to the mines before I marry someone he chooses."

"I don't recommend them."

She laughed but it didn't reach her eyes. "Of course not. At least he's preoccupied with you for the moment."

"Go. Thanks for this." I held up the drive.

"No problem." She didn't step through the door. I could see the indecision on her face. "Have you heard from him?"

"No, but he's alive."

"You're sure?"

I nodded. "Yes."

Her posture relaxed. "Thanks."

"Valeria, it's time. I'm leaving to retrieve Ev and the rest of my men as soon as I can."

The color drained from her face. She swallowed then nodded. "Good."

"I wish I could take you, but I need you here. Your father would wonder."

"I know." She glanced at her hands, spinning a ring around one of her fingers. "One way or another, we'll soon know the outcome of all our hopes." Valeria squared her shoulders. "Good journey, Am."

"Atua be with you, Valeria."

53

GOODBYE AGAIN: ELEENA

The days passed more quickly after I received the datacom. It didn't connect to the nets, so I hadn't been able to look up anything on the Hatana, but it had older photos of the royal family. Those pictures were almost twenty years old. Hatana Anaru stood beside a beautiful woman, his hand resting on the shoulder of a little boy of five or six years. The boy had lighter colored hair than Am. But the woman, and the little boy, had the same blue-gray eyes that he did. I wasn't sure, but my Am might be the Hatana.

Atua didn't confirm or deny. It made me antsy, but I couldn't decide if it was curiosity or fear. What would it mean if the man I'd fallen in love with over the years was the Hatana?

I tried to push the questions away and study to my heart's content, often staying up late into the night. Four days after being tested, I sat next to the window trying to see the stars. My room was dark except for the glow of the datacom in my lap.

A shadow moved outside, drawing my attention back to earth. The person kept to the hill. I guessed they were avoiding the palace lights in the background. I watched carefully, hoping it was Am coming to visit. Eventually, the shadow drew near my window and sat down.

"You're up late tonight," Am said.

He was here. All the pent-up energy, all the unanswered questions, everything I'd tried to lock away the last few days melted away. None of it mattered. Whoever he was, whatever happened, I loved him. I knew that with such clarity tears pricked my eyes.

"Eleena, what's wrong?"

"Nothing."

"Talk to me?" His brow creased as he leaned closer.

I needed a moment to find my words, so I turned off the datacom shifting us into darkness. It felt more intimate than when we'd spoken with the lights on. Perhaps it was because I'd finally admitted my feelings were more than a crush.

My continued silence must have concerned him because he rested his hand against the glass, his long fingers slightly curled, when he spoke again. "Please, are you alright?"

"Yes, I'm sorry to worry you. I," How to explain? "I just realized something, and it took me by surprise is all."

"Oh? Something good, or bad?"

I moved to my knees on the chair so I could place my hand next to his on the glass. "Good, but I have so many questions."

"I wish I could tell you everything, but I can't. Not yet." There was a note of desperation in his voice.

"I understand, really I do. How's Harper?"

"She's upset with me for visiting you."

I rested my head against the glass. Am really did have a nice voice. "Why is she mad?"

"She's afraid I'm putting you in danger, and she's right."

"I don't care." I'd rather he came to talk than stay away. I'd missed him the last few days.

"You should. Eleena, I wish you didn't have to stay in there." He ran his hands through his hair, making it stick up in the back. "Is it crazy that I feel like I've known you all my life?"

"No. You've known me a long time." There were so many things I wanted to say, but I changed the subject instead. "Is she alone?"

"Harper? There's someone with her, helping her adjust, and making sure she eats."

"That's good." I sighed, frustration welling up again.

"Eleena, I have to leave. When I come back," he paused, taking a deep breath, "things are going to change."

My heart rate sped up. "Where are you going?"

"I can't tell you, but will you pray for me?"

"I always do."

"Eleena, I…" He stopped and shook his head.

"I know."

Am rested his forehead against the glass and closed his eyes.

When he opened them, I could barely see them in the darkness. "Will you wish me peace?"

I leaned close. My gaze never left his. "Peace on your path, Amiran."

"Burn a light to guide me home, Eleena." He placed his hands on the glass and I matched both of them with mine.

For the first time in my life, I gazed into a man's eyes and felt an unspoken promise pass between us. It thrilled and scared me. He was real this time, but I could lose him as easily as Harper lost Iri.

Am pushed from the window and hurried toward the palace. Only then did I realize I had spoken his full name and he hadn't denied it. It didn't confirm he was the Hatana, but I was almost certain my Am carried a weight too heavy for anyone else.

54

LEAVING RAWIRI: AMIRAN

E leena called me Amiran. Did she know? I didn't dare ask, and it didn't matter. I'd seen the love in her eyes, heard her unspoken words with my heart. Every choice from here on out mattered more than anything else.

Corvey and I put on a show for Schirra until we boarded her glorywinger. We paraded through the streets of the city on our way to the spaceport, waving and smiling. Schirra watched our every move. Luckily we didn't have to act like we loved each other. He knew it was a marriage of convenience. A marriage to strengthen the empire and nothing more.

I didn't relax until we left orbit. Harper sat in the dining room with Corvey until my men finished sweeping the ship for amplifiers and recording devices. They found none, but we kept the jammers on just in case.

"I haven't been on a glorywinger since I left Manawa." I allowed myself to remember that dark day.

Harper patted my arm. "You did a lot of good before you left. If nothing else, I'll always be grateful to you for putting Eleena on Evander's ship. Without her, I'd be a different person."

"My Eleena?" Corvey grabbed Harper's free hand, her gaze jumping to me.

I answered, "I told you she made it off."

Harper stared at the other woman. "You know Leena?"

"We were best friends in school," Corvey nodded, "before the first evacuation."

"You're from Manawa?" Harper asked.

"Yes." Corvey turned to me. "Will you tell me where they are?"

"Who?" I asked.

"The Talrano's. Maybe they can meet us at Masaki's."

I saw Harper squeeze Corvey's shoulders tighter, but she let me clear things up. "Only Eleena made it off Manawa."

"She's been alone all this time?" More tears fell.

"No, Harper's been with her. She's had friends, people who loved her." I knew this to be true but felt the old sorrow that she'd lost her parents.

Harper glanced at me. "Does she know?"

"About what?" I asked.

Harper nodded toward Corvey. "How you feel about Eleena?"

Corvey's gaze shot toward me. "What?"

The small room became unbearably warm. "I haven't spoken of it to anyone. Only you have guessed. And Eleena."

"You saw her again?" Harper left Corvey's side. "You promised you wouldn't."

"Only to say goodbye for a few moments last night. She's lonely."

"Amiran," Harper clamped her lips shut and turned away. "You're gone now. That's probably the only way you can keep her safe."

Corvey interrupted, "She's in the barracks isn't she?"

"Yes."

Harper paced, brooding.

Corvey's brow furrowed. "How did it happen? You served in the fleet, and she would have been in a refugee camp."

I sighed. Everyone would want to know how it had happened. *And you will tell it many times.* I could almost hear laughter in Atua's voice.

"It's a long story," I said.

"It's a long trip." Corvey looked me in the eye.

Harper returned to her seat at the table. "I'd like to hear your side of it. Eleena used to talk about you a lot, but as she grew older she kept things closer to her heart. I suspect she talked less as her feelings deepened."

"I don't feel right talking about it when I haven't had more than five minutes to talk to Eleena. Please, be patient. After Birilu and Olea. If we put an end to Schirra's stranglehold on the empire, I'll satisfy both of your curiosity. But only after I've had the chance to tell Eleena once and for all how I feel for her first."

The women looked at each other, but it was Harper who spoke. "We can live with this."

Corvey stood. "I'm glad it's only a couple days to Birilu. Until then, I'm going to rest. Your mother will be happy to see you, Amiran."

My mother. I'd almost forgotten.

55

SIEGE: ELEENA

Although nothing in my daily routine changed, I knew when Am left. There was an emptiness that hadn't been there before. It happened late in the afternoon the day after he'd said goodbye.

I couldn't study. My mind didn't want to focus on anything other than thoughts of him.

"Snap out of it!" I had to stop. There was nothing I could do to change my life or his. Thinking about him would only make me lonelier.

I grabbed the datacom and browsed the fiction novels. I'd not had the luxury of a good story since leaving Mirimbia. Valeria had a taste for romance and suspense. Not helpful in my situation. I lived in constant suspense and I couldn't completely believe the stories of happily ever after. No matter how much I wanted to.

The day finally ended and I fell into a fitful sleep, waking just as tired and emotionally frantic as the day before.

I didn't feel hungry, but my stomach turned and clenched making me even more uncomfortable. I spent the day alternating between pacing, reading, and lying curled up on my bed.

Two days after Am left, the door to my room clicked open at breakfast time, but no one entered. I set the datacom down and tentatively pushed against the door. Ulla stood across the hall peeking at me from her room.

"Another meeting?" she asked.

"We haven't eaten." I felt hungry again, but the strange twisting of my stomach came and went.

The speakers popped. Valeria's voice came through next. "Ladies, if your door is unlocked it means your vitamin deficiencies are well in hand. You are free to go to the third floor and dine in the cafeteria."

"Finally." Ulla swung her door wide and stepped into the hall. "Even with things to study, it's far too quiet around here."

Relief flooded through me and I blinked away a few stupid tears as we headed up the stairs. It felt good to move. "They should really let us out to exercise. My muscles are going flabby."

Ulla laughed. "It looks good on you. Your face isn't so skinny anymore and you're developing breasts."

I glanced down. My tunic did fit more snugly across my chest and along my hips. It had only been a week and a half. What kind of vitamins were they giving us?

The question unnerved me, and I changed the subject. "What are you studying?"

"They've got me doing a refresher course in mathematics. It's so boring. I spend most of my time trying to hack the datacom to connect to the nets."

This time I laughed. We moved through a line where they handed us a tray and utensils. Then we could choose different food items. There were several things I didn't recognize. I chose fruit, eggs, and then I froze in place.

"Is that *taro nui?*" My mom used to make it as a special treat on my birthday.

"I don't know what that is." Ulla shrugged, but took a piece of the bread-like dish smothered in berries, sugar syrup, and whipped topping. "It looks good though."

I took one as well but struggled to accept this was my new life. Even though I was still trapped, there was *taro nui*. And books. Hot water, flushing toilets, and when I was lucky, Am.

"Eleena, let's sit over there." Ulla pointed and I followed lost in confusion.

How could I feel happy when I knew how many others had been tortured and killed? It didn't make sense, but I did. I was so grateful I felt close to tears.

"Are you okay?" Ulla stared at me.

"Yeah. Sorry, I've been overly emotional the last two days. It's probably connected to this stomach bug." I took a bite of the *taro nui* and let the tears stream down my face. It was wonderful. Sweet and comforting, exactly the way I remembered mother making it.

"Eleena, you should see the doctor. You've never been like this, and I don't know how you would have caught anything. Maybe they've messed up your pills." Ulla touched my elbow.

Tryla sat beside us. She pointed her spoon at me.

"You feeling strange mood swings? Crying a lot?" she asked me.

"Yeah." I cut my eyes toward Ulla.

"You ever had your cycle before?" Tryla continued to stare at me but didn't wait for an answer. "I bet now your body is healthy things are working the way they're supposed to."

"Oh." I hadn't thought of that. Surely, it would take longer for my body to change that much?

"You should—" Her words were cut short by a series of whistles.

Valeria and several other women ran into the room as the last shrill sounds faded away.

"To your rooms! Schirra's coming with soldiers!" We stared at each other, none of us moving until she yelled again. "He'll take you away if I don't lock you in for your protection. Go!"

The cafeteria became a mass of movement. Trays clattered to the ground. Women rushed to the exits. Ulla clung to my arm as we fought our way to the center stairs. We crammed inside with everyone else. Traffic bottlenecked as too many people tried to squeeze through at once.

"Leena!" Ulla struggled to keep from being pulled away from me.

Our hall was just as crowded. Women waved their arms in front of their doors to get them to open. We shoved our way to my door, and it felt like an eternity for the biosensor to recognize me and open. Ulla hovered behind me, but I stopped before she could get all the way in. Soldiers ran past my window.

"*Teina*, they've got guns," I almost sobbed. When would it end?

Ulla leaned into me. "We've got to get in so the door will lock."

A soldier veered toward the window. He looked straight at us then fired at the glass.

It cracked.

I screamed.

He kept firing until the window shattered.

I shoved Ulla backward and the door closed again. "What do we do?"

"My room doesn't have a window!" Ulla grabbed my arm and dragged me across the hall.

The sound of more windows breaking filled the air. Women screamed, but doors didn't open.

"Atua save us!" Ulla pulled me into her room. The lock clicked into place as soon as it closed. "Are we safe?"

"I don't know." How could we be? All that stood between us and the soldiers was a door.

BOOTS STOMPED up and down the hall. Men yelled at us to come out. Ulla and I huddled in a corner of her bed. When we didn't obey, they pounded on the door, but the steel enforced material held firm. Each time they hit it, the sound clanged and echoed through the room, rebounding through my chest.

Ulla cried, and I couldn't stop shaking.

Clang, clang…

"Leena, what will they do to us?"

I couldn't answer. Instead, I squeezed her tighter.

Clang…

She knew as well as I did they could do whatever they wanted. There was no one to stop them. Am had left.

Clang, clang…

He wasn't there to protect us, and I wasn't sure he could have anyway.

Dents appeared in the door around the locking mechanism.

Atua?

Clang.

My hand is stretched out to cover you.

Clang, clang…

"Ulla, Atua says he's with us."

"Does that mean they won't hurt us?"

"I don't know." The fear didn't go away.

Clang.

She started crying again, and I wished I could tell her differently. But I'd learned sometimes Atua picked up the broken pieces instead of protecting. That truth hurt but there was peace in knowing we weren't alone.

One last clang accompanied the grunt of men and the door flew open, bouncing off the wall. Two soldiers stood holding a large metal rod with handles. Their arms were thick with muscles, sweat dripped from their faces.

"Two in this one!" A soldier yelled down the hall before he moved to the next door.

A different soldier appeared in the doorway holding a pulse weapon. "Get up."

Ulla shook her head and the man frowned. He pointed the gun at us. "We don't need all of you. Get up."

I shoved Ulla to her feet. The man didn't look at us like the ones on Kahu had, but his eyes were cold, hard. He waved his weapon indicating where he wanted us to walk.

The hall was full of soldiers. Several pairs of burly men pounded on doors. Only the ones on the side of the hall without windows. I shivered to think why they didn't need in the rooms on the other side.

Two of the soldiers wandering the hall grabbed us and pushed us toward the far stairwell. The air was full of sobbing and the incessant pounding of the battering ram on metal.

Several women huddled at the base of the stairs. Ulla clung to me, but I didn't recognize anyone else. The men broke through another door and someone started screaming.

"Shut her up!" a soldier yelled.

A man ran toward the door, gun in hand. Instinct had me pulling away from Ulla, attempting to run down the hall to help. She gripped me tight and I only made it a step or two.

The man closest to me raised his weapon, aimed at me the same time the other soldier fired into the room.

"No!" I screamed. "You didn't have to do that! I could have convinced her to come out."

"Up the stairs or you'll be next." The soldier stalked forward.

Ulla continued to pull me back. "Leena, please."

Fear and anger collided, bringing on a full blown panic attack. The vice wrapped around my chest, cutting off my air. I gasped, but it didn't help. Arms wrapped around me and I heard Ulla as if from a distance.

"We're going." She spun me around, but I couldn't see through the darkness clouding my vision.

"Sounds like I'd be doing her a favor," the soldier taunted.

"Breathe, Leena." Ulla soothed and guided me forward. "We've got to make it up the stairs."

I nodded and concentrated on breathing. And not thinking. Just don't think about what they've done. What they keep doing.

Ulla put my hand on the rail. I slid my feet forward one at a time,

searching for the step. Women pressed around me and we were
herded up.

By the time we reached the mess hall, I could breathe a little
easier and had opened my eyes. The serving women sat at a table,
one soldier guarding them. They looked more angry than scared.

"Keep going," someone barked.

The hall to the outside world felt shorter than it had on the way
in. We didn't stop for showers or new clothes. There were no
medical exams. That moment when I felt the sun on my skin and the
breeze in my hair should have been joyous. But Schirra waited
for us.

The door burst open again and two men dragged Valeria outside.
Her red hair had fallen around her shoulders, her dress was ripped
on one side, and her lip looked swollen. She glared at Schirra, shoulders ridged.

"You have no right," Valeria howled.

"I have every right. Amiran has chosen a queen. They," he pointed
to us as the soldiers ordered us up the hill, "are now mine."

Amiran chose a queen? The pain in my chest changed. No longer
simply physical, it now ached deep into my soul.

"The Hatana wanted them shown mercy. Educated, freed."
Valeria didn't back down.

"When will you learn he is not in charge?" Schirra sneered.

Teina. I wanted Am to be the Hatana. Now, with all my heart I
prayed he wasn't. Simply because he hadn't chosen me.

"Where are they taking us?" Ulla whispered.

I'd forgotten she was there. We'd been marched away from
Valeria and Schirra. Their conversation no longer within hearing
range. We didn't pass the courtyard gardens but went around the
back of the palace toward the far side of the wall cutting it off from
the city proper.

"We'll find out soon enough." I trembled from head to foot. Am
was gone. Would he be able to find me? Would he even want to?

And why had Atua fallen silent?

56

BIRILU: AMIRAN

Congratulatory crowds and music met us on Birilu. Outwardly they looked as festive as those that sent us from Rawiri, but something felt subdued about the experience. Perhaps it was my own unease at the charade. It was wasted time. I only wanted to see my mother and get to Olea.

An escort drove us through the streets to the Masaki estate where the people were kept without the gates. Harper and I followed Corvey into the foyer where we met Masaki.

"Hatana, we are honored to have you visit." He bowed and waved toward a cozy sitting room filled with people.

There were several older women, but none who resembled my mother. The many men and women must have been family of Masaki. They all stood as if they didn't know what to expect.

"It is my honor to be in your home. Please, introduce me to your family and be comfortable. I know Corvey is not your daughter." I bowed in return. "In fact, I knew her on Manawa."

Masaki sighed, the tension easing from his shoulders. "How much do you know, Hatana?"

"Call me Amiran. I'd like to think I am among friends. There are few places I can relax."

Corvey led a man over to us. "Am, this is my fiancé, Nash."

"It's a pleasure to meet you. Forgive me for this ruse. It was the only way to leave Rawiri, and I knew she would not hold me to it."

Masaki moved closer and spoke low near my ear. "Hatana, are the rumors true? Do you know what can darken the moons?"

Love and gratitude filled my being. "Only Atua can do that and dry the oceans. And when he chooses, he can bring back the light as well as the rains."

Masaki's shoulders relaxed, he blinked and finally smiled. "Thank Atua for that."

He stepped back and resumed talking so the rest of the room could hear him. "It will be a while before dinner is ready."

"Thank you, but I can only stay an hour at most. However, everyone must think we are here for the week. Will you help me?" I focused on Masaki but saw Corvey whispering to Nash out of the corner of my eye.

"Yes, of course. There is something you should know. It might be helpful." Masaki turned to another man. "Hurry and collect the reports for the Hatana."

The man nodded and ran from the room.

"Reports?" I asked.

"I'm in the tech business. Mostly information gathering and reporting. Schirra has depended on me to keep track of all his men and assets for the last ten years." A twinkle entered Masaki's eye. "I may have fudged his reports."

"What do you mean?" My curiosity was piqued. Masaki's knowledge of weapons outposts and men would be invaluable.

"Eight years ago I exaggerated a few numbers. Not by much. Not enough for him to notice. Over the years we've run an algorithm allowing us to slowly increase those exaggerations."

"So Schirra thinks he's stronger than he really is?" My excitement grew.

Masaki nodded. "His numbers are now off by thousands."

"How has he missed this?"

"We never tweaked the numbers for his flagship," Masaki said it as if it explained everything. And it did.

"He never leaves his flagship. This is the weakness we've needed to find and it was in front of me all along." I paced, memories and possibilities vying for my attention. All my years in the fleet confirmed that Schirra didn't trust himself on any other ship. He never visited them and sent others for all inspections. "But how did no one else make the connection between the reports and smaller number of soldiers?"

"I only fudged Schirra's reports. All others went out correct."

"And Schirra doesn't talk to his subordinates?" That was a stupid mistake. Illogical and dangerous.

"Schirra doesn't share or trust," Masaki said.

"True."

The whispered conversations around us ceased. Even the swish of clothing from idle movements stopped. My gaze traveled the room to see people frozen and pale as a woman stepped from behind a tapestry.

She stood tall and every bit as regal as she did in the portrait in the palace. Her hair was now streaked with gray, but there was no doubt my mother stood before me.

Joy, sadness, an irrational urge to cry, and embarrassment washed through me. I don't remember moving, but somehow I'd crossed the room. Her hands rested in mine—soft, warm, and real.

"You're shorter than I remember." The stupidest words in history slipped from my lips.

Everyone laughed and the universe was a good place. I hugged her close, afraid if I let go she'd disappear.

"Mother," my voice cracked and she pulled back to place her hands on my face.

"You've grown into a man." She looked into my eyes as if trying to see my very soul. "More than anything I want to spend time with you, but I need to know one thing first."

"What?"

"The refugee women? What do you intend to do with them?"

"Set them free when it's safe." I watched her brow crease. "Why?"

Her gaze unfocused. "Do you know what's happening on Rawiri at this moment?"

Everyone in the room leaned closer. Masaki held his wife close, but it was Corvey who reached for my mother's arm and broke the eerie silence.

"Kuini, what do you see? Is it a vision?" Corvey whispered as she gazed into my mother's face.

Mother's eyes refocused on me. "Yes. She needs you. Schirra has taken her."

Fear and weakness had me gripping her hands tighter. "Eleena?"

"Is that her name?" Mother nodded. "Our reunion will have to wait. You must go straight to Olea and then to Rawiri. We will gather whatever help we can and follow."

"I'll go to Rawiri." I turned to Masaki, "can you go to Olea?"

Mother shook her head. "Don't let the emotion get the best of you. You will need your men if you wish to save her. Go to Olea. We will meet you on Rawiri."

Masaki nodded. "Kuini is right. Even with fewer men than he thinks, Schirra is strong. Especially on Rawiri."

Eleena would be at Schirra's mercy, and I knew he had none.

I couldn't stop my hands from shaking. "It will take three days to reach Olea. A week more to return to Rawiri. I need you to send a broad spectrum message."

"What should it say?" he asked.

Atua how long? We'll only get one chance.

Twelve days. Did Eleena have twelve days? His peace washed over me. *Have faith in my hand.*

"The moons have darkened and the oceans have gone dry. But Atua's hand shall bring light allowing the twelve rivers to refill *whenua.*"

Masaki repeated it, wished me luck and hurried from the room to send the message.

My mother hugged me again. "Have faith and I'll see you soon.

Nash stepped up. "I have a ship ready to go. Joba will send the reports to us there."

"I'm coming with you." Harper stood on the other side of Corvey, visibly shaking.

"Then let's go. We can coordinate the rest from the ship."

57

WORK CAMP: ELEENA

W e were loaded into a truck, left to stand, and packed in like animals. Valeria was shoved in with us. She wept at first, then grew quiet, her face devoid of emotion.

Hours passed. The air grew hot and thick the longer we drove. It smelled of fear—sweat and urine. Ulla and I clung to each other, taking turns leaning on the other when our legs grew too tired to support us any longer. Whenever the truck swayed, the mass of women standing shoulder to shoulder moved as one.

My stomach hurt. It churned and twisted. The pain radiated across my abdomen and lower back. I rested my head on Ulla's shoulder. I just wanted fresh air and the chance to sit.

I sobbed when I added my own body fluids to the stench in the air. I'd never been so humiliated.

After what felt like an eternity, the truck lurched to a stop. The motion threw us to the floor where we lay piled in a heap, too tired to care about the filth we lay in. The door opened. We'd traveled all day, and it was dark outside.

"Out." A voice ordered. "Turn on the lights!"

Spotlights flipped on one by one around the perimeter of an encampment. High fences surrounded a dirt courtyard and three wooden shacks. They didn't look much bigger than our original dorm tents on Jakaru.

"Out of the truck." This time he waved his weapon where we could see it.

The women closest to the opening managed to untangle themselves and climb or fall from the vehicle. The rest of us followed.

When it was my turn to climb down, I grabbed the side of the truck for support, but my knees buckled. I slid to the ground scraping my arms on the way down. Ulla tried to help me up.

"Keep moving. Building two."

Soldiers pointed guns in our direction. We shuffled toward the building with the number two on it. Another truck pulled into the compound. By the time Ulla and I reached the door, a second truck unloaded and joined us in the queue for the cabin.

The building was one empty room. No beds, chairs, blankets. Nothing. Ulla wrapped her arm around me and we stepped farther in. Many women cried quietly. We found somewhere to collapse and give in to our exhaustion.

ULLA and I huddled close until I could no longer ignore the need to relieve myself. The room remained dark, and the lights had been shut off outside. I made my way to the wall and walked the perimeter of the room. There was only the door we entered through.

I found a spot where someone else had relieved themselves in the back corner.

"Atua, what have we done to deserve this?" I whispered and squatted.

"You've done nothing." A woman's voice answered my question. The shape in front of me came closer. "Schirra is cruel simply for the sake of making others suffer."

I squeezed my eyes shut, hoping she couldn't hear me do my business. When I'd finished I moved toward her.

"Valeria?" I couldn't be sure in the dark.

"Yeah."

"Did he send you here for trying to help us?"

She sighed. "He thinks I'll change my mind if I spend time here."

"What about?"

"Him. The empire. Everything really. But I can never choose him over what's right." She paused and it looked like she stared straight up at the ceiling. "I hope he kills me when he figures that out."

I reached out for her arm. "Why would you wish for that?"

"Because he could do much worse."

My thoughts turned to Manawa. Yes, a man like that could do whatever he wanted.

"Did the Hatana choose a wife?" The question I'd tried to forget all day slipped from my lips.

"Schirra thinks so." Her shoulders moved in a shrug. "Why do you care?"

"No reason." I turned and made my way back to Ulla.

When I was close to the area I thought I'd woken from, I got down on my hands and knees to crawl through the bodies in the darkness.

"Ulla?" I called as loudly as I dared.

Women grunted and moved out of my way.

"Ulla?" I tried again.

"Leena?" her voice came to me from farther in the center of bodies.

I made my way to her only when I saw a shadow sit up.

"Sorry to wake you, but I couldn't find you any other way." I apologized.

"Where did you go?" she asked.

"Bathroom."

"Where?"

"Back corner. Step carefully."

"I'll wait 'til morning." She fell silent and I lay down, putting my hand next to hers, glad to know one person in the new *reinga* we found ourselves. Ulla patted my hand. "It'll be okay. We're survivors."

Yes, we were. But this time I felt wrung out. Drained of all hope. I'd adjust, but for the moment it was almost more than I could take. Everything had been taken from me. Even my silly dream of Am.

THE ROOM LIGHTENED from black to gray. I hadn't slept much. Most of the night had been spent trying to shut down my thoughts while trying to breathe evenly to ward off an attack. Ulla slept through it all.

I missed Harper. Was she still safe?

Women got up and paced, talking to each other in low whispers. There was an unspoken understanding that we avoided looking to the corner that had become our bathroom. Even so, I dreaded having to use it again. My chest tightened and my vision blurred.

"Hey." Ulla sat up. "You okay?"

I closed my eyes and breathed. "Yeah."

She touched my hand. "What's Atua say?"

The question took me off guard. Ulla had never been actively spiritual.

"I don't know. He's been quiet."

"Maybe you're too worked up to hear?" she asked.

"How do you know about that?" I felt the weight of failure.

Ulla shrugged. "Harper and I talked a lot on Meir's ship."

The memory of their whispered conversation felt like another lifetime ago.

"Why? Why did Harper tell you personal things like that?" I watched her closely, needing to learn her tells.

"I think she knew, and she didn't want you to be alone." Ulla kept eye contact.

"Knew? About the baby?"

"Yeah."

My heart split open again. Harper was going to have a baby. And I'd never see it. Warm tears ran down my cheeks and I wiped them away.

Atua, is Harper safe? I didn't care about me. But that innocent life deserved better than what we'd had the last few years.

I tried to block all my thoughts. Concentrating on how I felt, seeking the whisperings of the spirit.

They are in my hands. Atua's voice came loud and clear.

Sobs broke free. Atua was still there. Ulla looked uncomfortable, but she rubbed my arm. Someone else approached from behind to wrap me in a hug. I caught a glimpse of red hair right before she spoke.

"Shh, when Amiran learns what happened, he'll come for us." Valeria soothed, but her words brought more anxiety.

I didn't want him to see me like this. Tired, dirty, reeking of sweat and worse. I completely broke down. Valeria's grip tightened. She rocked me back and forth as I cried uncontrollably.

When I finally calmed down, I lay limply while Ulla's gaze bounced from me to Valeria. Her eyes wide, her brow furrowed.

"What is it, Ulla?" I finally asked since it didn't look like she was going to speak.

"Harper told me," she stopped and glanced at Valeria again.

"It's okay," I prompted.

"She told me you dreamed about a man named Am. Is he the Hatana?"

Valeria gasped.

I pulled myself out of her arms but didn't look at Valeria. I focused on Ulla. "I don't know, but I think he could be."

"Who are you?" Valeria asked. "Why do you think your Am is the Hatana?"

"Captain E told me Am was a great man, fighting for us as only he could."

"Evander?" her voice went all breathy.

"Yes." My heart pounded faster. "How did you know his name?"

Valeria's eyes filled with tears. "You were in Evander's camp? How long?"

I reached out to her in comfort, all while my mind screamed for her to spit out the answers I wanted. It took great effort to keep my voice calm, "Seven years."

She cried now. Other women noticed. Some moved away, clearly uncomfortable. Most hovered close, listening.

Valeria squeezed my hand. "I haven't seen him in six years. It was too dangerous after he decided to stay on as camp captain."

Valeria. Evander. Amiran. They all knew each other. Had known each other for years.

"Captain E's friend," I swallowed, "Am. Is he the Hatana?"

Ulla clutched me on one side, Valeria on the other. It was the only thing holding me together.

Teina. All this time. I'd been so stupid.

"Breathe," Ulla whispered.

Valeria turned to her. "You mentioned dreams. What's that about?"

"No, please don't." I found my voice.

"I won't." Ulla hugged me. "I'm sorry, Leena."

"You don't—" my words were cut off by the door being thrown open.

A soldier stepped in. "Time to work. If you cooperate, you will be fed. If not, we have no need for you." He hefted the blaster, making his meaning clear. "Everyone up and into the courtyard."

58

FINAL APPROACH: AMIRAN

"Am, sit down." Ev hovered at the other end of the table. He'd been pacing until a few moments ago.

"I can't." Two days had passed since we left Olea. Ev and De'truto joined me on Nash's ship. The rest of our men filled the other ships and were on different approaches to Rawiri. It couldn't look like we were coming in with a small fleet. Since it was unsafe to communicate with our sources in the palace, we were flying in blind.

We only knew what we saw on the news vids. Schirra made his move after I left. Valeria tried to protect the women and had been arrested for her efforts.

"There's no record he hurt them." Harper looked up from a datacom.

"There wouldn't be." My jaw hurt from clenching it.

We had another day before we reached orbit and rendezvoused with the others at Hebe's. The only good thing was Masaki's information had given us hope. Our numbers may have been few compared to those loyal to Schirra, but it wasn't as bad as we'd feared. Especially with the growing number of fleet officers hinting they were on my side.

"Schirra will want to look benevolent in front of Rawiri's citizens. I can't find any record they were shipped off the planet." De'truto rested a hand on my shoulder. "What does Atua tell you?"

"We are in his hands, they are in his hands. She is in his hands. But," I twisted away from his hold and paced again. "Anything could be happening to her. To them."

Corvey and Nash sat close together in the corner of the room. They'd been quiet most of the trip. Harper avoided looking at them, and as time dragged on, so did I. They were a constant reminder of what she'd lost and what I might never have.

De'truto growled. "Amiran, you're forgetting all you learned in the mines. Have faith. Trust in Atua's words, calm yourself, focus."

I stared at the bulkhead, refusing to face the others in the room. They didn't understand. I'd never had so much to lose. No one spoke. The hum of the ship's engines, breathing, and the occasional rustle of clothing were the only indications I wasn't alone.

De'truto was right. I couldn't help Eleena if I fell apart now.

"Have we heard from the men stationed around the fleet? Are they ready?" I tried to focus on the big picture. This wasn't about me, or Eleena. It was about shutting down Schirra's control of the fleet once and for all.

"That's more like it." De'truto grabbed another datacom from the conference table. "We've heard from the main contact on every ship and every outpost. The timeline is set to coincide with our arrival at the palace in thirty-six hours."

"Let's go through the plan again." I sat down, determined to get this right. "We can contact Timoti for Schirra's location once we get to Hebe's. He's the primary target, followed by the others on the list. Schirra must not escape."

"Agreed." Evander sat. "De'truto and I have put the best men in squads one through four. They'll split up and take one of the cardinal sides of the palace accompanied by secondary teams for reinforcement."

De'truto tapped the table. "Everyone moves at the designated time. We take out the fleet and outpost leadership loyal to Schirra."

"Then the fleet becomes a policing force instead of a conquering force," I spoke more to myself than the room. It was hard to concentrate. My thoughts more on the things out of my control than what we planned. "I wish he would let me see her."

Harper reached out and touched my arm. "Would that help or would it make things worse? And in the end, as long as she's alive, will it matter to you what she's going through right now?"

My hands fisted and my jaws clenched. The anger burning through my body. "It will only change how I punish those who have her."

"That's why Atua keeps those visions from you." Harper stood.

"She doesn't have to suffer the thing you fear most. The slightest harm would enrage you. Atua is protecting you from becoming what Schirra wanted all along."

Her words knocked the air from me.

Atua, is that true?

Love can bring out brutality quicker than any hate. His words were spoken softly to my mind. *Eleena needs your strength of faith. She needs the man you are, not the boy you were.*

I rested my head in my hands. Guilt coursing through me. I would have killed, tortured, done whatever it took to find and punish anyone who touched Eleena. Deep down, I knew I still might. It would make me as bad as Schirra. Judgment was Atua's.

But, there will be bloodshed. I thought. There was no way to stop Schirra and his men without taking a life. They would cut us down without a thought.

Yes, but not in the spirit of vengeance, Atua chastised.

I stood. "I need to be alone."

"Am?" Evander's brow rose.

"I need to meditate. Get myself in line with Atua's will before we reach Rawiri."

IT TOOK LONGER to land on Rawiri than we'd planned. Schirra had clearance checkpoints set up in orbit. Luckily, we had backstories in place for each ship, including destinations scattered around the globe so it wouldn't look like an invasion. Most ships had to back-track under the radar to return to the capital.

Nash put us down in an industrial spaceport east of the city proper. We boarded a transport and made our way to Hebe's for the rendezvous. I was the only one in disguise, and I hoped no one recognized Ev after so many years. We kept to back alleys as much as possible and slipped into the restaurant at the end of the busy lunch rush.

Hebe dipped his head my direction. "Fig, haven't seen you in a while. Looks like you've brought a crowd."

"It's been a hard week. I need something that will darken the moons." I watched him for a reaction, hoping my instincts about his allegiance was correct.

At first, I didn't think he was going to give the code phrase, but then he nodded toward a man cleaning tables. "I don't have anything like that out here. There is something strong enough to dry the oceans in the back. Shim, take over the counter."

"Thank Atua for that." I tried to smile.

"I should have known you'd come for the party." Hebe raised the section of counter that kept customers on their side and let us pass through.

"I called the party."

Hebe's eyes widened for a fraction of a second before a grin spread across his face. "You don't say. Should have known. It's always the quiet ones. Come on."

We followed. Every sense and nerve on high alert. Ev and De'truto flanked me, never looking in the same direction as each other, always scanning our surroundings. The sounds of the restaurant faded as we neared a door at the end of a short hallway. De'truto moved in front of me to enter first. Hebe's brow rose in interest, but he opened the door and led us inside.

Twenty of our men waited inside. It was a good start, but we needed more to pull this off.

"Do you need anything?" Hebe asked.

"A secure COM line?" I replied.

"Already set up on the back wall over there." He pointed.

"Thanks." I moved through the crowd with only one thought on my mind. Contact Timoti. Find out where Schirra was and take him out.

AN HOUR later we'd cycled ten squads through Hebe's back room. De'truto sent them off with orders to get into position around the palace even though we hadn't made contact with Timoti. A growing sense of dread pooled in my stomach.

"Am, we've come too far to back out now." Ev stood beside me.

"I know. What if he's not there?" I spoke my greatest fear.

"We've got men covering the spaceports. Schirra won't slip through our net." Ev sounded confident, but he hadn't spent five years watching Schirra in his element. The man always had multiple escape plans.

"If he has any idea we're here, and he probably does, this won't be easy." I grabbed my protective body armor and slid the vest on. With a flip of a switch, the nano shield expanded until my chest, arms, legs, and even my neck and head were protected.

"Then we go now." De'truto handed me a utility belt with battery pack and charger for the weapons. "Everyone's in position."

I nodded. "Let's do this."

Out of the corner of my eye, I saw Nash kiss Corvey goodbye. She and Harper reluctantly agreed to stay at Hebe's. I suspected we only got that much cooperation out of them because Eleena was no longer on the palace grounds. They would work with Hebe to locate the refugee women. There were clues, but no clear trail.

"Am, stay behind team one. Let them do their job." Evander waved the final two teams out the back door.

"No," I argued. "Rawiri needs to see I stand side by side with men from Allegiant and Coalition worlds. It's the only way to bring peace to the empire."

"They'll see that. What they really need to see is fleet soldiers and Coalition rebels both fighting to protect you." De'truto butted in.

"It's the same thing." I countered.

"It's not." Ev trotted beside me, as well as De'truto, Nash, and the rest of team one and five. "And you know it. Ask Atua."

I grumbled but didn't have to ask. Atua's voice had already told me to follow Ev's advice. We hadn't started the battle and I felt like a puppet.

Better my puppet than Schirra's, Atua whispered.

True.

Ev and De'truto both chuckled and I wondered what my expression looked like. I donned the visor that completed the body armor and darkened the faceplate so they could no longer see my face.

We left by way of a back alley, but we couldn't stay completely out of sight. The din of citizens going about their daily business ebbed and flowed on the streets. The stumble in cadence clear whenever our movements were noticed.

"If Schirra didn't know we were here, he does now. Step it up." I called out to those in front. "We can't wait for the coordinated attack on the fleet. We need to hit the palace now."

All the men gave up trying to stick to the shadows and we jogged the shortest route to our designated entry point at the palace. People scattered, taking cover as we passed.

The front gate of the palace was unmanned.

"Something's wrong." I stopped everyone from entering. I gave the next order over the mission frequency. "Everyone, set visors to record. Teams report."

"Holding position. No one has entered or left the palace since our arrival. Awaiting orders." Team two's leader answered. Team three was stationed with them.

Team four also chimed in. "All's quiet on our side. We haven't seen any movement."

"Same here." Team six checked in.

"Hold position and watch for anyone trying to escape." I switched back to the team channel. "Move in. The primary target is Schirra. Protect civilians where you can." I waved the men through the gate.

They scattered, clearing the courtyard before we hit the main entrance. It was too quiet. There should have been staff, civilians, and soldiers roaming everywhere. We moved forward silently, communicating only through hand signals until we reached the front doors.

They stood wide open.

Team one moved in first, team five stayed outside with Ev, Nash, and me. We waited for De'truto to give the all clear.

"Atua in heaven." His voice cut the silence inside my helmet. "Amiran, it's clear but it's not pretty."

I hurried inside. Men and women lay scattered throughout the large foyer. Their eyes glassy, faces frozen in one of two expressions —surprise or fear.

No one spoke. The teams spread out down the hall, clearing room after room. I stood still, flipping through their feeds on my visor. Bodies littered every room and corridor.

Timoti.

"Ev." I stopped the vids and raised my visor. "Your father. My suites."

We ran, Nash and De'truto calling for us to wait for the team. Evander had not stepped foot in the palace for nine years, but he knew the way. He was faster than me.

"Hurry, Am." He pounded on the bio-locked door uselessly.

When the door opened for me, I almost fell to my knees.

"No, no, no!" Ev's cries echoed the beating of my heart.

Timoti was strung up in his undergarments to some contraption. Blood dripped from cords piercing his skin at various places along his arms, legs, chest, and head. They held him up like a giant marionette. The dominant sound in the room was the rhythmic hiss of a ventilator, and the smell of blood and body fluids was overpowering.

Ev approached his father cautiously. I kept close, restraining myself from shoving him out of the way so I could get to Timoti faster.

"*Aukati*." Ev choked. "He's alive. Help me get him down!"

I reached for an arm, Ev took the other side.

"No." Timoti groaned and tried to raise his head. His next words were labored. "Only thing…keeping alive."

"I never should have left you." My guilt became a tangible force in the room.

Nash and De'truto entered my suite with half of team five.

"*Reinga*, what's this?" Nash halted just inside the door.

"Ev." Timoti managed to open his eyes. "Sorry."

"What happened?" Ev fidgeted like he didn't know what to do. His hands hovered over his father, but he didn't touch him. "Does it hurt?"

"Severed spinal column. No pain." Timoti's eyes moved to me. "He knows about Eleena."

The sadness weighing me down shattered to fear.

"How?" I fell to my knees. *Atua, why? I've done everything you asked.*

"Am." De'truto rested a hand on my shoulder.

I brushed him away.

"Jammer had…recording chip." Timoti closed his eyes, taking a long time to reopen them.

"When did this happen?" Ev concentrated on his father, but my mind had moved to Eleena.

It increased my guilt.

"This morning. Broke in. Retrieved. Recording." Timoti's breathing rattled, but the machine kept his lungs working despite his struggle. "He didn't…question me."

Why hadn't Atua pushed me to get here faster? We could have saved Timoti and the others.

Nash drew closer. "We've got a med team coming."

"Won't matter." Timoti stared at his son. "Let me go. Help Am. Valeria and Eleena need you."

My eyes stung. Timoti was dying.

Ev bowed his head. "I'm sorry I wasn't here for you."

"Been where Atua…wanted…you." Timoti's voice sounded weaker. "No regrets. Cut me loose."

"Ev?" I didn't know how to help.

He nodded and we moved back to his father's side. We each took an arm while the other men cut the cords. Timoti slumped to the ground, Ev cradling him.

"The rest." Timoti flicked his eyes toward the ventilator and another wire that plugged into the base of his skull.

I looked at Ev for confirmation in case he needed more time. Stupid, he'd always wish for more time.

"I'm ready." Ev whispered and tugged his father's body closer. "Atua be with you, dad."

My hand hovered over the switch for the ventilator. "I can't."

"You can…son." Timoti closed his eyes.

One deep breath, and on the inhale I flicked both of them. The ventilator hissed one last cycle.

"Thank you." Timoti smiled. "My boys. Together."

There was no pomp and circumstance. No struggle. Timoti's chest simply stopped moving. The other men stood still and silent. Only Ev and I allowed tears to fall.

I don't know how long we sat there. Me holding one of Timoti's hands while Ev rocked back and forth with his dad. Eventually, Ev stopped moving. He gently laid his father down, then looked at me.

"Let's finish this once and for all." His eyes held the same fire I'd feared would consume me on the ship.

"Yes." I agreed but vowed in my heart Evander would not be the one to strike Schirra. Not in revenge. Not if I could get to him first. "First we broadcast our video feeds. Let Rawiri and all the worlds know what Schirra has done. We need them on our side to find Eleena and the other women quickly."

De'truto stepped closer. "It's already done. I began streaming when I entered this room."

"Good." I faced De'truto and the camera in his visor. "People of Rawiri, it's time to put an end to Schirra's cruelty. If you cannot fight with me, at least come to care for the fallen so I can fight. And if you know where he's taken the refugee women, speak up."

I gave the kill sign and he tapped his visor.

"The nets are filling with conversations. If anyone knows where they are, we'll know soon." De'truto watched Ev and Nash carry Timoti's body into my bedroom.

"As soon as they're done, let's get to the ship so we're ready. How many teams can we route there?" I was ready to go now that I knew nothing could be done for Timoti.

"All six from the palace easily." De'truto tilted his head. "We're also getting reports from several operatives on the fleet ships. Some flipped loyalties easily. Others are still fighting for control."

"If we can take out Schirra quickly, the others should fold."

Evander stepped from my room. "Let's go."

59

SCHIRRA'S END GAME: ELEENA

We'd been at the work camp a little more than a week. Valeria became a fast friend, teaching me how to work the sewing machines in return for stories about Evander.

The third cabin in our compound was a large shower room. We were allowed in every three days to clean ourselves and our clothes. While we did that, our guards sprayed out our sleeping cabin, but we were never given dedicated toilet facilities.

Things were miserable, but they could have been worse.

Valeria, Ulla, and I bent over our machines, sewing fleet pants. I found them easier to sew than the jackets. My stitches were improving, and I had to pick out fewer seams every day.

A woman standing close to the door pressed her face against the rough wood.

"Something's coming!" She hissed and ran back to her seat.

No one had come or gone since we arrived. Valeria paled.

"What is it?" I asked.

"I don't know." She shook her head, but the terror was clear in her eyes. "Might be my father."

How could Valeria be related to Schirra, much less his daughter? I took her hand and squeezed it.

"Surely he won't hurt you?" I tried to sound confident, but uncertainty caused my voice to waver.

She stared at the wall. The lock turned in the door. We returned our gaze to our work.

"Eleena Talrano." The voice was familiar.

I trembled in my seat but didn't look up. Icy coldness ran down my arms and legs. How did he know my name?

Valeria stood. When she spoke, her voice carried more strength than I expected. "What do you want?"

"This experience hasn't taught you respect." The man stepped farther in, followed by several soldiers. I peeked up enough to see Schirra glaring down our row of machines. "Sit down, Valeria."

Her chin trembled, even as she stood straighter. "Or what father?"

Women gasped. She'd only told Ulla and me about her connection to Schirra.

He waved a hand toward his daughter.

Men spread out around the room. One of them grabbed Valeria. She twisted and fought as he dragged her toward the exit. When they reached the door, Valeria grabbed the doorjamb and held on.

"Why are you doing this?" she cried.

A second soldier stepped over to help push her through.

"Ten flicks." Schirra waited for the soldier to salute.

I glanced at Ulla, silently asking what a flick was. She shook her head, obviously at a loss as well.

"Eleena Talrano, stand up," Schirra ordered.

Ulla's hand gripped my leg, holding me down. The other women sat with their eyes riveted to a machine. I waited for one of them to rat me out.

The room grew heavy with anticipation.

"No?" Schirra studied the women one by one. "Fine. Kill that one." He pointed to a woman on his right.

I bolted out of my seat. It scared across the floor drawing every eye to me.

Schirra broke into a full smile. "Much better. We're going to send a message to the Hatana."

The breath stuck in my lungs. My fingertips tingled with the growing numbness, but my heart pounded for all it was worth.

A soldier grabbed my arm at the same time Schirra gave another command. "Kill the rest."

"No!" I reached for Ulla. Her eyes rounded, her lips quivered. *Atua stop him! Save them!*

Like Valeria, I was half dragged, half shoved, kicking and screaming to the door, never making contact with Ulla. The soldiers around the room lifted their blasters. The other women cried but there was nowhere to run.

I didn't look away from Ulla until Schirra closed the door behind him. Valeria howled in pain from somewhere I couldn't see, then blaster fire erupted inside.

We marched toward Valeria's tortured sounds as silence fell behind me. The soldiers exited the building.

"Burn it down. Amiran will have a harder time discovering she's not there." Schirra ordered and was obeyed without question.

My breaths came in short bursts as I struggled not to hyper-ventilate.

Ulla was gone.

"You should catch your breath." Schirra laughed. "You're going to need it."

We passed a truck and Valeria came into view. Her hands had been tied above her head to a tall pole. A man stood behind her with a long whip, buzzing with energy. He flicked it and added another red welt to her back.

She hung limply. The soldier flicked twice more even though she'd clearly passed out.

"Get the recorders. Cut Valeria down and string this one up." Schirra continued to give orders, unfazed by the sight of his daughter's suffering.

60

THE RESCUE: AMIRAN

B y the time we reached the ship, we had several tips on Eleena's location. The most promising from a driver that said he'd driven a truck of women to a small work camp in Gorda.

We were ten minutes from our destination when Nash stepped off of the flight deck. "Schirra's broadcasting."

"Which channel?" I flipped on the main viewer.

"All of them," he answered.

My heart clogged my throat. The screen showed two men dragging a woman to a post. They tied her up with her back to the camera, but it looked like Eleena. Schirra stood to the side watching.

"He's gone mad," De'truto moved closer. "He's not even trying to hide this action from the citizens."

"Why?" Ev asked.

"He doesn't think he can lose." My blood boiled with the determination to prove him wrong. To make him pay.

Schirra turned to the camera. "Amiran, I saw you got the message I left at the palace. I have another for you. Perhaps one more demonstration will teach you once and for all not to defy me."

The general walked to the post and grabbed the woman by the chin. He twisted her around to face the camera. It was Eleena. She tried to jerk free, the terror clear in her eyes.

"First Evander, now her. You've impressed me with your ability to keep secrets, but you'll learn you can't fight the inevitable."

"Nash! How long?" I yelled. My nerves thrummed with all he could do to hurt her all because of her connection to me.

"Five minutes," he answered.

Schirra beckoned the camera closer then spoke to Eleena. "You're going to scream nice and loud for me. I'm going to break Amiran, then I'll kill him. The people of Rawiri, of the empire, need someone stronger to lead them. I will be that leader."

"Am is stronger because Atua is with him." Eleena's voice came out strong but tears ran down her cheek. "You had your own daughter beaten. Am would never do that."

"She'll learn her lesson eventually." Schirra released Eleena and moved away.

"Valeria!" Ev gasped and pointed.

Only then did I notice the woman on the ground. Her face was turned away, but the red hair made Ev's guess valid. The back of her tunic had been shredded, the edges burned away.

Schirra waved offscreen and a man stepped into view with a vibrowhip in hand.

"Atua, no," I whispered. Valeria's wounds made sense, and I knew what Schirra had in store for Eleena.

"I'll work on the security bypass for the airlock. The doors will open before landing." Ev's voice shook with rage. He didn't wait for my answer, knowing every second gained would be needed to gain an advantaged over Schirra.

I wished for an excuse to walk away from the viewer, to not witness the pain coming for Eleena.

Schirra nodded. The man raised the whip. He turned on the switch for the current, and flicked his wrist.

Eleena's scream filled my ship as the current burned through cloth and skin. She arched her back, twisting in the effort to move out of the whip's range.

Her tormentor flicked again.

"Better hurry, Amiran, if you want to save her." Schirra laughed.

I saw red. By the time Ev and I finished with Schirra, there would be nothing left.

Amiran, judgment is mine.

I clenched my fists. *Now you speak? Why don't you stop him?*
You will stop him.

I tapped into the mission COM to speak to the other two ships flying with me. "Teams one through four, hit the ground running and neutralize Schirra's men. De'truto, how many?"

De'truto looked up from his datacom. "Schirra has two troop transports. Estimated thirty soldiers. It'll be an even fight."

Eleena shrieked as she was flicked again. Her sobs loud enough to be picked up by the recorder.

"Nash!" Her anguished cries pulsed through my veins.

"Descending now," he answered.

The man with the whip backed away from Eleena. Schirra looked to be giving his men orders as they moved into position around his location.

He knew we were coming. So be it.

"Turn it off." I gritted my teeth and headed for the airlock. "Take out as many as you can from the air. I'm not interested in prisoners. These are Schirra's most trust soldiers. They won't show us mercy."

De'truto and team five stayed close on my heels. Ev had bypassed the security protocols and opened the doors. We still wore our body armor. There was nothing to slow us down.

Schirra's men lifted their weapons.

All three of my ships opened fire from the air, cutting down the first line of soldiers. They scattered to take up more secure positions, clearing the way for us to leave our ships.

"Easy! Don't hit Eleena or Valeria." The wind from the open airlock whipped the sound away, and I hoped my mic had picked up the warning. "Keep up cover fire until we're down. Let's go!"

"Let team five go first," Ev yelled, the sound coming through clearly inside my helmet.

I ignored him and launched myself through the door, blaster in hand. Running toward Schirra, I only hit half my targets. I met a wall of soldiers blocking my way thirty feet from from the general.

"I need a path cleared." I yelled.

The COM crackled. "Team one approaching from left flank."

"Team four's right behind you."

"Team two requesting back up on the right flank."

"Three on the way."

"Just go!" I wanted to shut out the chatter, the distractions. Where was Schirra? He blended in with all the uniforms. I constantly scanned the motion of men fighting. Team five kept a defensive position around me the whole time.

There. Schirra stood by Eleena, sawing away at the ropes used to tie her up. Relief and fear battled for dominance. He hadn't killed her at my arrival, but that only meant he intended to use her for something else.

Let me get to her before he cuts her loose! I pled with Atua to let me have one thing go my way, then bulldozed my way past my security and straight through the line.

Schirra was faster.

He sliced through the rope, repositioning the knife at her neck as he spun to face me. Tears streamed down Eleena's face.

"Call off your men or she dies." Schirra grinned, stopping me in my tracks only ten feet away.

"Don't." Eleena's voice sounded raw. "He killed...the others."

Ev growled, "I'm going to make you pay for my father."

"If you'd stayed in the fleet he never would have died like that." Schirra squeezed Eleena tighter, the edge of the blade drawing blood. "Are you going to let your best friend get her killed? Come on, Amiran. *Hatana.*" He sneered. "Make a decision. Or will you be as weak as your father?"

"What?" He was toying with me. Why?

"You haven't figured it out?" Schirra took a step back, dragging Eleena with him. "He belonged to me because he fell in love. You have the same weakness."

Puzzle pieces from the last four months, from years, fell into place. Corvey's certainty Anaru loved my mother. Glimpses of approval I'd never been sure of. The fact I survived Manawa when Schirra probably hoped I'd die with the rest of the planet. Even the two years of freedom running from my father had been a gift. His way of giving me a chance to choose for myself.

Yes, Amiran. Atua confirmed the truth in my thoughts.

"I'm done playing. What will it be?" Schirra asked.

Valeria crawled to her feet and mouthed, "Get ready."

Jerking my gaze from her, every muscle in my body tensed for action. Fear rose like bile. The knife. Whatever Valeria planned would put Eleena in more danger.

"Will you step up and be strong," Schirra continued, unaware of his daughter behind him, "or let your affections make you weak."

"Wait—" I reached out but it was too late.

"Love isn't weakness," Valeria spoke loud and clear before launching herself into her father.

Schirra staggered. Eleena threw her hands out to catch herself as she fell. The general's arm slid across her body to stop his own fall, dragging the knife along her skin.

"Eleena!" I hurried forward, Ev rushed for Valeria.

Schirra scrambled for the knife.

"I said I wouldn't spare you," Schirra bellowed. He swung at his daughter but Ev blocked him.

Eleena crawled to one of the trucks. She touched her neck, her shoulder, her neck again.

"Eleena?" I grabbed her hand so I could see her neck. It was only nicked, but there was a downward slice across her collarbone.

"I'm okay," she gasped.

"Amiran, Schirra's men are converging on your location." The COM distracted me. "Teams one, two, four, and five have casualties. We're..."

"Am," Eleena pointed behind me, "watch out!"

I spun in time to aim and shoot at the soldiers running for us. Two went down, then my guard surrounded us. They fought off the rest while the other teams joined us.

Ev wasn't doing as well. Schirra's men dragged him off the general and pinned him down.

Schirra stood and aimed a blaster at Ev's head. "This time you'll stay dead."

"No!" Valeria screamed and rammed her father again. She clung to him until he dropped the gun.

The distraction was enough for Ev to break free from his captors. He grabbed one of the blasters from the ground as De'truto and the rest of our men rushed to his aid.

"Eleena, get under the truck." I tried to shove her toward safety.

"Am?"

"I'll be back." I'd lost sight of Schirra in the chaos but knew I had to end this now.

Eleena nodded and shimmied under the truck. I joined my men. COM chatter continued in a steady stream as my men fought the enemy. We were cutting them down, slowing gaining control.

"Amiran!" Schirra growled, drawing my attention. He stood, surrounded by a couple of his biggest men, brandishing a knife my direction. "Come on, you and me. Once and for all."

"Drop the knife." I nodded.

"The gun first."

I tossed my gun to the side. Schirra charged but kept the knife. I blocked, knocking it from his grip, the jolt of the impact ricocheted through me. We hit the ground, grappling for control. He was strong, with years more experience, but I had the image of Eleena being flicked on his orders in my mind.

Rage fueled me. I pinned him down. I bashed his face with my fist. And it felt good. One of his men knocked me off.

"We've got you, Am," someone spoke over the COM and the death blow I should have received never came.

Schirra, however was back up too.

"Am," it was Ev, "give the word and we'll take him down."

"He asked for a fair fight," I replied.

"He's not following the rules." This time it was De'truto.

Schirra and I circled each other.

"Stop talking and stay out of it. He's mine. The only other one that gets a shot is Ev. For Timoti." I flicked the COM button off.

Schirra used that moment to tackle me. Pain shot through my shoulder as I hit the ground again. He knocked the air out of me, giving him time to press his knees into my chest and lock his hands around my neck.

"Weak. Too worried about everyone else," Schirra gloated at my useless attempt to disengage his hold.

Someone screamed. Starbursts blurred my vision. I was tired, oxygen deprived, and ready for my men to disobey my last order.

Schirra jerked, clenching then releasing the pressure on my neck. He slumped over, crushing me with his full weight. His eyes were open but there was no life left. I shoved him to the side and he slid to the ground. Air rushed in. I sucked in a deep breath. Ev and De'truto saluted before splitting up—Ev to Valeria, De'truto to help the rest of our men.

The sounds of fighting had ceased. I flipped on my COM and it was quite as well.

"Report." My voice sounded raw.

"Cleaning up, full report in five," someone reported.

"Am?" Eleena's shaky voice was the last thing I expected to hear.

I craned my neck. She stood there, body shaking, staring at Schirra's body. Moving hurt like *reinga*, but I sat up, got to my feet and walked to her.

"Are you okay?" I noticed the blaster on the ground at her feet. "Why did you come out from the truck?"

"He was going to kill you." She peered up at me, lips trembling. "I couldn't let him kill you. Will Atua forgive me?"

"It was you?" I thought it had been Ev, maybe De'truto.

Her eyes were wide. She took a step away from me. "He." She struggled to catch her breath. "He was going to kill you."

"Eleena." I pulled her into my arms and she sobbed. She clung to me and I knew she cried for all she'd lost. And now for what she'd taken. "Atua knows what's in your heart. He knows you didn't want to kill anyone."

"But I did." She took a shuddering breath. "He wouldn't stop. He killed so many people. Ulla, Iri, all of Manawa."

I didn't know what to say. It was the truth and anyone on Rawiri would understand. *Atua?*

I will comfort when she comes to me for comfort.

"Eleena, Atua will be there for you. You know that." I held her and watched my men secured the area.

Too exhausted to stand any longer, I sunk to the ground, tugging her down with me.

"Are you hurt?" she asked, pulling back to look at me.

"Nothing some pain meds and a good sleep won't fix. I'm more worried about you." I outlined her face with my fingertips. She closed her eyes and leaned into my touch.

New tears trailed down her cheeks. "I'm trying not to think about the pain."

Nash approached us. "Your Highness, all of Schirra's men are dead. We're loading our wounded onto the ships."

I barely suppressed my groan. "You couldn't have told me that while I was still on my feet?"

Nash laughed and offered me a hand. "I figured you'd want to get Eleena to medical as soon as possible."

"Yes." I accepted the hand and then helped Eleena up, watching as she flinched with the movement. There was a lot that still needed to be done, but as soon as we reached the ship I was going to make her my top priority. That gave me five minutes to wrap up a few things with my teams. "Any updates on the fleet rebellions?"

61

REUNIONS: ELEENA

A m kept my hand in his. It was the only thing keeping me from falling apart. Ulla and the others were dead.

I killed Schirra.

Every time I thought about it my stomach twisted and it grew hard to breathe. Partly because I did it. Partly because I'd do it again if it would save Am.

I glanced at him. He listened intently as the man named Nash gave a report.

Nash's voice came from far away as I hovered on the edge of my own crisis. "The coordinated mutinies met with better success than we hoped. Sixty percent of the fleet is now under your control. We'll broadcast the news of Schirra's death and hope the others follow suit. However, we're worried about the flagship."

They were going to broadcast Schirra's death. Would everyone see me kill Schirra?

"We'll need to go after it." Am sounded tired.

"I'll give a more detailed report after you see to her wounds." Nash paused in the airlock. "Should I set course for the palace?"

"Yes." Am nodded then smiled at me. "Harper and Corvey will be waiting for us."

"Corvey?" I clung to his hand. "My Corvey?"

"It's a long story, and I'll let her tell it."

Nash went one way and we went another. Thoughts and feelings swirled inside. It was like I'd gotten stuck in the first moments of one of my anxiety attacks. Everything was fuzzy. It made it hard to think.

Corvey. Harper. Schirra. Each of them brought emotions that I didn't know how to deal with. And Am. The man Atua had sent visions of, had protected over the years, and had prepared to be Hatana.

My stomach turned and I thought I would be sick. If only I could catch my breath.

There was one way to feel better. I just didn't want to do it. But I had to if I wanted to be with Am.

Atua?

How could I ask for forgiveness if I wasn't sure I was sorry?

Atua, can I be forgiven?

A warmth seeped into my heart. *My child, in spite of what you think, you did not kill out of hatred. You acted out of love.*

But it's wrong to kill.

Yes, but for that moment you were my hand. Be at peace.

I wiped away a tear before Am could see.

I doubted I would forget the weight of the blaster, or the look in Schirra's eye as he died, but with Atua's blessing I planned to try.

"Here we are." Am led me into a small room where he helped me onto a table, then stood there clasping both my hands. His brow furrowed, and I reached out to smooth the wrinkles with my fingertips.

"What is it?" I asked.

"I hate that you got hurt." He reached out and touched my neck, then the slash across my shoulder.

A tremor rippled through me. "It's not your fault."

"I should have kept you safer," he whispered, still in my personal space.

"You showed up just in time." In spite of his nearness and the warm bubbles multiplying in my veins, my pain was becoming more unbearable. "My back is on fire, Am."

"We don't have a doctor or any other women on board." His wrinkles deepened. "We're all trained in combat medicine though."

"That's good." Why wasn't he fixing me already? The bubbles were evaporating.

"Would you rather someone else do this?"

"Oh." I finally understood his concern. The heat from my back curled over my shoulders and worked it's way up my neck to my face. "No." I maintained eye contact. "I trust you."

"Okay." He turned and pulled several things out of the drawer, including a pale green med gown. "Put this on and lay on your stomach."

Am handed me the fabric and turned to face the door. I dressed, tossing the filthy tunic to the floor. It had been a couple days since my last shower and I suddenly felt self-conscious.

"Eleena, are you ready?" He still faced the wall.

"Um," what to say? "I. We didn't. I mean the camp didn't have sanitation facilities."

He spun around, his face twisted in disgust? Anger? I wasn't sure.

"How did you, where? Did they even feed you?" he asked.

"Yes," I whispered. "We ate outside because of the stench where we slept."

Am stepped close, both hands cupping my face. "I'm so sorry. I'll never be able to tell you how sorry I am for all you've been through."

Reaching up, I placed my hands on the outside of his. "It wasn't your fault, Am."

"But,"

"No. You follow Atua. Schirra did not." The truth of those words comforted me as much as I wanted them to help Am.

"It's not that simple."

"It is. Now, please, give me something for the pain." I pushed his hands away and lay down.

"Dear Atua." He hissed. It must have looked as bad as it felt. Am unwrapped things and lay them beside the table on a little counter. "I'm going to give you a numbing agent so I can clean and bandage your back."

He pressed the hypospray into my shoulder. The medicine traveled like a river of ice to the damaged parts of my body.

"Can you feel this?" he asked.

"No."

"Okay, here we go."

I could hear him working but only felt a light pressure at times. The pile of bloody bandages grew beside me. Am sprayed something vile smelling, then covered my back with gauze.

"That'll have to do for now." He helped me sit up, concern all over his face. "Let me know when the pain returns and we'll get you more painkillers."

"Okay."

"I'll clean your neck and this other cut." He gently wiped at the crusted blood.

We didn't talk. We didn't need to.

He cleaned my wounds and I watched the emotions play on his face. I knew him so well, and yet it had been years since I'd seen expression on him. Each one was a wonder to me. I wanted to understand them all.

He looked up and caught me staring. "What?"

"It's good to see you relaxed. Not wearing that mask I saw in so many of the dreams."

"Atua willing, I'll never have to wear it again. Come." He helped me from the table and led me to another room with a real bed. It was rumpled, only half made.

"Who's room is this?" I asked.

"Mine. I usually make the bed, but we were going into battle." He shrugged, his smile reminding me of the young man who used to visit my family. Happy, carefree. But his eyes had changed forever. Tiny lines framed them. The pain and growth of the last seven years clear to be seen in their depths.

"Am?" There were so many things I wanted to ask. So much I wanted to say, but I didn't know where to begin.

"Rest until we reach the capital. I'll come back for you then." He turned to leave and the fear crushed me.

The attack that evaporated with Atua's forgiveness reared again. My breathing came in gasps. "Please. Don't. Leave."

I blinked and his arms were around me. Cradling me tenderly.

"I won't." He helped me to the bed. "But you need to rest."

We lay down and I curled into the crook of his arm. He was careful not to touch the bandages on my back, but he let his fingers trail up and down my arm. The sensations soothing me to sleep.

I woke to a light pressure on my forehead. It was gentle and warm but moved away too quickly to identify.

"Eleena, wake up." Am's voice pulled me into reality.

"Are we there?" I snuggled deeper into his embrace. How many times had I dreamt of him holding me like this?

"Almost. Corvey and Harper will be anxious to see you, and we can have a real doctor look at your injuries."

I could listen to him talk all day. Laying so close, his voice rumbled through my chest. The giddy joy made all the years of missing him bearable.

"Eleena, are you awake?" he teased.

I nodded. Even though I'd rather stay close to him, I scooted away. "I'm up. I was even listening. Harper, Corvey, doctor. I still can't believe you found Corvey."

He smiled and touched my hair. It was probably sticking up every which way. I tried to smooth it down, but he pulled my hands away.

"You look beautiful."

Too many emotions swirled inside. It felt like an anxiety attack, except pleasant. I still felt out of control, like it was hard to breathe, but I didn't wish for the sensation to go away.

"Am?" I breathed his name.

He rested his forehead on mine. "Not yet. Harper would kill me."

That made me laugh. I missed her so much. "And Corvey?"

"Probably." He moved off the bed before tugging me to standing as well.

"I can't go into public in a med gown." I looked around the room. "I should have showered too."

"Nash brought some of Corvey's clothes while you slept." He pointed to a chair with a pile of folded up fabric. "I'll see to food while you clean up. Try not to get your back wet."

The smile I felt probably took over my entire face. Warm water, clean clothes, and Am. I sighed with contentment. "I'll do my best."

Half an hour later, Am tapped on the door. "Eleena?"

"I'm ready." I finished running my fingers through my damp hair as the door opened.

"Do you want to join everyone in the common room? Valeria's there."

"How is she?"

"You can see for yourself."

I followed him to a room with a large table surrounded by chairs.

Captain E sat beside Valeria, holding one of her hands while she used the other to eat. He never took his eyes off of her, and she kept glancing at him as if he were a ghost ready to fade away. Nash and an older guy stood talking to each other.

I hurried to Valeria and hugged her carefully. "Are you okay?"

She smiled, glanced at Captain E, and replied, "Better than I've been in a long time."

My heart swelled with joy at her expression and the surety Captain E wasn't alone anymore.

"Eleena, this is De'truto." Am pointed to the older man.

298

"Oh! You were in the mines." The words spilled from my lips. I hadn't recognized him. He was clean, had shaved his beard, and cut his hair.

"How did you know that?" De'truto turned from me to Am. "I thought you said you hadn't seen her in years."

Am smiled. "Remember the dreams I told you about?"

"Yeah."

"Atua sent her dreams about me." Am wrapped his arm around my waist and tucked me close to his side, sending a thrill through me. "We might not have been on the same planet, but we've always been together."

"I knew it." A wicked little smile turned up Captain E's lips. "All those times you brushed me off, I saw it in your eyes when you said her name."

Am's gentle squeeze pulled at my bandages, but I didn't care.

"I didn't give you a hard time about Valeria, so why should I let you tease me." Am pointed to the last man. "Eleena, you remember Nash. He's Corvey's fiancé."

"I can't believe Corvey is connected to all of you. It's been so long since I've seen her. I have so many questions." My stomach growled loud enough for everyone to hear.

"They can wait. Sit and I'll bring you food." Am pulled out a chair for me before disappearing. He was only gone a minute before returning with two plates. "Has everyone else eaten?"

Captain E and the other two men nodded.

Nash spoke, "We're on final approach. We'll land in the field by the palace."

A weighted look passed between Am and De'truto. The older man nodded. "It's been taken care of."

"Thank you." Am sat beside me. He didn't say anything else, so I let it go.

I'd barely finished eating before we landed and headed to the airlock. I bounced from foot to foot while waiting for the doors to open.

"Eleena?" Am looked down at me. "Are you okay?"

"Yes, just excited to see my friends." A thread of sadness wove into my happiness. I'd have to tell Harper about Ulla and the others, but maybe I didn't have to tell them what I did to Schirra.

The doors opened and Harper stood with her arms interlocked with a blonde woman. Corvey had changed a lot over the years, but the eyes, the dimple in the cheeks belonged to the girl I remembered. They ran toward the ship, and I met them at the bottom of the ramp.

"Eleena!" Harper pulled me into a hug so tight I couldn't breathe. I tried not to gasp as her arms crushed and rubbed my back, but Corvey must have seen.

"Harper, you're hurting her," Corvey said it kindly, but Harper jerked away.

"Where are you hurt?" She looked me over from head to toe.

"It's her back." Am and the others joined us. Corvey rushed to Nash. "I want a real medic to check her over."

"Do I want to know?" Harper's face wrinkled in worry. I noticed she'd asked Am, not me.

He shook his head. "You didn't see Schirra's broadcast?"

"We were too busy taking care of the bodies," Harper answered.

"Bodies?" I looked at the barracks. They didn't look any different from where I stood, but I knew the other side must have damage from the soldiers breaking through the windows.

Am took my hand in his, rubbing them as if to warm them. "Schirra killed everyone in the palace before he came for you."

"Everyone?" This time I looked at Captain E. "Your father?"

He nodded and Valeria wrapped an arm around him.

"Eleena, let's get you and Valeria inside. You both need rest and medical attention." Am brushed my hair with his fingers, tucking the ends behind my ear. "There will be time to mourn, but I need to finish what I started."

"What do you mean?" I held on to his arm, not wanting him out of my sight.

"I have to go with my men. Most of the fleet is under my control, but there are a few holdouts that will cause a lot of trouble if we don't stop them now." Both his hands were on my face again.

My heart pounded. *Atua?*

Let him go, Eleena.

Will he come back? I blinked back my desperation.

Have faith.

62
_____

THE RETURN: AMIRAN

W e returned to Rawiri in the early morning hours. As we
descended into the atmosphere, I watched the sun rise
behind us. I asked Nash to land in the meadow by the palace instead
of the spaceport. The rest of the troops would go there in the larger
carriers, but Nash's ship was small. And I didn't care about
damaging the lawn. Ev and Nash agreed, wishing to see Valeria and
Corvey as much as I yearned for Eleena.

It had taken longer to subdue the flagship. In the end, the fleet
ships under my command converged on her and bombarded her
until she crumpled into pieces. After that, the smaller vessels still
fighting us surrendered. The fleet now belonged to me. I put
De'truto and Evander in charge of reorganizing the leadership and
mission of each ship.

During the long weeks, I had to satisfy myself with vid calls to
Eleena between battles. We'd only spoken twice before I headed
home. Now all I could think about was holding her and telling her
how I felt.

"We've landed." Nash left the flight deck, his pack slung over his
shoulder. "Where's Ev?"

"Here." Evander appeared near the corridor to the airlock. He too
carried his pack.

I didn't bother to gather my things. None of it mattered.
"Let's go."

We hurried into the cool morning, past where the barracks had stood. They'd been taken down while we were gone. A memorial garden planted in its place.

Near the center of the multi-colored flowers, an obelisk rose toward the sky. The names of the refugee women who'd been killed here and at the work camp filled one side. The other contained the names of others that had given their lives for Atua's cause. Timoti, Iri, Brindyn, and many others I'd met over the years. A third side was dedicated to the memory of Manawa, and the last contained a pledge to follow Atua.

I passed it, fighting the urge to break into a run. We walked up the hill and through the back entrance that led to the inner courtyard.

"Am!"

I looked up. Eleena leaned over a balcony two floors up. My will to walk evaporated and I ran inside. Evander and Nash close behind.

"Thank Atua!" Ev muttered. "I thought you were going to take your sweet time."

"I was trying to be an adult." I laughed and jogged up the staircase.

"That's a stupid reason." Ev continued.

"I know that now." I waved at him as we split ways at the top. Nash going the same direction as Ev but pulling ahead because he hadn't wasted breath talking.

Eleena met me halfway down the hall, running straight into my arms. I breathed her in, alternating between the need to hold her close and look at her. Her hair had grown some more, almost touching her shoulders. She'd gained weight. Her cheekbones no longer created sharp angles on her face, and her body held more curves that settled nicely in my arms.

A light floral scent hovered around her and tears glistened in her eyes.

"What's wrong?" I wiped one away before it trailed down her cheek.

"Nothing. I'm just relieved you're safe. Happy you're back."

"I missed you."

Her smile lit up my world. "I know, and I missed you. Now, are you going to kiss me?"

"With all my heart."

I leaned forward, pressing my lips to hers. They were warm, sweet. Eleena sighed and melted into me. She fit perfectly in my arms, my heart, and if she'd have me, in my life. I pulled her closer, deepening the kiss. She welcomed me in and my body warmed with need.

"Does this mean I get to plan a royal wedding?" the new voice was full of hope and joy.

I pulled back to see who had joined us in the hallway.

"Mother?"

Eleena laughed. "Kuini arrived right after you left. We've been getting to know each other while worrying over you."

My mother was home. And from the expression on her face, as enamored with Eleena as I was. Eleena stepped aside so I could embrace my mom. We stood there a long time, making up for missed years.

"Am, you've done it. Taken back the empire for Atua." She whispered. "Anaru would be proud."

"Do you think so?" I let her go and reached for Eleena's hand, needing to touch her.

"Yes. I wish you could have known him the way I did." She held up a small leather-bound book. "This will help. He gave it to me for safe keeping. It will answer many questions, but not all."

"Will it tell me how Schirra got so much power?" That had bothered me almost as much as why my father let things go so far.

"I'll let you read it for yourself." Her eyes sparkled as she glanced from Eleena and back to me. "Now, will we be making announcements?"

"I haven't asked yet." I wanted to do this right.

"Well, I'll leave you to it." Mother winked at Eleena. "Come visit later and we'll make plans."

Eleena leaned into hug Kuini. Then we watched her return to the rooms she must have claimed as her own.

When the hall was empty once more, Eleena turned to me. Although she smiled, there was a question in her eyes. "You don't have to ask because your mother told you too."

"I planned to ask, but not in a hallway." I led Eleena to a grouping of chairs a few feet away.

"You did?" She sat and I knelt in front of her, keeping her hand in mine.

I scooted close, not wanting even a chair between us. "Eleena, I've been in love with you for years."

"You have?"

I loved the way her voice had gone all breathy.

"At first, I didn't want to. I promised your father I'd take care of you, and falling in love didn't seem right. Maybe it was because you were so much younger than me."

"I'm still younger than you." A little wrinkle appeared on her brow.

I tried to figure out the right words. "Yes, but you're not a child anymore. You're old enough to know your own mind and choose for yourself what you want." She nodded and I continued. "Eleena, thanks to Atua, I've watched you grow into this strong woman of faith. When others crumbled under the pressure of fear, you stayed kind. You have no idea how much I need that, you, in my life. When I was in the fleet…"

"Shh." She placed a finger on my lips. "I know. Atua showed me how you tried to help people. He let me feel what was in your heart, including the helplessness. When I helped others, it wasn't just for Atua. It was for you too."

I didn't think I could love her more, but a surge of emotion over-whelmed me. *Atua, what did I do to earn such love?*

You listened when I called.

"Am, can you feel Atua with us?" Eleena's eyes sparkled with moisture. "We are in his hands as surely as my parents were. With his guidance, you can make the empire glorious."

"I know. I also believe he intended you to be here with me, helping me fulfill his will. Eleena Talrano, I don't want to do this without you. I need your strength, your comfort, your love. Will you marry me, be my queen, and help me bring peace to our worlds?"

Her smile told me the answer before she whispered the word, "Yes."

Rising on my knees, I pulled her in for another kiss. It was a promise of all I felt for her, all I wished to give her, and I felt her return that promise.

We were finally where we needed to be—in the hands of Atua.

63

EPILOGUE: ELEENA

2 0 Years Later

AMIRAN WAS AN EXCEPTIONAL HATANA. He brought peace to the Coalition and Allegiant worlds quickly. The mines of Cassia and Attalea became a paid job. Cities growing up around the wealthiest veins for the families of the men and women who chose to work there. Am made sure they were well compensated and strict safety protocols were enforced.

That and many other changes over the years made it easy for people to forget the price that was paid for the peace we'd achieved.

But we remembered.

The *Fortissimus II* circled Manawa several times. We searched for a place to build a memorial to all who sacrificed in that other lifetime. Am agreed with me in the end. Instead of placing it in my home city, the place we'd first met, we would put it by the seaside. The last place my parents had been before Manawa's destruction.

We landed and waited for the final radiation check. It was within acceptable limits for a short visit. We had twenty minutes to say what we wanted and return to the ship for decontamination.

It was surreal, standing on Manawa. Our children gathered around us, as did Harper and her husband with their children. The sky was clear blue, not a cloud in sight. There was no grass, bushes, or trees to tame the swift wind that scoured the surface of the planet. As far as I could see, only blackened rubble and mounded dirt stretched away from the sea. The ocean itself rolled into shore with relentless pounding as if it could cleanse the land if only it tried harder.

"Are you ready?" Am asked.

"Yes." I beckoned our children closer. Canto, Sora, Ulla, and Anaru were growing up fast, and they wouldn't be mine much longer. I was glad to share this with them. "Come, we'll watch the video as it plays for the first time on Manawa."

Harper's oldest son, Iri, kept his eye on his much younger siblings. He looked so much like his father, but this Iri could talk and debate with the best of them. I often wondered if his father would have been more like him if he'd been given different opportunities.

When everyone focused on the monument's screen, Am stepped forward.

"There is no way to memorialize every life that was extinguished twenty-seven years ago. However, we want the empire to remember what was lost. This video was sent to me days before the fleet's arrival. It represents all those who lived, loved, and sacrificed for that love. Let it stand as a testament that even in the face of certain death, we can rely on Atua. That it is better to be in his hands than on our own." He flipped the switch and the screen flared to life.

My father and mother stood on a beach, perhaps this one. The sun was setting over the ocean behind them, painting the sky in brilliant pinks, purples, and oranges. For the first time, I realized I was older than my mother. Tears started before my father spoke his first words.

"Amiran, thank you for getting Eleena to safety. We need you to tell her how much we love her." Popi hugged Mima as she cried beside him. The camera wobbled and Mima helped him hold it up. "There are no more ships. No way for us to join her until this is over." He choked on the last word.

Mima took over. "We know our chances aren't good." She wiped at her tears. "No matter what happens, tell Leena…tell her we've found peace knowing she is safe."

The screen zoomed in on Popi's face. "May Atua be with you, protecting and guiding you. Keep asking questions, Am. It's the only way to find your answers. And if possible, take care of Leena for us."

The video ended and the next couple of minutes were filled with screens setting down the history of Manawa. They were filled with beautiful pictures of the wildlife, flora, and fauna. City scenes, people walking, playing in the REC bubbles, swimming in the sea, and a hundred other vignettes of life. The final section of the memorial was the destruction itself.

I didn't want to watch it again. Instead, I curled into Am's embrace, grateful there was no sound. It allowed me to focus on the sound of the waves until the others started crying. My youngest daughter, Ulla, was only twelve. The same age I'd been when I last stood on this planet. She'd seen the vid before, but this time was harder. I understood and pulled her into our hug. Sora and Canto came on their own.

We huddled there, family groups holding each other. Grateful for all we had, vowing never to forget, and praying that we would always remain in Atua's hands.

THANK YOU!

Thank you for reading The Hand of Atua. Reviews are the best way to support an author and encourage them to keep writing. Please take a moment write a review on Amazon.

Join Charity's Street Team for the most up to date news on:

~New releases

~Sales and other promotions

~Giveaways and contests

~Opportunities to beta read and critique books before they're released to the public for free

https://www.subscribepage.com/e0e0x8

Or Text NEW READER to 444999 to Join!

FUN STUFF BEHIND THE SCENES

~I love to share little tidbits about my stories. Things like the songs I found myself listening to a lot while writing them. Almost every book I've ever written has its own "end credits song" if you will, like at the end of a movie. The song for THE HAND OF ATUA (HofA) doesn't sound remotely like a war song or sci-fi in any way. It's a Christian rock song by Skillet called Stars.

~Although the final product is nothing like the original idea, this story began as a blog hop piece. I wrote a scene about a captive queen waiting for her husband to return from war. She thought she hated him, but when she sees him she realizes she loves him. It was supposed to be an "almost kiss" scene. I started asking questions and eventually ended up here.

~That original short scene was also me playing with the idea of the Bible story Esther in a sci-fi setting. Once again, we've strayed far from that idea.

~Over the course of writing HofA I read a lot of news articles about what women suffer in refugee camps. I don't even scratch the surface in this story. Real life is often more horrible than we care to imagine.

~I ate nothing but protein bars for breakfast and lunch all summer in 2018. When I say protein bars I mean the gluten-free, high protein, low carb ones that taste like they're meant to keep you alive and nothing else. You know what? I lost weight and it didn't take long until I didn't feel hungry. Like, ever. Our bodies can adapt to crazy things. Granted I ate healthy dinners with vegetables and meat to round out the day.

~I also spent several hours in an underground paintball facility. This system of tunnels and caverns was fascinating and I wish I could describe the smells. My boys had a blast and I imagined what it would be like to live in such a place for a year.

ACKNOWLEDGMENTS

Writing a book is no longer a solitary experience. Sure, a lot of time is spent alone in front of a computer. However, there are hours spent in critique groups, commiserating online about writer's block, and all the insecurities that come with sharing your work. Then there are the wonderful readers who willingly read early versions of the story and give feedback for revisions. These people are worth their weight in gold.

My biggest fear is forgetting to thank someone who helped me during the three year process of writing this story. It's easy to remember the last readers, but there are always people at the beginning who may not have known your questions were "research." I want to tell all of those people thank you! Your contribution was just as important and I'm sorry my mind is like a sieve with the attention span of a five-year-old.

I can shout out to the Bithell boys for answering questions about how teen guys might look at certain situations. Katie and Kacey for frequently asking me if I'd finished this story yet. Sometimes knowing they wanted the ending was the only thing keeping me writing. Thank you!

Thank you to my writer's group for listening to the first five chapters four or five times! If you hadn't stuck with me who knows if I would have ever figured this one out. (Tamara, Tammy, Kiah, and Kirsten)

Even with a great critique group, sometimes a story can tie you in knots and give you fits. THE HAND OF ATUA was like that for me. I loved the story but always felt something was off. John aka Johan Twiss (author of the I AM SLEEPLESS series) helped me recognize many of those problem areas. Thanks for being a guy and seeing the obvious things I missed as a girl!

Thank you to my last beta readers: Dan, some students from Gravette High, and Kathy who helped me smooth the edges.

This story has come along way from the seed idea, and it's thanks to all of you.

ABOUT THE AUTHOR

Charity Bradford has been a voracious reader ever since her 5th grade teacher introduced her to the world of books with the *Where The Red Fern Grows* and *Summer Of The Monkeys*. She soon lost herself in the worlds created by Card, Bova, Asimov, Bradbury, Nagata and Niven. She lives in northwest Arkansas with her hubby and four kids that keep her on her toes. You can get all the latest news on her website: **http://charitywrites.com**

amazon.com/Charity-Bradford

bookbub.com/authors/charity-bradford

facebook.com/CharityWritesScienceFantasy

twitter.com/charitybradford

ALSO BY CHARITY BRADFORD

The Magic Wakes Series

The Magic Wakes Book 1 (2013, 2017)

Dawn of the Mages Book 2 (2015, 2017)

Demon Rising Book 3 (Coming 2019)

Birth of a Dragon Book 4 (Coming Soon)

Stellar Cloud: A short story collection

Fade Into Me—a modern day fairy tale

Charity Bradford also writes clean contemporary romance under the pen name River Ford.

Eureka In Love Series

Chocolate Kisses

Landscape Love

Teacher's Crush (Coming 2019)

Others

A Christmas Prayer (Previously part of A Merrily Matched Christmas 2017, Re-Released as a single—2018)

Christmas Magic (November 2018)

34495680R00179

Made in the USA
Middletown, DE
27 January 2019